PRAISE FOR THE *NEW YORK TIMES* AND *USA TODAY* BESTSELLING THRONE OF GLASS SERIES

THE ASSASSIN'S BLADE

"Fans will delight in this gorgeous edition. . . . Action-packed and full of insight into Celaena's character. . . . What a ride!" —*Booklist*

THRONE OF GLASS

A *Kirkus Reviews* Best Teen Book

A YALSA-ALA Best Fiction for Young Adults Book

★ "A thrilling read." —*Publishers Weekly*, starred review

"A must-read for lovers of epic fantasy and fairy tales." —*USA Today*

"Fans of Tamora Pierce and George R.R. Martin, pick up this book!" —*RT Book Reviews*, Top Pick

CROWN OF MIDNIGHT

★ "An epic fantasy readers will immerse themselves in and never want to leave." —*Kirkus Reviews*, starred review

"A thrill ride of epic fantasy proportions." —*USA Today*

HEIR OF FIRE

"Celaena is as much an epic hero as Frodo or Jon Snow!" —*New York Times* bestselling author Tamora Pierce

"Readers will devour Maas's latest entry. . . . A must-purchase." —*SLJ*

QUEEN OF SHADOWS

The Goodreads Choice Award Winner for Best Young Adult Fantasy and Science Fiction for 2015

"Beautifully written prose and brilliantly crafted plots come together in this entry of the awe-inspiring fantasy series that will leave readers anticipating the next volume." —*SLJ*

EMPIRE OF STORMS

"Tightly plotted, delightful escapism." —*Kirkus Reviews*

"Fans devoted to the series (and there are many) will be eager for this installment's cinematic action, twisty schemes, and intense revelations of secrets and legacies." —*Booklist*

TOWER OF DAWN

"Turns a corner from sprawling epic to thrilling psychological fantasy." —HuffPost

"Will leave readers spellbound." —*RT Book Reviews*

KINGDOM OF ASH

A *Time* Top Ten Fantasy Book

The Goodreads Choice Award Winner for Best Young Adult Fantasy and Science Fiction for 2018

"A worthy finale to one of the best fantasy book series of the past decade." —*Time* magazine

THE ASSASSIN'S BLADE

BOOKS BY SARAH J. MAAS

The Throne of Glass series

The Assassin's Blade
Throne of Glass
Crown of Midnight
Heir of Fire
Queen of Shadows
Empire of Storms
Tower of Dawn
Kingdom of Ash

•

The Throne of Glass Coloring Book

A Court of Thorns and Roses series

A Court of Thorns and Roses
A Court of Mist and Fury
A Court of Wings and Ruin
A Court of Frost and Starlight

•

A Court of Thorns and Roses Coloring Book

THE ASSASSIN'S BLADE

THE *Throne of Glass* NOVELLAS

SARAH J. MAAS

BLOOMSBURY
NEW YORK LONDON OXFORD NEW DELHI SYDNEY

First published in the United States of America in March 2014
by Bloomsbury YA
Paperback edition published in March 2015
www.bloomsbury.com

For information about permission to reproduce selections from this book, write to Permissions, Bloomsbury YA, 1385 Broadway, New York, New York 10018
Bloomsbury books may be purchased for business or promotional use. For information on bulk purchases please contact Macmillan Corporate and Premium Sales Department at specialmarkets@macmillan.com

The Library of Congress has cataloged the hardcover edition as follows:
Maas, Sarah J.
[Novellas. Selections]
The assassin's blade : the Throne of glass novellas / by Sarah J. Maas.
pages cm
Contains four previously published e-books: The assassin and the pirate lord, The assassin and the desert, The assassin and the underworld, and The assassin and the empire, plus one never-before-published novella, The assassin and the healer.
Summary: In these five prequel novellas to *Throne of Glass*, feared assassin Celaena embarks on daring missions that take her from remote islands to hostile deserts, where she fights to liberate slaves and avenge tyranny.
ISBN 978-1-61963-361-2 (hardcover) • ISBN 978-1-61963-221-9 (e-book)
[1. Fantasy. 2. Assassins—Fiction.] I. Title.
PZ7.M111575As 2014 [Fic]—dc23 2013041954

ISBN 978-1-61963-517-3 (paperback)

Book design by Regina Flath
Typeset by Westchester Book Composition
Printed and bound in the U.S.A. by Berryville Graphics Inc., Berryville, Virginia
16 18 20 19 17

All papers used by Bloomsbury Publishing, Inc., are natural, recyclable products made from wood grown in well-managed forests. The manufacturing processes conform to the environmental regulations of the country of origin.

This one's for the phenomenal worldwide team at Bloomsbury:
thank you for making my dreams come true

And for my cunning and brilliant editor, Margaret:
thank you for believing in Celaena from page one

TABLE OF CONTENTS

Erilea
Amaroth
Frozen Wastes
The Ruins of Morla
Jungle of Morla
The Western Wastes
The Witch Kingdom
Briarcliff
Bogdano Jungle
The Deserted Land
Gulf of Oro
The Singing Sands
Yurpa
The Red Desert
Silent Assassins
Oasis of Barg
The Cleaver
Xandria
Noll
The Black Dunes
The Black Sands of Roth
volcano Flows

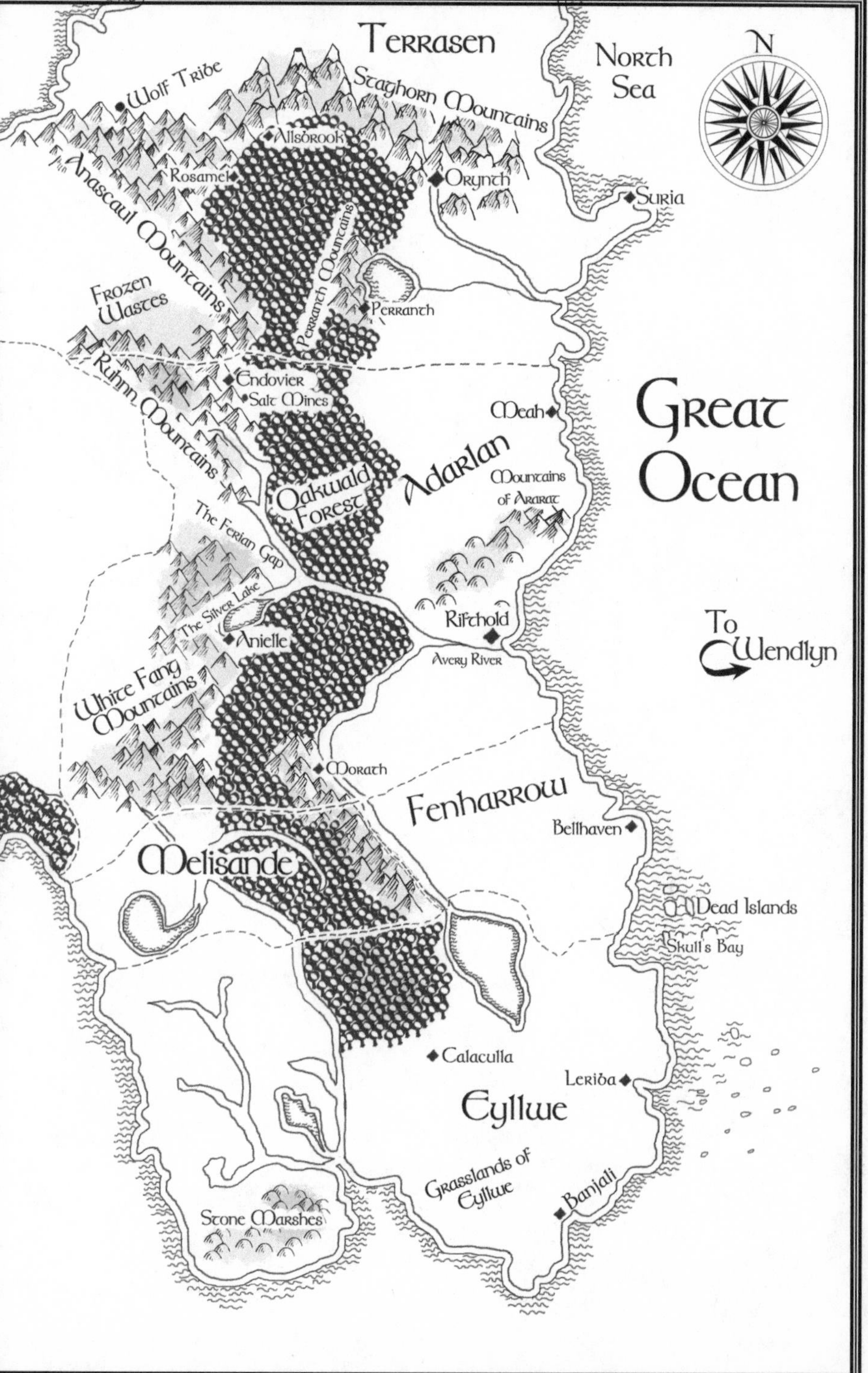

Terrasen
North Sea
N
Wolf Tribe
Staghorn Mountains
Allsbrook
Rosamel
Orynth
Suria
Anascaul Mountains
Perranth Mountains
Frozen Wastes
Perranth
Endovier
Salt Mines
Ruhnn Mountains
Meah
Great Ocean
Adarlan
Oakwald Forest
Mountains of Ararat
The Ferian Gap
The Silver Lake
Anielle
Rifthold
Avery River
To Wendlyn
White Fang Mountains
Morath
Fenharrow
Bellhaven
Melisande
Dead Islands
Skull's Bay
Calaculla
Leriba
Eyllwe
Grasslands of Eyllwe
Banjali
Stone Marshes

THE ASSASSIN AND THE PIRATE LORD

CHAPTER 1

Seated in the council room of the Assassins' Keep, Celaena Sardothien leaned back in her chair. "It's past four in the morning," she said, adjusting the folds of her crimson silk dressing gown and crossing her bare legs beneath the wooden table. "This had better be important."

"Perhaps if you hadn't been reading all night, you wouldn't be so exhausted," snapped the young man seated across from her. She ignored him and studied the four other people assembled in the underground chamber.

All male, all far older than she, and all refusing to meet her stare. A chill that didn't have to do with the drafty room ran down her spine. Picking at her manicured nails, Celaena schooled her features into neutrality. The five assassins gathered at the long table—including herself—were five of Arobynn Hamel's seven most trusted companions.

This meeting was undeniably important. She'd known that from the moment the serving girl pounded on her door, insisting Celaena come downstairs and not even bother to get dressed. When Arobynn summoned you, you didn't keep him waiting. Thankfully, her sleepwear was as exquisite as her daytime wardrobe—and cost nearly as much. Still, being sixteen in a room with men made her keep an eye on the neckline of her robe. Her beauty was a weapon—one she kept honed—but it could also be a vulnerability.

Arobynn Hamel, King of the Assassins, lounged at the head of the table, his auburn hair shining in the light from the glass chandelier. His silver eyes met hers, and he frowned. It might have just been the late hour, but Celaena could have sworn that her mentor was paler than usual. Her stomach twisted.

"Gregori's been caught," Arobynn finally said. Well, that would explain one person missing from this meeting. "His mission was a trap. He's now being held in the royal dungeons."

Celaena sighed through her nose. *This* was why she'd been awakened? She tapped a slippered foot on the marble floor. "Then kill him," she said.

She'd never liked Gregori, anyway. When she was ten, she'd fed his horse a bag of candy and he'd thrown a dagger at her head for it. She'd caught the dagger, of course, and ever since, Gregori had borne the scar on his cheek from her return throw.

"*Kill* Gregori?" demanded Sam, the young man seated at Arobynn's left—a place that usually went to Ben, Arobynn's second-in-command. Celaena knew very well what Sam Cortland thought of her. She'd known since they were children, when Arobynn took her in and declared her—not Sam—to be his protégée and heir. That hadn't stopped Sam from trying to undermine her at every turn. And now, at seventeen, Sam was still a year older than she, and he still hadn't forgotten that he would always be second best.

She bristled at the sight of Sam in Ben's seat. Ben would probably throttle Sam for it when he arrived. Or she could just save Ben the effort and do it herself.

Celaena looked to Arobynn. Why hadn't *he* reprimanded Sam for sitting in Ben's place? Arobynn's face, still handsome despite the silver starting to show in his hair, remained impassive. She hated that unreadable mask, especially when controlling her own expressions—and temper—remained a tad difficult.

"If Gregori's been caught," Celaena drawled, brushing back a strand of her long, golden hair, "then the protocol's simple: send an apprentice to slip something into his food. Nothing painful," she added as the men around her tensed. "Just enough to silence him before he talks."

Which Gregori might very well do, if he was in the royal dungeons. Most criminals who went in there never came out again. Not alive. And not in any recognizable shape.

The location of the Assassins' Keep was a well-guarded secret, one she'd been trained to keep until her last breath. But even if she didn't, no one was likely to believe that an elegant manor house on a very respectable street in Rifthold was home to some of the greatest assassins in the world. What better place to hide than in the middle of the capital city?

"And if he's already talked?" challenged Sam.

"And if Gregori's already talked," she said, "then kill everyone who heard." Sam's brown eyes flashed as she gave him a little smile that she knew made him irate. Celaena turned to Arobynn. "But you didn't need to drag us here to decide this. You already gave the order, didn't you?"

Arobynn nodded, his mouth a thin line. Sam choked back his objection and looked toward the crackling hearth beside the table. The firelight cast the smooth, elegant panes of Sam's face into light and shadow—a face, she'd been told, that could have earned him a fortune if he'd followed in his mother's footsteps. But Sam's mother had opted instead to leave him with assassins, not courtesans, before she died.

Silence fell, and a roaring noise filled her ears as Arobynn took a breath. Something was wrong.

"What else?" she asked, leaning forward. The other assassins focused on the table. Whatever had happened, they knew. Why hadn't Arobynn told her first?

Arobynn's silver eyes became steel. "Ben was killed."

Celaena gripped the arms of her chair. "What?" *Ben*—Ben, the ever-smiling assassin who had trained her as often as Arobynn had. Ben, who had once mended her shattered right hand. Ben, the seventh and final member of Arobynn's inner circle. He was barely thirty years old. Celaena's lips pulled back from her teeth. "What do you mean, 'killed'?"

Arobynn eyed her, and a glimmer of grief flashed across his face. Five years Ben's senior, Arobynn had grown up with Ben. They'd been trained together; Ben had seen to it that his friend became the unrivaled King of the Assassins, and never questioned his place as Arobynn's Second. Her throat closed up.

"It was supposed to be Gregori's mission," Arobynn said quietly. "I don't know why Ben was involved. Or who betrayed them. They found his body near the castle gates."

"Do you have his body?" she demanded. She had to see it—had to see him one last time, see how he'd died, how many wounds it had taken to kill him.

"No," Arobynn said.

"Why the hell not?" Her fists clenched and unclenched.

"Because the place was swarming with guards and soldiers!" Sam burst out, and she whipped her head to him. "How do you think we learned about this in the first place?"

Arobynn had sent *Sam* to see why Ben and Gregori were missing?

"If we'd grabbed his body," Sam said, refusing to back down from her glare, "it would have led them right to the Keep."

"You're assassins," she growled at him. "You're *supposed* to be able to retrieve a body without being seen."

"If you'd been there, you would have done the same."

Celaena pushed her chair back so hard it flipped over. "If I'd been there, I would have killed *all of them* to get Ben's body back!" She slammed her hands on the table, rattling the glasses.

Sam shot to his feet, a hand on the hilt of his sword. "Oh, listen to you. Ordering us about like *you* run the Guild. But not yet, Celaena." He shook his head. "Not yet."

"*Enough*," Arobynn snapped, rising from his chair.

Celaena and Sam didn't move. None of the other assassins spoke, though they gripped their various weapons. She'd seen firsthand what fights at the Keep were like; the weapons were as much for the bearers' own safety as they were to prevent her and Sam from doing serious damage to each other.

"I said, *enough*."

If Sam took one step toward her, drew his sword a fraction of an inch, that concealed dagger in her robe would find itself a new home in his neck.

Arobynn moved first, grabbing Sam's chin in one hand, forcing the young man to look at him. "Check yourself, or I'll do it for you, boy," he murmured. "You're a fool for picking a fight with her tonight."

Celaena bit down on her reply. She could handle Sam tonight—or any other night, for that matter. If it came down to a fight, she'd win—she always beat Sam.

But Sam released the hilt of his sword. After a moment, Arobynn removed his grip on Sam's face, but didn't step away. Sam kept his gaze on the floor as he strode to the far side of the council room.

Crossing his arms, he leaned against the stone wall. She could still reach him—one flick of her wrist, and his throat would spout blood.

"Celaena," Arobynn said, his voice echoing in the silent room.

Enough blood had been spilled tonight; they didn't need another dead assassin.

Ben. Ben was dead and gone, and she'd never again run into him in the halls of the Keep. He'd never set her injuries with his cool, deft hands, never coax a laugh from her with a joke or a lewd anecdote.

"Celaena," Arobynn warned again.

"I'm done," Celaena snapped. She rolled her neck, running a hand through her hair. She stalked to the door, but paused on the threshold.

"Just so you know," she said, speaking to all of them but still watching Sam, "I'm going to retrieve Ben's body." A muscle feathered in Sam's jaw, though he wisely kept his eyes averted. "But don't expect me to extend the same courtesy to the rest of you when your time comes."

With that, she turned on her heel and ascended the spiral staircase to the manor above. Fifteen minutes later, no one stopped her when she slipped out the front gate and into the silent city streets.

CHAPTER 2

Two months, three days, and about eight hours later, the clock on the mantel chimed noon. Captain Rolfe, Lord of the Pirates, was late. Then again, so were Celaena and Sam, but Rolfe had no excuse, not when they were already two hours behind schedule. Not when they were meeting in *his* office.

And it wasn't *her* fault for being tardy. She couldn't control the winds, and those skittish sailors had certainly taken their time sailing into the archipelago of the Dead Islands. She didn't want to think about how much gold Arobynn had spent bribing a crew to sail into the heart of pirate territory. But Skull's Bay was on an island, so they hadn't really had a choice about their mode of transportation.

Celaena, concealed behind a far-too-stuffy black cloak, tunic, and ebony mask, rose from her seat before the Pirate Lord's desk. How dare he make her wait! He knew precisely why they were here, after all.

Three assassins had been found murdered by pirate hands, and Arobynn had sent her to be his personal dagger—to extract retribution, preferably the gold kind, for what their deaths would cost the Assassins' Guild.

"With every minute he makes us wait," Celaena said to Sam, the mask making her words low and soft, "I'm adding an extra ten gold pieces to his debt."

Sam, who didn't wear a mask over his handsome features, crossed his arms and scowled. "You'll do no such thing. Arobynn's letter is sealed, and it's going to remain that way."

Neither of them had been particularly happy when Arobynn announced that Sam would be sent to the Dead Islands with Celaena. Especially when Ben's body—which Celaena *had* retrieved—had barely been in the ground for two months. The sting of losing him hadn't exactly worn off.

Her mentor had called Sam an escort, but Celaena knew what his presence meant: a watchdog. Not that she'd do anything bad when she was about to meet the Pirate Lord of Erilea. It was a once-in-a-lifetime chance. Even though the tiny, mountainous island and ramshackle port city hadn't really made much of an impression so far.

She'd been expecting a manor house like the Assassins' Keep, or at least a fortified, aging castle, but the Pirate Lord occupied the entire top floor of a rather suspect tavern. The ceilings were low, the wooden floors creaked, and the cramped room combined with the already-sizzling temperature of the southern islands meant Celaena was sweating buckets beneath her clothing. But her discomfort was worth it: as they'd strode through Skull's Bay, heads had turned at the sight of her—the billowing black cape, the exquisite clothing, and the mask transformed her into a whisper of darkness. A little intimidation never did any harm.

Celaena walked to the wooden desk and picked up a piece of paper, her black-gloved hands turning it over to read the contents. A weather log. How dull.

"What are you doing?"

Celaena lifted another piece of paper. "If His Pirateness can't be bothered to clean for us, then I don't see why I can't have a look."

"He'll be here any second," Sam hissed. She picked up a flattened map, examining the dots and markings along the coastline of their continent. Something small and round gleamed beneath the map, and she slipped it into her pocket before Sam could notice.

"Oh, hush," she said, opening the hutch on the wall adjacent to the desk. "With these creaky floors, we'll hear him a mile off." The hutch was crammed with rolled scrolls, quills, the odd coin, and some very old, very expensive-looking brandy. She pulled out a bottle, swirling the amber liquid in the sunlight streaming through the tiny porthole window. "Care for a drink?"

"No," Sam snapped, half-twisting in his seat to watch the door. "Put it back. *Now.*"

She cocked her head, twirled the brandy once more in its crystal bottle, and set it down. Sam sighed. Beneath her mask, Celaena grinned.

"He can't be a very good lord," she said, "if *this* is his personal office." Sam gave a stifled cry of dismay as Celaena plopped into the giant armchair behind the desk and set about opening the pirate's ledgers and turning over his papers. His handwriting was cramped and near-illegible, his signature nothing more than a few loops and jagged peaks.

She didn't know what she was looking for, exactly. Her brows rose a bit at the sight of a piece of purple, perfumed paper, signed by someone named Jacqueline. She leaned back in the chair, propping her feet on the desk, and read it.

"Damn it, Celaena!"

She raised her brows, but realized he couldn't see. The mask and clothes were a necessary precaution, one that made it far easier to protect her identity. In fact, all of Arobynn's assassins had been sworn to secrecy about who she was—under the threat of endless torture and eventual death.

Celaena huffed, though her breath only made the interior of the insufferable mask hotter. All that the world knew about Celaena Sardothien, Adarlan's Assassin, was that she was female. And she wanted to keep it that way. How else would she be able to stroll the broad avenues of Rifthold or infiltrate grand parties by posing as foreign nobility? And while she wished that Rolfe could have the chance to admire her lovely face, she had to admit that the disguise also made her rather imposing, especially when the mask warped her voice into a growling rasp.

"Get back in your seat." Sam reached for a sword that wasn't there. The guards at the entrance to the inn had taken their weapons. Of course, none of them had realized that Sam and Celaena were weapons themselves. They could kill Rolfe just as easily with their bare hands.

"Or you'll fight me?" She tossed the love letter onto the desk. "Somehow, I don't think that'd make a favorable impression on our new acquaintances." She crossed her arms behind her head, gazing at the turquoise sea visible between the dilapidated buildings that made up Skull's Bay.

Sam half-rose from his chair. "Just get back in your seat."

"I've spent the past ten days at sea. Why should I sit in that uncomfortable chair when this one's far more suited to my tastes?"

Sam let out a growl. Before he could speak, the door opened.

Sam froze, but Celaena only inclined her head in greeting as Captain Rolfe, Lord of the Pirates, entered his office.

"I'm glad to see you've made yourself at home." The tall,

dark-haired man shut the door behind him. Bold move, considering who was waiting in his office.

Celaena remained where she sat. Well, *he* certainly wasn't what she'd expected. It wasn't every day that she was surprised, but . . . she'd imagined him to be a bit dirtier—and far more flamboyant. Considering the tales she'd heard of Rolfe's wild adventures, she had trouble believing that this man—lean but not wiry, well dressed but not overtly so, and probably in his late twenties—was the legendary pirate. Perhaps he, too, kept his identity a secret from his enemies.

Sam stood, bowing his head slightly. "Sam Cortland," he said by way of greeting.

Rolfe extended a hand, and Celaena watched his tattooed palm and fingers as they clasped Sam's broad hand. The map—*that* was the mythic map that he'd sold his soul to have inked on his hands. The map of the world's oceans—the map that changed to show storms, foes . . . and treasure.

"I suppose *you* don't need an introduction." Rolfe turned to her.

"No." Celaena leaned back farther in his desk chair. "I suppose I don't."

Rolfe chuckled, a crooked smile spreading across his tanned face. He stepped to the hutch, giving her the chance to examine him further. Broad shoulders, head held high, a casual grace to his movements that came with knowing he had all the power here. He didn't have a sword, either. Another bold move. Wise, too, given that they could easily use his weapons against him. "Brandy?" he asked.

"No, thank you," Sam said. Celaena felt Sam's eyes hard upon her, willing her to take her feet off Rolfe's desk.

"With that mask on," Rolfe mused, "I don't think you could have a drink, anyway." He poured brandy for himself and took a long sip. "You must be boiling in all that clothing."

Celaena lowered her feet to the ground as she ran her hands

along the curved edge of his desk, stretching out her arms. "I'm used to it."

Rolfe drank again, watching her for a heartbeat over the rim of his glass. His eyes were a striking shade of sea green, as bright as the water just a few blocks away. Lowering the glass, he approached the end of the desk. "I don't know how you handle things in the North, but down here, we like to know who we're speaking to."

She cocked her head. "As you said, I don't need an introduction. And as for the privilege of seeing my beautiful face, I'm afraid that's something few men receive."

Rolfe's tattooed fingers tightened on the glass. "Get out of my chair."

Across the room, Sam tensed. Celaena examined the contents of Rolfe's desk again. She clicked her tongue, shaking her head. "You really need to work on organizing this mess."

She sensed the pirate grabbing for her shoulder and was on her feet before his fingers could graze the black wool of her cloak. He stood a good head taller than her. "I wouldn't do that if I were you," she crooned.

Rolfe's eyes gleamed with the challenge. "You're in *my* city, and on *my* island." Only a handbreadth separated them. "You're not in any position to give me orders."

Sam cleared his throat, but Celaena stared up into Rolfe's face. His eyes scanned the blackness beneath the hood of her cloak—the smooth black mask, the shadows that concealed any trace of her features. "Celaena," Sam warned, clearing his throat again.

"Very well." She sighed loudly, and stepped around Rolfe as if he were nothing but a piece of furniture in her way. She sank into the chair beside Sam, who flashed her a glare that burned enough to melt the entirety of the Frozen Wastes.

She could feel Rolfe watching their every movement, but he merely adjusted the lapels of his midnight-blue tunic before sitting down. Silence fell, interrupted only by the cry of gulls circling above the city and the shouting of pirates calling to one another in the filthy streets.

"Well?" Rolfe rested his forearms on the desk.

Sam glanced at her. Her move.

"You know precisely why we're here," Celaena said. "But perhaps all that brandy's gone to your head. Shall I refresh your memory?"

Rolfe gestured with his green, blue, and black hand for her to continue, as if he were a king on his throne listening to the complaints of the rabble. *Ass.*

"Three assassins from our Guild were found dead in Bellhaven. The one that got away told us they were attacked by pirates." She draped an arm along the back of her chair. "*Your* pirates."

"And how did the survivor know they were *my* pirates?"

She shrugged. "Perhaps it was the tattoos that gave them away." All of Rolfe's men had their wrists tattooed with an image of a multicolored hand.

Rolfe opened a drawer in his desk, pulling out a piece of paper and reading the contents. He said, "Once I caught wind that Arobynn Hamel might blame me, I had the shipyard master of Bellhaven send me these records. It seems the incident occurred at three in the morning at the docks."

This time Sam answered. "That's correct."

Rolfe set down the paper and lifted his eyes skyward. "So if it was three in the morning, and it took place at the docks—which have no street lamps, as I'm sure you know"—she didn't—"then *how* did your assassin see all of their tattoos?"

Beneath her mask, Celaena scowled. "Because it happened three weeks ago—during the full moon."

"Ah. But it's early spring. Even up in Bellhaven, nights are still cold. Unless my men were without coats, there was no way for—"

"Enough," Celaena snapped. "I suppose that piece of paper has ten different paltry excuses for your men." She grabbed the satchel from the floor and yanked out the two sealed documents. "These are for you." She tossed them on the desk. "From our master."

A smile tugged on Rolfe's lips, but he pulled the documents to him, studying the seal. He held it up to the sunlight. "I'm surprised it hasn't been tampered with." His eyes glimmered with mischief. Celaena could sense Sam's smugness oozing out of him.

With two deft flicks of his wrist, Rolfe sliced open both envelopes with a letter-knife she somehow hadn't spotted. How had she missed it? A fool's mistake.

In the silent minutes that passed as Rolfe read the letters, his only reaction was the occasional drumming of his fingers on the wooden desk. The heat was suffocating, and sweat slipped down her back. They were supposed to be here for three days—long enough for Rolfe to gather the money he owed them. Which, judging by the growing frown on Rolfe's face, was quite a lot.

Rolfe let out a long breath when he finished and shuffled the papers into alignment.

"Your master drives a hard bargain," Rolfe said, looking from Celaena to Sam. "But his terms aren't unfair. Perhaps you should have read the letter before you started flinging accusations at me and my men. There will be no retribution for those dead assassins. Whose deaths, your master agrees, were not my fault in the least. He must have some common sense, then." Celaena quelled the urge to lean forward. If Arobynn wasn't demanding payment for the death of those assassins, then what *were* they doing here? Her face burned. She'd looked like a fool, hadn't she? If Sam smiled just the slightest bit . . .

Rolfe drummed his inked fingers again and ran a hand through his shoulder-length dark hair. "As for the trade agreement he's outlined . . . I'll have my accountant draw up the necessary fees, but you'll have to tell Arobynn that he can't expect any profits until *at least* the second shipment. Possibly the third. And if he has an issue with that, then he can come down here himself to tell me."

For once, Celaena was grateful for the mask. It sounded like they'd been sent for some sort of business investment. Sam nodded at Rolfe—as if he knew exactly what the Pirate Lord was talking about. "And when can we tell Arobynn to expect the first shipment?" he asked.

Rolfe stuffed Arobynn's letters into a desk drawer and locked it. "The slaves will be here in two days—ready for your departure the day after. I'll even loan you my ship, so you can tell that trembling crew of yours they're free to return to Rifthold tonight, if it pleases them."

Celaena stared at him. Arobynn had sent them here for . . . for *slaves*? How could he stoop so disgustingly low? And to tell her she was going to Skull's Bay for one thing but to really send her here for *this* . . . She felt her nostrils flare. Sam had known about this deal, but he'd somehow forgotten to mention the truth behind their visit—even during the ten days they'd spent at sea. As soon as she got him alone, she'd make him regret it. But for now . . . she couldn't let Rolfe catch on to her ignorance.

"You'd better not botch this," Celaena warned the Pirate Lord. "Arobynn won't be pleased if anything goes awry."

Rolfe chuckled. "You have my word that it will all go according to plan. I'm not Lord of the Pirates for nothing, you know."

She leaned forward, flattening her voice into the even tones of a business partner concerned about her investment. "How long, exactly, have you been involved in the slave trade?" It couldn't have been long. Adarlan had only started capturing and selling slaves two years ago—most of them prisoners of war from whatever territories dared rebel against their conquest. Many of them were from Eyllwe, but there were still prisoners from Melisande and Fenharrow, or the isolated tribe in the White Fang Mountains. The majority of slaves went to Calaculla or Endovier, the continent's largest and most notorious labor camps, to mine for salt and precious metals. But more and more slaves were making their way into the households of Adarlan's nobility. And for Arobynn to make a filthy trade agreement—some sort of black market deal . . . It would sully the Assassins' Guild's entire reputation.

"Believe me," Rolfe said, crossing his arms, "I have enough experience. You should be more concerned about your master. Investing in the slave trade is a guaranteed profit, but he might need to expend more of his resources than he'd like in order to keep our business from reaching the wrong ears."

Her stomach turned over, but she feigned disinterest as best she could and said, "Arobynn is a shrewd businessman. Whatever you can supply, he'll make the most of it."

"For his sake, I hope that's true. I don't want to risk my name for nothing." Rolfe stood, and Celaena and Sam rose with him. "I'll have the documents signed and returned to you tomorrow. For now . . ." He pointed toward the door. "I have two rooms prepared for you."

"We only need one," she interrupted.

Rolfe's eyebrows rose suggestively.

Beneath her mask, her face burned, and Sam choked on a laugh. "One room, *two* beds."

Rolfe chuckled, striding to the door and opening it for them. "As you wish. I'll have baths drawn for you as well." Celaena and Sam followed him out into the narrow, dark hallway. "You could both use one," he added with a wink.

It took all of her self-restraint to keep from punching him below the belt.

CHAPTER 3

It took them five minutes to search the cramped room for any spy-holes or signs of danger; five minutes for them to lift the framed paintings on the wood-paneled walls, tap at the floorboards, seal the gap between the door and the floor, and cover the window with Sam's weatherworn black cloak.

When she was certain that no one could either hear or see her, Celaena ripped off her hood, untied the mask, and whirled to face him.

Sam, seated on his small bed—which seemed more like a cot—raised his palms to her. "Before you bite my head off," he said, keeping his voice quiet just in case, "let me say that I went into that meeting knowing as little as you."

She glared at him, savoring the fresh air on her sticky, sweaty face. "Oh, really?"

"You're not the only one who can improvise." Sam kicked off his boots and hoisted himself farther onto the bed. "That man's as much in love with himself as you are; the last thing we need is for him to know that he had the upper hand in there."

Celaena dug her nails into her palms. "Why would Arobynn send us here without telling us the true reason? Reprimand Rolfe . . . for a crime that had nothing to do with him! Maybe Rolfe was lying about the content of the letter." She straightened. "*That* might very well be—"

"He was *not* lying about the content of the letter, Celaena," Sam said. "Why would he bother? He has more important things to do."

She grumbled a slew of nasty words and paced, her black boots clunking against the uneven floorboards. Pirate Lord indeed. *This* was the best room he could offer them? She was Adarlan's Assassin, the right arm of Arobynn Hamel—not some backstreet harlot!

"Regardless, Arobynn has his reasons." Sam stretched out on his bed and closed his eyes.

"Slaves," she spat, dragging a hand through her braided hair. Her fingers caught in the plait. "What business does Arobynn have getting involved in the slave trade? We're better than that—we don't *need* that money!"

Unless Arobynn was lying; unless all of his extravagant spending was done with nonexistent funds. She'd always assumed that his wealth was bottomless. He'd spent a king's fortune on her upbringing—on her wardrobe alone. Fur, silk, jewels, the weekly cost of just keeping herself *looking* beautiful . . . Of course, he'd always made it clear that she was to pay him back, and she'd been giving him a cut of her wages to do so, but . . .

Maybe Arobynn wanted to increase what wealth he already had. If Ben were alive, he wouldn't have stood for it. Ben would have been as disgusted as she was. Being hired to kill corrupt government officials was one thing, but taking prisoners of war, brutalizing them until they stopped fighting back, and sentencing them to a lifetime of slavery . . .

Sam opened an eye. "Are you going to take a bath, or can I go first?"

She hurled her cloak at him. He caught it with a single hand and tossed it to the ground. She said, "I'm going first."

"Of course you are."

She shot him a dirty look and stormed into the bathroom, slamming the door behind her.

Of all the dinners she'd ever attended, this was by far the worst. Not because of the company—which was, she grudgingly admitted, somewhat interesting—and not because of the food, which looked and smelled wonderful, but simply because she couldn't *eat* anything, thanks to that confounded mask.

Sam, of course, seemed to take second helpings of everything solely to mock her. Celaena, seated at Rolfe's left, half-hoped the food was poisoned. Sam had only served himself from the array of meats and stews after watching Rolfe eat some himself, so the likelihood of that wish coming true was rather low.

"Mistress Sardothien," Rolfe said, his dark brows rising high on his forehead. "You must be famished. Or is my food not pleasing enough for your refined palate?"

Beneath the cape and the cloak and the dark tunic, Celaena was not just famished, but also hot and tired. And thirsty. Which, combined with her temper, usually turned out to be a lethal combination. Of course, they couldn't see any of that.

"I'm quite fine," she lied, swirling the water in her goblet. It lapped against the sides, taunting her with each rotation. Celaena stopped.

"Maybe if you took off your mask, you might have an easier time eating," Rolfe said, taking a bite of roasted duck. "Unless what lies beneath it will make us lose our appetites."

The five other pirates—all captains in Rolfe's fleet—sniggered.

"Keep talking like that"—Celaena gripped the stem of her goblet—"and I might give *you* a reason to wear a mask." Sam kicked her under the table, and she kicked him back, a deft blow to his shins—hard enough that he choked on his water.

Some of the assembled captains stopped laughing, but Rolfe chuckled. She rested her gloved hand atop the stained dining table. The table was freckled with burns and deep gouges; it had clearly seen its fair share of brawls. Didn't Rolfe have *any* taste for luxury? Perhaps he wasn't so well off, if he was resorting to the slave trade. But Arobynn . . . Arobynn was as rich as the King of Adarlan himself.

Rolfe flicked his sea-green eyes to Sam, who was frowning yet again. "Have you seen her without the mask?"

Sam, to her surprise, grimaced. "Once." He gave her an all too believably wary look. "And that was enough."

Rolfe studied Sam for a heartbeat, then took another bite of his meat. "Well, if you won't show me your face, then perhaps you'll indulge us with the tale of how, exactly, you became protégée to Arobynn Hamel?"

"I trained," she said dully. "For years. We aren't all lucky enough to have a magic map inked on our hands. Some of us had to climb to the top."

Rolfe stiffened, and the other pirates halted their eating. He stared at her long enough for Celaena to want to squirm, and then set down his fork.

Sam leaned a bit closer to her, but, she realized, only to see better as Rolfe laid both of his hands palm up on the table.

Together, his hands formed a map of their continent—and only that.

"This map hasn't moved for eight years." His voice was a low growl. A chill went down her spine. Eight years. Exactly the time that had passed since the Fae had been banished and executed, when Adarlan had conquered and enslaved the rest of the continent and magic had disappeared. "Don't think," Rolfe continued, withdrawing his hands, "that I haven't had to claw and kill my way as much as you."

If he was nearly thirty, then he'd probably done even more killing than she had. And, from the many scars on his hands and face, it was easy to tell that he'd done a *lot* of clawing.

"Good to know we're kindred spirits," she said. If Rolfe was already used to getting his hands dirty, then trading slaves wasn't a stretch. But he was a filthy pirate. They were Arobynn Hamel's assassins—educated, wealthy, refined. Slavery was beneath them.

Rolfe gave her that crooked smile. "Do you act like this because it's actually in your nature, or is it just because you're afraid of dealing with people?"

"I'm the world's greatest assassin." She lifted her chin. "I'm not afraid of anyone."

"Really?" Rolfe asked. "Because I'm the world's greatest pirate, and I'm afraid of a great number of people. That's how I've managed to stay alive for so long."

She didn't deign to reply. *Slave-mongering pig.* He shook his head, smiling in exactly the same way she smirked at Sam when she wanted to piss him off.

"I'm surprised Arobynn hasn't made you check your arrogance," Rolfe said. "Your companion seems to know when to keep his mouth shut."

Sam coughed loudly and leaned forward. "How did you become Pirate Lord, then?"

Rolfe ran a finger along a deep groove in the wooden table. "I killed every pirate who was better than me." The three other captains—all older, all more weathered and far less attractive than him—huffed, but didn't refute it. "Anyone arrogant enough to think they couldn't possibly lose to a young man with a patchwork crew and only one ship to his name. But they all fell, one by one. When you get a reputation like that, people tend to flock to you." Rolfe glanced between Celaena and Sam. "You want my advice?" he asked her.

"No."

"I'd watch your back around Sam. You might be the best, Sardothien, but there's always someone waiting for you to slip."

Sam, the traitorous bastard, didn't hide his smirk. The other pirate captains chuckled.

Celaena stared hard at Rolfe. Her stomach twisted with hunger. She'd eat later—swipe something from the tavern kitchens. "You want *my* advice?"

He waved a hand, beckoning her to go on.

"Mind your own business."

Rolfe gave her a lazy smile.

"I don't mind Rolfe," Sam mused later into the pitch darkness of their room. Celaena, who'd taken first watch, glared toward where his bed lay against the far wall.

"Of course you don't," she grumbled, relishing the free air on her face. Seated on her bed, she leaned against the wall and picked at the threads on the blanket. "He told you to assassinate me."

Sam chuckled. "It *is* wise advice."

She rolled up the sleeves of her tunic. Even at night, this rotten place was scorching hot. "Perhaps it isn't a wise idea for *you* to go to sleep, then."

Sam's mattress groaned as he turned over. "Come on—you can't take a bit of teasing?"

"Where my life is concerned? No."

Sam snorted. "Believe me, if I came home without you, Arobynn would skin me alive. Literally. If I'm going to kill you, Celaena, it'll be when I can actually get away with it."

She scowled. "I appreciate that." She fanned her sweating face with a hand. She'd sell her soul to a pack of demons for a cool breeze right now, but they had to keep the window covered—unless she wanted some spying pair of eyes to discover what she looked like. Though, now that she thought about it, she'd *love* to see the look on Rolfe's face if he found out the truth. Most already knew that she was a young woman, but if he knew he was dealing with a sixteen-year-old, his pride might never recover.

They'd only be here for three nights; they could both go without a little sleep if it meant keeping her identity—and their lives—safe.

"Celaena?" Sam asked into the dark. "*Should* I worry about going to sleep?"

She blinked, then laughed under her breath. At least Sam took her threats somewhat seriously. She wished she could say the same for Rolfe. "No," she said. "Not tonight."

"Some other night, then," he mumbled. Within minutes, he was out.

Celaena rested her head against the wooden wall, listening to the sound of his breathing as the long hours of the night stretched by.

CHAPTER 4

Even when her turn to sleep came, Celaena lay awake. In the hours she'd spent watching over their room, one thought had become increasingly problematic.

The slaves.

Perhaps if Arobynn had sent someone else—perhaps if it was just a business deal that she found out about later, when she was too busy to care—she might not have been so bothered by it. But to send her to retrieve a shipment of slaves . . . people who had done nothing wrong, only dared to fight for their freedom and the safety of their families . . .

How could Arobynn expect her to do that? If Ben had been alive, she might have found an ally in him; Ben, despite his profession, was the most compassionate person she knew. His death left a vacancy that she didn't think could ever be filled.

She sweated so much that her sheets became damp, and slept so little that when dawn came, she felt like she'd been trampled by a herd of wild horses from the Eyllwe grasslands.

Sam finally nudged her—a none-too-gentle prodding with the pommel of his sword. He said, "You look horrible."

Deciding to let that set the tone for the day, Celaena got out of bed and promptly slammed the bathroom door.

When she emerged a while later, as fresh as she could get using only the washbasin and her hands, she understood one thing with perfect clarity.

There was no way—no way in any realm of Hell—that she was going to bring those slaves to Rifthold. Rolfe could keep them for all she cared, but she wouldn't be the one to transport them to the capital city.

That meant she had two days to figure out how to ruin Arobynn and Rolfe's deal.

And find a way to come out of it alive.

She slung her cape over her shoulders, silently bemoaning the fact that the yards of fabric concealed much of her lovely black tunic—especially its delicate golden embroidery. Well, at least her cape was also exquisite. Even if it was a bit dirty from so much traveling.

"Where are you going?" Sam asked. He sat up from where he lounged on the bed, cleaning his nails with the tip of a dagger. Sam definitely wouldn't help her. She'd have to find a way to get out of the deal on her own.

"I have some questions to ask Rolfe. Alone." She fastened her mask and strode to the door. "I want breakfast waiting for me when I return."

Sam went rigid, his lips forming a thin line. "What?"

Celaena pointed to the hallway, toward the kitchen. "Breakfast," she said slowly. "I'm hungry."

Sam opened his mouth, and she waited for the retort, but it never came. He bowed deeply. "As you wish," he said. They swapped particularly vulgar gestures before she stalked down the hallway.

Dodging puddles of filth, vomit, and the gods knew what else, Celaena found it just a *tad* difficult to match Rolfe's long stride. With rain clouds gathering overhead, many of the people in the street—raggedy pirates swaying where they stood, prostitutes stumbling past after a long night, barefoot orphans running amok—had begun migrating into the various ramshackle buildings.

Skull's Bay wasn't a beautiful city by any definition, and many of the leaning and sagging buildings seemed to have been constructed from little more than wood and nails. Aside from its denizens, the city was most famous for Ship-Breaker, the giant chain that hung across the mouth of the horseshoe-shaped bay.

It had been around for centuries, and was so large that, as its name implied, it could snap the mast of any ship that came up against it. While mostly designed to discourage any attacks, it also kept anyone from sneaking off. And given that the rest of the island was covered with towering mountains, there weren't many other places for a ship to safely dock. So, any ship that wanted to enter or exit the harbor had to wait for it to be lowered under the surface—and be ready to pay a hefty fee.

"You have three blocks," Rolfe said. "Better make them count."

Was he deliberately walking fast? Steadying her rising temper, Celaena focused on the jagged, lush mountains hovering around the city, on the glittering curve of the bay, on the hint of sweetness in the air. She'd found Rolfe just about to leave the tavern to go to a business meeting, and he'd agreed to let her ask questions as he walked.

"When the slaves arrive," she said, trying to sound as inconvenienced as possible, "will I get the chance to inspect them, or can I trust that you're giving us a good batch?"

He shook his head at her impertinence, and Celaena jumped over the outstretched legs of an unconscious—or dead—drunk in her path. "They'll arrive tomorrow afternoon. I was *planning* to inspect them myself, but if you're so worried about the quality of your wares, I'll allow you to join me. Consider it a privilege."

She snorted. "Where? On your ship?" Better to get a good sense of how everything worked, and then build her plan from there. Knowing how things operated might create some ideas for how to make the deal fall apart with as little risk as possible.

"I've converted a large stable at the other end of the town into a holding facility. I usually examine all the slaves there, but since you're leaving the next morning, we'll examine yours on the ship itself."

She clicked her tongue loudly enough for him to hear it. "And how long can I expect this to take?"

He raised an eyebrow. "You have better things to do?"

"Just answer the question." Thunder rumbled in the distance.

They reached the docks, which were by far the most impressive thing about the town. Ships of all shapes and sizes rocked against the wooden piers, and pirates scurried along the decks, tying down various things before the storm hit. On the horizon, lightning flashed above the lone watchtower perched along the northern entrance to the bay—the watchtower from which Ship-Breaker was raised and lowered. In the flash, she'd also seen the two catapults atop one of the tower landings. If Ship-Breaker didn't destroy a boat, then those catapults finished the job.

"Don't worry, Mistress Sardothien," Rolfe said, striding past the various taverns and inns that lined the docks. They had two blocks left. "Your time won't be wasted. Though getting through a hundred slaves will take a while."

A hundred slaves on one ship! Where did they all *fit*?

"As long as you don't try to fool me," she snapped, "I'll consider it time well spent."

"So you don't find reasons to complain—and I'm sure you'll try your best to do just that—I have another shipment of slaves being inspected at the holding facility tonight. Why don't you join me? That way, you can have something to compare them to tomorrow."

That would be perfect, actually. Perhaps she could merely claim the slaves weren't up to par and refuse to do business with him. And then leave, no harm done to either of them. She'd still have to face Sam—and then Arobynn—but . . . she'd figure them out later.

She waved a hand. "Fine, fine. Send someone for me when it's time." The humidity was so thick she felt as if she were swimming through it. "And after Arobynn's slaves are inspected?" Any bit of information could later be used as a weapon against him. "Are they mine to look after on the ship, or will your men be watching them for me? Your pirates might very well think they're free to take whatever slaves they wish."

Rolfe clenched the hilt of his sword. It glinted in the muted light, and she admired the intricate pommel, shaped like a sea dragon's head. "If I give the order that no one is to touch your slaves, then no one will touch them," Rolfe said through his teeth. His annoyance was an unexpected delight. "However, I'll arrange to have a few guards on the ship, if that will make you sleep easier. I wouldn't want Arobynn to think I don't take his investment seriously."

They approached a blue-painted tavern, where several men in dark tunics lounged out front. At the sight of Rolfe, they straightened, saluting him. His guards? Why hadn't anyone escorted him through the streets?

"That will be fine," she said crisply. "I don't want to be here any longer than necessary."

"I'm sure you're eager to return to your clients in Rifthold." Rolfe stopped in front of the faded door. The sign above it, swinging in the growing storm winds, said THE SEA DRAGON. It was also the name of his famed ship, which was docked just behind them, and really didn't look all that spectacular, anyway. Perhaps *this* was the Pirate Lord's headquarters. And if he was making her and Sam stay at that tavern a few blocks away, then perhaps he trusted them as little as they trusted him.

"I think I'm more eager to return to civilized society," she said sweetly.

Rolfe let out a low growl and stepped onto the threshold of the tavern. Inside, it was all shadows and murmuring voices—and reeked of stale ale. Other than that, she could see nothing.

"One day," Rolfe said, too quietly, "someone's really going to make you pay for that arrogance." Lightning made his green eyes flicker. "I just hope I'm there to see it."

He shut the tavern door in her face.

Celaena smiled, and her smile grew wider as fat drops of rain splattered on the rust-colored earth, instantly cooling the muggy air.

That had gone surprisingly well.

"Is it poisoned?" she asked Sam, plopping down on her bed as a clap of thunder shook the tavern to its foundations. The teacup rattled in its saucer, and she breathed in the smell of fresh-baked bread, sausage, and porridge as she threw back her hood and removed her mask.

"By them, or by me?" Sam was sitting on the floor, his back against the bed.

Celaena sniffed all her food. "Do I detect . . . belladonna?"

Sam gave her a flat stare, and Celaena smirked as she tore a bite from the bread. They sat in silence for a few minutes, the only sounds the scrape of her utensils against the chipped plates, the drumming of the rain on the roof, and the occasional groan of a thunderhead breaking.

"So," Sam said. "Are you going to tell me what you're planning, or should I warn Rolfe to expect the worst?"

She sipped daintily at her tea. "I don't have the faintest idea what you're talking about, Sam Cortland."

"What sort of 'questions' did you ask him?"

She set down her teacup. Rain lashed the shutters, muffling the clink of her cup against the saucer. "Polite ones."

"Oh? I didn't think you knew what polite meant."

"I can be polite when it pleases me."

"When it gets you what you want, you mean. So what is it you want from Rolfe?"

She studied her companion. *He* certainly didn't seem to have any qualms about the deal. While he might not trust Rolfe, it didn't bother him that a hundred innocent souls were about to be traded like cattle. "I wanted to ask him more about the map on his hands."

"Damn it, Celaena!" Sam slammed his fist onto the wooden floor. "Tell me the truth!"

"Why?" she asked, giving him a pout. "And how do you know I'm *not* telling the truth?"

Sam got to his feet and began pacing the length of their small room. He undid the top button of his black tunic, revealing the skin beneath. Something about it felt strangely intimate, and Celaena found herself quickly looking away from him.

"We've grown up together." Sam stopped at the foot of her bed. "You think I don't know how to tell when you're cooking up some scheme? What do you want from Rolfe?"

If she told him, he'd do everything in his power to prevent her from ruining the deal. And having one enemy was enough. With her plan still unformed, she *had* to keep Sam out of it. Besides, if worse came to worst, Rolfe might very well kill Sam for being involved. Or simply for knowing her.

"Maybe I'm just unable to resist how handsome he is," she said.

Sam went rigid. "He's twelve years older than you."

"So?" He didn't think she was *serious*, did he?

He gave her a look so scathing it could have turned her to ash, and he stalked to the window, ripping his cloak down.

"What are you doing?"

He flung open the wooden shutters to reveal a sky full of rain and forked lightning. "I'm sick of suffocating. And if you're interested in Rolfe, he's bound to find out what you look like at some point, isn't he? So why bother slowly roasting to death?"

"Shut the window." He only crossed his arms. "*Shut it,*" she growled.

When he made no move to close the window, she jumped to her feet, upsetting the tray of food on her mattress, and shoved him aside hard enough for him to take a step back. Keeping her head down, she shut the window and shutters and threw his cape over the whole thing.

"Idiot," she seethed. "What's gotten into you?"

Sam stepped closer, his breath hot on her face. "I'm tired of all the melodrama and nonsense that happens whenever you wear that ridiculous mask and cloak. And I'm even more tired of you ordering me around."

So *that's* what this was about. "Get used to it."

She made to turn to her bed, but he grabbed her wrist. "Whatever plan you're concocting, whatever bit of intrigue you're about to drag me into, just remember that you're not head of the Assassins' Guild *yet*. You still answer to Arobynn."

She rolled her eyes, yanking her wrist out of his grasp. "Touch me again," she said, striding to her bed and picking up the spilled food, "and you'll lose that hand."

Sam didn't speak to her after that.

CHAPTER 5

Dinner with Sam was silent, and Rolfe appeared at eight to bring them both to the holding facility. Sam didn't even ask where they were going. He just played along, as if he'd known the whole time.

The holding facility was an enormous wooden warehouse, and even from down the block, something about the place made Celaena's instincts scream at her to get away. The sharp reek of unwashed bodies didn't hit her until they stepped inside. Blinking against the brightness of the torches and crude chandeliers, it took her a few heartbeats to sort out what she was seeing.

Rolfe, striding ahead of them, didn't falter as he passed cell after cell packed with slaves. Instead, he walked toward a large open space in the rear of the warehouse, where a nut-brown Eyllwe man stood before a cluster of four pirates.

Beside her, Sam let out a breath, his face wan. If the smell wasn't bad enough, the people in the cells, clinging to the bars or cowering against the walls or clutching their children—*children*—ripped at every shred of her being.

Aside from some occasional muffled weeping, the slaves were silent. Some of their eyes widened at the sight of her. She'd forgotten how she must appear—faceless, cloak waving behind her, striding past them like Death itself. Some of the slaves even sketched invisible marks in the air, warding off whatever evil they thought she was.

She took in the locks on the pens, counting the number of people crammed into each cell. They hailed from all the kingdoms on the continent. There were even some orange-haired, gray-eyed mountain clansmen—wild-looking men who tracked her movements. And women—some of them barely older than Celaena herself. Had they been fighters, too, or just in the wrong place at the wrong time?

Celaena's heart pounded faster. Even after all these years, people still defied Adarlan's conquest. But what right did Adarlan—or Rolfe, or anyone—have to treat them like this? Conquest wasn't enough; no, Adarlan had to *break* them.

Eyllwe, she'd heard, had taken the brunt of it. Though their king had yielded his power to the King of Adarlan, Eyllwe soldiers still could be found fighting in the rebel groups that plagued Adarlan's forces. But the land itself was too vital for Adarlan to abandon. Eyllwe boasted two of the most prosperous cities on the continent; its territory—rich in farmland, waterways, and forests—was a crucial vein in trade routes. Now, it seemed, Adarlan had decided that it might make money off its people, too.

The men standing around the Eyllwe prisoner parted as Rolfe approached, bowing their heads. She recognized two of the men from dinner the previous night: the short, bald Captain Fairview and the one-eyed, hulking Captain Blackgold. Celaena and Sam stopped beside Rolfe.

The Eyllwe man had been stripped naked, his wiry body already bruised and bleeding.

"This one fought back a bit," said Captain Fairview. Though sweat gleamed on the slave's skin, he kept his chin high, his eyes upon some distant sight. He must have been around twenty. Did he have a family?

"Keep him in irons, though, and he'll fetch a good price," Fairview went on, wiping his face on the shoulder of his crimson tunic. The gold embroidery was fraying, and the fabric, which had probably once been rich with color, was faded and stained. "I'd send him to the market in Bellhaven. Lots of rich men there needing strong hands to do their building. Or women needing strong hands for something else entirely." He winked in Celaena's direction.

Unyielding rage boiled up so fast the breath was knocked from her. She didn't realize her hand was moving toward her sword until Sam knotted his fingers through hers. It was a casual-enough gesture, and to anyone else, it might have looked affectionate. But he squeezed her fingers tightly enough for her to know that he was well aware of what she was about to do.

"How many of these slaves will actually be deemed useful?" Sam asked, releasing her gloved fingers. "Ours are all going to Rifthold, but you're dividing this batch up?"

Rolfe said, "You think your master is the first to strike a deal with me? We have other agreements in different cities. My partners in Bellhaven tell me what the wealthy are looking for, and I supply them. If I can't think of a good place to sell the slaves, I'll send them to Calaculla. If your master has leftovers, sending them to Endovier might be a good option. Adarlan's stingy with what they'll offer when buying slaves for the salt mines, but it's better than making no money at all."

So Adarlan wasn't just snatching prisoners from battlefields and their homes—they were *buying* slaves for the Salt Mines of Endovier, too.

"And the children?" she asked, keeping her voice was neutral as possible. "Where do they go?"

Rolfe's eyes darkened a bit at that, glimmering with enough guilt that Celaena wondered if the slave trade had been a last resort for him. "We try to keep the children with their mothers," he said quietly. "But at the auction block, we can't control whether they're separated."

She fought the retort on her tongue, and just said, "I see. Are they a burden to sell? And how many children can we expect in our shipment?"

"We have about ten here," Rolfe said. "Your shipment shouldn't contain more than that. And they're not a burden to sell, if you know where to sell them."

"Where?" Sam demanded.

"Some wealthy households might want them for scullery maids or stableboys." Though his voice remained steady, Rolfe studied the ground. "A brothel madam might show up at the auction, too."

Sam's face went white with fury. If there was one thing that set him off, one subject she *knew* she could always rely upon to rile him, it was this.

His mother, sold at eight to a brothel, had spent her too-short twenty-eight years clawing her way up from an orphan to one of the most successful courtesans in Rifthold. She'd had Sam only six years before she'd died—murdered by a jealous client. And though she'd amassed some money, it hadn't been enough to liberate her from her brothel—or to provide for Sam. But she'd been a favorite of Arobynn's, and when he'd learned that she wanted Sam to be trained by him, he'd taken the boy in.

"We'll take that into consideration," Sam said sharply.

It wasn't enough for Celaena to ensure the deal fell apart. No, that wasn't *nearly* enough. Not when all of these people were imprisoned here. Her blood pounded in her veins. Death, at least, was quick. Especially when dealt by her hand. But slavery was unending suffering.

"Very well," she said, lifting her chin. She had to get out of here—and get *Sam* out of here before he snapped. A deadly gleam was growing in his eyes. "I look forward to seeing our shipment tomorrow night." She inclined her head toward the pens behind her. "When will these slaves be sent out?" It was such a dangerous, stupid question.

Rolfe looked to Captain Fairview, who rubbed his dirty head. "This lot? We'll divvy them up, and they'll be loaded onto a new ship tomorrow, probably. They'll sail around the same time you do, I bet. We need to assemble crews." He and Rolfe started off on a conversation about manning the ships, and Celaena took that as her cue to leave.

With a final look at the slave still standing there, Celaena strode out of the warehouse that stank of fear and death.

"Celaena, *wait*!" Sam called, panting as he walked after her.

She couldn't wait. She'd just started walking, and walking, and walking, and now, as she reached the empty beach far from the lights of Skull's Bay, she wouldn't stop walking until she reached the water.

Not too far down the curve in the bay, the watchtower stood guard, Ship-Breaker hanging across the water for the duration of the night. The moon illuminated the powder-fine sand and turned the calm sea into a silver mirror.

She removed her mask and dropped it behind her, then ripped off her cloak, boots, and tunic. The damp breeze kissed her bare skin, fluttering her delicate white undershirt.

"*Celaena!*"

Bath-warm waves flooded past her, and she kicked up a spray of water as she kept walking. Before she could get deeper than her calves, Sam grabbed her arm.

"What are you doing?" he demanded. She yanked on her arm, but he held firm.

In a single, swift movement, she twirled, swinging her other arm. But he knew the move—because he'd practiced it right alongside her for years—and he caught her other hand. "*Stop*," he said, but she swept her foot. She caught him behind the knee, sending him tumbling down. Sam didn't release her, and water and sand sprayed as they hit the ground.

Celaena landed on top of him, but Sam didn't pause for a moment. Before she could give him a sharp elbow to the face, he flipped her. The air whooshed out of her lungs. Sam lunged for her, and she had the sense to bring her feet up just as he leapt. She kicked him square in the stomach. He cursed as he dropped to his knees. The surf broke around him, a shower of silver.

She sprang into a crouch, the sand hissing beneath her feet as she made to tackle him.

But Sam had been waiting, and he twisted away, catching her by the shoulders and throwing her to the ground.

She knew she'd been caught before he even finished slamming her into the sand. He pinned her wrists, his knees digging into her thighs to keep her from getting her legs under her again.

"*Enough!*" His fingers dug painfully into her wrists. A rogue wave reached them, soaking her.

She thrashed, her fingers curling, straining to draw blood, but they couldn't reach his hands. The sand shifted enough that she could scarcely get a steady surface to support herself, to flip him. But Sam knew her—he knew her movements, knew what tricks she liked to pull.

"*Stop*," he said, his breathing ragged. "Please."

In the moonlight, his handsome face was strained. "Please," he repeated hoarsely.

The sorrow—the defeat—in his voice made her pause. A wisp of cloud passed over the moon, illuminating the strong panes of his cheekbones, the curve of his lips—the kind of rare beauty that had made his mother so successful. Far above his head, stars flickered faintly, nearly invisible in the glow of the moon.

"I'm not going to let go until you promise to stop attacking me," Sam said. His face was inches away, and she felt the breath of every one of his words on her mouth.

She took an uneven breath, then another. She had no reason to attack Sam. Not when he'd kept her from gutting that pirate in the warehouse. Not when he'd gotten so riled about the slave children. Her legs trembled with pain.

"I promise," she mumbled.

"Swear it."

"I swear on my life."

He watched her for a second longer, then slowly eased off her. She waited until he was standing, then got to her feet. Both of them were soaked and crusted with sand, and she was fairly certain her hair had come half out of her braid and she looked like a raging lunatic.

"So," he said, taking off his boots and tossing them onto the sand behind them. "Are you going to explain yourself?" He rolled his pants up to the knees and took a few steps into the surf.

Celaena began pacing, waves splattering at her feet. "I just . . . ," she began, but waved an arm, shaking her head fiercely.

"You what?" His words were almost drowned out by the crashing waves.

She whirled to face him. "How can you bear to look at those people and not do anything?"

"The slaves?"

She resumed her pacing. "It makes me sick. It makes me . . . makes me so mad I think I might . . ." She couldn't finish the thought.

"Might what?" Splashing steps sounded, and she looked over her shoulder to find him approaching. He crossed his arms, bracing for a fight. "Might do something as foolish as attacking Rolfe's men in their own warehouse?"

It was now or never. She hadn't wanted to involve him, but . . . now that her plans had changed, she needed his help.

"I might do something as foolish as freeing the slaves," she said.

Sam went so still that he might have been turned into stone. "I knew you were thinking up something—but *freeing* them . . ."

"I'm going to do it with or without you." She'd only intended to ruin the deal, but from the moment she'd walked into that warehouse tonight, she'd known she couldn't leave the slaves there.

"Rolfe will kill you," Sam said. "Or Arobynn will, if Rolfe doesn't first."

"I have to try," she said.

"Why?" Sam stepped close enough that she needed to tilt her head back to see his face. "We're assassins. We *kill* people. We destroy lives every day."

"We have a choice," she breathed. "Maybe not when we were children—when it was Arobynn or death—but now . . . Now you and I have a *choice* in the things we do. Those slaves were just *taken*. They were fighting for their freedom, or lived too close to a battlefield, or some mercenaries passed through their town and *stole* them. They're innocent people."

"And we weren't?"

Something icy pierced her heart at the glimmer of memory. "We kill corrupt officials and adulterous spouses; we make it quick and clean. These are entire families being ripped apart. Every one of these people used to be somebody."

Sam's eyes glowed. "I'm not disagreeing with you. I don't like the idea of this at all. Not just the slaves, but Arobynn's involvement.

And those children . . ." He pinched the bridge of his nose. "But we're just two people—surrounded by Rolfe's pirates."

She gave him a crooked grin. "Then it's good that we're the best. And," she added, "it's good that I've been asking him so many questions about his plans for the next two days."

Sam blinked. "You realize this is the most reckless thing you've ever done, right?"

"Reckless, but maybe the most meaningful, too."

Sam stared at her long enough for heat to flood her cheek, as if he could see right inside of her—see everything. The fact that he didn't turn away from whatever he saw made her blood thrum in her veins. "I suppose if we're going to die, it should be for a noble cause," he said.

She snorted, using it as an excuse to step away from him. "We're not going to die. At least, not if we follow my plan."

He groaned. "You already have a plan?"

She grinned, then told him everything. When she finished, he only scratched his head. "Well," he admitted, sitting on the sand, "I suppose that'd work. We'd have to time it right, but . . ."

"But it could work." She sat beside him.

"When Arobynn finds out . . ."

"Leave Arobynn to me. I'll figure out how to deal with him."

"We could always just . . . *not* return to Rifthold," Sam suggested.

"What, run away?"

Sam shrugged. Though he kept his eyes on the waves, she could have sworn a blush darkened his cheeks. "He might very well kill us."

"If we ran away, he'd hunt us for the rest of our lives. Even if we took different names, he'd find us." As if she could leave her entire life behind! "He's invested too much money in us—and we've yet to pay him back entirely. He'd see it as a bad investment."

Sam's gaze drifted northward, as if he could see the sprawling capital city and its towering glass castle. "I think there's more at work here than this trade agreement."

"What do you mean?"

Sam traced circles in the sand between them. "I mean, why send the two of us here in the first place? His excuse for sending us was a lie. We're not instrumental to this deal. He could just as easily have sent two other assassins who aren't at each other's throats all the time."

"What are you implying?"

Sam shrugged. "Perhaps Arobynn wanted us out of Rifthold right now. Needed to get us out of the city for a month."

A chill went through her. "Arobynn wouldn't do that."

"Wouldn't he?" Sam asked. "Did we ever find out why Ben was there the night Gregori got captured?"

"If you're implying that Arobynn somehow set Ben up to—"

"I'm not implying anything. But some things don't add up. And there are questions that haven't been answered."

"We're not supposed to question Arobynn," she murmured.

"And since when do you ever follow orders?"

She stood. "Let's get through the next few days. Then we'll consider whatever conspiracy theories you're inventing."

Sam was on his feet in an instant. "I don't have any *theories*. Just questions that you should be asking yourself, too. *Why* did he want us gone this month?"

"We can trust Arobynn." Even as the words left her mouth, she felt stupid for saying them.

Sam stooped to pick up his boots. "I'm going back to the tavern. Are you coming?"

"No. I'm staying here for a little longer."

Sam gave her an appraising look, but nodded. "We're to examine Arobynn's slaves on their ship at four tomorrow afternoon. Try not to stay out here the whole night. We need all the rest we can get."

She didn't reply, and turned away before she could watch him head toward the golden lights of Skull's Bay.

She walked along the curve of the shoreline, all the way to the lone watchtower. After studying it from the shadows—the two catapults near its top, the giant chain anchored above them—she continued on. She walked until there was nothing in the world but the grumble and hiss of the waves, the sigh of the sand beneath her feet, and the glare of the moon on the water.

She walked until a surprisingly cold breeze swept past her. She halted.

Slowly, Celaena turned north, toward the source of the breeze, which smelled of a faraway land she hadn't seen in eight years. Pine and snow—a city still in winter's grasp. She breathed it in, staring across the leagues of lonely, black ocean, seeing, somehow, that distant city that had once, long ago, been her home. The wind ripped the strands of hair from her braid, lashing them across her face. Orynth. A city of light and music, watched over by an alabaster castle with an opal tower so bright it could be viewed for miles.

The moonlight vanished behind a thick cloud. In the sudden dark, the stars glowed brighter.

She knew all the constellations by heart, and she instinctively sought out the Stag, Lord of the North, and the immovable star that crowned his head.

Back then, she hadn't had any choice. When Arobynn offered her this path, it was either that, or death. But now . . .

She took a shuddering breath. No, she was as limited in her choices as she'd been when she was eight years old. She was Adarlan's Assassin, Arobynn Hamel's protégée and heir—and she would always be.

It was a long walk back to the tavern.

CHAPTER 6

After yet another miserably hot and sleepless night, Celaena spent the following day with Sam, walking through the streets of Skull's Bay. They kept their pace leisurely, pausing at various vendors' carts and popping into the occasional shop, but all the while tracing each step of their plan, going over every detail that they'd need to orchestrate perfectly.

From the fishermen along the docks, they learned that the rowboats tied to the piers belonged to nobody in particular, and that tomorrow's morning tide came in just after sunrise. Not advantageous, but better than midday.

From flirting with the harlots along the main street, Sam learned that every once in a while, Rolfe covered the tab for all the pirates in his service, and the revelry lasted for days. Sam also picked up a few other pointers that he refused to tell Celaena about.

And from the half-drunk pirate languishing in an alley, Celaena learned how many men guarded the slave ships, what manner of weapons they carried, and where the slaves were kept.

When four o'clock rolled around, Celaena and Sam were standing aboard the ship Rolfe had promised them, watching and counting as the slaves stumbled onto the wide deck. Ninety-three. Mostly men, most of them young. The women were a broader range of ages, and there were only a handful of children, just as Rolfe had said.

"Do they meet your refined tastes?" Rolfe asked as he approached.

"I thought you said there'd be more," she replied coldly, keeping her eyes upon the chained slaves.

"We had an even hundred, but seven died on the journey."

She bit back the anger that flared. Sam, knowing her far too well for her liking, cut in. "And how many can we expect to lose on the journey to Rifthold?" His face was relatively neutral, though his brown eyes flashed with annoyance. Fine—he was a good liar. As good as she was, maybe.

Rolfe ran a hand through his dark hair. "Don't you two ever stop *questioning*? There's no way of predicting how many slaves you'll lose. Just keep them watered and fed."

A low growl slipped through her teeth, but Rolfe was already walking to his group of guards. Celaena and Sam followed him, observing as the last of the slaves were shoved onto the deck.

"Where are the slaves from yesterday?" Sam asked.

Rolfe waved a hand. "Most are on that ship, and will leave tomorrow." He pointed to a nearby ship and ordered one of the slave drivers to start the inspection.

They waited until a few slaves had been looked over, offering remarks on how fit a slave was, where he'd fetch a good price in Rifthold. Each word tasted fouler than the last.

"Tonight," she said to the Pirate Lord, "you can guarantee that this ship's protected?" Rolfe sighed loudly and nodded. "That watchtower across the bay," she pressed. "I assume that they'll also be responsible for monitoring this ship, too?"

"Yes," Rolfe snapped. Celaena opened her mouth, but he interrupted. "And before you ask, let me say that we change the watch just before dawn." So they'd have to target the morning watch instead, to avoid any alarm being raised at dawn—at high tide. Which was a slight hitch in her plan, but they could easily fix it.

"How many of the slaves speak our language?" she asked.

Rolfe raised a brow. "Why?"

She could feel Sam tense beside her, but she shrugged. "It might add to their value."

Rolfe studied her a bit too closely, then whirled to face a slave woman standing nearby. "Do you speak the common tongue?"

She looked this way and that, clutching her scraps of clothing to her—a mix of fur and wool undoubtedly worn to keep her warm in the frigid mountain passes of the White Fangs.

"Do you understand what I'm saying?" Rolfe demanded. The woman lifted her shackled hands. Raw, red skin lay around the iron.

"I think the answer is no," Sam offered.

Rolfe glared at him, then walked through the stables. "Can any of you speak the common tongue?" He repeated himself, and was about to turn back when an older Eyllwe man—reed thin and covered with cuts and bruises—stepped forward.

"I can," he said.

"That's it?" Rolfe barked at the slaves. "No one else?" Celaena approached the man who had spoken, committing his face to memory. He recoiled at her mask and her cloak.

"Well, at least he might fetch a higher price," Celaena said over her shoulder to Rolfe. Sam summoned Rolfe with a question about the mountain-woman in front of him, providing enough distraction. "What's your name?" Celaena asked the slave.

"Dia." His long, frail fingers trembled slightly.

"You're fluent?"

He nodded. "My—my mother was from Bellhaven. My father was a merchant from Banjali. I grew up with both languages."

And he'd probably never worked a day in his life. How had *he* gotten caught up in this mess? The other slaves on the deck hung back, huddling together, even some of the larger men and women whose scars and bruises marked them as fighters—prisoners of war. Had they already seen enough of slavery to break them? For both her sake and theirs, she hoped not.

"Good," she said, and strode away.

Hours later, no one noticed—or if they did, they certainly didn't care—when two cloaked figures slipped into two rowboats and headed toward the slave ships hovering several hundred yards offshore. A few lanterns illuminated the behemoth vessels, but the moon was bright enough for Celaena to easily make out the *Golden Wolf* as she rowed toward it.

To her right, Sam rowed as quietly as he could to the *Loveless*, where the slaves from yesterday were being held. Silence was their only hope and ally, though the town behind them was already in the midst of revelry. It hadn't taken long for word to get out that Arobynn Hamel's assassins had opened a celebratory tab at the tavern, and even as they had strode to the docks, pirates were already streaming the other way toward the inn.

Panting through her mask, Celaena's arms ached with each stroke. It wasn't the town she was worried about, but the solitary watchtower to her left. A fire burned in its jagged turret, faintly illuminating the catapults and the ancient chain across the narrow bay mouth. If they were to be caught, the first alarm would be sounded from there.

It might have been easier to escape now—take down the watchtower, overpower the slave ships, and set sail—but the chain was only the first in a line of defenses. The Dead Islands were nearly impossible to navigate at night, and at low tide . . . They'd get a few miles and run aground on a reef or a sandbank.

Celaena drifted the last few feet to the *Golden Wolf* and grasped the rung of a wooden ladder to keep the boat from thudding too hard against the hull.

They were better off at first light tomorrow, when the pirates would be too drunk or unconscious to notice, and when they had high tide on their side.

Sam flashed a compact mirror, indicating he'd made it to the *Loveless*. Catching the light in her own mirror, she signaled him back, then flashed twice, indicating that she was ready.

A moment later, Sam returned the same signal. Celaena took a long, steadying breath.

It was time.

CHAPTER 7

Nimble as a cat and smooth as a snake, Celaena climbed the wooden ladder built into the side of the ship.

The first guard didn't notice she was upon him until her hands were around his neck, striking the two points that sent him into unconsciousness. He slumped to the deck, and she caught him by his filthy tunic, softening his fall. Quiet as mice, quiet as the wind, quiet as the grave.

The second guard, stationed at the helm, saw her coming up the staircase. He managed to emit a muffled cry before the pommel of her dagger slammed into his forehead. Not as neat, and not as quiet: he hit the deck with a thud that made the third guard, stationed at the prow, whirl to see.

But it was shadowy, and there were yards of ship between them. Celaena crouched low to the deck, covering the fallen guard's body with her cloak.

"Jon?" the third guard called across the deck. Celaena winced at the sound. Not too far away, the *Loveless* was silent.

Celaena grimaced at the reek from Jon's unwashed body.

"Jon?" the guard said, and thumping steps followed. Closer and closer. He'd see the first guard soon.

Three . . . two . . . one . . .

"What in *hell*?" The guard tripped over the first guard's prostrate body.

Celaena moved.

She swung over the railing fast enough that the guard didn't look up until she'd landed behind him. All it took was a swift blow to the head and she was easing his body down atop the first guard's. Her heart hammering through every inch of her, she sprinted to the prow of the ship. She flashed the mirror three times. Three guards down.

Nothing.

"Come on, Sam." She signaled again.

Far too many heartbeats later, a signal greeted her. The air rushed from her lungs in a breath she hadn't realized she'd been holding. The guards on the *Loveless* were unconscious, too.

She signaled once. The watchtower was still quiet. If the guards were up there, they hadn't seen anything. She had to be quick, had to get this done before her disappearance was noticed.

The guard outside the captain's quarters managed to kick the wall hard enough to wake the dead before she knocked him out, but it didn't stop Captain Fairview from squealing when she slipped into his office and shut the door.

When Fairview was secured in the brig, gagged and bound and fully aware that his cooperation and the cooperation of his guards meant his life, she crept down to the cargo area.

The passages were cramped, but the two guards at the door still didn't notice her until she took the liberty of rendering them unconscious.

Silently as she could, she grabbed a lantern hanging from a peg on the wall and opened the door. The reek almost brought her to her knees.

The ceiling was so low she almost grazed it with her head. The slaves had all been chained, sitting, to the floor. No latrines, no source of light, no food or water.

The slaves murmured, squinting against the sudden brightness of the torchlight leaking in from the hallway.

Celaena took the ring of keys she'd stolen from the captain's quarters and stepped into the cargo chamber. "Where is Dia?" she asked. They said nothing, either because they didn't understand, or out of solidarity.

Celaena sighed, stepping farther into the chamber, and some of the wild-eyed mountain men murmured to one another. While they might have only recently declared themselves Adarlan's enemies, the people of the White Fang Mountains had long been known for their unyielding love of violence. If she were to meet with any trouble in here, it would be from them. "Where is Dia?" she asked more loudly.

A trembling voice came from the back of the cargo area. "Here." Her eyes strained to spy his narrow, fine features. "I'm here."

She strode carefully through the crowded darkness. They were so close together that there was no room to move, and hardly any air to breathe. No wonder seven had died on the voyage here.

She took out Captain Fairview's key and freed the shackles at Dia's feet, then his manacles, before offering him a hand up. "You're going to translate for me." The mountain folk and whoever else didn't speak either the common tongue or Eyllwe could figure out enough on their own.

Dia rubbed his wrists, which were bleeding and scabbed in places. "Who are you?"

Celaena unlocked the chains of the too-thin woman beside Dia, then held out the keys in her direction. "A friend," she said. "Tell her to unlock everyone, but tell them *not* to leave this room."

Dia nodded, and spoke in Eyllwe. The woman, mouth slightly open, looked at Celaena, then took the keys. Without a word, she set about freeing her companions. Dia then addressed the entire cargo bay, his voice soft but fierce.

"The guards are unconscious," she said. Dia translated. "The captain has been locked in the brig, and tomorrow, should you choose to act, he will guide you through the Dead Islands and to safety. He knows that the penalty for bad information is death."

Dia translated, his eyes growing wider and wider. Somewhere near the back, one of the mountain men began translating. And then two others translated, too—one in the language of Melisande, and another in a language she didn't recognize. Had it been clever or cowardly of them not to speak up last night when she asked who spoke the common tongue?

"When I am done explaining our plan of action," she said, her hands shaking a bit as she suddenly recalled what, exactly, lay before them, "you may leave this room, but do not set foot on the decks. There are guards in the watchtower, and guards monitoring this ship from land. If they see you on the deck, they will warn everyone."

She let Dia and the others finish before going on.

"My colleague is already aboard the *Loveless*, another slave ship set to sail tomorrow." She swallowed hard. "When I am done here, he and I will return to the town and create a distraction large enough that when the dawn breaks, you will have enough time to sail out of the harbor. You need the full day to sail out of the Dead Islands before dark—or else you'll be caught in their labyrinth."

Dia translated, but a woman spoke from nearby. Dia frowned as he turned to Celaena. "She has two questions. What of the chain at the entrance to the bay? And how will we sail the ship?"

Celaena nodded. "Leave the chain to us. We'll have it down before you reach it."

When Dia and the others translated, murmurs broke out. Shackles were still thudding to the ground as slave after slave was unlocked.

"As for sailing the ship," she went on above the noise, "are any of you sailors? Fishermen?"

Some hands went up. "Captain Fairview will give you specific instructions. You'll have to row out of the bay, though. Everyone who has the strength will be needed on the oars, or you won't have a shot of outrunning Rolfe's ships."

"What of his fleet?" another man asked.

"Leave it to me." Sam was probably already rowing over to the *Golden Wolf.* They had to get back to shore *now.* "No matter if the chain is still up, no matter what might be happening in town, the moment the sun slips over the horizon, you start rowing like hell."

A few voices objected to Dia's translation, and he gave a sharp, short reply before turning to her. "We will sort out specifics on our own."

She lifted her chin. "Discuss it among yourselves. Your fate is yours to decide. But no matter what plan you choose, I *will* have the chain down, and will buy you as much time as I can at dawn."

She bowed her head in farewell as she left the cargo hold, beckoning Dia along with her. Discussion started behind them—muffled, at least.

In the hallway, she could see how thin he was, how filthy. She pointed down the hall. "That is where the brig is; there you'll find Captain Fairview. Get him out before dawn, and don't be afraid to bloody him up a bit if he refuses to talk. There are three unconscious guards tied up on the deck, a guard outside Fairview's quarters, and the two here. Do whatever you want with them; the choice is yours."

"I'll have someone take them to the brig," Dia said quickly. He rubbed at the stubble on his face. "How much time will we have to get away? How long before the pirates notice?"

"I don't know. I'll try to disable their ships, which might slow them down." They reached the narrow stairs that led to the upper decks. "There's one thing I need you to do," she continued, and he looked up at her, his eyes bright. "My colleague doesn't speak Eyllwe. I need you to take a rowboat to the other ship and tell them all that I've told you, and unlock their chains. We have to return to shore now, so you'll have to go alone."

Dia sucked in a breath, but nodded. "I will."

After Dia told the people in the cargo bay to take the unconscious guards to the brig, he crept with Celaena onto the empty deck. He cringed at the sight of the unconscious guards, but didn't object when she swept Jon's cloak over his shoulders and concealed his face in the folds of the cloak. Or when she gave him Jon's sword and dagger.

Sam was already waiting at the side of the ship, hidden from the far-seeing eyes of the watchtower. He helped Dia into the first rowboat before climbing into the second and waiting for Celaena to get aboard.

Blood gleamed on Sam's dark tunic, but they'd both packed a change of clothes. Silently, Sam picked up the oars. Celaena cleared her throat. Dia turned back to her.

She inclined her head east, toward the mouth of the bay. "Remember: you *must* start rowing at sunrise, even if the chain is up. Every moment you delay means losing the tide."

Dia grasped the oars. "We will be ready."

"Then good luck," she said. Without another word, Dia began rowing to the other ship, his strokes a bit too loud for her liking, but not enough to be detected.

Sam, too, started rowing, slipping around the curve of the prow and heading toward the docks at a casual, unsuspicious pace.

"Nervous?" he asked, his voice barely audible above the steady slice of his oars through the calm bay.

"No," she lied.

"Me, too."

Ahead of them were the golden lights of Skull's Bay. Hoots and cheers echoed across the water. Word had certainly spread about the free ale.

She smiled slightly. "Get ready to unleash hell."

CHAPTER 8

Though the chant of the crowd roared around them, Rolfe and Sam had their eyes closed in concentration as their throats moved up and down, down and up, chugging their mugs of ale. And Celaena, watching it from behind her mask, could not stop laughing.

It wasn't that hard to pretend Sam was drunk and they were having the grandest time in the world. Mostly because of her mask, but also because Sam played the part very, very well.

Rolfe slammed his mug on the table, letting out a satisfied "Ah!" and wiping his wet mouth on his sleeve as the gathered crowd cheered. Celaena cackled, her masked face oozing sweat. Like everyplace else on this island, the tavern was suffocatingly hot, and the odor of ale and unwashed bodies poured from every crevice and stone.

It was packed to capacity. A three-man ensemble made up of an accordion, a fiddle, and a tambourine played raucously in the corner by the hearth. Pirates swapped stories and called for their favorite songs. Peasants and lowlifes drank themselves into oblivion and gambled on rigged games of chance. Harlots patrolled the room, milling around tables and sitting on laps.

Across from her, Rolfe grinned, and Sam drained the last from his mug. Or so Rolfe thought. Given how often drinks were spilled and splashed, no one really noticed the constant puddle around Sam's mug, and the hole he'd drilled into the bottom of it was too small to detect.

The crowd dispersed, and Celaena laughed as she raised her hand. "Another round, gentlemen?" she cried, signaling for the barmaid.

"Well," Rolfe said, "I think it's safe to say that I prefer you like this to when we're discussing business."

Sam leaned in, a conspirator's grin on his face. "Oh, I do, too. She's horrible most of the time."

Celaena kicked him—hard enough, because she knew it wasn't entirely a lie—and Sam yelped. Rolfe chuckled.

She flipped the barmaid a copper as the woman refilled Rolfe's and Sam's mugs.

"So, will I ever get to see the face behind the legendary Celaena Sardothien?" Rolfe leaned forward to rest his arms on the sodden table. The clock behind the bar read three thirty in the morning. They had to act soon. Given how crowded the tavern was, and how many of the pirates were already halfway unconscious, it was a miracle there was any ale left in Skull's Bay. If Arobynn and Rolfe didn't kill her for freeing the slaves, then Rolfe might very well murder her for starting a tab with not nearly enough money to pay for it all.

She leaned closer to Rolfe. "If you make my master and me as much money as you claim, I'll show you my face."

Rolfe glanced at the tattooed map on his hands.

"Did you really sell your soul for that?" she asked.

"When you show me your face, I'll tell you the truth."

She extended her hand. "Deal." He shook it. Sam raised his mug—already drained half an inch from the small hole in the bottom—and saluted their promise before both men drank. She fished out a pack of cards from a cloak pocket. "Care for a game of Kings?"

"If you aren't beggared by the time this night is over," Rolfe said, "then playing against me will guarantee it."

She clicked her tongue. "Oh, I highly doubt that." She broke and shuffled the deck three times and dealt the cards.

The hours passed by in a series of clanking glasses and perfect card suites, group singing sessions and tales of lands far and near, and as the clock was silenced by the never-ending music, Celaena found herself leaning into Sam's shoulder, laughing as Rolfe finished his crude and absurd story of the farmer's wife and her stallions.

She banged her fist on the table, howling—and that wasn't entirely an act, either. As Sam slipped a hand around her waist, his touch somehow sending a bright-hot flame through her, she had to wonder if he was still pretending, too.

In terms of cards, it turned out to be Sam who took them for everything they were worth, and by the time the clock hands pointed to five, Rolfe had shifted into a foul mood.

Unfortunately for him, that mood wasn't about to improve. Sam gave Celaena a nod, and she tripped a passing pirate, who spilled his drink on an already belligerent man, who in turn tried to punch him in the face but hit the man next to him instead. By luck, at that moment, a trick card fell out of a man's sleeve, a prostitute slapped a pirate wench, and the tavern exploded into a brawl.

People wrestled one another to the ground, some pirates drawing swords and daggers to try to duel their way across the floor. Others jumped from the mezzanine to join the fight, swinging themselves across the railing, either attempting to land on tables or aiming for the iron chandelier and missing badly.

The music still played, and the musicians rose and backed farther into the corner. Rolfe, half-standing, put a hand on his hilt. Celaena gave him a nod before drawing her sword and charging into the brawling crowd.

With deft flicks of her wrist, she cut someone's arm and ripped another's leg open, but didn't actually kill anyone. She just needed to keep the fight going—and escalate it enough—to hold all eyes on the town.

As she made to slip toward the exit, someone grabbed her around the waist and threw her into a wooden pillar so hard she knew she'd have a bruise. She squirmed in the red-faced pirate's grasp, nearly gagging as his sour breath seeped through her mask. She got her arm free enough to thrust the pommel of her sword between his legs. He dropped to the ground like a stone.

Celaena barely got a step away before a hairy fist slammed into her jaw. Pain blinded her like lightning, and she tasted blood in her mouth. She quickly felt her mask to ensure it wasn't cracked or about to fall off.

Dodging the next blow, she swept her foot behind the man's knee and sent him careening into a yowling cluster of harlots. She didn't know where Sam had gone, but if he was sticking to the plan, then she didn't need to worry about him. Weaving through the snarls of fighting pirates, Celaena headed toward the exit, clashing her blade against several unskilled swords.

A pirate with a frayed eye patch raised a clumsy hand to strike her, but Celaena caught it and kicked him in the stomach, sending him flying into another man. They both hit a table, flipped over it, and began fighting between themselves. *Animals.* Celaena stalked through the crowd and out the front door of the tavern.

To her delight, the streets weren't much better. The fight had spread with astonishing speed. Up and down the avenue, pouring out of the other taverns, pirates wrestled and dueled and rolled on the ground. Apparently, she hadn't been the only one eager for a fight.

Reveling in the mayhem, she was halfway down the street, headed toward the meet-up point with Sam, when Rolfe's voice boomed out from behind her.

"*ENOUGH!*"

Everyone lifted whatever they had in their hands—a mug, a sword, a clump of hair—and saluted.

And then promptly resumed fighting.

Laughing to herself, Celaena hurried down an alley. Sam was already there, blood seeping from his nose, but his eyes were bright.

"I'd say that went pretty well," he said.

"I never knew you were such an expert card player." She looked him up and down. His stance was steady. "Or an expert drunkard."

He grinned. "There's a lot you don't know about me, Celaena Sardothien." He grabbed her shoulder, suddenly closer than she'd like. "Ready?" he asked, and she nodded, looking to the lightening sky.

"Let's go." She pulled out of his grasp and yanked off her gloves, stuffing them in her pocket. "The watch at the tower must have changed by now. We've got until dawn to disable that chain and the catapults." They'd debated for a while about whether it would be more useful to just destroy the chain from its unguarded opposite side. But even if they did, they'd still have the catapults to contend with. It was better to risk the guards and take out both the chain and the catapults at once.

"If we live through this, Celaena," Sam said, heading toward the side street that led to the docks, "remind me to teach you how to play cards properly."

She cursed colorfully enough to make him laugh, and launched into a run.

They turned onto a quiet street just as someone stepped out of the shadows.

"Going somewhere?"

It was Rolfe.

CHAPTER 9

Down the slope of the street, Celaena could perfectly see the two slave ships sitting—still unmoving—in the bay. And the mast-snapping chain not too far from them. Unfortunately, from his angle, so could Rolfe.

The sky had turned light gray. Dawn.

Celaena bowed her head to the Pirate Lord. "I'd rather not get my hands dirty in that mess."

Rolfe's lips formed a thin line. "Funny, given that you tripped the man who started the brawl."

Sam glared at her. She'd been subtle, damn it!

Rolfe drew his sword, the dragon's eyes gleaming in the growing light. "And also funny, since you've been spoiling for a fight for days, that you suddenly decided to vanish when everyone's attention is elsewhere."

Sam raised his hands. "We don't want any trouble."

Rolfe chuckled, a harsh, humorless sound. "Maybe you don't, Sam Cortland, but *she* does." Rolfe stepped toward her, his sword dangling at his side. "She's wanted trouble since the moment she got here. What was your plan? Steal treasure? Information?"

From the corner of her eye, something shifted in the ships. Like a bird flexing its wings, a row of oars shot out from their sides. They were ready. And the chain was still up.

Don't look, don't look, don't look . . .

But Rolfe looked, and Celaena's breathing turned shallow as he scanned the ships.

Sam tensed, his knees bending slightly.

"I am going to kill you, Celaena Sardothien," Rolfe breathed. And he meant it.

Celaena's fingers tightened around her sword, and Rolfe opened his mouth, lungs filling with air as he prepared to shout a warning.

Quick as a whip, she did the only thing she could think of to distract him.

Her mask clattered to the ground, and she shook off her hood. Her golden hair gleamed in the growing light.

Rolfe froze. "You . . . You're . . . What sort of trickery is this?"

Beyond them, the oars began moving, churning the water as the boats turned toward the chain—and the freedom beyond it. "Go," she murmured to Sam. "*Now.*"

Sam only nodded before he sprinted down the street.

Alone with Rolfe, Celaena raised her sword. "Celaena Sardothien, at your service."

The pirate was still staring at her, his face pale with rage. "How *dare* you deceive me?"

She sketched a bow. "I did nothing of the sort. I *told* you I was beautiful."

Before she could stop him, Rolfe shouted, "They're trying to steal our ships! To your boats! To the watchtower!"

A roar erupted around them, and Celaena prayed that Sam could reach the watchtower before the pirates caught him.

Celaena began circling the Pirate Lord. He circled her, too. He wasn't drunk in the least.

"How old are you?" Each of his steps was carefully placed, but she noticed that he kept shifting to expose his left side.

"Sixteen." She didn't bother to keep her voice low and gravelly.

Rolfe swore. "Arobynn sent a sixteen-year-old to deal with me?"

"He sent the best of the best. Consider that an honor."

With a growl, the Pirate Lord lunged.

She danced back, swinging up her sword to block the blow he aimed for her throat. She didn't need to kill him right away—just to distract him long enough to prevent him from further organizing his men. And keep him away from the ships. She had to buy Sam enough time to disable the chain and the catapults. The ships were already turning toward the mouth of the bay.

Rolfe launched himself again, and she let him land two strikes on her sword before she ducked the third blow and slammed into him. She swept her foot, and Rolfe staggered back a step. Not missing a beat, she pulled out her long hunting knife, slashing for his chest. She let her blow fall short, ripping through the fine blue material of his tunic instead.

Rolfe stumbled into the wall of a building behind him, but caught his footing and dodged the blow that would have taken off his head. The vibrations of her sword hitting stone stung her hand, but she kept hold of the hilt.

"What was the plan?" Rolfe panted above the roar of the pirates rushing toward the docks. "Steal my slaves and take all the profit?"

She laughed, feinting to his right, but sweeping for his unprotected left with her dagger. To her surprise, Rolfe deflected both moves in a swift, sure motion.

"To free them," she said. Beyond the chain, beyond the mouth of the bay, the clouds on the horizon began to color with the light of the coming dawn.

"Fool," Rolfe spat, and this time feinted so well that even Celaena couldn't avoid the rake of his sword across her arm. Warm blood seeped through her black tunic. She hissed, darting away a few steps. A careless mistake.

"You think freeing two hundred slaves will solve anything?" Rolfe kicked a fallen bottle of liquor at her. She knocked it aside with the flat of her sword, her right arm screaming in pain. Glass shattered behind her. "There are thousands of slaves out there. Are you going to march into Calaculla and Endovier and free them, too?"

Behind him, the steady strokes of the oars propelled the ships toward the chain. Sam had to hurry.

Rolfe shook his head. "Stupid girl. If I don't kill you, your master will."

Not him giving the luxury of a warning, she threw herself at him. She ducked, twirling, and Rolfe barely turned before she slammed the pommel of her sword into the back of his head.

The Pirate Lord crumpled to the dirt street just as a crowd of bloodied and filthy pirates appeared around the corner. Celaena only had time to throw her hood over her head, hoping the shadows concealed enough of her face, before she took off at a run.

It didn't take much to get away from a group of half-drunk battle-crazed pirates. She only had to lead them down a few twisted streets, and then she lost them. But the wound on her arm still slowed her considerably as she ran for the watchtower. Sam was already far ahead. Releasing the chain was now in his hands.

Pirates raged up and down the docks, seeking *any* boat that was in working order. That had been the final leg of her journey last night: disabling the rudders in all of the ships along the docks, including Rolfe's own ship, the *Sea Dragon*—which honestly deserved to be tampered with, given that security on board had been so lax. But, despite the damage, some pirates managed to find rowboats and piled into them, brandishing swords or cutlasses or axes and shouting profanities to the high heavens. The ramshackle buildings blurred as she sprinted toward the watchtower. Her breath was ragged in her throat, a night of no sleep already taking its toll. She burst past pirates on the docks, too busy bemoaning their ruined boats to notice her.

The slaves still rowed for the chain as if demons from every Hellrealm were upon them.

Celaena charged down the road, heading for the edge of the town. With the sloping, wide-open road, she could see Sam racing far ahead—and a large group of pirates not too far behind him. The cut on her arm throbbed, but she pushed herself to run faster.

Sam had mere minutes to get that chain down, or else the slaves' ships would shatter upon it. Even if the slaves' ships were able to stop before they hit it, there were enough smaller boats heading out that the pirates would overpower them. The pirates had weapons. Aside from whatever was onboard the ships, the slaves were unarmed, even if many of them had been warriors and rebels.

There was a flash of movement from the half-crumbling tower. Steel glimmered, and there was Sam, charging up the staircase that wound up the outside of the tower.

Two pirates rushed down the steps, swords raised. Sam dodged one, knocking him down with a swift strike to the spine. Before the pirate had even finished falling, Sam's blade skewered the other man clean through the middle.

But there was still Ship-Breaker to disable, along with the two catapults, and—

And the dozen pirates who had now reached the foot of the tower.

Celaena cursed. She was still too far. There was no way she could make it in time to disable the chain—the ships would crash into it long before she got there.

She swallowed the pain in her arm, focusing on her breathing as she ran and ran, not daring to take her eyes off the tower ahead. Sam, still a tiny figure in the distance, reached the top of the tower and the expanse of open stone where the anchor to the chain lay. Even from here, she could tell it was gargantuan. And as Sam rushed around it, hacking at whatever he could, throwing himself against the enormous lever, both of them realized the horrible truth, the one thing she'd overlooked: the chain was too heavy for one man to move.

The slaves' ships were close now. So close that stopping . . . stopping was impossible.

They were going to die.

But the slaves didn't cease rowing.

The dozen pirates were climbing the stairs. Sam had been trained to engage multiple men in combat, but a dozen pirates . . . Damn Rolfe and his men for delaying her!

Sam glanced toward the stairs. He knew about the pirates, too.

She could see everything with such maddening clarity. Sam remained atop the tower. A level below him, perched on a platform jutting out over the sea, sat the two catapults. And in the bay, the two ships that rowed with increasing speed. Freedom or death.

Sam slung himself down to the catapult level, and Celaena staggered a step as he hurled himself against the rotating platform on which the catapult sat, pushing, pushing, pushing until the catapult began to move—not toward the sea, but toward the tower itself, toward the spot in the stone wall where the chain was anchored.

She didn't dare take her attention from the tower as Sam heaved the catapult into position. A boulder had already been loaded, and in the glare of the rising sun, she could just make out the rope stretched taut to secure the catapult.

The pirates were almost at the catapult level. The two ships rowed faster and faster, the chain so close that its shadow loomed over them.

Celaena sucked in a breath as pirates poured onto the catapult landing, weapons held high.

Sam raised his sword. Light from the sunrise gleamed off the blade, bright as a star.

A warning cry broke from her lips as a pirate's dagger flipped toward Sam.

Sam brought his sword down on the catapult rope, doubling over. The catapult snapped so fast she could hardly follow the motion. The boulder slammed into the tower, shattering stone, wood, and metal. Rock exploded, dust clouding the air.

And with a boom that echoed across the bay, the chain collapsed, taking out a chunk of the tower—taking out the spot where she'd last seen Sam.

Celaena, reaching the tower at last, paused to watch as the white sails of the slaves' ships unfurled, glowing golden in the sunrise.

The wind filled their sails and set them cruising, flying swiftly from the mouth of the bay and into the ocean beyond it. By the time the pirates fixed their ships, the slaves would be too far away to catch.

She murmured a prayer for them to find a safe harbor, her words carrying on the wings of the wind, and wished them well.

A block of stone crashed near her. Celaena's heart gave a lurch. Sam.

He couldn't be dead. Not from that dagger, or those dozen pirates, or from the catapult. No, Sam couldn't be *so* stupid that he'd get himself killed. She'd . . . she'd . . . Well, she'd kill him if he was dead.

Drawing her sword despite the ache in her arm, she made to rush into the half-wrecked tower, but a dagger pressed against her neck halted her in her tracks.

"I don't think so," Rolfe whispered in her ear.

CHAPTER 10

"You make a move, and I'll spill your throat on the ground," Rolfe hissed, his free hand ripping Celaena's dagger from its sheath and tossing it into the brush. Then he took her sword, too.

"Why not just kill me right now?"

Rolfe's breathy laugh tickled her ear. "Because I want to take a long, long while to enjoy killing you."

She stared at the half-ruined tower, at the dust still swirling from the catapult's destruction. How could Sam have survived that?

"Do you know how much your attempt at playing hero cost me?" Rolfe pushed his blade into her neck, and her skin split open with a stinging burst. "Two hundred slaves, plus two ships, plus the seven ships you disabled in the harbor, plus countless lives."

She snorted. "Don't forget the ale from last night."

Rolfe shifted his blade, digging in and making Celaena wince despite herself. "I'll take that from your flesh, too, don't worry."

"How'd you find me?" She needed time. Needed something to work with. If she moved the wrong way, she'd find herself with a cut throat.

"I knew you'd follow Sam. If you were so set on freeing the slaves, then you certainly wouldn't leave your companion to die alone. Though I think you arrived a bit too late for that."

In the dense jungle, the cries of birds and beasts slowly returned. But the watchtower remained silent, interrupted only by the hiss of crumbling stone.

"You're going to return with me," Rolfe said. "And after I'm done with you, I'll contact your master to come pick up the pieces."

Rolfe took a step, pivoting them toward the town, but Celaena had been waiting.

Throwing her back into his chest, she hooked her foot behind his. Rolfe stumbled, tripping over her leg, and she wedged her hand between her neck and his dagger just as he remembered to act on his promise to slit her throat.

Blood from her palm splattered down her tunic, but she shoved the pain aside and butted her elbow into his stomach. Rolfe's breath whooshed out of him, and he doubled over, only to meet her knee slamming into his face. A faint *crack* sounded as her kneecap connected with his nose. When she hurled Rolfe to the dirt, blood was on her pant leg—his blood.

She grabbed his fallen dagger as the Pirate Lord reached for his sword. He scrambled to his knees, lunging for her, but she stomped her foot down upon his sword, sending it crashing to the ground. Rolfe raised his head just in time for her to knock him onto his back. Crouching over him, she held his dagger to his neck.

"Well, *that* didn't go the way you expected, did it?" she asked, listening for a moment to ensure no pirates were about to come crashing down the road. But the animals still hooted and screeched, the insects still hummed. They were alone. Most of the pirates were probably brawling in the town.

Her hand throbbed, blood pouring out as she grasped the collar of his tunic to lift his head closer to hers.

"So," she said, her smirk widening at the blood dripping from his nose. "This is what's going to happen." She dropped his collar and fished out the two papers from inside her tunic. Compared to the pain in her hand, the injury on her arm had faded to a dull pulsing. "You are going to sign these and stamp each with your seal."

"I refuse," Rolfe seethed.

"You don't even know what they say." She pushed the tip of the dagger into his heaving throat. "So allow me to clarify: one of these is a letter to my master. It says that the deal is over, that you won't be sending him slaves, and if you catch him entering into another slave-trade agreement with anyone else, you'll bring your whole armada to punish him."

Rolfe choked. "You're insane."

"Maybe," she said. "But I'm not done yet." She picked up the second letter. "This one . . . I wrote this one for you. I did my best to try to write it in *your* voice, but you'll forgive me if it's a tad more elegant than you're used to being." Rolfe struggled, but she pushed the blade a little harder, and he stopped. "Basically," she said, sighing dramatically, "this one says that you, Captain Rolfe, bearer of the magical map inked on your hands, will never, *ever* sell a slave again. And if you catch any pirates selling or transporting or trading slaves, you'll hang, burn, or drown them yourself. And that Skull's Bay is forevermore a safe haven for any slaves fleeing Adarlan's clutches."

Rolfe practically had steam blowing out his ears. "I won't sign either of them, you stupid girl. Don't you know who I am?"

"Fine," she said, angling the blade to sink into his flesh more easily. "I memorized your signature when I was in your office that first day. It won't be hard to forge. And as for your seal ring . . ." She removed something else from her pocket. "I also took that the first day in your office, just in case I needed it. Turns out I was right." Rolfe croaked as she held it up in her free hand, the garnet flashing in the light. "I figure I can return to town and tell your cronies that you decided to set sail after those slaves, and to expect you back in . . . I don't know—six months? A year? Long enough that they won't notice the grave I'll dig for you right off the road here. Frankly, you've seen who I am, and I *should* end your life for it. But consider it a favor—and a promise that if you *don't* follow my orders, I'll change my decision to spare you."

Rolfe's eyes narrowed to slits. "Why?"

"You'll have to clarify that."

He took a breath. "Why go to so much trouble for slaves?"

"Because if we don't fight for them, who will?" She pulled a fountain pen from her pocket. "Sign the papers."

Rolfe raised an eyebrow. "And how will you know that I'm holding true to my word?"

She removed the dagger from his throat, using the blade to brush back a strand of his dark hair. "I have my sources. And if I hear that you're trading slaves, no matter where you go, no matter how far you run, I *will* hunt you down. That's twice now I've disabled you. The third time, you won't be so lucky. I swear that on my name. I'm almost seventeen, and I can already wallop you; imagine how good I'll be in a few years." She shook her head. "I don't think you'll want to try me now—and certainly not then."

Rolfe stared at her for a few heartbeats. "If you ever set foot in my territory again, your life is forfeit." He paused, then muttered, "May the gods help Arobynn." He took the pen. "Any other requests?"

She eased off him, but kept the dagger in her hand. "Why, yes," she said. "A ship would be nice."

Rolfe only glared at her before he grabbed the documents.

When Rolfe had signed, stamped, and handed the documents to Celaena, she took the liberty of knocking him out again. Swift blows to two points in his neck did the trick, and he'd be out long enough for her to accomplish what she needed: to find Sam.

She raced up the half-crumbling stairs of the tower, leaping over pirate corpses and chunks of stone, not stopping until she found the crushed bodies of the dozen pirates who were closest to Sam and the ruins of the catapults. Blood, bone, squished bits of flesh that she didn't particularly care to look at for too long . . .

"Sam!" she shouted, slipping over a bit of debris. She heaved a slab of wood off the side, scanning the landing for any sign of him. "Sam!"

Her hand began bleeding again, leaving smears of blood as she turned over stone and wood and metal. Where *was* he?

It had been *her* plan. If one of them had to die for it, it should have been her. Not him.

She reached the second catapult, its entire frame snapped in half from a fallen piece of tower. She'd last seen him here. A slab of stone jutted up from where it had hit the landing. It was large enough to have squashed someone beneath.

She hurled herself against it, her feet sliding against the ground as she pushed and pushed and pushed. The stone didn't move.

Grunting, gasping, she shoved harder. Still the stone was too large.

Cursing, she beat a fist against the gray surface, her injured hand aching in protest. The pain snapped something open, and she struck the stone again and again, clenching her jaw to keep the building scream inside of her.

"For some reason, I don't think that's going to make the rock move," said a voice, and Celaena whirled.

Emerging from the other side of the landing was Sam. He was covered head to toe in gray dust, and blood leaked from a cut in his forehead, but he was . . .

She lifted her chin. "I've been shouting for you."

Sam shrugged, sauntering over to her. "I figured you could wait a few minutes, given that I saved the day and all." His brows rose high on his ash-covered face.

"Some hero." She gestured to the ruin of the tower around them. "I've never seen such sloppy work."

Sam smiled, his brown eyes turning golden in the dawn. It was such a *Sam* look, the twinkle of mischief, the hint of exasperation, the kindness that would always, *always* make him a better person than she was.

Before she knew what she was doing, Celaena threw her arms around him and held him close.

Sam stiffened, but after a heartbeat, his arms came around her. She breathed him in—the smell of his sweat, the tang of the dust and rock, the metallic odor of his blood . . . Sam rested his cheek on her head. She couldn't remember—honestly couldn't recall—the last time anyone had held her. No, wait—it had been a year ago. With Ben, after she'd come back from a mission two hours late and with a sprained ankle. He'd been worried, and given how close she'd come to being captured by the royal guards, she was more than a bit shaken.

But embracing Sam was different, somehow. Like she wanted to curl into his warmth, like for one moment, she didn't have to worry about anything or anybody.

"Sam," she murmured into his chest.

"Hmm?"

She peeled away from him, stepping out of his arms. "If you ever tell anyone about me embracing you . . . I'll gut you."

Sam gaped at her, then tipped his head back and laughed. He laughed and laughed, until dust lodged in his throat and he launched into a coughing fit. She let him suffer through it, not finding it very funny at all.

When he could breathe again, Sam cleared his throat. "Come on, Sardothien," he said, slinging an arm around her shoulders. "If you're done liberating slaves and destroying pirate cities, then let's go home."

Celaena glanced at him sidelong and grinned.

THE ASSASSIN AND THE HEALER

CHAPTER 1

The strange young woman had been staying at the White Pig Inn for two days now and had hardly spoken to anyone save for Nolan, who had taken one look at her fine night-dark clothes and bent over backward to accommodate her.

He gave her the best room at the Pig—the room he only offered to patrons he intended to bleed dry—and didn't seem at all bothered by the heavy hood the young woman wore or the assortment of weapons that gleamed along her long, lean body. Not when she tossed him a gold coin with a casual flick of her gloved fingers. Not when she was wearing an ornate gold brooch with a ruby the size of a robin's egg.

Then again, Nolan was never really afraid of anyone, unless they seemed likely not to pay him—and even then, it was anger and greed, not fear, that won out.

Yrene Towers had been watching the young woman from the safety of the taproom bar. Watching, if only because the stranger was young and unaccompanied and sat at the back table with such stillness that it was impossible *not* to look. Not to wonder.

Yrene hadn't seen her face yet, though she'd caught a glimpse every now and then of a golden braid glinting from the depths of her black hood. In any other city, the White Pig Inn would likely be considered the lowest of the low as far as luxury and cleanliness were concerned. But here in Innish, a port town so small it wasn't on most maps, it was considered the finest.

Yrene glanced at the mug she was currently cleaning and tried not to wince. She did her best to keep the bar and taproom clean, to serve the Pig's patrons—most of them sailors or merchants or mercenaries who often thought *she* was up for purchase as well—with a smile. But Nolan still watered down the wine, still washed the sheets only when there was no denying the presence of lice and fleas, and sometimes used whatever meat could be found in the back alley for their daily stew.

Yrene had been working here for a year now—eleven months longer than she had intended—and the White Pig still sickened her. Considering that she could stomach almost anything (a fact that allowed both Nolan and Jessa to demand *she* clean up the most disgusting messes of their patrons), that was really saying something.

The stranger at the back table lifted her head, signaling with a gloved finger for Yrene to bring another ale. For someone who didn't seem older than twenty, the young woman drank an ungodly amount—wine, ale, whatever Nolan bade Yrene bring over—but never seemed to lose herself to it. It was impossible to tell with that heavy hood, though. These past two nights she'd merely stalked back to her room with a feline grace, not stumbling over herself like most of the patrons on their way out after last call.

Yrene quickly poured ale into the mug she'd just been drying and set it on a tray. She added a glass of water and some more bread, since the girl hadn't touched the stew she'd been given for dinner. Not a single bite. Smart woman.

Yrene wove through the packed taproom, dodging the hands that tried to grab her. Halfway through her trek, she caught Nolan's eye from where he sat by the front door. An encouraging nod, his mostly bald head gleaming in the dim light. *Keep her drinking. Keep her buying.*

Yrene avoided rolling her eyes, if only because Nolan was the sole reason she wasn't walking the cobblestone streets with the other young women of Innish. A year ago, the stout man had let her convince him that he needed more help in the tavern below the inn. Of course, he'd only accepted when he realized he'd be receiving the better end of the bargain.

But she'd been eighteen and desperate, and had gladly taken a job that offered only a few coppers and a miserable little bed in a broom closet beneath the stairs. Most of her money came from tips, but Nolan claimed half of them. And then Jessa, the other barmaid, usually claimed two-thirds of what remained, because, as Jessa often said, *she* was the *pretty face that gets the men to part with their money, anyway.*

One glance into a corner revealed that pretty face and its attendant body perched on the lap of a bearded sailor, giggling and tossing her thick brown curls. Yrene sighed through her nose but didn't complain, because Jessa was Nolan's favorite, and Yrene had nowhere—absolutely nowhere—left to go. Innish was her home now, and the White Pig was her haven. Outside of it, the world was too big, too full of splintered dreams and armies that had crushed and burned everything Yrene held dear.

Yrene at last reached the stranger's table and found the young woman looking up at her. "I brought you some water and bread, too," Yrene stammered by way of greeting. She set down the ale, but hesitated with the other two items on her tray.

The young woman just said, "Thank you." Her voice was low and cool—cultured. Educated. And completely uninterested in Yrene.

Not that there was anything about her that was remotely interesting, with her homespun wool dress doing little for her too-slim figure. Like most who hailed from southern Fenharrow, Yrene had golden-tan skin and absolutely ordinary brown hair and was of average height. Only her eyes, a bright gold-brown, gave her any source of pride. Not that most people saw them. Yrene did her best to keep her eyes down most of the time, avoiding any invitation for communication or the wrong kind of attention.

So, Yrene set down the bread and water and took the empty mug from where the girl had pushed it to the center of the table. But curiosity won out, and she peered into the black depths beneath the young woman's cowl. Nothing but shadows, a gleam of gold hair, and a hint of pale skin. She had so many questions—so, so many questions. *Who are you? Where do you come from? Where are you going? Can you use all those blades you carry?*

Nolan was watching the entire encounter, so Yrene curtsied and walked back to the bar through the field of groping hands, eyes downcast as she plastered a distant smile on her face.

Celaena Sardothien sat at her table in the absolutely worthless inn, wondering how her life had gone to hell so quickly.

She hated Innish. Hated the reek of trash and filth, hated the heavy blanket of mist that shrouded it day and night, hated the second-rate merchants and mercenaries and generally miserable people who occupied it.

No one here knew who she was, or why she'd come; no one knew that the girl beneath the hood was Celaena Sardothien, the most notorious assassin in Adarlan's empire. But then again, she didn't want them to know. *Couldn't* let them know, actually. And didn't want them knowing that she was just over a week away from turning seventeen, either.

She'd been here for two days now—two days spent either holed up in her despicable room (a "suite," the oily innkeeper had the nerve to call it), or down here in the taproom that stank of sweat, stale ale, and unwashed bodies.

She would have left if she'd had any choice. But she was forced to be here, thanks to her master, Arobynn Hamel, King of the Assassins. She'd always been proud of her status as his chosen heir—always flaunted it. But now . . . This journey was her punishment for destroying his atrocious slave-trade agreement with the Pirate Lord of Skull's Bay. So unless she wanted to risk the trek through the Bogdano Jungle—the feral bit of land that bridged the continent to the Deserted Land—sailing across the Gulf of Oro was the only way. Which meant waiting here, in this dump of a tavern, for a ship to take her to Yurpa.

Celaena sighed and took a long drink of her ale. She almost spat it out. Disgusting. Cheap as cheap could be, like the rest of this place. Like the stew she hadn't touched. Whatever meat was in there wasn't from any creature worth eating. Bread and mild cheese it was, then.

Celaena sat back in her seat, watching the barmaid with the brown-gold hair slip through the labyrinth of tables and chairs. The girl nimbly dodged the men who groped her, all without disturbing the tray she carried over her shoulder. What a waste of swift feet, good balance, and intelligent, stunning eyes. The girl wasn't dumb. Celaena had noted the way she watched the room and its patrons—the way she watched Celaena herself. What personal hell had driven her to work here?

Celaena didn't particularly care. The questions were mostly to drive the boredom away. She'd already devoured the three books she'd carried with her from Rifthold, and not one of the shops in Innish had a single book for sale—only spices, fish, out-of-fashion clothing, and nautical gear. For a port town, it was pathetic. But the Kingdom of Melisande had fallen on hard times in the past eight and a half years—since the King of Adarlan had conquered the continent and redirected trade through Eyllwe instead of Melisande's few eastern ports.

The whole world had fallen on hard times, it seemed. Celaena included.

She fought the urge to touch her face. The swelling from the beating Arobynn had given her had gone down, but the bruises remained. She avoided looking in the sliver of mirror above her dresser, knowing what she'd see: mottled purple and blue and yellow along her cheekbones, a vicious black eye, and a still-healing split lip.

It was all a reminder of what Arobynn had done the day she returned from Skull's Bay—proof of how she'd betrayed him by saving two hundred slaves from a terrible fate. She had made a powerful enemy of the Pirate Lord, and she was fairly certain she'd ruined her relationship with Arobynn, but she had been right. It was worth it; it would always be worth it, she told herself.

Even if she was sometimes so angry that she couldn't think straight. Even if she'd gotten into not one, not two, but three bar fights in the two weeks that she'd been traveling from Rifthold to the Red Desert. One of the brawls, at least, had been rightfully provoked: a man had cheated at a round of cards. But the other two . . .

There was no denying it: she'd merely been spoiling for a fight. No blades, no weapons. Just fists and feet. Celaena supposed she should feel bad about it—about the broken noses and jaws, about the heaps of unconscious bodies in her wake. But she didn't.

She couldn't bring herself to care, because those moments she spent brawling were the few moments she felt like herself again.

When she felt like Adarlan's greatest assassin, Arobynn Hamel's chosen heir.

Even if her opponents were drunks and untrained fighters; even if she should know better.

The barmaid reached the safety of the counter, and Celaena glanced about the room. The innkeeper was still watching her, as he had for the past two days, wondering how he could squeeze even more money out of her purse. There were several other men observing her, too. Some she recognized from previous nights, while others were new faces that she quickly sized up. Was it fear or luck that had kept them away from her so far?

She'd made no secret of the fact that she carried money with her. And her clothes and weapons spoke volumes about her wealth, too. The ruby brooch she wore practically begged for trouble—she wore it to *invite* trouble, actually. It was a gift from Arobynn on her sixteenth birthday; she *hoped* someone would try to steal it. If they were good enough, she might just let them. So it was only a matter of time, really, before one of them tried to rob her.

And before she decided she was bored of fighting only with fists and feet. She glanced at the sword by her side; it glinted in the tavern's dank light.

But she would be leaving at dawn—to sail to the Deserted Land, where she'd make the journey to the Red Desert to meet the Mute Master of Assassins, with whom she was to train for a month as further punishment for her betrayal of Arobynn. If she were being honest with herself, though, she'd started entertaining the thought of *not* going to the Red Desert.

It was tempting. She could take a ship somewhere else—to the southern continent, perhaps—and start a new life. She could leave behind Arobynn, the Assassins' Guild, the city of Rifthold, and Adarlan's damned empire. There was little stopping her, save for the feeling that Arobynn would hunt her down no matter how far she went. And the fact that Sam . . . well, she didn't know what had happened to her fellow assassin that night the world had gone to hell. But the lure of the unknown remained, the wild rage that begged her to cast off the last of Arobynn's shackles and sail to a place where she could establish her *own* Assassins' Guild. It would be so, so easy.

But even if she decided not to take the ship to Yurpa tomorrow and instead took one bound for the southern continent, she was still left with another night in this awful inn. Another sleepless night where she could only hear the roar of anger in her blood as it thrashed inside her.

If she were smart, if she were levelheaded, she would avoid any confrontation tonight and leave Innish in peace, no matter where she went.

But she wasn't feeling particularly smart, or levelheaded—certainly not once the hours passed and the air in the inn shifted into a hungry, wild thing that howled for blood.

CHAPTER 2

Yrene didn't know how or when it happened, but the atmosphere in the White Pig changed. It was as if all the gathered men were waiting for something. The girl at the back was still at her table, still brooding. But her gloved fingers were tapping on the scarred wooden surface, and every now and then, she shifted her hooded head to look around the room.

Yrene couldn't have left even if she wanted to. Last call wasn't for another forty minutes, and she'd have to stay an hour after that to clean up and usher intoxicated patrons out the door. She didn't care where they went once they passed the threshold—didn't care if they wound up facedown in a watery ditch—just as long as they got out of the taproom. And stayed gone.

Nolan had vanished moments ago, either to save his own hide or to do some dark dealings in the back alley, and Jessa was still in that sailor's lap, flirting away, unaware of the shift in the air.

Yrene kept looking at the hooded girl. So did many of the tavern's patrons. Were they waiting for her to get up? There were some thieves that she recognized—thieves who had been circling like vultures for the past two days, trying to figure out whether the strange girl could use the weapons she carried. It was common knowledge that she was leaving tomorrow at dawn. If they wanted her money, jewelry, weapons, or something far darker, tonight would be their last chance.

Yrene chewed on her lip as she poured a round of ales for the table of four mercenaries playing Kings. She should warn the girl—tell her that she might be better off sneaking to her ship right now, before she wound up with a slit throat.

But Nolan would throw Yrene out into the streets if he knew she had warned her. Especially when many of the cutthroats were beloved patrons who often shared their ill-gained profits with him. And she had no doubt that he'd send those very men after her if she betrayed him. How had she become so adjusted to these people? When had Nolan and the White Pig become a place and position she wanted so desperately to keep?

Yrene swallowed hard, pouring another mug of ale. Her mother wouldn't have hesitated to warn the girl.

But her mother had been a good woman—a woman who never wavered, who never turned away a sick or wounded person, no matter how poor, from the door of their cottage in southern Fenharrow. Never.

As a prodigiously gifted healer blessed with no small amount of magic, her mother had always said it wasn't right to charge people for what she'd been given for free by Silba, the Goddess of Healing. And the only time she'd seen her mother falter was the day the soldiers from Adarlan surrounded their house, armed to the teeth and bearing torches and wood.

They hadn't bothered to listen when her mother explained that her power, like Yrene's, had already disappeared months before, along with the rest of the magic in the land—abandoned by the gods, her mother had claimed.

No, the soldiers hadn't listened at all. And neither had any of those vanished gods to whom her mother and Yrene had pleaded for salvation.

It was the first—and only—time her mother took a life.

Yrene could still see the glint of the hidden dagger in her mother's hand, still feel the blood of that soldier on her bare feet, hear her mother scream at her to *run*, smell the smoke of the bonfire as they burned her gifted mother alive while Yrene wept from the nearby safety of Oakwald Forest.

It was from her mother that Yrene had inherited her iron stomach—but she'd never thought those solid nerves would wind up keeping her here, claiming this hovel as her home.

Yrene was so lost in thought and memory that she didn't notice the man until a broad hand was wrapped around her waist.

"We could use a pretty face at this table," he said, grinning up at her with a wolf's smile. Yrene stepped back, but he held firm, trying to yank her into his lap.

"I've work to do," she said as blandly as possible. She'd detangled herself from situations like this before—countless times now. It had stopped scaring her long ago.

"You can go to work on me," said another of the mercenaries, a tall man with a worn-looking blade strapped to his back. Calmly, she pried the first mercenary's fingers off her waist.

"Last call is in forty minutes," she said pleasantly, stepping back—as far as she could without irritating the men grinning at her like wild dogs. "Can I get you anything else?"

"What are you doing after?" said another.

"Going home to my husband," she lied. But they looked at the ring on her finger—the ring that now passed for a wedding band. It had belonged to her mother, and her mother's mother, and all the great women before her, all such brilliant healers, all wiped from living memory.

The men scowled, and taking that as a cue to leave, Yrene hurried back to the bar. She didn't warn the girl—didn't make the trek across the too-big taproom, with all those men waiting like wolves.

Forty minutes. Just another forty minutes until she could kick them all out.

And then she could clean up and tumble into bed, one more day finished in this living hell that had somehow become her future.

Honestly, Celaena was a little insulted when none of the men in the taproom made a grab for her, her money, her ruby brooch, or her weapons as she stalked between the tables. The bell had just finished ringing for last call, and even though she wasn't tired in the slightest, she'd had enough of waiting for a fight or a conversation or anything to occupy her time.

She supposed she could go back to her room and reread one of the books she'd brought. As she prowled past the bar, flipping a silver coin to the dark-haired serving girl, she debated the merits of instead going out onto the streets and seeing what adventure found her.

Reckless and stupid, Sam would say. But Sam wasn't here, and she didn't know if he was dead or alive or beaten senseless by Arobynn. It was a safe bet Sam had been punished for the role he'd played in liberating the slaves in Skull's Bay.

She didn't want to think about it. Sam had become her friend, she supposed. She'd never had the luxury of friends, and never particularly wanted any. But Sam had been a good contender, even if he didn't hesitate to say exactly what he thought about her, or her plans, or her abilities.

What would *he* think if she just sailed off into the unknown and never went to the Red Desert, or never even returned to Rifthold? He might celebrate—especially if Arobynn appointed *him* as his heir. Or she could poach him, maybe. He'd suggested that they try to run away when they were in Skull's Bay, actually. So once she was settled someplace, once she had established a new life as a top assassin in whatever land she made her home, she could ask him to join her. And they'd never put up with beatings and humiliations again. Such an easy, inviting idea—such a temptation.

Celaena trudged up the narrow stairs, listening for any thieves or cutthroats that might be waiting. To her disappointment, the upstairs hall was dark and quiet—and empty.

Sighing, she slipped into her room and bolted the door. After a moment, she shoved the ancient chest of drawers in front of it, too. Not for her own safety. Oh, no. It was for the safety of whatever fool tried to break in—and would then find himself split open from navel to nose just to satisfy a wandering assassin's boredom.

But after pacing for fifteen minutes, she pushed aside the furniture and left. Looking for a fight. For an adventure. For anything to take her mind off the bruises on her face and the punishment Arobynn had given her and the temptation to shirk her obligations and instead sail to a land far, far away.

Yrene lugged the last of the rubbish pails into the misty alley behind the White Pig, her back and arms aching. Today had been longer than most.

There hadn't been a fight, thank the gods, but Yrene still couldn't shake her nerves and that sense of something being *off*. But she was glad—so, so glad—there hadn't been a brawl at the Pig. The last thing she wanted to do was spend the rest of the night mopping blood and vomit off the floor and hauling broken furniture into the alley. After she'd rung the last-call bell, the men had finished their drinks, grumbling and laughing, and dispersed with little to no harassment.

Unsurprisingly, Jessa had vanished with her sailor, and given that the alley was empty, Yrene could only assume the young woman had gone elsewhere with him. Leaving her, yet again, to clean up.

Yrene paused as she dumped the less-disgusting rubbish into a neat pile along the far wall. It wasn't much: stale bread and stew that would be gone by morning, snatched up by the half-feral urchins roaming the streets.

What would her mother say if she knew what had become of her daughter?

Yrene had been only eleven when those soldiers burned her mother for her magic. For the first six and a half years after the horrors of that day, she'd lived with her mother's cousin in another village in Fenharrow, pretending to be an absolutely ungifted distant relative. It wasn't a hard disguise to maintain: her powers truly had vanished. But in those days fear had run rampant, and neighbor had turned on neighbor, often selling out anyone formerly blessed with the gods' powers to whatever army legion was closest. Thankfully, no one had questioned Yrene's small presence; and in those long years, no one looked her way as she helped the family farm struggle to return to normal in the wake of Adarlan's forces.

But she'd wanted to be a healer—like her mother and grandmother. She'd started shadowing her mother as soon as she could talk, learning slowly, as all the traditional healers did. And those years on that farm, however peaceful (if tedious and dull), hadn't been enough to make her forget eleven years of training, or the urge to follow in her mother's footsteps. She hadn't been close to her cousins, despite their charity, and neither party had really tried to bridge the gap caused by distance and fear and war. So no one objected when she took whatever money she'd saved up and walked off the farm a few months before her eighteenth birthday.

She'd set out for Antica, a city of learning on the southern continent—a realm untouched by Adarlan and war, where rumor claimed magic still existed. She'd traveled on foot from Fenharrow, across the mountains into Melisande, through Oakwald, eventually winding up at Innish—where rumor also claimed one could find a boat to the southern continent, to Antica. And it was precisely here that she'd run out of money.

It was why she'd taken the job at the Pig. First, it had just been temporary, to earn enough to afford the passage to Antica. But then she'd worried she wouldn't have any money when she arrived, and then that she wouldn't have any money to pay for her training at the Torre Cesme, the great academy of healers and physicians. So she'd stayed, and weeks had turned into months. Somehow the dream of sailing away, of attending the Torre, had been set aside. Especially as Nolan increased the rent on her room and the cost of her food and found ways to lower her salary. Especially as that healer's stomach of hers allowed her to endure the indignities and darkness of this place.

Yrene sighed through her nose. So here she was. A barmaid in a backwater town with hardly two coppers to her name and no future in sight.

There was a crunch of boots on stone, and Yrene glared down the alley. If Nolan caught the urchins eating his food—however stale and disgusting—he'd blame her. He'd say he wasn't a charity and take the cost out of her paycheck. He'd done it once before, and she'd had to hunt down the urchins and scold them, make them understand that they had to wait until the middle of the night to get the food she so carefully laid out.

"I told you to wait until it's past—" she started, but paused as four figures stepped from the mist.

Men. The mercenaries from before.

Yrene was moving for the open doorway in a heartbeat, but they were fast—faster.

One blocked the door while another came up behind her, grabbing her tight and pulling her against his massive body. "Scream and I'll slit your throat," he whispered in her ear, his breath hot and reeking of ale. "Saw you making some hefty tips tonight, girl. Where are they?"

Yrene didn't know what she would have done next: fought or cried or begged or actually tried to scream. But she didn't have to decide.

The man farthest from them was yanked into the mist with a strangled cry.

The mercenary holding her whirled toward him, dragging Yrene along. There was a ruffle of clothing, then a thump. Then silence.

"Ven?" the man blocking the door called.

Nothing.

The third mercenary—standing between Yrene and the mist—drew his short sword. Yrene didn't have time to cry out in surprise or warning as a dark figure slipped from the mist and grabbed him. Not in front, but from the side, as if they'd just *appeared* out of thin air.

The mercenary threw Yrene to the ground and drew the sword from across his back, a broad, wicked-looking blade. But his companion didn't even shout. More silence.

"Come out, you bleedin' coward," the ringleader growled. "Face us like a proper man."

A low, soft laugh.

Yrene's blood went cold. Silba, protect her.

She knew that laugh—knew the cool, cultured voice that went with it.

"Just like how you proper men surrounded a defenseless girl in an alley?"

With that, the stranger stepped from the mist. She had two long daggers in her hands. And both blades were dark with dripping blood.

CHAPTER 3

Gods. Oh, gods.

Yrene's breath came quickly as the girl stepped closer to the two remaining attackers. The first mercenary barked a laugh, but the one by the door was wide-eyed. Yrene carefully, so carefully, backed away.

"You killed my men?" the mercenary said, blade held aloft.

The young woman flipped one of her daggers into a new position. The kind of position that Yrene thought would easily allow the blade to go straight up through the ribs and into the heart. "Let's just say your men got what was coming to them."

The mercenary lunged, but the girl was waiting. Yrene knew she should run—run and run and not look back—but the girl was only armed with two daggers, and the mercenary was enormous, and—

It was over before it really started. The mercenary got in two hits, both met with those wicked-looking daggers. And then she knocked him out cold with a swift blow to the head. So fast—unspeakably fast and graceful. A wraith moving through the mist.

He crumpled into the fog and out of sight, and Yrene didn't listen too hard as the girl followed where he'd fallen.

Yrene whipped her head to the mercenary in the doorway, preparing to shout a warning to her savior. But the man was already sprinting down the alley as fast as his feet could carry him.

Yrene had half a mind to do that herself when the stranger emerged from the mist, blades clean but still out. Still ready.

"Please don't kill me," Yrene whispered. She was ready to beg, to offer everything in exchange for her useless, wasted life.

But the young woman just laughed under her breath and said, "What would have been the point in saving you, then?"

Celaena hadn't meant to save the barmaid.

It had been sheer luck that she'd spotted the four mercenaries creeping about the streets, sheer luck that they seemed as eager for trouble as she was. She had hunted them into that alley, where she found them ready to hurt that girl in unforgivable ways.

The fight was over too quickly to really be enjoyable, or be a balm to her temper. If you could even call it a fight.

The fourth one had gotten away, but she didn't feel like chasing him, not as the servant girl stood in front of her, shaking from head to toe. Celaena had a feeling that hurling a dagger after the sprinting man would only make the girl start screaming. Or faint. Which would . . . complicate things.

But the girl didn't scream or faint. She just pointed a trembling finger at Celaena's arm. "You—you're bleeding."

Celaena frowned down at the little shining spot on her bicep. "I suppose I am."

A careless mistake. The thickness of her tunic had stopped it from being a troublesome wound, but she'd have to clean it. It would be healed in a week or less. She made to turn back to the street, to see what else she could find to amuse her, but the girl spoke again.

"I—I could bind it up for you."

She wanted to shake the girl. Shake her for about ten different reasons. The first, and biggest, was because she was trembling and scared and had been utterly useless. The second was for being stupid enough to *stand* in that alley in the middle of the night. She didn't feel like thinking about all the other reasons—not when she was already angry enough.

"I can bind myself up just fine," Celaena said, heading for the door that led into the White Pig's kitchens. Days ago, she'd scoped out the inn and its surrounding buildings, and now could navigate them blindfolded.

"Silba knows what was on that blade," the girl said, and Celaena paused. Invoking the Goddess of Healing. Very few did that these days—unless they were . . .

"I—my mother was a healer, and she taught me a few things," the girl stammered. "I could—I could . . . Please let me repay the debt I owe you."

"You wouldn't owe me anything if you'd used some common sense."

The girl flinched as though Celaena had struck her. It only annoyed her even more. Everything annoyed her—this town, this kingdom, this cursed world.

"I'm sorry," the girl said softly.

"What are you apologizing to me for? Why are you apologizing at all? Those men had it coming. But you should have been smarter on a night like this—when I'd bet all my money that you could taste the aggression in that filthy damned taproom."

It wasn't the girl's fault, she had to remind herself. Not her fault at all that she didn't know how to fight back.

The girl put her face in her hands, her shoulders curving inward. Celaena counted down the seconds until the girl burst into sobs, until she fell apart.

But the tears didn't come. The girl just took a few deep breaths, then lowered her hands. "Let me clean your arm," she said in a voice that was . . . different, somehow. Stronger, clearer. "Or you'll wind up losing it."

And the slight change in the girl was interesting enough that Celaena followed her inside.

She didn't bother about the three bodies in the alley. She had a feeling no one but the rats and carrion-feeders would care about them in this town.

CHAPTER 4

Yrene brought the girl to her room under the stairs, because she was half-afraid that the mercenary who'd gotten away would be waiting for them upstairs. And Yrene didn't want to see any more fighting or killing or bleeding, strong stomach or no.

Not to mention she was also half-afraid to be locked in the suite with the stranger.

She left the girl sitting on her sagging bed and went to fetch two bowls of water and some clean bandages—supplies that would be taken out of her paycheck when Nolan realized they were gone. It didn't matter, though. The stranger had saved her life. This was the least she could do.

When Yrene returned, she almost dropped the steaming bowls. The girl had removed her hood and cloak and tunic.

Yrene didn't know what to remark on first:

That the girl was young—perhaps two or three years younger than Yrene—but *felt* old.

That the girl was beautiful, with golden hair and blue eyes that shone in the candlelight.

Or that the girl's face would have been even more beautiful had it not been covered in a patchwork of bruises. Such horrible bruises, including a black eye that had undoubtedly been swollen shut at some point.

The girl was staring at her, quiet and still as a cat.

It wasn't Yrene's place to ask questions. Especially not when this girl had dispatched three mercenaries in a matter of moments. Even if the gods had abandoned her, Yrene still believed in them; they were still somewhere, still watching. She believed, because how else could she explain being saved just now? And the thought of being alone—truly alone—was almost too much to bear, even when so much of her life had gone astray.

The water sloshed in the bowls as Yrene set them down on the tiny table beside her bed, trying to keep her hands from trembling too much.

The girl said nothing while Yrene inspected the cut on her bicep. Her arm was slender, but rock-hard with muscle. The girl had scars everywhere—small ones, big ones. She offered no explanation for them, and it seemed to Yrene that the girl wore her scars the way some women wore their finest jewelry.

The stranger couldn't have been older than seventeen or eighteen, but . . . but Adarlan had made them all grow up fast. Too fast.

Yrene set about washing the wound, and the girl hissed softly. "Sorry," Yrene said quickly. "I put some herbs in there as an antiseptic. I should have warned you." Yrene kept a stash of them with her at all times, along with other herbs her mother had taught her about. Just in case. Even now, Yrene couldn't turn away from a sick beggar in the street, and often walked toward the sound of coughing.

"Believe me, I've been through worse."

"I do," Yrene said. "Believe you, I mean." Those scars and her mangled face spoke volumes. And explained the hood. But was it vanity or self-preservation that made her wear it? "What's your name?"

"It's none of your concern, and it doesn't matter."

Yrene bit her tongue. Of course it was none of her business. The girl hadn't given a name to Nolan, either. So she was traveling on some secret business, then. "My name is Yrene," she offered. "Yrene Towers."

A distant nod. Of course, the girl didn't care, either.

Then the stranger said, "What's the daughter of a healer doing in this piece of shit town?"

No kindness, no pity. Just blunt, if not almost bored, curiosity.

"I was on my way to Antica to join their healers' academy and ran out of money." She dipped the rag into the water, wrung it out, and resumed cleaning the shallow wound. "I got work here to pay for the passage over the ocean, and . . . Well, I never left. I guess staying here became . . . easier. Simpler."

A snort. "This place? It's certainly simple, but easy? I think I'd rather starve in the streets of Antica than live here."

Yrene's face warmed. "It—I . . ." She didn't have an excuse.

The girl's eyes flashed to hers. They were ringed with gold—stunning. Even with the bruises, the girl was alluring. Like wildfire, or a summer storm swept in off the Gulf of Oro.

"Let me give you a bit of advice," the girl said bitterly, "from one working girl to another: Life isn't easy, no matter where you are. You'll make choices you think are right, and then suffer for them." Those remarkable eyes flickered. "So if you're going to be miserable, you might as well go to Antica and be miserable in the shadow of the Torre Cesme."

Educated and possibly extremely well-traveled, then, if the girl knew the healers' academy by name—and she pronounced it perfectly.

Yrene shrugged, not daring to voice her dozens of questions. Instead, she said, "I don't have the money to go now, anyway."

It came out sharper than she intended—sharper than was smart, considering how lethal this girl was. Yrene didn't try to guess what manner of working girl she might be—mercenary was about as dark as she'd let herself imagine.

"Then steal the money and go. Your boss deserves to have his purse lightened."

Yrene pulled back. "I'm no thief."

A roguish grin. "If you want something, then go take it."

This girl wasn't *like* wildfire—she *was* wildfire. Deadly and uncontrollable. And slightly out of her wits.

"More than enough people believe that these days," Yrene ventured to say. Like Adarlan. Like those mercenaries. "I don't need to be one of them."

The girl's grin faded. "So you'd rather rot away here with a clean conscience?"

Yrene didn't have a reply, so she didn't say anything as she set down the rag and bowl and pulled out a small tin of salve. She kept it for herself, for the nicks and scrapes she got while working, but this cut was small enough that she could spare a bit. As gently as she could, she smeared it onto the wound. The girl didn't flinch this time.

After a moment, the girl asked, "When did you lose your mother?"

"Over eight years ago." Yrene kept her focus on the wound.

"That was a hard time to be a gifted healer on this continent, especially in Fenharrow. The King of Adarlan didn't leave much of its people—or royal family—alive."

Yrene looked up. The wildfire in the girl's eyes had turned into a scorching blue flame. *Such rage*, she thought with a shiver. *Such simmering rage*. What had she been through to make her look like that?

She didn't ask, of course. And she didn't ask how the young woman knew where she was from. Yrene understood that her golden skin and brown hair were probably enough to mark her as being from Fenharrow, if her slight accent didn't give her away.

"If you managed to attend the Torre Cesme," the girl said, her anger shifting as if she had shoved it down deep inside her, "what would you do afterward?"

Yrene picked up one of the fresh bandages and began wrapping it around the girl's arm. She'd dreamed about it for years, contemplated a thousand different futures while she washed dirty mugs and swept the floors. "I'd come back. Not to here, I mean, but to the continent. Go back to Fenharrow. There are a . . . a lot of people who need good healers these days."

She said the last part quietly. For all she knew, the girl might support the King of Adarlan—might report her to the small town guard for just speaking ill of the king. Yrene had seen it happen before, far too many times.

But the girl looked toward the door with its makeshift bolt that Yrene had constructed, at the closet that she called her bedroom, at the threadbare cloak draped over the half-rotted chair against the opposite wall, then finally back at her. It gave Yrene a chance to study her face. Seeing how easily she'd trounced those mercenaries, whoever had harmed her must be fearsome indeed.

"You'd really come back to this continent—to the empire?"

There was such quiet surprise in her voice that Yrene met her eyes.

"It's the right thing to do," was all Yrene could think of to say.

The girl didn't reply, and Yrene continued wrapping her arm. When she was finished, the girl shrugged on her shirt and tunic, tested her arm, and stood. In the cramped bedroom, Yrene felt so much smaller than the stranger, even if there were only a few inches' difference between them.

The girl picked up her cloak but didn't don it as she took a step toward the closed door.

"I could find something for your face," Yrene blurted.

The girl paused with a hand on the doorknob and looked over her shoulder. "These are meant to be a reminder."

"For what? Or—to whom?" She shouldn't pry, shouldn't have even asked.

She smiled bitterly. "For me."

Yrene thought of the scars she'd seen on her body and wondered if those were all reminders, too.

The young woman turned back to the door, but stopped again. "Whether you stay, or go to Antica and attend the Torre Cesme and return to save the world," she mused, "you should probably learn a thing or two about defending yourself."

Yrene eyed the daggers at the girl's waist, the sword she hadn't even needed to draw. Jewels embedded in the hilt—real jewels—glinted in the candlelight. The girl had to be fabulously wealthy, richer than Yrene could ever conceive of being. "I can't afford weapons."

The girl huffed a laugh. "If you learn these maneuvers, you won't need them."

Celaena took the barmaid into the alley, if only because she didn't want to wake the other inn guests and get into yet another fight. She didn't really know why she'd offered to teach her to defend herself. The last time she'd helped anybody, it had just turned around to beat the hell out of her. Literally.

But the barmaid—Yrene—had looked so earnest when she talked about helping people. About being a healer.

The Torre Cesme—any healers worth their salt knew about the academy in Antica where the best and brightest, no matter their station, could study. Celaena had once dreamed of dwelling in the fabled cream-colored towers of the Torre, of walking the narrow, sloping streets of Antica and seeing wonders brought in from lands she'd never heard of. But that was a lifetime ago. A different person ago.

Not now, certainly. And if Yrene stayed in this gods-forsaken town, other people were bound to try to attack her again. So here Celaena was, cursing her own conscience for a fool as they stood in the misty alley behind the inn.

The bodies of the three mercenaries were still out there, and Celaena caught Yrene cringing at the sound of scurrying feet and soft squeaking. The rats hadn't wasted any time.

Celaena gripped the girl's wrist and held up her hand. "People—men—usually don't hunt for the women who look like they'll put up a fight. They'll pick you because you look off-guard or vulnerable or like you'd be sympathetic. They'll usually try to move you to another location where they won't need to worry about being interrupted."

Yrene's eyes were wide, her face pale in the light of the torch Celaena had dropped just outside the back door. Helpless. What was it like to be helpless to defend yourself? A shudder that had nothing to do with the rats gnawing on the dead mercenaries went through her.

"*Do not* let them move you to another location," Celaena continued, reciting from the lessons that Ben, Arobynn's Second, had once taught her. She'd learned self-defense before she'd ever learned to attack anyone, and to first fight without weapons, too.

"Fight back enough to convince them that you're not worth it. And make as much noise as you can. In a shit-hole like this, though, I bet no one will bother coming to help you. But you should still start screaming your head off about a fire—not rape, not theft, not something that cowards would rather hide from. And if shouting doesn't discourage them, then there are a few tricks to outsmart them.

"Some might make them drop like a stone, some might get them down temporarily, but as soon as they let go of you, your *biggest* priority is getting the hell away. You understand? They let you go, you *run*."

Yrene nodded, still wide-eyed. She remained that way as Celaena took the hand she'd lifted and walked her through the eye-gouge, showing her how to shove her thumbs into the corner of someone's eyes, crook her thumbs back behind the eyeballs, and—well, Celaena couldn't actually finish that part, since she liked her own eyeballs very much. But Yrene grasped it after a few times, and did it perfectly when Celaena grabbed her from behind again and again.

She then showed her the ear clap, then how to pinch the inside of a man's upper thigh hard enough to make him scream, where to stomp on the most delicate part of the foot, what soft spots were the best to hit with her elbow (Yrene actually hit her so hard in the throat that Celaena gagged for a good minute). And then told her to go for the groin—always try to go for a strike to the groin.

And when the moon was setting, when Celaena was convinced that Yrene might stand a chance against an assailant, they finally stopped. Yrene seemed to be holding herself a bit taller, her face flushed.

"If they come after you for money," Celaena said, jerking her chin toward where the mercenaries lay in a heap, "throw whatever coins you have far away from you and run in the opposite direction. Usually they'll be so occupied by chasing after your money that you'll have a good chance of escape."

Yrene nodded. "I should—I should teach all this to Jessa."

Celaena didn't know or care who Jessa was, but she said, "If you get the chance, teach it to any female who will take the time to listen."

Silence fell between them. There was so much more to learn, so much else to teach her. But dawn was about two hours away, and she should probably go back to her room now, if only to pack and go. Go, not because she was ordered to or because she found her punishment acceptable, but . . . because she needed to. She needed to go to the Red Desert.

Even if it was only to see where the Wyrd planned to lead her. Staying, running away to another land, avoiding her fate . . . she wouldn't do that. She couldn't be like Yrene, a living reminder of loss and shoved-aside dreams. No, she'd continue to the Red Desert and follow this path, wherever it led, however much it stung her pride.

Yrene cleared her throat. "Did you—did you ever have to use these maneuvers? Not to pry. I mean, you don't have to answer if—"

"I've used them, yes—but not because I was in that kind of situation. I . . ." She knew she shouldn't say it, but she did. "I'm usually the one who does the hunting."

Yrene, to her surprise, just nodded, if a bit sadly. There was such irony, she realized, in them working together—the assassin and the healer. Two opposite sides of the coin.

Yrene wrapped her arms around herself. "How can I ever repay you for—"

But Celaena held up a hand. The alley was empty, but she could feel them, could hear the shift in the fog, in the scurrying of the rats. Pockets of quiet.

She met Yrene's stare and flicked her eyes toward the back door, a silent command. Yrene had gone white and stiff. It was one thing to practice, but to put lessons into action, to use them . . . Yrene was more of a liability. Celaena jerked her chin at the door, an order now.

There were at least five men—two on either end of the alley converging upon them, and one more standing guard by the busier end of the street.

Yrene was through the back door by the time Celaena drew her sword.

CHAPTER 5

In the darkened kitchen, Yrene leaned against the back door, a hand on her hammering heart as she listened to the melee outside. Earlier, the girl had the element of surprise—but how could she face them again?

Her hands trembled as the sound of clashing blades and shouts filtered through the crack beneath the door. Thumps, grunts, growls. What was happening?

She couldn't stand it, not knowing what was happening to the girl.

It went against every instinct to open up the back door and peer out.

Her breath caught in her throat at the sight:

The mercenary who had escaped earlier had returned with more friends—more skilled friends. Two were facedown on the cobblestones, pools of blood around them. But the remaining three were engaged with the girl, who was—was—

Gods, she moved like a black wind, such lethal grace, and—

A hand closed over Yrene's mouth as someone grabbed her from behind and pressed something cold and sharp against her throat. There had been another man; he came in through the inn.

"Walk," he breathed in her ear, his voice rough and foreign. She couldn't see him, couldn't tell anything about him beyond the hardness of his body, the reek of his clothes, the scratch of a heavy beard against her cheek. He flung open the door and, still holding the dagger to Yrene's neck, strode into the alley.

The young woman stopped fighting. Another mercenary had gone down, and the two before her had their blades pointed at her.

"Drop your weapons," the man said. Yrene would have shaken her head, but the dagger was pressed so close that any movement she made would have slit her own throat.

The young woman eyed the men, then Yrene's captor, then Yrene herself. Calm—utterly calm and cold as she bared her teeth in a feral grin. "Come and get them."

Yrene's stomach dropped. The man had only to shift his wrist and he'd spill her life's blood. She wasn't ready to die—not now, not in Innish.

Her captor chuckled. "Bold and foolish words, girl." He pushed the blade harder, and Yrene winced. She felt the dampness of her blood before she realized he'd cut a thin line across her neck. Silba save her.

But the girl's eyes were on Yrene, and they narrowed slightly. In challenge, in a command. *Fight back,* she seemed to say. *Fight for your miserable life.*

The two men with the swords circled closer, but she didn't lower her blade.

"Drop your weapons before I cut her open," Yrene's captor growled. "Once we're done making you pay for our comrades, for all the money you cost us with their deaths, maybe we'll let *her* live." He squeezed Yrene tighter, but the young woman just watched him. The mercenary hissed. "*Drop your weapons.*"

She didn't.

Gods, she was going to let him kill her, wasn't she?

Yrene couldn't die like this—not here, not as a no-name barmaid in this horrible place. *Wouldn't* die like this. Her mother had gone down swinging—her mother had *fought* for her, had killed that soldier so Yrene could have a chance to flee, to make something of her life. To do some good for the world.

She wouldn't die like this.

The rage hit, so staggering that Yrene could hardly see through it, could hardly see anything except a year in Innish, a future beyond her grasp, and a life she was not ready to part with.

She gave no warning before she stomped down as hard as she could on the bridge of the man's foot. He jerked, howling, but Yrene brought up her arms, shoving the dagger from her throat with one hand as she drove her elbow into his gut. Drove it with every bit of rage she had burning in her. He groaned as he doubled over, and she slammed her elbow into his temple, just as the girl had shown her.

The man collapsed to his knees, and Yrene bolted. To run, to help, she didn't know.

But the girl was already standing in front of her, grinning broadly. Behind her, the two men lay unmoving. And the man on his knees—

Yrene dodged aside as the young woman grabbed the gasping man and dragged him into the dark mist beyond. There was a muffled scream, then a thump.

And despite her healer's blood, despite the stomach she'd inherited, Yrene barely made it two steps before she vomited.

When she was done, she found the young woman watching her again, smiling faintly. "Fast learner," she said. Her fine clothes, even her darkly glittering ruby brooch, were covered with blood. Not her own, Yrene noted with some relief. "You sure you want to be a healer?"

Yrene wiped her mouth on the corner of her apron. She didn't want to know what the alternative was—what this girl might be. No, all she wanted was to smack her. Hard.

"You could have dispatched them without me! But you let that man hold a knife to my throat—you *let him!* Are you insane?"

The girl smiled in such a way that said yes, she was most certainly insane. But she said, "Those men were a joke. I wanted you to get some real experience in a controlled environment."

"You call that *controlled*?" Yrene couldn't help shouting. She put a hand to the already clotted slice in her neck. It would heal quickly, but might scar. She'd have to inspect it immediately.

"Look at it this way, Yrene Towers: now you know you can do it. That man was twice your weight and had almost a foot on you, and you downed him in a few heartbeats."

"You said those men were a joke."

A fiendish grin. "To me, they are."

Yrene's blood chilled. "I—I've had enough of today. I think I need to go to bed."

The girl sketched a bow. "And I should probably be on my way. Word of advice: wash the blood out of your clothes and don't tell anyone what you saw tonight. Those men might have more friends, and as far as I'm concerned, they were the unfortunate victims of a horrible robbery." She held up a leather pouch heavy with coins and stalked past Yrene into the inn.

Yrene spared a glance at the bodies, felt a heavy weight drop into her stomach, and followed the girl inside. She was still furious with her, still shaking with the remnants of terror and desperation.

So she didn't say good-bye to the deadly girl as she vanished.

CHAPTER 6

Yrene did as the girl said and changed into another gown and apron before going to the kitchens to wash the blood from her clothes. Her hands were shaking so badly that it took longer than usual to wash the clothing, and by the time she finished, the pale light of dawn was creeping through the kitchen window.

She had to be up in . . . well, now. Groaning, she trudged back to her room to hang the wet clothes to dry. If someone saw her laundry drying, it would only raise suspicion. She supposed she'd have to be the one to pretend to find the bodies, too. Gods, what a mess.

Wincing at the thought of the long, long day ahead of her, trying to make sense of the night she'd just had, Yrene entered her room and softly shut the door. Even if she told someone, they probably wouldn't believe her.

It wasn't until she was done hanging her clothes on the hooks embedded in the wall that she noticed the leather pouch on the bed, and the note pinned beneath it.

She knew what was inside, could easily guess based on the lumps and edges. Her breath caught in her throat as she pulled out the note.

There, in elegant, feminine handwriting, the girl had written:

For wherever you need to go—and then some. The world needs more healers.

No name, no date. Staring at the paper, she could almost picture the girl's feral smile and the defiance in her eyes. This note, if anything, was a challenge—a dare.

Hands shaking anew, Yrene dumped out the contents of the pouch.

The pile of gold coins shimmered, and Yrene staggered back, collapsing into the rickety chair across from the bed. She blinked, and blinked again.

Not just gold, but also the brooch the girl had been wearing, its massive ruby smoldering in the candlelight.

A hand to her mouth, Yrene stared at the door, at the ceiling, then back at the small fortune sitting on her bed. Stared and stared and stared.

The gods had vanished, her mother had once claimed. But had they? Had it been some god who had visited tonight, clothed in the skin of a battered young woman? Or had it merely been their distant whispers that prompted the stranger to walk down that alley? She would never know, she supposed. And maybe that was the whole point.

Wherever you need to go . . .

Gods or fate or just pure coincidence and kindness, it was a gift. This was a gift. The world was wide-open—wide-open and hers for the taking, if she dared. She could go to Antica, attend the Torre Cesme, go anywhere she wished.

If she dared.

Yrene smiled.

An hour later, no one stopped Yrene Towers as she walked out of the White Pig and never looked back.

Washed and dressed in a new tunic, Celaena boarded the ship an hour before dawn. It was her own damn fault that she felt hollow and light-headed after a night without rest. But she could sleep today—sleep the whole journey across the Gulf of Oro to the Deserted Land. She *should* sleep, because once she landed in Yurpa, she had a trek across blistering, deadly sands—a week, at least, through the desert before she reached the Mute Master and his fortress of Silent Assassins.

The captain didn't ask questions when she pressed a piece of silver into his palm and went belowdecks, following his directions to find her stateroom. With the hood and blades, she knew none of the sailors would bother her. And while she now had to be careful with the money she had left, she knew she'd hand over another silver piece or two before the voyage was done.

Sighing, Celaena entered her cabin—small but clean, with a little window that looked out onto the dawn-gray bay. She locked the door behind her and slumped onto the tiny bed. She'd seen enough of Innish; she didn't need to bother watching the departure.

She'd been on her way out of the inn when she'd passed that horrifically small closet Yrene called a bedroom. While Yrene had tended to her arm, Celaena had been astounded by the cramped conditions, the rickety furniture, the too-thin blankets. She'd planned to leave some coins for Yrene anyway—if only because she was certain the innkeeper would make Yrene pay for those bandages.

But Celaena had stood in front of that wooden door to the bedroom, listening to Yrene wash her clothes in the nearby kitchen. She found herself unable to turn away, unable to stop thinking about the would-be healer with the brown-gold hair and caramel eyes, of what Yrene had lost and how helpless she'd become. There were so many of them now—the children who had lost everything to Adarlan. Children who had now grown into assassins and barmaids, without a true place to call home, their native kingdoms left in ruin and ash.

Magic had been gone all these years. And the gods were dead, or simply didn't care anymore. Yet there, deep in her gut, was a small but insistent *tug.* A tug on a strand of some invisible web. So Celaena decided to tug back, just to see how far and wide the reverberations would go.

It was a matter of moments to write the note and then stuff most of her gold pieces into the pouch. A heartbeat later, she'd set it on Yrene's sagging cot.

She'd added Arobynn's ruby brooch as a parting thought. She wondered if a girl from ravaged Fenharrow wouldn't mind a brooch in Adarlan's royal colors. But Celaena was glad to be rid of it, and hoped Yrene would pawn the piece for the small fortune it was worth. Hoped that an assassin's jewel would pay for a healer's education.

So maybe it was the gods at work. Maybe it was some force beyond them, beyond mortal comprehension. Or maybe it was just for what and who Celaena would never be.

Yrene was still washing her bloodied clothes in the kitchen when Celaena slipped out of her room, then down the hall, and left the White Pig behind.

As she stalked through the foggy streets toward the ramshackle docks, Celaena had prayed Yrene Towers wasn't foolish enough to tell anyone—especially the innkeeper—about the money. Prayed Yrene Towers seized her life with both hands and set out for the pale-stoned city of Antica. Prayed that somehow, years from now, Yrene Towers would return to this continent, and maybe, just maybe, heal their shattered world a little bit.

Smiling to herself in the confines of her cabin, Celaena nestled into the bed, pulled her hood low over her eyes, and crossed her ankles. By the time the ship set sail across the jade-green gulf, the assassin was fast asleep.

THE ASSASSIN AND THE DESERT

CHAPTER 1

There was nothing left in the world except sand and wind.

At least, that's how it seemed to Celaena Sardothien as she stood atop the crimson dune and gazed across the desert. Even with the wind, the heat was stifling, and sweat made her many layers of clothes cling to her body. But sweating, her nomad guide had told her, was a good thing—it was when you didn't sweat that the Red Desert became deadly. Sweat reminded you to drink. When the heat evaporated your perspiration before you could realize you were sweating, that's when you could cross into dehydration and not know it.

Oh, the *miserable* heat. It invaded every pore of her, made her head throb and her bones ache. The muggy warmth of Skull's Bay had been nothing compared to this. What she wouldn't give for just the briefest of cool breezes!

Beside her, the nomad guide pointed a gloved finger toward the southwest. "The *sessiz suikast* are there." *Sessiz suikast.* The Silent Assassins—the legendary order that she'd been sent here to train with.

"To learn obedience and discipline," Arobynn Hamel had said. *In the height of summer in the Red Desert* was what he'd failed to add. It was a punishment. Two months ago, when Arobynn had sent Celaena along with Sam Cortland to Skull's Bay on an unknown errand, they'd discovered that he'd actually dispatched them to trade in slaves. Needless to say, that hadn't sat well with Celaena or Sam, despite their occupation. So they'd freed the slaves, deciding to damn the consequences. But now . . . As punishments went, this was probably the worst. Given the bruises and cuts that were still healing on her face a month after Arobynn had bestowed them, that was saying something.

Celaena scowled. She pulled the scarf a bit higher over her mouth and nose as she took a step down the dune. Her legs strained against the sliding sand, but it was a welcome freedom after the harrowing trek through the Singing Sands, where each grain had hummed and whined and moaned. They'd spent a whole day monitoring each step, careful to keep the sand beneath them ringing in harmony. Or else, the nomad had told her, the sands could dissolve into quicksand.

Celaena descended the dune, but paused when she didn't hear her guide's footsteps. "Aren't you coming?"

The man remained atop the dune, and pointed again to the horizon. "Two miles that way." His use of the common tongue was a bit unwieldy, but she understood him well enough.

She pulled down the scarf from her mouth, wincing as a gust of sand stung her sweaty face. "I paid you to take me there."

"Two miles," he said, adjusting the large pack on his back. The scarf around his head obscured his tanned features, but she could still see the fear in his eyes.

Yes, yes, the *sessiz suikast* were feared and respected in the desert. It had been a miracle that she'd found a guide willing to take her this close to their fortress. Of course, offering gold had helped. But the nomads viewed the *sessiz suikast* as little less than shadows of death—and apparently, her guide would go no farther.

She studied the westward horizon. She could see nothing beyond dunes and sand that rippled like the surface of a windblown sea.

"Two miles," the nomad said behind her. "They will find you."

Celaena turned to ask him another question, but he had already disappeared over the other side of the dune. Cursing him, she tried to swallow, but failed. Her mouth was too dry. She had to start now, or else she'd need to set up her tent to sleep out the unforgiving midday and afternoon heat.

Two miles. How long could that take?

Taking a sip from her unnervingly light waterskin, Celaena pulled her scarf back over her mouth and nose and began walking.

The only sound was the wind hissing through the sand.

Hours later, Celaena found herself using all of her self-restraint to avoid leaping into the courtyard pools or kneeling to drink at one of the little rivers running along the floor. No one had offered her water upon her arrival, and she didn't think her current escort was inclined to do so either as he led her through the winding halls of the red sandstone fortress.

The two miles had felt more like twenty. She had been just about to stop and set up her tent when she'd crested a dune and the lush green trees and adobe fortress had spread before her, hidden in an oasis nestled between two monstrous sand dunes.

After all that, she was parched. But she was Celaena Sardothien. She had a reputation to uphold.

She kept her senses alert as they walked farther into the fortress—taking in exits and windows, noting where sentries were stationed.

They passed a row of open-air training rooms in which she could see people from all kingdoms and of all ages sparring or exercising or just sitting quietly, lost in meditation. They climbed a narrow flight of steps that went up and up into a large building. The shade of the stairwell was wonderfully cool. But then they entered a long, enclosed hall, and the heat wrapped around her like a blanket.

For a fortress of supposedly silent assassins, the place was fairly noisy, with the clatter of weapons from the training rooms, the buzzing of insects in the many trees and bushes, the chatter of birds, the gurgle of all that crystal-clear water running through every room and hall.

They approached an open set of doors at the end of the hallway. Her escort—a middle-aged man flecked with scars that stood out like chalk against his tan skin—said nothing to her. Beyond the doors, the interior was a mixture of shadow and light. They entered a giant chamber flanked by blue-painted wooden pillars that supported a mezzanine on either side. A glance into the darkness of the balcony informed her that there were figures lurking there—watching, waiting. There were more in the shadows of the columns. Whoever they thought she was, they certainly weren't underestimating her. Good.

A narrow mosaic of green and blue glass tiles wove through the floor toward the dais, echoing the little rivers on the lower level. Atop the dais, seated among cushions and potted palms, was a white-robed man.

The Mute Master. She had expected him to be ancient, but he seemed to be around fifty. She kept her chin held high as they approached him, following the tile path in the floor. She couldn't tell if the Master's skin had always been that tan or if it was from the sun. He smiled slightly—he'd probably been handsome in his youth. Sweat oozed down Celaena's spine. Though the Master had no visible weapons, the two servants fanning him with palm leaves were armed to the teeth. Her escort stopped a safe distance from the Master and bowed.

Celaena did the same, and when she raised herself, she removed the hood from over her hair. She was sure it was a mess and disgustingly greasy after two weeks in the desert with no water to bathe in, but she wasn't here to impress him with her beauty.

The Mute Master looked her up and down, and then nodded. Her escort nudged her with an elbow, and Celaena cleared her dry throat as she stepped forward.

She knew the Mute Master wouldn't say anything; his self-imposed silence was well-known. It was incumbent upon her to make the introduction. Arobynn had told her exactly what to say—*ordered* her was more like it. There would be no disguises, no masks, no fake names. Since she had shown such disregard for Arobynn's best interests, he no longer had any inclination to protect hers. She'd debated for weeks how she might find a way to protect her identity—to keep these strangers from knowing who she was—but Arobynn's orders had been simple: she had one month to win the Mute Master's respect. And if she didn't return home with his letter of approval—a letter about *Celaena Sardothien*—she'd better find a new city to live in. Possibly a new continent.

"Thank you for granting me an audience, Master of the Silent Assassins," she said, silently cursing the stiffness of her words.

She put a hand over her heart and dropped to both knees. "I am Celaena Sardothien, protégée of Arobynn Hamel, King of the Northern Assassins." Adding "Northern" seemed appropriate; she didn't think the Mute Master would be much pleased to learn that Arobynn called himself King of *all* the Assassins. But whether or not it surprised him, his face revealed nothing, though she sensed some of the people in the shadows shifting on their feet.

"My master sent me here to beseech you to train me," she said, chafing at the words. Train *her*! She lowered her head so the Master wouldn't see the ire on her face. "I am yours." She tilted her palms faceup in a gesture of supplication.

Nothing.

Warmth worse than the heat of the desert singed her cheeks. She kept her head down, her arms still upheld. Cloth rustled, then near-silent steps echoed through the chamber. At last, two bare, brown feet stopped before her.

A dry finger tilted her chin up, and Celaena found herself staring into the sea-green eyes of the Master. She didn't dare move. With one movement, the Master could snap her neck. This was a test—a test of trust, she realized.

She willed herself into stillness, focusing on the details of his face to avoid thinking about how vulnerable she was. Sweat beaded along the border of his dark hair, which was cropped close to his head. It was impossible to tell what kingdom he hailed from; his hazelnut skin suggested Eyllwe. But his elegant, almond-shaped eyes suggested one of the countries in the distant southern continent. Regardless, how had he wound up here?

She braced herself as his long fingers pushed back the loose strands of her braided hair, revealing the yellowing bruises still lingering around her eyes and cheeks, and the narrow arc of the scab along her cheekbone. Had Arobynn sent word that she would be coming? Had he told him the circumstances under which she'd been packed off? The Master didn't seem at all surprised by her arrival.

But the Master's eyes narrowed, his lips forming a tight line as he looked at the remnants of the bruises on the other side of her face. She was lucky that Arobynn was skilled enough to keep his blows from permanently marring her. A twinge of guilt went through her as she wondered if Sam had healed as well. In the three days following her beating, she hadn't seen him around the Keep. She'd blacked out before Arobynn could deal with her companion. And since that night, even during her trip out here, everything had been a haze of rage and sorrow and bone-deep weariness, as if she were dreaming while awake.

She calmed her thundering heart just as the Master released her face and stepped back. He motioned with a hand for her to rise, which she did, to the relief of her aching knees.

The Master gave her a crooked smile. She would have echoed the expression—but an instant later he snapped his fingers, triggering four men to charge at her.

CHAPTER 2

They didn't have weapons, but their intent was clear enough. The first man, clad in the loose, layered clothing that everyone here wore, reached her, and she dodged the sweeping blow aimed at her face. His arm shot past her, and she grabbed it by the wrist and bicep, locking and twisting his arm so he grunted with pain. She whirled him around, careening him into the second attacker hard enough that the two men went tumbling to the ground.

Celaena leapt back, landing where her escort had been standing only seconds before, careful to avoid crashing into the Master. This was another test—a test to see at what level she might begin her training. And if she was worthy.

Of course she was worthy. She was Celaena Sardothien, gods be damned.

The third man pulled out two crescent-shaped daggers from the folds of his beige tunic and slashed at her. Her layered clothing was too cumbersome for her to dart away fast enough, so as he swiped for her face, she bent back. Her spine strained, but the two blades passed overhead, slicing through an errant strand of her hair. She dropped to the ground and lashed out with a leg, sweeping the man off his feet.

The fourth man, though, had come up behind her, a curved blade flashing in his hand as he made to plunge it through her head. She rolled, and the sword struck stone, sparking.

By the time she got to her feet, he'd raised the sword again. She caught his feint to the left before he struck at her right. She danced aside. The man was still swinging when she drove the base of her palm straight into his nose and slammed her other fist into his gut. The man dropped to the floor, blood gushing from his nose. She panted, the air ragged in her already-burning throat. She really, *really* needed water.

None of the four men on the ground moved. The Master began smiling, and it was then that the others gathered around the chamber stepped closer to the light. Men and women, all tan, though their hair showed the range of the various kingdoms on the continent. Celaena inclined her head. None of them nodded back. Celaena kept one eye on the four men before her as they got to their feet, sheathed their weapons, and stalked back to the shadows. Hopefully they wouldn't take it personally.

She scanned the shadows again, bracing herself for more assailants. Nearby, a young woman watched her, and she flashed Celaena a conspirator's grin. Celaena tried not to look too interested, though the girl was one of the most stunning people she'd ever beheld. It wasn't just her wine-red hair or the color of her eyes, a red-brown Celaena had never seen before. No, it was the girl's armor that initially caught her interest: ornate to the point of probably being useless, but still a work of art.

The right shoulder was fashioned into a snarling wolf's head, and her helmet, tucked into the crook of her arm, featured a wolf hunched over the noseguard. Another wolf's head had been molded into the pommel of her broadsword. On anyone else, the armor might have looked flamboyant and ridiculous, but on the girl . . . There was a strange, boyish sort of carelessness to her.

Still, Celaena wondered how it was possible not to be sweltering to death inside all that armor.

The Master clapped Celaena on the shoulder and beckoned to the girl to come forward. Not to attack—a friendly invitation. The girl's armor clinked as it moved, but her boots were near-silent.

The Master used his hands to form a series of motions between the girl and Celaena. The girl bowed low, then gave her that wicked grin again. "I'm Ansel," she said, her voice bright, amused. She had a barely perceptible lilt to her accent that Celaena couldn't place. "Looks like we're sharing a room while you're here." The Master gestured again, his calloused, scarred fingers creating rudimentary gestures that Ansel could somehow decipher. "Say, how long will that be, actually?"

Celaena fought her frown. "One month." She inclined her head to the Master. "If you allow me to stay that long."

With the month that it took to get here, and the month it would take to get home, she'd be away from Rifthold three months before she returned.

The Master merely nodded and walked back to the cushions atop the dais. "That means you can stay," Ansel whispered, and then touched Celaena's shoulder with an armor-clad hand. Apparently not all the assassins here were under a vow of silence—or had a sense of personal space. "You'll start training tomorrow," Ansel went on. "At dawn."

The Master sank onto the cushions, and Celaena almost sagged with relief. Arobynn had made her think that convincing him to train her would be nearly impossible. Fool. Pack her off to the desert to suffer, would he!

"Thank you," Celaena said to the Master, keenly aware of the eyes watching her in the hall as she bowed again. He waved her away.

"Come," Ansel said, her hair shimmering in a ray of sunlight. "I suppose you'll want a bath before you do anything else. *I* certainly would, if I were you." Ansel gave her a smile that stretched the splattering of freckles across the bridge of her nose and cheeks.

Celaena glanced sidelong at the girl and her ornate armor, and followed her from the room. "That's the best thing I've heard in weeks," she said.

Alone with Ansel as they strode through the halls, Celaena keenly felt the absence of the long daggers usually sheathed in her belt. But they'd been taken from her at the gate, along with her sword and her pack. She let her hands dangle at her sides, ready to react to the slightest movement from her guide. Whether or not Ansel noticed Celaena's readiness to fight, the girl swung her arms casually, her armor clanking with the movement.

Her roommate. That was an unfortunate surprise. Sharing a room with Sam for a few nights was one thing. But a month with a complete stranger? Celaena studied Ansel out of the corner of her eye. She was slightly taller, but Celaena couldn't see much else about her, thanks to the armor. She'd never spent much time around other girls, save the courtesans that Arobynn invited to the Keep for parties or took to the theater, and most of them were not the sort of person that Celaena cared to know. There were no other female assassins in Arobynn's guild. But here . . . in addition to Ansel, there had been just as many women as men. In the Keep, there was no mistaking who she was. Here, she was only another face in the crowd.

For all she knew, Ansel might be better than her. The thought didn't sit well.

"So," Ansel said, her brows rising. "Celaena Sardothien."

"Yes?"

Ansel shrugged—or at least shrugged as well as she could, given the armor. "I thought you'd be . . . more dramatic."

"Sorry to disappoint," Celaena said, not sounding very sorry at all. Ansel steered them up a short staircase, then down a long hall. Children popped in and out of the rooms along the passage, buckets and brooms and mops in hand. The youngest looked about eight, the eldest about twelve.

"Acolytes," Ansel said in response to Celaena's silent question. "Cleaning the rooms of the older assassins is part of their training. Teaches them responsibility and humility. Or something like that." Ansel winked at a child who gaped up at her as she passed. Indeed, several of the children stared after Ansel, their eyes wide with wonder and respect; Ansel must be well regarded, then. None of them bothered to look at Celaena. She raised her chin.

"And how old were you when you came here?" The more she knew the better.

"I had barely turned thirteen," Ansel said. "So I narrowly missed having to do the drudgery work."

"And how old are you now?"

"Trying to get a read on me, are you?"

Celaena kept her face blank.

"I just turned eighteen. You look about my age, too."

Celaena nodded. She certainly didn't have to yield any information about herself. Even though Arobynn had ordered her not to hide her identity here, that didn't mean she had to give away details. And at least Celaena had started her training at eight; she had several years on Ansel. That had to count for something. "Has training with the Master been effective?"

Ansel gave her a rueful smile. "I wouldn't know. I've been here for five years, and he's still refused to train me personally. Not that I care. I'd say I'm pretty damn good with or without his expertise."

Well, *that* was certainly odd. How had she gone so long without working with the Master? Though, many of Arobynn's assassins never received private lessons with him, either. "Where are you from, originally?" Celaena asked.

"The Flatlands." The Flatlands . . . Where in hell were the Flatlands? Ansel answered for her. "Along the coast of the Western Wastes—formerly known as the Witch Kingdom."

The Wastes were certainly familiar. But she'd never heard of the Flatlands.

"My father," Ansel went on, "is Lord of Briarcliff. He sent me here for training, so I might 'make myself useful.' But I don't think five hundred years would be enough to teach me that."

Despite herself, Celaena chuckled. She stole another glance at Ansel's armor. "Don't you get hot in all that armor?"

"Of course," Ansel said, tossing her shoulder-length hair. "But you have to admit it's rather striking. And very well suited for strutting about a fortress full of assassins. How else am I to distinguish myself?"

"Where did you get it from?" Not that she might want some for herself; she had no use for armor like that.

"Oh, I had it made for me." So—Ansel had money, then. Plenty of it, if she could throw it away on armor. "But the sword"—Ansel patted the wolf-shaped hilt at her side—"belongs to my father. His gift to me when I left. I figured I'd have the armor match it—wolves are a family symbol."

They entered an open walkway, the heat of the midafternoon sun slamming into them with full force. Yet Ansel's face remained jovial, and if the armor did indeed make her uncomfortable, she didn't show it. Ansel looked her up and down. "How many people have you killed?"

Celaena almost choked, but kept her chin high. "I don't see how that is any of your concern."

Ansel chuckled. "I suppose it'd be easy enough to find out; you must leave *some* indication if you're so notorious." Actually, it was Arobynn who usually saw to it that word got out through the proper channels. She left very little behind once her job was finished. Leaving a sign felt somewhat . . . cheap. "I'd want *everyone* to know that I'd done it," Ansel added.

Well, Celaena *did* want everyone to know that she was the best, but something about the way Ansel said it seemed different from her own reasoning.

"So, which of you looks worse?" Ansel asked suddenly. "You, or the person who gave those to you?" Celaena knew that she meant the fading bruises and cuts on her face.

Her stomach tightened. It was getting to be a familiar feeling.

"Me," Celaena said quietly.

She didn't know why she admitted it. Bravado might have been the better option. But she was tired, and suddenly so heavy with the weight of that memory.

"Did your master do that to you?" Ansel asked. This time, Celaena stayed silent, and Ansel didn't push her.

At the other end of the walkway, they took a spiral stone staircase down into an empty courtyard where benches and little tables stood in the shade of the towering date trees. Someone had left a book lying atop one of the wooden tables, and as they passed by, Celaena glimpsed the cover. The title was in a scrawling, strange script that she didn't recognize.

If she'd been alone, she might have paused to flip through the book, just to see words printed in a language so different from anything she knew, but Ansel continued on toward a pair of carved wooden doors.

"The baths. It's one of the places here where silence is actually enforced, so try to keep quiet. Don't splash too much, either. Some of the older assassins can get cranky about even that." Ansel pushed one of the doors open. "Take your time. I'll see to it that your things are brought to our room. When you're done, ask an acolyte to take you there. Dinner isn't for a few hours; I'll come by the room then."

Celaena gave her a long look. The idea of Ansel—or anyone—handling the weapons and gear she'd left at the gate wasn't appealing. Not that she had anything to hide—though she did cringe inwardly at the thought of the guards pawing at her undergarments as they searched her bag. Her taste for very expensive and very delicate underwear wouldn't do much for her reputation.

But she was here at their mercy, and her letter of approval depended on her good behavior. And good attitude.

So Celaena merely said "Thank you," before striding past Ansel and into the herb-scented air beyond the doors.

While the fortress had communal baths, they were thankfully separated between men and women, and at that point in the day, the women's baths were empty.

Hidden by towering palms and date trees sagging with the weight of their fruit, the baths were made from the same sea green and cobalt tiles that had formed the mosaic in the Master's chamber, kept cool by white awnings jutting out from the walls of the building. There were multiple large pools—some steamed, some bubbled, some steamed *and* bubbled—but the one Celaena slipped into was utterly calm and clear and cold.

Celaena stifled a groan as she submerged herself and stayed under until her lungs ached. While modesty was a trait she'd learned to live without, she still kept herself low in the water. Of course, it had nothing to do with the fact that her ribs and arms were peppered with fading bruises, and that the sight of them made her sick. Sometimes it was sick with anger; other times it was with sorrow. Often, it was both. She wanted to go back to Rifthold—to see what had happened to Sam, to resume the life that had splintered in a few agonizing minutes. But she also dreaded it.

At least, here at the edge of the world, that night—and all of Rifthold and the people it contained—seemed very far away.

She stayed in the pool until her hands turned uncomfortably pruny.

Ansel wasn't in their tiny, rectangular room when Celaena arrived, though someone had unpacked Celaena's belongings. Aside from her sword and daggers, some undergarments, and a few tunics, she hadn't brought much—and hadn't bothered to bring her finer clothing. Which she was grateful for, now that she'd seen how quickly the sand had worn through the bulky clothes the nomad had made her wear.

There were two narrow beds, and it took her a moment to figure out which was Ansel's. The red stone wall behind it was bare. Aside from the small iron wolf figurine on the bedside table, and a human-sized dummy that must be used to store Ansel's extraordinary armor, Celaena would have had no idea that she was sharing a room with anyone.

Peeking through Ansel's chest of drawers was equally futile. Burgundy tunics and black pants, all neatly folded. The only things that offset the monotony were several white tunics—garb that many of the men and women had been wearing. Even the undergarments were plain—and folded. Who folded their undergarments? Celaena thought of her enormous closet back home, exploding with color and different fabrics and patterns, all tossed together. Her undergarments, while expensive, usually wound up in a heap in their drawer.

Sam probably folded his undergarments. Though, depending on how much of him Arobynn had left intact, he might not even be able to now. Arobynn would never permanently maim *her*, but Sam might have fared worse. Sam had always been the expendable one.

She shoved the thought away and nestled farther into the bed. Through the small window, the silence of the fortress lulled her to sleep.

~

She'd never seen Arobynn so angry, and it was scaring the hell out of her. He didn't yell, and he didn't curse—he just went very still and very quiet. The only signs of his rage were his silver eyes, glittering with a deadly calm.

She tried not to flinch in her chair as he stood from the giant wooden desk. Sam, seated beside her, sucked in a breath. She couldn't speak; if she started talking, her trembling voice would betray her. She couldn't endure that kind of humiliation.

"Do you know how much money you've cost me?" Arobynn asked her softly.

Celaena's palms began sweating. It was worth it, *she told herself. Freeing those two hundred slaves was worth it. No matter what was about to happen, she'd never regret doing it.*

"It's not her fault," Sam cut in, and she flashed him a warning glare. "We both thought it was—"

"Don't lie to me, Sam Cortland," Arobynn growled. "The only way you

became involved in this was because she decided to do it—and it was either let her die trying, or help her."

Sam opened his mouth to object, but Arobynn silenced him with a sharp whistle through his teeth. His office doors opened. Wesley, Arobynn's bodyguard, peered in. Arobynn kept his eyes on Celaena as he said, "Get Tern, Mullin, and Harding."

This wasn't a good sign. She kept her face neutral, though, as Arobynn continued watching her. Neither she nor Sam dared speak in the long minutes that passed. She tried not to shake.

At last, the three assassins—all men, all cut from muscle and armed to the teeth—filed in. "Shut the door," Arobynn said to Harding, the last one to enter. Then he told the others, "Hold him."

Instantly, Sam was dragged out of his chair, his arms pinned back by Tern and Mullin. Harding took a step in front of them, his fist flexing.

"No," Celaena breathed as she met Sam's wide-eyed stare. Arobynn wouldn't be that cruel—he wouldn't make her watch as he hurt Sam. Something tight and aching built in her throat.

But Celaena kept her head high, even as Arobynn said quietly to her, "You are not going to enjoy this. You will not forget this. And I don't want you to."

She whipped her head back to Sam, a plea for Harding not to hurt him on her lips.

She sensed the blow only a heartbeat before Arobynn struck her.

She toppled out of her chair and didn't have time to raise herself properly before Arobynn grabbed her by the collar and swung again, his fist connecting with her cheek. Light and darkness reeled. Another blow, hard enough that she felt the warmth of her blood on her face before she felt the pain.

Sam began screaming something. But Arobynn hit her again. She tasted blood, yet she didn't fight back, didn't dare to. Sam struggled against Tern and Mullin. They held him firm, Harding putting a warning arm in front of Sam to block his path.

Arobynn hit her—her ribs, her jaw, her gut. And her face. Again and again and again. Careful blows—blows meant to inflict as much pain as possible without doing permanent damage. And Sam kept roaring, shouting words she couldn't quite hear over the agony.

The last thing she remembered was a pang of guilt at the sight of her blood staining Arobynn's exquisite red carpet. And then darkness, blissful darkness, full of relief that she hadn't seen him hurt Sam.

CHAPTER 3

Celaena dressed in the nicest tunic she'd brought—which wasn't really anything to admire, but the midnight blue and gold *did* bring out the turquoise hues in her eyes. She went so far as to apply some cosmetics to her eyes, but opted to avoid putting anything on the rest of her face. Even though the sun had set, the heat remained. Anything she put on her skin would likely slide right off.

Ansel made good on her promise to retrieve her before dinner and pestered Celaena with questions about her journey during the walk to the dining hall. As they walked, there were some areas where Ansel talked normally, others where she kept her voice at a whisper, and others where she signaled not to speak at all. Celaena couldn't tell why certain rooms demanded utter silence and others did not—they all seemed the same. Still exhausted despite her nap, and unsure when she could speak, Celaena kept her answers brief. She wouldn't have minded missing dinner and just sleeping all night.

Staying alert as they entered the hall was an effort of will. Yet even with her exhaustion, she instinctively scanned the room. There were three exits—the giant doors through which they entered, and two servants' doors on either end. The hall was packed wall-to-wall with long wooden tables and benches full of people. At least seventy of them in total. None of them looked at Celaena as Ansel ambled toward a table near the front of the room. If they knew who she was, they certainly didn't care. She tried not to scowl.

Ansel slid into place at a table and patted the empty spot on the bench beside her. The nearest assassins looked up from their meal—some had been talking quietly and others were silent—as Celaena stood before them.

Ansel waved a hand in Celaena's direction. "Celaena, this is everyone. Everyone, this is Celaena. Though I'm sure you gossips know everything about her already." She spoke softly, and even though some assassins in the hall were talking, they seemed to hear her just fine. Even the clank of their utensils seemed hushed.

Celaena scanned the faces of those around her; they all seemed to be watching her with benign, if not amused, curiosity. Carefully, too aware of each of her movements, Celaena sat on the bench and surveyed the table. Platters of grilled, fragrant meats; bowls full of spherical, spiced grains; fruits and dates; and pitcher after pitcher of water.

Ansel helped herself, her armor glinting in the light of the ornate glass lanterns dangling from the ceiling, and then piled the same food on Celaena's plate. "Just start eating," she whispered. "It all tastes good, and none of it is poisoned." To emphasize her point, Ansel popped a cube of charred lamb into her mouth and chewed. "See?" she said between bites. "Lord Berick might want to kill us, but he knows better than to try to get rid of us through poisons. We're far too skilled to fall for that sort of thing. Aren't we?" The assassins around her grinned.

"Lord Berick?" Celaena asked, now staring at her plate and all the food on it.

Ansel made a face, gobbling down some saffron-colored grains. "Our local villain. Or I suppose we're *his* local villains, depending on who is telling the story."

"He's the villain," said a curly-haired, dark-eyed man across from Ansel. He was handsome in a way, but had a smile far too much like Captain Rolfe's for Celaena's liking. He couldn't have been older than twenty-five. "No matter *who* is telling the story."

"Well, *you* are ruining *my* story, Mikhail," Ansel said, but grinned at him. He tossed a grape at Ansel, and she caught it in her mouth with ease. Celaena still didn't touch her food. "Anyway," Ansel said, dumping more food onto Celaena's plate, "Lord Berick rules over the city of Xandria, and *claims* that he rules this part of the desert, too. Of course, we don't quite agree with that, but . . . To shorten a long and frightfully dull story, Lord Berick has wanted us all dead for years and years. The King of Adarlan set an embargo on the Red Desert after Lord Berick failed to send troops into Eyllwe to crush some rebellion, and Berick has been dying to get back in the king's good graces ever since. He somehow got it into his thick skull that killing all of us—and sending the head of the Mute Master to Adarlan on a silver platter—would do the trick."

Ansel took another bite of meat and went on. "So, every now and then, he tries some tactic or other: sending asps in baskets, sending soldiers posing as our beloved foreign dignitaries"—she pointed to a table at the end of the hall, where the people were dressed in exotic clothing—"sending troops in the dead of night to fire flaming arrows at us . . . Why, two days ago, we caught some of his soldiers trying to dig a tunnel beneath our walls. Ill-conceived plan from the start."

Across the table, Mikhail chuckled. "Nothing's worked yet," he said. Hearing the noise of their conversation, an assassin at a nearby table pivoted to raise a finger to her lips, shushing them. Mikhail gave them an apologetic shrug. The dining hall, Celaena gleaned, must be a silence-is-requested-but-not-required sort of place.

Ansel poured a glass of water for Celaena, then one for herself, and spoke more quietly. "I suppose that's the problem with attacking an impenetrable fortress full of skilled warriors: you have to be smarter than us. Though . . . Berick is almost brutal enough to make up for it. The assassins that have fallen into his hands came back in pieces." She shook her head. "He enjoys being cruel."

"And Ansel knows that firsthand," Mikhail chimed in, though his voice was little more than a murmur. "She's had the pleasure of meeting him."

Celaena raised a brow, and Ansel made a face. "Only because I'm the most charming of you lot. The Master sometimes sends me to Xandria to meet with Berick—to try to negotiate some sort of accord between us. Thankfully, he still won't dare violate the terms of parlay, but . . . one of these days, I'll pay for my courier duties with my hide."

Mikhail rolled his eyes at Celaena. "She likes to be dramatic."

"That I do."

Celaena gave them both a weak smile. It had been a few minutes, and Ansel certainly wasn't dead. She bit into a piece of meat, nearly moaned at the array of tangy-smoky spices, and set about eating. Ansel and Mikhail began chattering to each other, and Celaena took the opportunity to glance down the table.

Outside of the markets in Rifthold and the slave ships at Skull's Bay, she'd never seen such a mix of different kingdoms and continents. And though most of the people here were trained killers, there was an air of peace and contentment—of joy, even. She flicked her eyes to the table of foreign dignitaries that Ansel had pointed out.

Men and women, hunched over their food, whispered with one another and occasionally watched the assassins in the room.

"Ah," Ansel said quietly. "They're just squabbling over which of us they want to make a bid for."

"Bid?"

Mikhail leaned forward to see the ambassadors through the crowd. "They come here from foreign courts to offer us positions. They make offers for the assassins that most impress them—sometimes for one mission, other times for a lifelong contract. Any of us are free to go, if we wish. But not all of us want to leave."

"And you two . . . ?"

"Ach, no," Ansel said. "My father would wallop me from here to the ends of the earth if I bound myself to a foreign court. He'd say it's a form of prostitution."

Mikhail laughed under his breath. "Personally, I like it here. When I want to leave, I'll let the Master know I'm available. But until then . . ." He glanced at Ansel, and Celaena could have sworn the girl's face flushed slightly. "Until then, I've got my reasons to stay."

Celaena asked, "What courts do the dignitaries hail from?"

"None in Adarlan's grip, if that's what you're asking." Mikhail scratched the day's worth of stubble on his face. "Our Master knows well enough that everything from Eyllwe to Terrasen is *your* Master's territory."

"It certainly is." She didn't know why she said it. Given what Arobynn had done to her, she hardly felt defensive of the assassins in Adarlan's empire. But . . . but to see all these assassins gathered here, so much collective power and knowledge, and to know that they wouldn't dare intrude on Arobynn's—on *her*—territory . . .

Celaena went on eating in silence as Ansel and Mikhail and a few others around them talked quietly. Vows of silence, Ansel had explained earlier, were taken for as long as each person saw fit. Some spent weeks in silence; others, years. Ansel claimed she'd once sworn to be silent for a month, and had only lasted two days before she gave up. She liked talking too much. Celaena didn't have any trouble believing that.

A few of the people around them were pantomiming. Though it often took them a few tries to discern the vague gestures, it seemed like Ansel and Mikhail could interpret the movements of their hands.

Celaena felt someone's attention on her, and tried not to blink when she noticed a dark-haired, handsome young man watching her from a few seats down. Stealing glances at her was more like it, since his sea-green eyes kept darting to her face, then back to his companions. He didn't open his mouth once, but pantomimed to his friends. Another silent one.

Their eyes met, and his tan face spread into a smile, revealing dazzlingly white teeth. Well, he was certainly desirable—as desirable as Sam, maybe.

Sam—when had she ever thought of him as *desirable*? He'd laugh until he died if he ever knew she thought of him like that.

The young man inclined his head slightly in greeting, then turned back to his friends.

"That's Ilias," Ansel whispered, leaning closer than Celaena would like. Didn't she have any sense of personal space? "The Master's son."

That explained the sea-green eyes. Though the Master had an air of holiness, he must not be celibate.

"I'm surprised you caught Ilias's eye," Ansel teased, keeping her voice low enough for only Celaena and Mikhail to hear. "He's usually too focused on his training and meditating to notice anyone—even pretty girls."

Celaena raised her brows, biting back a reply that she didn't want to know *any* of this.

"I've known him for years, and he's never been anything but aloof with me," Ansel continued. "But maybe he has a thing for blondes." Mikhail snorted.

"I'm not here for anything like that," Celaena said.

"And I bet you have a flock of suitors back home, anyway."

"I certainly do not."

Ansel's mouth popped open. "You're lying."

Celaena took a long, long sip of water. It was flavored with slices of lemon—and was unbelievably delicious. "No, I'm not."

Ansel gave her a quizzical look, then fell back into conversation with Mikhail. Celaena pushed around the food on her plate. It wasn't that she wasn't romantic. She'd been infatuated with a few men before—from Archer, the young male courtesan who'd trained with them for a few months when she was thirteen, to Ben, Arobynn's now-deceased Second, back when she was too young to really understand the impossibility of such a thing.

She dared another look at Ilias, who was laughing silently at something one of his companions had said. It was flattering that he even considered her worthy of second thought; she'd avoided looking in the mirror in the month since that night with Arobynn, only checking to ensure nothing was broken or out of place.

"So," Mikhail said, shattering her thoughts as he pointed a fork at her, "when your master beat the living daylights out of you, did you actually deserve it?"

Ansel shot him a dark look, and Celaena straightened. Even Ilias was now listening, his lovely eyes fixed on her face. But Celaena stared right at Mikhail. "I suppose it depends on who is telling the story."

Ansel chuckled.

"If Arobynn Hamel is telling the story, then yes, I suppose I did deserve it. I cost him a good deal of money—a kingdom's worth of riches, probably. I was disobedient and disrespectful, and completely remorseless about what I did."

She didn't break her stare, and Mikhail's smile faltered.

"But if the two hundred slaves that I freed are telling the story, then no, I suppose I didn't deserve it."

None of them were smiling anymore. "Holy gods," Ansel whispered. True silence fell over their table for a few heartbeats.

Celaena resumed eating. She didn't feel like talking to them after that.

~

Under the shade of the date trees that separated the oasis from the sand, Celaena stared out at the expanse of desert stretching before them. "Say that again," she said flatly to Ansel. After the hushed dinner last night and the utterly silent fortress walkways that had brought them here, speaking normally grated on her ears.

But Ansel, who was wearing a white tunic and pants, and boots wrapped in camel pelts, just grinned and fastened her white scarf around her red hair. "It's a three-mile run to the next oasis." Ansel handed Celaena the two wooden buckets she'd brought with her. "These are for you."

Celaena raised her brows. "I thought I was going to be training with the Master."

"Oh, no. Not today," Ansel said, picking up two buckets of her own. "When he said 'training' he meant this. You might be able to wallop four of our men, but you still smell like the northern wind. Once you start reeking like the Red Desert, then he'll bother to train you."

"That's ridiculous. Where is he?" She looked toward the fortress towering behind them.

"Oh, you won't find him. Not until you prove yourself. Show that you're willing to leave behind all that you know and all that you were. Make him think you're worth his time. Then he'll train you. At least, that's what I've been told." Ansel's mahogany eyes gleamed with amusement. "Do you know how many of us have begged and groveled to just have *one* lesson with him? He picks and chooses as he sees fit. One morning, he might approach an acolyte. The next, it might be someone like Mikhail. I'm still waiting for *my* turn. I don't think even Ilias knows the method behind his father's decisions."

This wasn't at all what Celaena had planned. "But I need him to write me a letter of approval. I *need* him to train me. I'm *here* so he can train me—"

Ansel shrugged. "So are we all. If I were you, though, I'd suggest training with me until he decides that you're worth it. If anything, I can get you into the rhythm of things. Make it seem more like you care about us, and less like you're here just for that letter of approval. Not that we *all* don't have our own secret agenda." Ansel winked, and Celaena frowned. Panicking now wouldn't do her any good. She needed time to come up with a logical plan of action. She'd try to speak to the Master later. Perhaps he hadn't understood her yesterday. But for now . . . she'd tag along after Ansel for the day. The Master had been at dinner the night before; if she needed to, she could corner him in the dining hall tonight.

When Celaena didn't object further, Ansel held up a bucket. "So this bucket is for your journey back from the oasis—you'll need it. And this one"—she held up the other—"is just to make the trip hell."

"Why?"

Ansel hooked the buckets into the yoke across her shoulders. "Because if you can run three miles across the dunes of the Red Desert, then three miles back, you can do almost anything."

"Run?" Celaena's throat dried up at the thought of it. All around them, assassins—mostly the children, plus a few others a bit older than her—began running for the dunes, their buckets clacking along.

"Don't tell me the infamous Celaena Sardothien can't run three miles!"

"If you've been here for so many years, doesn't the three miles seem like nothing now?"

Ansel rolled her neck like a cat stretching out in the sun. "Of course it does. But the running keeps me in shape. You think I was just *born* with these legs?" Celaena ground her teeth as Ansel gave her a fiendish grin. She'd never met anyone who smiled and winked so much.

Ansel began jogging, leaving the shade of the date trees overhead, kicking up a wave of red sand behind her. She glanced over her shoulder. "If you walk, it'll take all day! And then you'll certainly never impress anyone!" Ansel pulled her scarf over her nose and mouth and took off at a gallop.

Taking a deep breath, cursing Arobynn to Hell, Celaena hooked the buckets onto the yoke and ran.

If it had been three flat miles, even three miles up grassy knolls, she might have made it. But the dunes were enormous and unwieldy, and Celaena made it one measly mile before she had to slow to a walk, her lungs near to combusting. It was easy enough to find the way—the dozens of footprints from the people racing ahead showed her where she needed to go.

She ran when she could and walked when she couldn't, but the sun rose higher and higher, toward that dangerous noontime peak. Up one hill, down the other. One foot in front of the next. Bright flashes flitted across her vision, and her head pounded.

The red sand shimmered, and she draped her arms over the yoke. Her lips became filmy, cracking in places, and her tongue turned leaden in her mouth.

Each step made her head throb, and the sun rose higher and higher . . .

One more dune. Just one more dune.

But many more dunes later, she was still trudging along, following the smattering of footprints in the sand. Had she somehow tracked the *wrong* group?

Even as she thought it, assassins appeared atop the dune before her, already running back to the fortress, their buckets heavy with water.

She kept her head high as they passed and didn't look any of them in the face. Most of them didn't bother looking at her, though a few spared her a mortifyingly pitying glance. Their clothes were sodden.

She crested a dune so steep she had to use one hand to brace herself, and just when she was about to sink to her knees atop it, she heard splashing.

A small oasis, mostly a ring of trees and a giant pool fed by a shimmering stream, was barely an eighth of a mile away.

She was Adarlan's Assassin—at least she'd *made* it here.

In the shallows of the pool, many disciples splashed or bathed or sat, cooling themselves. No one spoke—and hardly anyone gestured. Another of the absolutely silent places, then. She spotted Ansel with her feet in the water, tossing dates into her mouth. None of the others paid Celaena any heed. And for once, she was glad. Perhaps she should have found a way to defy Arobynn's order and come here under an alias.

Ansel waved her over. If she gave her one look that hinted at her being so slow . . .

But Ansel merely held up a date, offering it to her.

Celaena, trying to control her panting, didn't bother taking the date as she strode into the cool water until she was completely submerged.

Celaena drank an entire bucket before she was even halfway back to the fortress, and by the time she reached the sandstone complex and its glorious shade, she'd consumed all of the second.

At dinner, Ansel didn't mention that it'd taken Celaena a long, long while to return. Celaena had had to wait in the shade of the palms until later in the afternoon to leave—and wound up walking the whole way back. She'd reached the fortress near dusk. A whole day spent "running."

"Don't look so glum," Ansel whispered, taking a forkful of those delightful spiced grains. She was wearing her armor again. "You know what happened my first day out there?"

Some of the assassins seated at the long table gave knowing grins.

Ansel swallowed and braced her arms on the table. Even the gauntlets of her armor were delicately engraved with a wolf motif. "My first run, I collapsed. Mile two. Completely unconscious. Ilias found me on his way back and carried me here. In his arms and everything." Ilias's eyes met with Celaena's, and he smiled at her. "If I hadn't been about to die, I would have been swooning," Ansel finished and the others grinned, some of them laughing silently.

Celaena blushed, suddenly too aware of Ilias's attention, and took a sip from her cup of lemon water. As the meal wore on, her blush remained as Ilias continued flicking his eyes toward her.

She tried not to preen too much. But then she remembered how miserably she'd performed today—how she hadn't even gotten a chance to train—and the swagger died a bit.

She kept an eye on the Master, who dined at the center of the room, safely ensconced within rows of his deadly assassins. He sat at a table of acolytes, whose eyes were so wide that Celaena could only assume his presence at their table was an unexpected surprise.

She waited and waited for him to stand, and when he did, Celaena made her best attempt to look casual as she, too, stood and bid everyone good night. As she turned away, she noticed that Mikhail took Ansel's hand and held it in the shadows beneath the table.

The Master was just leaving the hall when she caught up to him.

With everyone still eating, the torch-lit halls were empty. She took a loud step, unsure if he'd appreciate if she tried being mute, and how, exactly, to address him.

The Master paused, his white clothes rustling around him. He offered her a little smile. Up close, she could certainly see his resemblance to his son. There was a pale line around one of his fingers—perhaps where a wedding ring had once been. Who was Ilias's mother?

Of course, it wasn't at all the time for questions like that. Ansel had told her to try to impress him—to make him think she *wanted* to be here. Perhaps silence would work. But how to communicate what needed to be said? She gave him her best smile, even though her heart raced, and began making a series of motions, mostly just her best impression of running with the yoke, and a lot of shaking her head and frowning that she hoped he'd take to mean "I came here to train with *you*, not with the others."

The Master nodded, as if he already knew. Celaena swallowed, her mouth still tasting of those spices they used to season their meat. She gestured between the two of them several times, taking a step closer to indicate her wanting to work *only* with him. She might have been more aggressive with her motions, might have really let her temper and exhaustion get the better of her, but . . . that confounded letter!

The Master shook his head.

Celaena ground her teeth, and tried the gesturing between the two of them again.

He shook his head once more, and bobbed his hands in the air, as if he were telling her to slow down—to wait. To wait for him to train her.

She reflected the gesture, raising an eyebrow as if to say, "Wait for you?" He nodded. How on earth to ask him "Until when?" She exposed her palms, beseeching, doing her best to look confused. Still, she couldn't keep the irritation from her face. She was only here for a month. How long would she have to wait?

The Master understood her well enough. He shrugged, an infuriatingly casual gesture, and Celaena clenched her jaw. So Ansel had been right—she was to wait for him to send for her. The Master gave her that kind smile and turned on his heel, resuming his walk. She took a step toward him, to beg, to shout, to do whatever her body seized up to do, but someone grabbed her arm.

She whirled, already reaching for her daggers, but found herself looking into Ilias's sea-green eyes.

He shook his head, his gaze darting from the Master to her and back again. She was not to follow him.

So perhaps Ilias hadn't paid attention to her out of admiration, but because he didn't trust her. And why should he? Her reputation didn't exactly lend itself to trust. He must have followed her out of the hall the moment he saw her trailing his father. Had their positions been reversed—had *he* been visiting Rifthold—she wouldn't have dared leave him alone with Arobynn.

"I have no plans to hurt him," she said softly. But Ilias gave her a half smile, his brows rising as if to ask if she could blame him for being protective of his father.

He slowly released her arm. He wore no weapons at his side, but she had a feeling he didn't need them. He was tall—taller than Sam, even—and broad-shouldered. Powerfully built, yet not bulky. His smile spread a bit more as he extended his hand toward her. A greeting.

"Yes," she said, fighting her own smile. "I don't suppose we've been properly introduced."

He nodded, and put his other hand on his heart. Scars peppered his hand—small, slender scars that suggested years of training with blades.

"You're Ilias, and I'm Celaena." She put a hand on her own chest. Then she took his extended hand and shook it. "It's nice to meet you."

His eyes were vivid in the torchlight, his hand firm and warm around hers. She let go of his fingers. The son of the Mute Master and the protégée of the King of the Assassins. If there was anyone here who was at all similar to her, she realized, it was Ilias. Rifthold might be her realm, but this was his. And from the easy way he carried himself, from the way she'd seen his companions gazing at him with admiration and respect, she could tell that he was utterly at home here—as if this place had been made for him, and he never needed to question his spot in it. A strange sort of envy wended its way through her heart.

Ilias suddenly began making a series of motions with his long, tan fingers, but Celaena laughed softly. "I have no idea what you're trying to say."

Ilias looked skyward and sighed through his nose. Throwing his hands in the air in mock defeat, he merely patted her on the shoulder before passing by—following his father, who had disappeared down the hall.

Though she walked back toward her room—in the other direction—she didn't once believe that the son of the Mute Master wasn't still watching her, making sure she wasn't going to follow his father.

Not that you have anything to worry about, she wanted to shout over her shoulder. She couldn't run six measly miles in the desert.

As she walked back to her room, Celaena had a horrible feeling that here, being Adarlan's Assassin might not count for much.

Later that night, when she and Ansel were both in their beds, Ansel whispered into the darkness: "Tomorrow will be better. It might be only a foot more than today, but it will be a foot longer that you can run."

That was easy enough for Ansel to say. *She* didn't have a reputation to uphold—a reputation that might be crumbling around her. Celaena stared at the ceiling, suddenly homesick, strangely wishing Sam was with her. At least if she were to fail, she'd fail with him.

"So," Celaena said suddenly, needing to get her mind off everything—especially Sam. "You and Mikhail . . ."

Ansel groaned. "It's that obvious? Though I suppose we don't really make that much of an effort to hide it. Well, *I* try, but he doesn't. He *was* rather irritated when he found out I suddenly had a roommate."

"How long have you been seeing him?"

Ansel was silent for a long moment before answering. "Since I was fifteen."

Fifteen! Mikhail was in his midtwenties, so even if this had started almost three years ago, he still would have been far older than Ansel. It made her a little queasy.

"Girls in the Flatlands are married as early as fourteen," Ansel said.

Celaena choked. The idea of being anyone's *wife* at fourteen, let alone a mother soon after . . . "Oh," was all she managed to get out.

When Celaena didn't say anything else, Ansel drifted into sleep. With nothing else to distract her, Celaena eventually returned to thinking about Sam. Even weeks later, she had no idea how she'd somehow gotten attached to him, what he'd been shouting when Arobynn beat her, and why Arobynn had thought he'd need three seasoned assassins to restrain him that day.

CHAPTER 4

Though Celaena didn't want to admit it, Ansel was right. She did run farther the next day. And the day after that, and the one following that. But it still took her so long to get back that she didn't have time to seek out the Master. Not that she could. He'd send for *her.* Like a lackey.

She did manage to find *some* time late in the afternoon to attend drills with Ansel. The only guidance she received there was from a few older-looking assassins who positioned her hands and feet, tapped her stomach, and slapped her spine into the correct posture. Occasionally, Ilias would train alongside her, never *too* close, but close enough for her to know his presence was more than coincidental.

Like the assassins in Adarlan, the Silent Assassins weren't known for any skill in particular—save the uncannily quiet way they moved. Their weapons were mostly the same, though their bows and blades were slightly different in length and shape. But just watching them—it seemed that there was a good deal less . . . *viciousness* here.

Arobynn encouraged cutthroat behavior. Even when they were children, he'd set her and Sam against each other, use their victories and failures against them. He'd made her see everyone but Arobynn and Ben as a potential enemy. As allies, yes, but also as foes to be closely watched. Weakness was never to be shown at any cost. Brutality was rewarded. And education and culture were equally important—words could be just as deadly as steel.

But the Silent Assassins . . . Though they, too, might be killers, they looked to one another for learning. Embraced collective wisdom. Older warriors smiled as they taught the acolytes; seasoned assassins swapped techniques. And while they were all competitors, it appeared that an invisible link bound them together. Something had brought them to this place at the ends of the earth. More than a few, she discovered, were actually mute from birth. But all of them seemed full of secrets. As if the fortress and what it offered somehow held the answers they sought. As if they could find whatever they were looking for in the silence.

Still, even as they corrected her posture and showed her new ways to control her breathing, she tried her best not to snarl at them. She knew plenty—she wasn't Adarlan's Assassin for nothing. But she needed that letter of good behavior as proof of her training. These people might all be called upon by the Mute Master to give an opinion of her. Perhaps if she demonstrated that she was skilled enough in these practices, the Master might take notice of her.

She'd get that letter. Even if she had to hold a dagger to his throat while he wrote it.

The attack by Lord Berick happened on her fifth night. There was no moon, and Celaena had no idea how the Silent Assassins spotted the thirty or so soldiers creeping across the dark dunes. Mikhail had burst into their room and whispered to come to the fortress battlements. Hopefully, this would turn out to be another opportunity to prove herself. With just over three weeks left, she was running out of options. But the Master wasn't at the battlements. And neither were many of the assassins. She heard a woman question another, asking how Berick's men had known that a good number of the assassins would be away that night, busy escorting some foreign dignitaries back to the nearest port. It was too convenient to be coincidental.

Crouched atop the parapet, an arrow nocked into her bow, Celaena peered through one of the crenels in the wall. Ansel, squatting beside her, also twisted to look. Up and down the battlements, assassins hid in the shadow of the wall, clothed in black and with bows in hand. At the center of the wall, Ilias knelt, his hands moving quickly as he conveyed orders down the line. It seemed more like the silent language of soldiers than the basic gestures used to represent the common tongue.

"Get your arrow ready," Ansel murmured, dipping her cloth-covered arrow tip into the small bowl of oil between them. "When Ilias gives the signal, light it on the torch as fast as you can and fire. Aim for the ridge in the sand just below the soldiers."

Celaena glanced into the darkness beyond the wall. Rather than give themselves away by extinguishing the lights of the fortress, the defenders had kept them on—which made focusing in the dark nearly impossible. But she could still make out the shapes against the starlit sky—thirty men on their stomachs, poised to do whatever they had planned. Attack the assassins outright, murder them in their sleep, burn the place to the ground . . .

"We're not going to kill them?" Celaena whispered back. She weighed the weapon in her hands. The bow of the Silent Assassins was different—shorter, thicker, harder to bend.

Ansel shook her head, watching Ilias down the line. "No, though

I wish we could." Celaena didn't particularly care for the casual way she said it, but Ansel went on. "We don't want to start an all-out battle with Lord Berick. We just need to scare them off. Mikhail and Ilias rigged that ridge last week; the line in the sand is a rope soaking in a trough of oil."

Celaena was beginning to see where this was going. She dipped her arrow into the dish of oil, drenching the cloth around it thoroughly. "That's going to be a long wall of fire," she said, following the course of the ridge.

"You have no idea. It stretches around the whole fortress." Ansel straightened, and Celaena glanced over her shoulder to see Ilias's arm make a neat, slicing motion.

Instantly, they were on their feet. Ansel reached the torch in the nearby bracket before Celaena did, and was at the battlements a heartbeat later. Swift as lightning.

Celaena nearly dropped her bow as she swiped her arrow through the flame and heat bit at her fingers. Lord Berick's men started shouting, and over the crackle of the ignited arrows, Celaena heard twangs as the soldiers fired their own ammunition.

But Celaena was already at the wall, wincing as she drew the burning arrow back far enough for it to singe her fingers. She fired.

Like a wave of shooting stars, their flaming arrows went up, up, up, then dropped. But Celaena didn't have time to see the ring of fire erupt between the soldiers and the fortress. She ducked against the wall, throwing her hands over her head. Beside her, Ansel did the same.

Light burst all around them, and the roar of the wall of flame drowned out the hollering of Lord Berick's men. Black arrows rained from the sky, ricocheting off the stones of the battlements. Two or three assassins grunted, swallowing their screams, but Celaena kept her head low, holding her breath until the last of the enemy's arrows had fallen.

When there was nothing but the muffled moaning of the injured assassins and the crackling of the wall of fire, Celaena dared to look at Ansel. The girl's eyes were bright. "Well," Ansel breathed, "wasn't *that* fun?"

Celaena grinned, her heart racing. "Yes." Pivoting, she spied Lord Berick's men fleeing back across the dunes. "Yes, it was."

Near dawn, when Celaena and Ansel were back in their room, a soft knock sounded. Ansel was instantly on her feet, and opened the door only wide enough for Celaena to spy Mikhail on the other side. He handed Ansel a sealed scroll. "You're to go to Xandria today and give him this." Celaena saw Ansel's shoulders tense. "Master's orders," he added.

She couldn't see Ansel's face as she nodded, but Celaena could have sworn Mikhail brushed her cheek before he turned away. Ansel let out a long breath and shut the door. In the growing light of predawn, Celaena saw Ansel wipe the sleep from her eyes. "Care to join me?"

Celaena hoisted herself up onto her elbows. "Isn't that two days from here?"

"Yes. Two days through the desert, with only yours truly to keep you company. Unless you'd rather stay here, running every day and waiting like a dog for the Master to notice you. In fact, coming with me might help get him to consider training you. He'd certainly see your dedication to keeping us safe." Ansel wriggled her eyebrows at Celaena, who rolled her eyes.

It was actually sound reasoning. What better way to prove her dedication than to sacrifice four days of her precious time in order to help the Silent Assassins? It was risky, yes, but . . . it might be bold enough to catch his attention. "And what will we be doing in Xandria?"

"That's for you to find out."

From the mischief twinkling in Ansel's red-brown eyes, Celaena could only wonder what might await them.

CHAPTER 5

Celaena lay on her cloak, trying to imagine that the sand was her down mattress in Rifthold, and that she wasn't completely exposed to the elements in the middle of the desert. The last thing she needed was to wake up with a scorpion in her hair. Or worse.

She flipped onto her side, cradling her head in the nook of her arm.

"Can't sleep?" Ansel asked from a few feet away. Celaena tried not to growl. They'd spent the entire day trudging across the sand, stopping only at midday to sleep under their cloaks and avoid the mind-crisping glare of the sun.

And a dinner of dates and bread hadn't been exactly filling, either. But Ansel had wanted to travel light, and said that they could pick up more food once they got to Xandria tomorrow afternoon. When Celaena complained about *that*, Ansel just told her that she should be grateful it wasn't sandstorm season.

"I've got sand in every crevice of my body," Celaena muttered, squirming as she felt it grind against her skin. How in hell had sand gotten inside her clothes? Her white tunic and pants were layered enough that *she* couldn't even find her skin beneath.

"Are you *sure* you're Celaena Sardothien? Because I don't think she'd actually be this fussy. I bet she's used to roughing it."

"I'm plenty used to roughing it," Celaena said, her words sucked into the dunes rising around them. "That doesn't mean I have to *enjoy* it. I suppose that someone from the Western Wastes would find this luxurious."

Ansel chuckled. "You have no idea."

Celaena quit her taunting as curiosity seized her. "Are your lands as cursed as they claim?"

"Well, the Flatlands used to be part of the Witch Kingdom. And yes, I suppose you could say they're somewhat cursed." Ansel sighed loudly. "When the Crochan Queens ruled five hundred years ago, it was very beautiful. At least, the ruins all over the place seem like they would have been beautiful. But then the three Ironteeth Clans destroyed it all when they overthrew the Crochan Dynasty."

"Ironteeth?"

Ansel let out a low hiss. "Some witches, like the Crochans, were gifted with ethereal beauty. But the Ironteeth Clans have iron teeth, sharp as a fish's. Actually, their iron fingernails are more dangerous; those can gut you in one swipe."

A chill went down Celaena's spine.

"But when the Ironteeth Clans destroyed the kingdom, they say the last Crochan Queen cast a spell that turned the land against any that flew under the banners of the Ironteeth—so that no crops would grow, the animals withered up and died, and the waters turned muddy. It's not like that now, though. The land has been fertile ever since the Ironteeth Clans journeyed east . . . toward your lands."

"So . . . so have *you* ever seen one of the witches?"

Ansel was quiet for a moment before she said, "Yes."

Celaena turned toward her, propping her head on a hand. Ansel remained looking at the sky.

"When I was eight and my sister was eleven, she and I and Maddy, one of her friends, snuck out of Briarcliff Hall. A few miles away, there was a giant tor with a lone watchtower on top. The upper bits were all ruined because of the witch-wars, but the rest of it was still intact. See, there was this archway that went through the bottom of the watchtower—so you could see through it to the other side of the hill. And one of the stable boys told my sister that if you looked through the archway on the night of the summer solstice, then you might see into another world."

The hair on Celaena's neck stood. "So you went inside?"

"No," Ansel said. "I got near the top of the tor and became so terrified that I wouldn't set foot on it. I hid behind a rock, and my sister and Maddy left me there while they went the rest of the way. I can't remember how long I waited, but then I heard screaming.

"My sister came running. She just grabbed my arm and we ran. It didn't come out at first, but when we got to my father's hall, she told them what had happened. They had gone under the archway of the tower and seen an open door leading to its interior. But an old woman with metal teeth was standing in the shadows, and she grabbed Maddy and dragged her into the stairwell."

Celaena choked on a breath.

"Maddy began screaming, and my sister ran. And when she told my father and his men, they raced for the tor. They arrived at dawn, but there was no trace of Maddy, or the old woman."

"Gone?" Celaena whispered.

"They found one thing," Ansel said softly. "They climbed the tower, and on one of the landings, they found the bones of a child. White as ivory and picked clean."

"Gods above," Celaena said.

"After that, my father walloped us within an inch of our lives, and we were on kitchen duty for six months, but he knew my sister's guilt would be punishment enough. She never really lost that haunted gleam in her eyes."

Celaena shuddered. "Well, now I certainly won't be able to sleep tonight."

Ansel laughed. "Don't worry," she said, nestling down on her cloak. "I'll tell you a valuable secret: the only way to kill a witch is to cut off her head. Besides, I don't think an Ironteeth witch stands much of a chance against us."

"I hope you're right," Celaena muttered.

"I am right," Ansel said. "They might be vicious, but they're not invincible. And if I had an army of my own . . . if I had even twenty of the Silent Assassins at my command, I'd hunt down all the witches. They wouldn't stand a chance." Her hand thumped against the sand; she must have struck the ground. "You know, these assassins have been here for ages, but what do they *do*? The Flatlands would *prosper* if they had an army of assassins to defend them. But no, they just sit in their oasis, silent and thoughtful, and whore themselves out to foreign courts. If *I* were the Master, I'd use our numbers for greatness—for glory. We'd defend every unprotected realm out there."

"So noble of you," Celaena said. "Ansel of Briarcliff, Defender of the Realm."

Ansel only laughed, and soon was asleep.

Celaena, though, stayed awake a while longer, unable to stop imagining what that witch had done when she dragged Maddy into the shadows of the tower.

~

It was Market Day in Xandria, and though the city had long suffered from Adarlan's embargo, it still seemed that there were vendors from all the kingdoms on the continent—and beyond. They were crammed into every possible space in the small, walled port city. All around Celaena were spices and jewels and clothes and food, some sold right out of brightly painted wagons, others spread on blankets in shadowy alcoves. There was no sign that anyone knew anything about the ill-fated attack on the Silent Assassins the other night.

She kept close to Ansel as they walked along, the red-haired girl weaving through the crowd with a kind of casual grace that Celaena, despite herself, envied. No matter how many people shoved into Ansel, or stepped in her path, or cursed her for stepping in theirs, she didn't falter, and her boyish grin only grew. Many people stopped to stare at her red hair and matching eyes, but Ansel took it in stride. Even without her armor, she was stunning. Celaena tried not to think about how few people bothered to notice *her*.

With the bodies and the heat, Celaena was oozing sweat by the time Ansel stopped near the edge of the souk. "I'm going to be a couple hours," Ansel said, and waved a long, elegant hand to the sandstone palace hovering above the small city. "The old beast likes to talk and talk and talk. Why don't you do some shopping?"

Celaena straightened. "I'm not going with you?"

"Into Berick's palace? Of course not. It's the Master's business."

Celaena felt her nostrils flare. Ansel clapped her on the shoulder. "Believe me, you'd much rather spend the next few hours in the souk than waiting in the stables with Berick's men leering at you. Unlike us"—Ansel flashed that grin—"they don't have access to baths whenever they please."

Ansel kept glancing at the palace, still a few blocks away. Nervous that she'd be late? Or nervous that she was going to confront Berick on behalf of the Master? Ansel brushed the remnants of red sand from the layers of her white clothes. "I'll meet you at that fountain at three. Try not to get into *too* much trouble."

And with that, Ansel vanished into the press of bodies, her red hair gleaming like a hot brand. Celaena contemplated trailing her. Even if she was an outsider, why let her accompany Ansel on the journey if she was just going to have to sit around? What could be so important and secret that Ansel wouldn't allow her to partake in the meeting? Celaena took a step toward the palace, but passing people jostled her to and fro, and then a vendor began cooking something that smelled divine, and Celaena found herself following her nose instead.

She spent the two hours wandering from vendor to vendor. She cursed herself for not bringing more money with her. In Rifthold, she had a line of credit at all her favorite stores, and never had to bother carrying money, aside from small coppers and the occasional silver coin for tips and bribes. But here . . . well, the pouch of silver she'd brought felt rather light.

The souk wound through every street, great and small, down narrow stairways and onto half-buried alleys that had to have been there for a thousand years. Ancient doors opened onto courtyards jammed with spice vendors or a hundred lanterns, glittering like stars in the shadowy interior. For such a remote city, Xandria was teeming with life.

She was standing under the striped awning of a vendor from the southern continent, debating if she had enough to buy the pair of curled-toe shoes before her *and* the lilac perfume she'd smelled at a wagon owned by white-haired maidens. The maidens claimed they were the priestesses of Lani, the goddess of dreams—and perfume, apparently.

Celaena ran a finger down the emerald silk thread embroidered on the delicate shoes, tracing the curve of the point as it swept upward and curled over the shoe itself. They'd certainly be eye-catching in Rifthold. And no one else in the capital would have them. Though, in the filthy city streets, these would easily get ruined.

She reluctantly put the shoes down, and the vendor raised his brows. She shook her head, a rueful smile on her face. The man held up seven fingers—one less than the original asking price, and she chewed on her lip, signing back, "Six coppers?"

The man spat on the ground. Seven coppers. Seven coppers was laughably cheap.

She looked at the souk around her, then back at the beautiful shoes. "I'll come back later," she lied, and with one final, mournful glance, she continued along. The man began shouting after her in a language she'd never heard before, undoubtedly offering the shoes for six coppers, but she forced herself to keep walking. Besides, her pack was heavy enough; lugging the shoes around would be an additional burden. Even if they were lovely and different and not *that* heavy. And the thread detailing along the sides was as precise and beautiful as calligraphy. And really, she could just wear them *inside*, so she—

She was about to turn around and walk right back to the vendor when something glistening in the shadows beneath an archway between buildings caught her eye. There were a few hired guards standing around the covered wagon, and a tall, lean man stood behind the table displayed in front of it. But it wasn't the guards or the man or his wagon that grabbed her attention.

No, it was what was *on* his table that knocked the breath from her and made her curse her too-light money purse.

Spidersilk.

There were legends about the horse-sized stygian spiders that lurked in the woods of the Ruhnn Mountains of the north, spinning their thread for hefty costs. Some said they offered it in exchange for human flesh; others claimed the spiders dealt in years and dreams, and could take either as payment. Regardless, it was as delicate as gossamer, lovelier than silk, and stronger than steel. And she'd never seen so much of it before.

It was so rare that if you wanted it, odds were you had to go and get it for yourself. But here it was, yards of raw material waiting to be shaped. It was a kingdom's ransom.

"You know," the merchant said in the common tongue, taking in Celaena's wide-eyed stare, "you're the first person today to recognize it for what it is."

"I'd know what that is even if I were blind." She approached the table, but didn't dare to touch the sheets of iridescent fabric. "But what are you doing here? Surely you can't get much business in Xandria."

The man chuckled. He was middle-aged, with close-cropped brown hair and midnight-blue eyes that seemed haunted, though they now sparkled with amusement. "I might also ask what a girl from the North is doing in Xandria." His gaze flicked to the daggers tucked into the brown belt slung across her white clothes. "And with such beautiful weapons."

She gave him a half smile. "At least your eye is worthy of your wares."

"I try." He sketched a bow, then beckoned her closer. "So, tell me, girl from the North, when have you seen Spidersilk?"

She clenched her fingers into fists to keep from touching the priceless material. "I know a courtesan in Rifthold whose madam had a handkerchief made from it—given to her by an extraordinarily wealthy client."

And that handkerchief had probably cost more than most peasants made in a lifetime.

"That was a kingly gift. She must have been skilled."

"She didn't become madam of the finest courtesans in Rifthold for nothing."

The merchant let out a low laugh. "So if you associate with the finest courtesans in Rifthold, then what brings you to this bit of desert scrub?"

She shrugged. "This and that." In the dim light beneath the canopy, the Spidersilk still glittered like the surface of the sea. "But I would like to know how *you* came across so much of this. Did you buy it, or find the stygian spiders on your own?"

He traced a finger down the plane of fabric. "I went there myself. What else is there to know?" His midnight eyes darkened. "In the depths of the Ruhnn Mountains, everything is a labyrinth of mist and trees and shadows. So you don't find the stygian spiders—they find you."

Celaena stuffed her hands in her pockets to keep from touching the Spidersilk. Though her fingers were clean, there were still grains of red sand under her nails. "So why are you here, then?"

"My ship to the southern continent doesn't leave for two days; why not set up shop? Xandria might not be Rifthold, but you never know who might approach your stall." He winked at her. "How old are you, anyway?"

She raised her chin. "I turned seventeen two weeks ago." And what a miserable birthday that had been. Trudging across the desert with no one to celebrate with except her recalcitrant guide, who just patted her shoulder when she announced it was her birthday. Horrible.

"Not much younger than me," he said. She chuckled, but paused when she didn't find him smiling.

"And how old are *you*?" she asked. There was no mistaking it—he *had* to be at least forty. Even if his hair wasn't sprinkled with silver, his skin was weathered.

"Twenty-five," he said. She gave a start. "I know. Shocking."

The yards of Spidersilk lifted in a breeze from the nearby sea.

"Everything has a price," he said. "Twenty years for a hundred yards of Spidersilk. I thought they meant to take them off the end of my life. But even if they'd warned me, I would have said yes." She eyed the caravan behind him. This much Spidersilk was enough to enable him to live what years he had left as a very, very wealthy man.

"Why not take it to Rifthold?"

"Because I've seen Rifthold, and Orynth, and Banjali. I'd like to see what a hundred yards of Spidersilk might fetch me outside of Adarlan's empire."

"Is there anything to be done about the years you lost?"

He waved a hand. "I followed the western side of the mountains on my way here, and met an old witch along the way. I asked if she could fix me, but she said what was taken was taken, and only the death of the spider who consumed my twenty years could return them to me." He examined his hands, already lined with age. "For a copper more, she told me that only a great warrior could slay a stygian spider. The greatest warrior in the land . . . Though perhaps an assassin from the North might do."

"How did you—"

"You can't honestly think no one knows about the *sessiz suikast*? Why else would a seventeen-year-old girl bearing exquisite daggers be here unescorted? And one who holds such fine company in Rifthold, no less. Are you here to spy for Lord Berick?"

Celaena did her best to quell her surprise. "Pardon me?"

The merchant shrugged, glancing toward the towering palace. "I heard from a city guard that strange dealings go on between Berick and some of the Silent Assassins."

"Perhaps," was all Celaena said. The merchant nodded, not all that interested in it anymore. But Celaena tucked the information away for later. Were some of the Silent Assassins actually working *for* Berick? Perhaps that was why Ansel had insisted on keeping the meeting so secret—maybe the Master didn't want the names of the suspected traitors getting out.

"So?" the merchant asked. "Will you retrieve my lost years for me?"

She bit her lip, thoughts of spies instantly fading away. To journey into the depths of the Ruhnn Mountains, to slay a stygian spider. She could certainly see herself battling the eight-legged monstrosities. And witches. Though after Ansel's story, meeting a witch—especially one belonging to the Ironteeth Clans—was the last thing she ever wanted to do. For a heartbeat, she wished Sam were with her. Even if she told him about this encounter, he'd never believe her. But would *anyone* ever believe her?

As if he could read her daydreams, he said: "I could make you rich beyond your wildest imaginings."

"I'm already rich. And I'm unavailable until the end of the summer."

"I won't be back from the southern continent for at least a year, anyway," he countered.

She examined his face, the gleam in his eyes. Adventure and glory aside, anyone who'd sell twenty years of his life for a fortune couldn't be trusted. But . . .

"The next time you're in Rifthold," she said slowly, "seek out Arobynn Hamel." The man's eyes widened. She wondered how he'd react if he knew who *she* was. "He'll know where to find me." She turned from the table.

"But what's your name?"

She looked over her shoulder. "He'll know where to find me," she repeated, and began walking back toward the stall with the pointed shoes.

"Wait!" She paused in time to see him fumbling with the folds of his tunic. "Here." He set down a plain wooden box on the table. "A reminder."

Celaena flipped open the lid and her breath caught. A folded bit of woven Spidersilk lay inside, no larger than six square inches. She could buy ten horses with it. Not that she'd ever sell it. No, this was an heirloom to be passed down from generation to generation. If she ever had children. Which seemed highly unlikely.

"A reminder of what?" She shut the lid and tucked the small box into the inner pocket of her white tunic.

The merchant smiled sadly. "That everything has a price."

A phantom pain flashed through her face. "I know," she said, and left.

~

She wound up buying the shoes, though it was nearly impossible to pass over the lilac perfume, which smelled even more lovely the second time she approached the priestesses' stall. When the city bells pealed three o'clock, she was sitting on the lip of the fountain, munching on what she *hoped* was mashed beans inside a warm bread pocket.

Ansel was fifteen minutes late, and didn't apologize. She merely grabbed Celaena's arm and began leading her through the still-packed streets, her freckled face gleaming with sweat.

"What is it?" Celaena asked. "What happened in your meeting?"

"That's none of your business," Ansel said a bit sharply. Then she added, "Just follow me."

They wound up sneaking inside the Lord of Xandria's palace walls, and Celaena knew better than to ask questions as they crept across the grounds. But they didn't head to the towering central building. No—they approached the stables, where they slipped around the guards and entered the pungent shadows within.

"There had better be a good reason for this," Celaena warned as Ansel crept toward a pen.

"Oh, there is," she hissed back, and stopped at a gate, waving Celaena forward.

Celaena frowned. "It's a horse." But even as the words left her mouth, she knew it wasn't.

"It's an Asterion horse," Ansel breathed, her red-brown eyes growing huge.

The horse was black as pitch, with dark eyes that bored into Celaena's own. She'd heard of Asterion horses, of course. The most ancient breed of horse in Erilea. Legend claimed that the Fae had made them from the four winds—spirit from the north, strength from the south, speed from the east, and wisdom from the west, all rolled into the slender-snouted, high-tailed, lovely creature that stood before her.

"Have you ever seen anything so beautiful?" Ansel whispered. "Her name is Hisli." Mares, Celaena remembered, were more prized, as Asterion pedigrees were traced through the female line. "And that one," Ansel said, pointing to the next stall, "is named Kasida—it means 'drinker of the wind' in the desert dialect."

Kasida's name was fitting. The slender mare was a dapple gray, with a sea-foam white mane and thundercloud coat. She huffed and stomped her forelegs, staring at Celaena with eyes that seemed older than the earth itself. Celaena suddenly understood why the Asterion horses were worth their weight in gold.

"Lord Berick got them today. Bought them from a merchant on his way to Banjali." Ansel slipped into Hisli's pen. She cooed and murmured, stroking the horse's muzzle. "He's planning on testing them out in half an hour." That explained why they were already saddled.

"And?" Celaena whispered, holding out a hand for Kasida to smell. The mare's nostrils flared, her velvety nose tickling Celaena's fingertips.

"And then he's either going to give them away as a bribe, or lose interest and let them languish here for the rest of their lives. Lord Berick tends to tire of his playthings rather quickly."

"What a waste."

"Indeed it is," Ansel muttered from inside the stall. Celaena lowered her fingers from Kasida's muzzle and peered into Hisli's pen. Ansel was running a hand down Hisli's black flank, her face still full of wonder. Then she turned. "Are you a strong rider?"

"Of course," Celaena said slowly.

"Good."

Celaena bit down on her cry of alarm as Ansel unlocked the stall door and guided Hisli out of her pen. In a smooth, quick motion, the girl was atop the horse, clutching the reins in one hand. "Because you're going to have to ride like hell."

With that, Ansel sent Hisli into a gallop, heading straight for the stable doors.

Celaena didn't have time to gape or really even to process what she was about to do as she unlocked Kasida's pen, yanked her out, and heaved herself into the saddle. With a muffled curse, she dug her heels into the mare's sides and took off.

Chapter 6

The guards didn't know what was happening until the horses had already rushed past them in a blur of black and gray, and they were through the main palace gate before the guards' cries finished echoing. Ansel's red hair shone like a beacon as she broke for the side exit from the city, people leaping aside to let them pass.

Celaena looked back through the crowded streets only once—and that was enough to see the three mounted guards charging after them, shouting.

But the girls were already through the city gate and into the sea of red dunes that spread beyond, Ansel riding as if the denizens of Hell were behind her. Celaena could only race after her, doing her best to keep in the saddle.

Kasida moved like thunder and turned with the swiftness of lightning. The mare was so fast that Celaena's eyes watered in the wind. The three guards, astride ordinary horses, were still far off, but not nearly far enough for comfort. In the vastness of the Red Desert, Celaena had no choice but to follow Ansel.

Celaena clung to Kasida's mane as they took dune after dune, up and down, down and up, until there was only the red sand and the cloudless sky and the rumble of hooves, hooves, hooves rolling through the world.

Ansel slowed enough for Celaena to catch up, and they galloped along the broad, flat top of a dune.

"Are you out of your damned mind?" Celaena shouted.

"I don't want to walk home! We're taking a shortcut!" Ansel shouted back. Behind them, the three guards still charged onward.

Celaena debated slamming Kasida into Hisli to send Ansel tumbling onto the dunes—leaving her for the guards to take care of—but the girl pointed over Hisli's dark head. "Live a little, Sardothien!"

And just like that, the dunes parted to reveal the turquoise expanse of the Gulf of Oro. The cool sea breeze kissed her face, and Celaena leaned into it, almost moaning with pleasure.

Ansel let out a whoop, careening down the final dune and heading straight toward the beach and the breaking waves. Despite herself, Celaena smiled and held on tighter.

Kasida hit the hard-packed red sand and gained speed, faster and faster.

Celaena had a sudden moment of clarity then, as her hair ripped from her braid and the wind tore at her clothes. Of all the girls in all the world, here she was on a spit of beach in the Red Desert, astride an Asterion horse, racing faster than the wind. Most would never experience this—*she* would never experience anything like this again. And for that one heartbeat, when there was nothing more to it than that, she tasted bliss so complete that she tipped her head back to the sky and laughed.

The guards reached the beach, their fierce cries nearly swallowed up by the booming surf.

Ansel cut away, surging toward the dunes and the giant wall of rock that arose nearby. The Desert Cleaver, if Celaena knew her geography correctly—which she did, as she'd studied maps of the Deserted Land for weeks now. A giant wall that arose from the earth and stretched from the eastern coast all the way to the black dunes of the south—split clean down the middle by an enormous fissure. They'd come around it on the way from the fortress, which was on the other side of the Cleaver, and that was what had made their journey so insufferably long. But today . . .

"Faster, Kasida," she whispered in the horse's ear. As if the mare understood her, she took off, and soon Celaena was again beside Ansel, cutting up dune after dune as they headed straight for the red wall of rock. "What are you doing?" she called to Ansel.

Ansel gave her a fiendish grin. "We're going through it. What good is an Asterion horse if it can't jump?"

Celaena's stomach dropped. "You can't be serious."

Ansel glanced over her shoulder, her red hair streaming past her face. "They'll chase us to the doors of the fortress if we go the long way!" But the guards couldn't make the jump, not with ordinary horses.

A narrow opening in the wall of red rock appeared, twisting away from sight. Ansel headed straight toward it. How *dare* she make such a reckless, stupid decision without consulting Celaena first?

"You planned this the whole time," Celaena snapped. Though the guards still remained a good distance away, they were close enough for Celaena to see the weapons, including longbows, strapped to them.

Ansel didn't reply. She just sent Hisli flying forward.

Celaena had to choose between the unforgiving walls of the Cleaver and the three guards behind them. She could take the guards in a few seconds—if she slowed enough to draw her daggers. But they were mounted, and aiming might be impossible. Which meant she'd have to get close enough to kill them, as long as they didn't start firing at her first. They probably wouldn't shoot at Kasida, not when she was worth more than all of their lives put together, but Celaena couldn't bring herself to risk the magnificent beast. And if she killed the guards, that still left her alone in the desert, since Ansel surely wouldn't stop until she was on the other side of the Cleaver. Since she had no desire to die of thirst . . .

Cursing colorfully, Celaena plunged after Ansel into the passage through the canyon.

The passage was so narrow that Celaena's legs nearly grazed the rain-smoothed orange walls. The beating hooves echoed like firecrackers, the sound only worsening as the three guards entered the canyon. It would have been nice, she realized, to have Sam with her. He might be a pain in her ass, but he'd proven himself to be more than handy in a fight. Extraordinarily skilled, if she felt like admitting it.

Ansel wove and turned with the passage, fast as a stream down a mountainside, and it was all Celaena could do to hold on to Kasida as they followed.

A twang snapped through the canyon, and Celaena ducked low to Kasida's surging head—just as an arrow ricocheted off the rock a few feet away. So much for not firing at the horses. Another sharp turn set her in the clear, but the relief was short-lived as she beheld the long, straight passage—and the ravine beyond it.

Celaena's breath lodged in her throat. The jump had to be thirty feet at least—and she didn't want to know how long a fall it was if she missed.

Ansel barreled ahead; then her body tensed, and Hisli leapt from the cliff edge.

The sunlight caught in Ansel's hair as they flew over the ravine, and she loosed a joyous cry that set the whole canyon humming. A moment later, she landed on the other side, with only inches to spare.

There wasn't enough room for Celaena to stop—even if she tried, they wouldn't have enough space to slow down, and they'd go right over the edge. So she began praying to anyone, anything. Kasida gave a sudden burst of speed, as if she, too, understood that only the gods would see them safely over.

And then they were at the lip of the ravine, which went down, down, down to a jade river hundreds of feet below. And Kasida was soaring, only air beneath them, nothing to keep her from the death that now wrapped around her completely.

Celaena could only hold on and wait to fall, to die, to scream as she met her horrible end . . .

But then there was rock under them, solid rock. She gripped Kasida tighter as they landed in the narrow passage on the other side, the impact exploding through her bones, and kept galloping.

Back across the ravine, the guards had pulled to a halt, and cursed at them in a language she was grateful she didn't understand.

Ansel let out another whoop when they came out the other end of the Cleaver, and she turned to find Celaena still riding close behind her. They rode across the dunes, heading west, the setting sun turning the entire world bloodred.

When the horses were too winded to keep running, Ansel finally stopped atop a dune, Celaena pulling up beside her. Ansel looked at Celaena, wildness still rampant in her eyes. "Wasn't that wonderful?"

Breathing hard, Celaena didn't say anything as she punched Ansel so hard in the face that the girl went flying off her horse and tumbled onto the sand.

Ansel just clutched her jaw and laughed.

Though they could have made it back before midnight, and though Celaena pushed her to continue riding, Ansel insisted on stopping for the night. So when their campfire was nothing but embers and the horses were dozing behind them, Ansel and Celaena lay on their backs on the side of a dune and stared up at the stars.

Her hands tucked behind her head, Celaena took a long, deep breath, savoring the balmy night breeze, the exhaustion ebbing from her limbs. She rarely got to see stars so bright—not with the lights of Rifthold. The wind moved across the dunes, and the sand sighed.

"You know," Ansel said quietly, "I never learned the constellations. Though I think ours are different from yours—the names, I mean."

It took Celaena a moment to realize that by "ours" she didn't mean the Silent Assassins—she meant her people in the Western Wastes. Celaena pointed to a cluster of stars to their left. "That's the dragon." She traced the shape. "See the head, legs, and tail?"

"No." Ansel chuckled.

Celaena nudged her with an elbow and pointed to another grouping of stars. "That's the swan. The lines on either side are the wings, and the arc is its neck."

"What about that one?" Ansel said.

"That's the stag," Celaena breathed. "The Lord of the North."

"Why does he get a fancy title? What about the swan and the dragon?"

Celaena snorted, but the smile faded when she stared at the familiar constellation. "Because the stag remains constant—no matter the season, he's always there."

"Why?"

Celaena took a long breath. "So the people of Terrasen will always know how to find their way home. So they can look up at the sky, no matter where they are, and know Terrasen is forever with them."

"Do you ever want to return to Terrasen?"

Celaena turned her head to look at Ansel. She hadn't told her she was from Terrasen. Ansel said, "You talk about Terrasen the way my father used to talk about our land."

Celaena was about to reply when she caught the word. *Used to.*

Ansel's attention remained on the stars. "I lied to the Master when I came here," she whispered, as if afraid someone else would hear them in the emptiness of the desert. Celaena looked back to the sky. "My father never sent me to train. And there is no Briarcliff, or Briarcliff Hall. There hasn't been for five years."

A dozen questions sprung up, but Celaena kept her mouth shut, letting Ansel speak.

"I was twelve," Ansel said, "when Lord Loch took several territories around Briarcliff, and then demanded we yield to him as well—that we bow to him as High King of the Wastes. My father refused. He said there was one tyrant already conquering everything east of the mountains—he didn't want one in the west, too." Celaena's blood went cold as she braced herself for what she was certain was coming. "Two weeks later, Lord Loch marched into our land with his men, seizing our villages, our livelihood, our people. And when he got to Briarcliff Hall . . ."

Ansel drew a shuddering breath. "When he arrived at Briarcliff Hall, I was in the kitchen. I saw them from the window and hid in a cupboard as Loch walked in. My sister and father were upstairs, and Loch stayed in the kitchen as his men brought them down and . . . I didn't dare make a sound as Lord Loch made my father watch as he . . ." She stumbled, but forced it out, spitting it as if it were poison. "My father begged on his hands and knees, but Loch still made my father watch as he slit my sister's throat, then his. And I just hid there, even as they killed our servants, too. I hid there and did nothing.

"And when they were gone, I took my father's sword from his

corpse and ran. I ran and ran until I couldn't run anymore, at the foothills of the White Fang Mountains. And that's when I collapsed at the campfire of a witch—one of the Ironteeth. I didn't care if she killed me. But she told me that it was not my fate to die there. That I should journey south, to the Silent Assassins in the Red Desert, and there . . . there I would find my fate. She fed me, and bound my bleeding feet, and gave me gold—gold that I later used to commission my armor—then sent me on my way."

Ansel wiped at her eyes. "So I've been here ever since, training for the day when I'm strong enough and fast enough to return to Briarcliff and take back what is mine. Someday, I'll march into High King Loch's hall and repay him for what he did to my family. With my father's sword." Her hand grazed the wolf-head hilt. "This sword will end his life. Because this sword is all I have left of them."

Celaena hadn't realized she was crying until she tried to take a deep breath. Saying that she was sorry didn't feel adequate. She knew what this sort of loss was like, and words didn't do anything at all.

Ansel slowly turned to look at her, her eyes lined with silver. She traced Celaena's cheekbone, where the bruises had once been. "Where do men find it in themselves to do such monstrous things? How do they find it acceptable?"

"We'll make them pay for it in the end." Celaena grasped Ansel's hand. The girl squeezed back hard. "We'll see to it that they pay."

"Yes." Ansel shifted her gaze back to the stars. "Yes, we will."

CHAPTER 7

Celaena and Ansel knew their little escapade with the Asterion horses would have consequences. Celaena had at least expected to have enough time to tell a decent lie about how they acquired the horses. But when they returned to the fortress and found Mikhail waiting, along with three other assassins, she knew that word of their stunt had somehow already reached the Master.

She kept her mouth shut as she and Ansel knelt at the foot of the Master's dais, heads bowed, eyes on the floor. She certainly wouldn't convince him to train her now.

His receiving chamber was empty today, and each of his steps scraped softly against the floor. She knew he could be silent if he wished. He wanted them to feel the dread of his approach.

And Celaena felt it. She felt each footstep, the phantom bruises on her face throbbing with the memory of Arobynn's fists. And suddenly, as the memory of that day echoed through her, she remembered the words Sam kept screaming at Arobynn as the King of the Assassins beat her, the words that she somehow had forgotten in the fog of pain: *I'll kill you!*

Sam had said it like he meant it. He'd bellowed it. Again and again and again.

The clear, unexpected memory was almost jarring enough for her to forget where she was—but then the snow-white robes of the Master came into view. Her mouth went dry.

"We only wanted to have some fun," Ansel said quietly. "We can return the horses."

Celaena, head still lowered, glanced toward Ansel. She was staring up at the Master as he towered over them. "I'm sorry," Celaena murmured, wishing she could convey it with her hands, too. Though silence might have been preferable, she needed him to hear her apology.

The Master just stood there.

Ansel was the first to break under his stare. She sighed. "I know it was foolish. But there's nothing to worry about. I can handle Lord Berick; I've been handling him for ages."

There was enough bitterness in her words that Celaena's brows rose slightly. Perhaps his refusal to train her wasn't easy for Ansel to bear. She was never outright competitive about getting the Master's attention, but . . . After so many years of living here, being stuck as the mediator between the Master and Berick didn't exactly seem like the sort of glory Ansel was interested in. Celaena certainly wouldn't have enjoyed it.

The Master's clothes whispered as they moved, and Celaena flinched when she felt his calloused fingers hook under her chin. He lifted her head so she was forced to look at him, his face lined with disapproval. She remained perfectly still, bracing herself for the strike, already praying he wouldn't damage her too significantly. But then the Master's sea-green eyes narrowed ever so slightly, and he gave her a sad smile as he released her.

Her face burned. He hadn't been about to hit her. He'd wanted her to look at him, to tell him her side of the story. But even if he wasn't going to strike her, he still might punish them. And if he kicked out Ansel for what they'd done . . . Ansel needed to be here, to learn all that these assassins could teach her, because Ansel wanted to *do* something with her life. Ansel had a purpose. And Celaena . . .

"It was my idea," Celaena blurted, her words too loud in the empty chamber. "I didn't feel like walking back here, and I thought it would be useful to have horses. And when I saw the Asterion mares . . . I thought we might as well travel in style." She gave him a shaky half grin, and the Master's brows rose as he looked between them. For a long, long moment, he just watched them.

Whatever he saw on Ansel's face suddenly made him nod. Ansel quickly bowed her head. "Before you decide on a punishment . . ." She turned to Celaena, then looked back at the Master. "Since we like horses so much, maybe we could . . . be on stable duty? For the morning shift. Until Celaena leaves."

Celaena almost choked, but she schooled her features into neutrality.

A faint glimmer of amusement shone in his eyes, and he considered Ansel's words for a moment. Then he nodded again. Ansel loosened a breath. "Thank you for your lenience," she said. The Master glanced toward the doors behind them. They were dismissed.

Ansel got to her feet, and Celaena followed suit. But as Celaena turned, the Master grabbed her arm. Ansel paused to watch as the Master made a few motions with his hand. When he finished, Ansel's brows rose. He repeated the motions again—slower, pointing to Celaena repeatedly. When it seemed she was certain she understood him, Ansel turned to Celaena.

"You're to report to him at sunset tomorrow. For your first lesson."

Celaena bit back her sigh of relief, and gave the Master a genuine grin. He returned a hint of a smile. She bowed deeply, and couldn't stop smiling as she and Ansel left the hall and headed to the stables. She had three and a half weeks left—that would be more than enough time to get that letter.

Whatever he had seen in her face, whatever she had said . . . somehow, she'd proven herself to him at last.

It turned out that they weren't just responsible for shoveling horse dung. Oh, no—they were responsible for cleaning the pens of *all* the four-legged livestock in the fortress, a task that took them from breakfast until noon. At least they did it in the morning, before the afternoon heat really made the smell atrocious.

Another benefit was that they didn't have to go running. Though after four hours of shoveling animal droppings, Celaena would have begged to take the six-mile run instead.

Anxious as she was to be out of the stables, she couldn't contain her growing trepidation as the sun arced across the sky, heading toward sunset. She didn't know what to expect; even Ansel had no idea what the Master might have in mind. They spent the afternoon sparring as usual—with each other, and with whatever assassins wandered into the shade of the open-air training courtyard. And when the sun finally hovered near the horizon, Ansel gave Celaena squeeze on the shoulder and sent her to the Master's hall.

But the Master wasn't in his receiving hall, and when she ran into Ilias, he just gave her his usual smile and pointed toward the roof. After taking a few staircases and then climbing a wooden ladder and squeezing through a hatch in the ceiling, she found herself in the open air high atop the fortress.

The Master stood by the parapet, gazing across the desert. She cleared her throat, but he remained with his back to her.

The roof couldn't have been more than twenty square feet, and the only thing on it was a covered reed basket placed in the center. Torches burned, illuminating the rooftop.

Celaena cleared her throat again, and the Master finally turned. She bowed, which, strangely, was something she felt he actually deserved, rather than something she ought to do. He gave her a nod and pointed to the reed basket, beckoning her to open the lid. Doing her best not to look skeptical, hoping there was a beautiful new weapon inside, she approached. She stopped when she heard the hissing.

Unpleasant, don't-come-closer hissing. From inside the basket.

She turned to the Master, who hopped onto one of the merlons, his bare feet dangling in the gap between one block of stone and the next, and beckoned her again. Palms sweating, Celaena took a deep breath and snatched back the lid.

A black asp curled into itself, head drawn back low as it hissed.

Celaena leapt away a yard, making for the parapet wall, but the Master let out a low click of his tongue.

His hands moved, flowing and winding through the air like a river—like a snake. *Observe it*, he seemed to tell her. *Move with it.*

She looked back at the basket in time to see the slender, black head of the asp slide over the rim, then down to the tiled roof.

Her heart thundered in her chest. It was poisonous, wasn't it? It had to be. It looked poisonous.

The snake slithered across the roof, and Celaena inched back from it, not daring to look away for even a heartbeat. She reached for a dagger, but the Master again clicked his tongue. A glance in his direction was enough for her to understand the meaning of the sound.

Don't kill it. Absorb.

The snake moved effortlessly, lazily, and tasted the evening air with its black tongue. With a deep, steadying breath, Celaena observed.

She spent every night that week on the roof with the asp, watching it, copying its movements, internalizing its rhythm and sounds until she could move like it moved, until they could face each other and she could anticipate how it would lunge; until she could strike like the asp, swift and unflinching.

After that, she spent three days dangling from the rafters of the fortress stables with the bats. It took her longer to figure out their strengths—how they became so silent that no one noticed they were there, how they could drown out the external noise and focus only on the sound of their prey. And after that, it was two nights spent with jackrabbits on the dunes, learning their stillness, absorbing how they used their speed and dexterity to evade talons and claws, how they slept above ground to better hear their enemies approaching. Night after night, the Master watched from nearby, never saying a word, never doing anything except occasionally pointing out how an animal moved.

As the remaining weeks passed, she saw Ansel only during meals and for the few hours they spent each morning shoveling manure. And after a long night spent sprinting or hanging upside down or running sideways to see why crabs bothered moving like that, Celaena was usually in no mood to talk. But Ansel was merry—almost gleeful, more and more with every passing day. She never said why, exactly, but Celaena found it rather infectious.

And every day, Celaena went to sleep after lunch and dozed until the sun went down, her dreams full of snakes and rabbits and chirping desert beetles. Sometimes she spotted Mikhail training the acolytes, or found Ilias meditating in an empty training room, but she rarely got the chance to spend time with them.

They had no more attacks from Lord Berick, either. Whatever Ansel had said during that meeting with him in Xandria, whatever the Master's letter had contained, it seemed to have worked, even after the theft of his horses.

There were quiet moments also, when she wasn't training or toiling with Ansel. Moments when her thoughts drifted back to Sam, to what he'd said. He'd threatened to *kill* Arobynn. For hurting her. She tried to work through it, tried to figure out what had changed in Skull's Bay to make Sam dare say such a thing to the King of the Assassins. But whenever she caught herself thinking about it too much, she shoved those thoughts into the back of her mind.

CHAPTER 8

"You mean to tell me you do this *every day*?" Ansel said, her brows high on her forehead as Celaena brushed rouge onto the girl's cheeks.

"Sometimes twice a day," Celaena said, and Ansel opened an eye. They were sitting on Celaena's bed, a scattering of cosmetics between them—a small fraction of Celaena's enormous collection back in Rifthold. "Besides being useful for my work, it's fun."

"Fun?" Ansel opened her other eye. "Smearing all this gunk on your face is fun?"

Celaena set down her pot of rouge. "If you don't shut up, I'll draw a mustache on you."

Ansel's lips twitched, but she closed her eyes again as Celaena raised the little container of bronze powder and dusted some on her eyelids.

"Well, it *is* my birthday. And Midsummer Eve," Ansel said, her eyelashes fluttering beneath the tickle of Celaena's delicate brush. "We so rarely get to have fun. I suppose I should look nice."

Ansel always looked nice—better than nice, actually—but Celaena didn't need to tell her that. "At a minimum, at least you don't smell like horse droppings."

Ansel let out a breathy chuckle, the air warm on Celaena's hands as they hovered near her face. She kept quiet while Celaena finished with the powder, then held still as she lined her eyes with kohl and darkened her lashes.

"All right," Celaena said, sitting back so she could see Ansel's face. "Open."

Ansel opened her eyes, and Celaena frowned.

"What?" Ansel said.

Celaena shook her head. "You're going to have to wash it all off."

"Why?"

"Because you look better than I do."

Ansel pinched Celaena's arm. Celaena pinched her back, laughter on her lips. But then the single remaining week that Celaena had left loomed before her, brief and unforgiving, and her chest tightened at the thought of leaving. She hadn't even dared ask the Master for her letter yet. But more than that . . . Well, she'd never had a female friend—never really had *any* friends—and somehow, the thought of returning to Rifthold without Ansel was a tad unbearable.

The Midsummer Eve festival was like nothing Celaena had ever experienced. She'd expected music and drinking and laughter, but instead, the assassins gathered in the largest of the fortress courtyards. And all of them, including Ansel, were totally silent. The moon provided the only light, silhouetting the date trees swaying along the courtyard walls.

But the strangest part was the dancing. Even though there was no music, most of the people danced—some of the dances foreign and strange, some of them familiar. Everyone was smiling, but aside from the rustle of clothing and the scrape of merry feet against the stones, there was no sound.

But there *was* wine, and she and Ansel found a table in a corner of the courtyard and fully indulged themselves.

Though she loved, loved, *loved* parties, Celaena would have rather spent the night training with the Master. With only one week left, she wanted to spend every waking moment working with him. But he'd insisted she go to the party—if only because *he* wanted to go to the party. The old man danced to a rhythm Celaena could not hear or make out, and looked more like someone's benevolent, clumsy grandfather than the master of some of the world's greatest assassins.

She couldn't help but think of Arobynn, who was all calculated grace and restrained aggression—Arobynn who danced with a select few, and whose smile was razor-sharp.

Mikhail had dragged Ansel to the dancing, and she was grinning as she twirled and bobbed and bounced from partner to partner, all of the assassins now keeping the same, silent beat. Ansel had experienced such horror, and yet she was still so carefree, so keenly alive. Mikhail caught her in his arms and dipped her, low enough for Ansel's eyes to widen.

Mikhail truly liked Ansel—that much was obvious. He always found excuses to touch her, always smiled at her, always looked at her as if she were the only person in the room.

Celaena sloshed the wine around in her glass. If she were being honest, sometimes she thought Sam looked at her that way. But then he'd go and say something absurd, or try to undermine her, and she'd chide herself for even thinking that about him.

Her stomach tightened. What had Arobynn done to him that

night? She should have inquired after him. But in the days afterward, she'd been so busy, so wrapped in her rage . . . She hadn't dared look for him, actually. Because if Arobynn had hurt Sam the way he'd hurt her—if he'd hurt Sam *worse* than that . . .

Celaena drained the rest of her wine. During the two days after she'd awoken from her beating, she'd used a good chunk of her savings to purchase her own apartment, away and well hidden from the Assassins' Keep. She hadn't told anyone—partially because she was worried she might change her mind while she was away—but with each day here, with each lesson with the Master, she was more and more resolved to tell Arobynn she was moving out. She was actually eager to see the look on his face. She still owed him money, of course—he'd seen to it that her debts would keep her with him for a while—but there was no rule that said she had to live *with* him. And if he ever laid a hand on her again . . .

If Arobynn ever laid a hand on her *or* Sam again, she'd see to it that he lost that hand. Actually, she'd see to it that he lost everything up to the elbow.

Someone touched her shoulder, and Celaena looked up from her empty wine goblet to find Ilias standing behind her. She hadn't seen much of him in the past few days, aside from at dinner, where he still glanced at her and gave her those lovely smiles. He offered his hand.

Celaena's face instantly warmed and she shook her head, trying her best to convey a sense of not knowing these dances.

Ilias shrugged, his eyes bright. His hand remained extended.

She bit her lip and glanced pointedly at his feet. Ilias shrugged again, this time as if to suggest that his toes weren't all that valuable, anyway.

Celaena glanced at Mikhail and Ansel, spinning wildly to a beat only the two of them could hear. Ilias raised his brows. *Live a little,*

Sardothien! Ansel had said that day they stole the horses. Why not live a little tonight, too?

Celaena gave him a dramatic shrug and took his hand, tossing a wry smile his way. *I suppose I could spare a dance or two*, she wanted to say.

Even though there was no music, Ilias led her through the dances with ease, each of his movements sure and steady. It was hard to look away—not just from his face, but also from the contentment that radiated from him. And he looked back at her so intently that she had to wonder if he'd been watching her all these weeks not only to protect his father.

They danced until well after midnight; wild dances that weren't at all like the waltzes she'd learned in Rifthold. Even when she switched partners, Ilias was always there, waiting for the next dance. It was almost as intoxicating as the oddity of dancing to no music, to hearing a collective, silent rhythm—to letting the wind and the sighing sand outside the fortress provide the beat and the melody. It was lovely and strange, and as the hours passed, she often wondered if she'd strayed into some dream.

When the moon was setting, Celaena found herself leaving the dance floor, doing her best to convey how exhausted she was. It wasn't a lie. Her feet hurt, and she hadn't had a proper night's rest in weeks and weeks. Ilias tried pulling her back onto the floor for one last dance, but she nimbly slipped out of his grasp, grinning as she shook her head. Ansel and Mikhail were still dancing, holding each other closer than any other pair on the dance floor. Not wanting to interrupt her friend, Celaena left the hall, Ilias in tow.

She couldn't deny that her racing heartbeat wasn't just from the dancing as they walked down the empty hall. Ilias strolled beside her, silent as ever, and she swallowed tightly.

What would he say—that is, if he could speak—if he knew that Adarlan's Assassin had never been kissed? She'd killed men, freed slaves, stolen horses, but she'd never kissed anyone. It was ridiculous, somehow. Something that she should have gotten out of the way at some point, but she'd never found the right person.

All too quickly, they were standing outside the door to her room. Celaena didn't touch the door handle, and tried to calm her breathing as she turned to face Ilias.

He was smiling. Maybe he didn't mean to kiss her. His room was, after all, just a few doors down.

"Well," she said. After so many hours of silence, the word was jarringly loud. Her face burned. He stepped closer, and she tried not to flinch as he slipped a hand around her waist. It would be so simple to kiss him, she realized.

His other hand slid against her neck, his thumb caressing her jaw as he gently tilted her head back. Her blood pounded through every inch of her. Her lips parted . . . but as Ilias inclined his head, she went rigid and stepped back.

He immediately withdrew, his brows crossed with concern. She wanted to seep into the stones and disappear. "I'm sorry," she said thickly, trying not to look too mortified. "I—I can't. I mean, I'm leaving in a week. And . . . and you live here. And I'm in Rifthold, so . . ." She was babbling. She should stop. Actually, she should just stop talking. Forever.

But if he sensed her mortification, he didn't show it. Instead, he bowed his head and squeezed her shoulder. Then he gave her one of those shrugs, which she interpreted to mean, *If only we didn't live thousands of miles apart. But can you blame me for trying?*

With that, he strode the few feet to his room. He gave her a friendly wave before disappearing inside.

Alone in the hallway, Celaena watched the shadows cast by the torches. It hadn't been the mere impossibility of a relationship with Ilias that had made her pull away.

No; it was the memory of Sam's face that had stopped her from kissing him.

Ansel didn't come back to their room that night. And when she stumbled into the stables the following morning, still wearing her clothes from the party, Celaena could assume she'd either spent the whole night dancing, or with Mikhail. From the flush on Ansel's freckled cheeks, Celaena thought it might be both.

Ansel took one look at the grin on Celaena's face and glowered. "Don't you even start."

Celaena shoveled a heap of manure into the nearby wagon. Later she'd cart it to the gardens, where it would be used for fertilizer. "What?" Celaena said, grinning even wider. "I wasn't going to say anything."

Ansel snatched her shovel from where it leaned against the wooden wall, several pens down from where Kasida and Hisli now had their new homes. "Good. I got enough of it from the others while I was walking here."

Celaena leaned against her shovel in the open gate. "I'm sure Mikhail will get his fair share of teasing, too."

Ansel straightened, her eyes surprisingly dark. "No, he won't. They'll congratulate him, just like they always do, for a conquest well made." She let out a long sigh from her nose. "But me? I'll get teased until I snap at them. It's always the same."

They continued their work in silence. After a moment, Celaena spoke. "Even though they tease you, you still want to be with Mikhail?"

Ansel shrugged again, flinging dung into the pile she'd gathered into the wagon. "He's an amazing warrior; he's taught me far more than I would have learned without him. So they can tease me all they want, but at the end of the day, he's still the one giving me extra attention when we train."

That didn't sit well with Celaena, but she opted to keep her mouth shut.

"Besides," Ansel said, glancing sidelong at Celaena, "not all of us can so easily convince the Master to train us."

Celaena's stomach twisted a little. Was Ansel jealous of that? "I'm not entirely sure why he changed his mind."

"Oh?" Ansel said, sharper than Celaena had ever heard her. It scared her, surprisingly. "The noble, clever, beautiful assassin from the North—the *great* Celaena Sardothien, has no idea why he'd want to train her? No idea that he might want to leave his mark on you, too? To have a hand in shaping your glorious fate?"

Celaena's throat tightened, and she cursed herself for feeling so hurt by the words. She didn't think the Master felt that way at all, but she still hissed, "Yes, my glorious fate. Shoveling dung in a barn. A worthy task for me."

"But certainly a worthy task for a girl from the Flatlands?"

"I didn't say that," Celaena said through her teeth. "Don't put words in my mouth."

"Why not? I know you think it—and you know I'm telling the truth. I'm not good enough for the Master to train me. I began seeing Mikhail to get extra attention during lessons, and I certainly don't have a notorious name to flaunt around."

"Fine," Celaena said. "Yes: most of the people in the kingdoms know my name—know to fear me." Her temper rose with dizzying speed. "But you . . . You want to know the truth about you, Ansel? The truth is, even if you go home and get what you want, no one will give a damn if you take back your speck of territory—no one will even hear about it. Because no one except for *you* will even care."

She regretted the words the instant they left her mouth. Ansel's face went white with anger, and her lips trembled as she pressed them together. Ansel threw down her shovel. For a moment, Celaena thought that she'd attack, and even went as far as slightly bending her knees in anticipation of a fight.

But Ansel stalked past her and said, "You're just a spoiled, selfish bitch." With that, she left Celaena to finish their morning chores.

CHAPTER 9

Celaena couldn't focus on her lesson with the Master that night. All day, Ansel's words had been ringing in her ears. She hadn't seen her friend for hours—and dreaded the moment when she'd have to return to her room and face her again. Though Celaena hated to admit it, Ansel's parting claim had felt true. She *was* spoiled. And selfish.

The Master snapped his fingers, and Celaena, who was yet again studying an asp, looked up. Though she'd been mirroring the snake's movements, she hadn't noticed it was slowly creeping toward her.

She leapt back a few feet, crouching close to the roof 's wall, but stopped when she felt the Master's hand on her shoulder. He motioned to leave the snake be and sit beside him on the merlons that ran around the roof. Grateful for a break, she hopped up, trying not to glance down at the ground far, far below. Though she was well acquainted with heights, and had no problems with balance, sitting on an edge never really felt *natural*.

The Master raised his eyebrows. *Talk*, he seemed to say.

She tucked her left foot under her right thigh, making sure to keep an eye on the asp, which slithered into the shadows of the roof.

But telling him about her fight with Ansel felt so . . . childish. As if the Master of the Silent Assassins would want to hear about a petty squabble.

Cicadas buzzed in the trees of the keep, and somewhere in the gardens, a nightingale sang her lament. *Talk*. Talk about what?

She didn't have anything to say, so they sat on the parapet in silence for a while—until even the cicadas went to sleep, and the moon slipped away behind them, and the sky began to brighten. *Talk*. Talk about what had been haunting her these months. Haunting every thought, every dream, every breath. *Talk*.

"I'm scared to go home," she said at last, staring out at the dunes beyond the walls.

The predawn light was bright enough for her to see the Master's brows rise. *Why*?

"Because everything will be different. Everything is already different. I think everything changed when Arobynn punished me, but . . . Some part of me still thinks that the world will go back to the way it was before that night. Before I went to Skull's Bay."

The Master's eyes shone like emeralds. Compassionate—sorrowful.

"I'm not sure I *want* it to go back to the way it was before," she admitted. "And I think . . . I think that's what scares me the most."

The Master smiled at her reassuringly, then rolled his neck and stretched his arms over his head before standing atop the merlon.

Celaena tensed, unsure if she should follow.

But the Master didn't look at her as he began a series of movements, graceful and winding, as elegant as a dance and deadly as the asp that lurked on the roof.

The asp.

Watching the Master, she could see each of the qualities she had copied for the past few weeks—the contained power and swiftness, the cunning and the smooth restraint.

He went through the motions again, and it took only a glance in her direction to get her to her feet atop the parapet wall. Mindful of her balance, she slowly copied him, her muscles singing with the *rightness* of the movements. She grinned as night after night of careful observation and mimicry clicked into place.

Again and again, the sweep and curve of her arm, the twisting of her torso, even the rhythm of her breathing. Again and again, until she became the asp, until the sun broke over the horizon, bathing them in red light.

Again and again, until there was nothing left but the Master and her as they greeted the new day.

An hour after sunup, Celaena crept into her room, bracing herself for another fight, but found Ansel already gone to the stables. Since Ansel had abandoned her to do the chores by herself yesterday, Celaena decided to return the favor. She sighed with contentment as she collapsed atop her bed.

She was later awoken by someone shaking her shoulder—someone who smelled like manure.

"It had better be afternoon," Celaena said, rolling onto her stomach and burying her face in her pillow.

Ansel chuckled. "Oh, it's almost dinner. And the stables and pens are in good order, no thanks to you."

"You left me to do it all yesterday," Celaena mumbled.

"Yes, well . . . I'm sorry."

Celaena peeled her face from the pillow to look at Ansel, who stood over the bed. Ansel twisted her hands. She was wearing her armor again. At the sight of it, Celaena winced as she recalled what she'd said about her friend's homeland.

Ansel tucked her red hair behind her ears. "I shouldn't have said those things about you. I don't think you're spoiled or selfish."

"Oh, don't worry. I am—very much so." Celaena sat up. Ansel gave her a weak smile. "But," she went on, "I'm sorry for what I said, too. I didn't mean it."

Ansel nodded, glancing toward the shut door, as if she expected someone to be there. "I have lots of friends here, but you're the first *true* friend I've had. I'll be sorry to see you go."

"I still have five days," Celaena said. Given how popular Ansel was, it was surprising—and somewhat relieving—to hear that she'd also felt slightly alone.

Ansel flicked her eyes to the door again. What was she nervous about? "Try to remember me fondly, will you?"

"I'll try. But it might be hard."

Ansel let out a quiet laugh and took two goblets from the table beneath the window. "I brought us some wine." She handed one to Celaena. Ansel lifted her copper goblet. "To making amends—and fond memories."

"To being the most fearsome and imposing girls the world has ever seen." Celaena raised her goblet high before she drank.

As she swallowed a large mouthful of wine, she had two thoughts.

The first was that Ansel's eyes were now filled with unmasked sorrow.

And the second—which explained the first—was that the wine tasted strange.

But Celaena didn't have time to consider what poison it was before she heard her own goblet clatter to the floor, and the world spun and went black.

Chapter 10

Someone was hammering against an anvil somewhere very, very close to her head. So close that she felt each beat in her body, the sound shattering through her mind, stirring her from sleep.

With a jolt, Celaena sat up. There was no hammer and no anvil—just a pounding headache. And there was no assassins' fortress, only endless miles of red dunes, and Kasida standing watch over her. Well, at least she wasn't dead.

Cursing, she got to her feet. What had Ansel done?

The moon illuminated enough of the desert for her to see that the assassins' fortress was nowhere in sight, and that Kasida's saddlebags were full of her belongings. Except for her sword. She searched and searched, but it wasn't there. Celaena reached for one of her two long daggers, but stiffened when she felt a scroll of paper tucked into her belt.

Someone had also left a lantern beside her, and it took only a few moments for Celaena to get it lit and nestled into the dune. Kneeling before the dim light, she unrolled the paper with shaking hands.

It was in Ansel's handwriting, and wasn't long.

I'm sorry it had to end this way. The Master said it would be easier to let you go like this, rather than shame you by publicly asking you to leave early. Kasida is yours—as is the Master's letter of approval, which is in the saddlebag. Go home.

I will miss you,
Ansel

Celaena read the letter three times to make sure she hadn't missed something. She was being let go—but why? She had the letter of approval, at least, but . . . but what had she done that made it so urgent to get rid of her that he'd drug her and then dump her in the middle of the desert? She had five days left; he couldn't have waited for her to leave?

Her eyes burned as she sorted through the events of the past few days for ways she might have offended the Master. She got to her feet and rifled through the saddlebags until she pulled out the letter of approval. It was a folded square of paper, sealed with sea-green wax—the color of the Master's eyes. A little vain, but . . .

Her fingers hovered over the seal. If she broke it, then Arobynn might accuse her of tampering with the letter. But what if it said horrid things about her? Ansel said it was a letter of approval, so it couldn't be that bad. Celaena tucked the letter back into the saddlebag.

Perhaps the Master had also realized that she was spoiled and selfish. Maybe everyone had just been tolerating her, and . . . maybe they'd heard of her fight with Ansel and decided to send her packing. It wouldn't surprise her. They were looking out for their own, after all. Never mind that for a while, *she* had felt like one of their own—felt, for the first time in a long, long while, like she had a place where she belonged. Where she might learn something more than deceit and how to end lives.

But she'd been wrong. Somehow, realizing that hurt far worse than the beating Arobynn had given her.

Her lips trembled, but she squared her shoulders and scanned the night sky until she found the Stag and the crowning star that led north. Sighing, Celaena blew out the lantern, mounted Kasida, and rode into the night.

She rode toward Xandria, opting to find a ship there instead of braving the northern trek across the Singing Sands to Yurpa—the port she'd originally sailed into. Without a guide, she didn't really have much of a choice. She took her time, often walking instead of riding Kasida, who seemed as sad as she was to leave the Silent Assassins and their luxurious stables.

The next day, she was a few miles into her late afternoon trek when she heard the *thump*, *thump*, *thump*. It grew louder, the movements now edged with clashing and clattering and deep voices. She hopped onto Kasida's back and crested a dune.

In the distance, at least two hundred men were marching—straight into the desert. Some bore red and black banners. Lord Berick's men. They marched in a long column, with mounted soldiers galloping along the flanks. Though she had never seen Berick, a quick examination of the host showed no signs of a lord being present. He must have stayed behind.

But there was nothing out here. Nothing except for . . .

Celaena's mouth went dry. Nothing except for the assassins' fortress.

A mounted soldier paused his riding, his black mare's coat gleaming with sweat. He stared toward her. With her white clothes concealing all of her but her eyes, he had no way of identifying her, no way of telling what she was.

Even from the distance, she could see the bow and quiver of arrows he bore. How good was his aim?

She didn't dare to move. The last thing she needed was the attention of all those soldiers on her. They all possessed broadswords, daggers, shields, and arrows. This definitely wasn't going to be a friendly visit, not with this many men.

Was that why the Master had sent her away? Had he somehow known this would happen and didn't want her caught up in it?

Celaena nodded to the soldier and continued riding toward Xandria. If the Master didn't want anything to do with her, then she certainly didn't need to warn them. Especially since he probably knew. And he had a fortress full of assassins. Two hundred soldiers were nothing compared to seventy or so of the *sessiz suikast*.

The assassins could handle themselves. They didn't need her. They'd made that clear enough.

Still, the muffled thump of Kasida's steps away from the fortress became more and more difficult to bear.

The next morning, Xandria was remarkably quiet. At first, Celaena thought it was because the citizens were all waiting for news about the attack on the assassins, but she soon realized she found it quiet because she had only seen it on Market Day. The winding, narrow streets that had been crammed with vendors were now empty, littered with errant palm fronds and piles of sand that slithered in the fierce winds from the sea.

She bought passage on a ship that would sail to Amier, the port in

Melisande across the Gulf of Oro. She'd hoped for a ship to Innish, another port, so she could inquire after a young healer she'd met on her journey here, but there were none. And with the embargo on ships from Xandria going to other parts of Adarlan's empire, a distant, forgotten port like Amier would be her best bet. From there, she'd travel on Kasida back to Rifthold, hopefully catching another boat somewhere on the long arm of the Avery River that would take her the last leg to the capital.

The ship didn't leave until high tide that afternoon, which left Celaena with a few hours to wander the city. The Spidersilk merchant was long gone, along with the cobbler and the temple priestesses.

Nervous the mare would be identified in the city, but more worried that someone would steal Kasida if she left her unguarded, Celaena led the horse through back alleys until she found a near-private trough for Kasida. Celaena leaned against a sandstone wall as her horse drank her fill. Had Lord Berick's men reached the fortress yet? At the rate they were going, they would probably arrive this night or early tomorrow morning. She just hoped the Master was prepared—and that he had at least restocked the flaming wall after the last attack from Berick. Had he sent her away for her own safety, or was he about to be blindsided?

She glanced up at the palace towering over the city. Berick hadn't been with his men. Delivering the Mute Master's head to the King of Adarlan would surely get the embargo lifted from his city. Was he doing it for the sake of his people, or for himself?

But the Red Desert also needed the assassins—and the money and the trade the foreign emissaries brought in, too.

Berick and the Master had certainly been communicating in the past few weeks. What had gone wrong? Ansel had made another trip a week ago to see him, and hadn't mentioned trouble. She'd seemed quite jovial, actually.

Celaena didn't really know why a chill snaked down her spine in that moment. Or why she found herself suddenly digging through the saddlebags until she pulled out the Master's letter of approval, along with the note Ansel had written her.

If the Master had known about the attack, he would have been fortifying his defenses already; he wouldn't have sent Celaena away. She was Adarlan's greatest assassin, and if two hundred men were marching on his fortress, he'd *need* her. The Master wasn't proud—not like Arobynn. He truly loved his disciples; he looked after and nurtured them. But he'd never trained Ansel. Why?

And with so many of his loved ones in the fortress, why send only Celaena away? Why not send them all?

Her heart beat so fast it stumbled, and Celaena tore open the letter of approval.

It was blank.

She flipped the paper over. The other side was also blank. Holding it up to the sun revealed no hidden ink, no watermark. But it had been sealed by him, hadn't it? That was *his* seal on the—

It was easy to steal a signet ring. She'd done it with Captain Rolfe. And she'd seen the white line around the Master's finger—his ring *had* been missing.

But if Ansel had drugged her, and given her a document sealed with the Master's signet ring . . .

No, it wasn't possible. And it didn't make sense. Why would Ansel send her away and pretend the Master had done it? Unless . . .

Celaena looked up at Lord Berick's palace. Unless Ansel hadn't been visiting Lord Berick on behalf of the Master at all. Or maybe she had at first, long enough to gain the Master's trust. But while the Master thought she was mending the relationships between them, Ansel was really doing quite the opposite. And that Spidersilk merchant had mentioned something about a spy among the assassins—a spy working for Berick. But why?

Celaena didn't have time to ponder it. Not with two hundred men so close to the fortress. She might have questioned Lord Berick, but that, too, would take precious time.

One warrior might not make a difference against two hundred, but she was Celaena Sardothien. That had to count for something. That *did* count for something.

She mounted Kasida and turned her toward the city gates.

"Let's see how fast you can run," she whispered into the mare's ear, and took off.

CHAPTER 11

Like a shooting star across a red sky, Kasida flew over the dunes, and made the jump across the Cleaver as if she were leaping over a brook. They paused only long enough for the horse to rest and fill up on water, and though Celaena apologized to the mare for pushing her so hard, Kasida never faltered. She, too, seemed to sense the urgency.

They rode through the night, until the crimson dawn broke over the dunes and smoke stained the sky, and the fortress spread before them.

Fires burned here and there, and shouts rang out, along with the clashing of weapons. The assassins hadn't yielded yet, though their walls had been breached. A few bodies littered the sand leading up to the gates, but the gates themselves showed no sign of a forced entry—as if someone had left them unlocked.

Celaena dismounted Kasida before the final dune, leaving the horse to either follow or find her own path, and crept the rest of the way into the fortress. She paused long enough to swipe a sword from a dead soldier and tuck it into her belt. It was cheaply made and unbalanced, but the point was sharp enough to do the job. From the muffled clopping of hooves behind her, she knew Kasida had followed. Still, Celaena didn't dare take her eyes away from the scene before her as she drew her two long daggers.

Inside the walls, bodies were everywhere—assassin and soldier alike. Otherwise, the main courtyard was empty, its little rivers now flowing red. She tried her best not to look too closely at the faces of the fallen.

Fires smoldered, most of them just smoking piles of ash. Charred remnants of arrows revealed that they'd probably been ablaze when they hit. Every step into the courtyard felt like a lifetime. The shouts and clanging weapons came from other parts of the fortress. Who was winning? If all the soldiers had gotten in with so few dead on the sand, then someone *had* to have let them in—probably in the dead of night. How long had it taken before the night watch spotted the soldiers creeping inside? . . . Unless the night watch had been dispatched before they could sound the alarm.

But, as Celaena took step after step, she realized that the question she *should* be asking was far worse. *Where is the Master*?

That was what Lord Berick had wanted—the Master's head.

And Ansel . . .

Celaena didn't want to finish that thought. Ansel hadn't sent her away because of this. Ansel couldn't be behind this. But . . .

Celaena started sprinting for the Master's greeting room, heedless of the noise. Blood and destruction were everywhere. She passed courtyards full of soldiers and assassins, locked in deadly battle.

She was halfway up the stairs to the Master's room when a soldier came rushing down them, his blade drawn. She ducked the blow for her head and struck low and deep, her long dagger burying itself into his gut. With the heat, the soldiers had forgone metal armor—and their leather armor couldn't turn a blade made with Adarlanian steel.

She jumped aside as he groaned and tumbled down the steps. She didn't bother sparing him a final look as she continued her ascent. The upper level was completely silent.

Her breath sharp in her throat, she careened toward the open doors of the greeting room. The two hundred soldiers were meant to destroy the fortress—and provide a distraction. The Master could have been unguarded with everyone focused on the attack. But he was still the Master. How could Ansel expect to best him?

Unless she used that drug on him as well. How else would she be able to disarm him and catch him unawares?

Celaena hurled herself through the open wooden doors and nearly tripped on the body prostrate between them.

Mikhail lay on his back, his throat slit, eyes staring up at the tiled ceiling. Dead. Beside him was Ilias, struggling to rise as he clutched his bleeding belly. Celaena bit back her cry, and Ilias raised his head, blood dripping from his lips. She made to kneel beside him, but he grunted, pointing to the room ahead.

To his father.

The Master lay on his side atop the dais, his eyes open and his robes still unstained by blood. But he had the stillness of one drugged—paralyzed by whatever Ansel had given him.

The girl stood over him, her back to Celaena as she talked, swift and quiet. Babbling. She clenched her father's sword in one hand, the bloodied blade drooping toward the floor. The Master's eyes shifted to Celaena's face, then to his son. They were filled with pain. Not for himself, but for Ilias—for his bleeding boy. He looked back to Celaena's face, his sea-green eyes now pleading. *Save my son.*

Ansel took a deep breath and the sword rose in the air, making to slice off the Master's head.

Celaena had a heartbeat to flip the knife in her hands. She cocked her wrist and let it fly.

~

The dagger slammed into Ansel's forearm, exactly where Celaena had aimed. Ansel let out a cry, her fingers splaying. Her father's sword clattered to the ground. Her face went white with shock as she whirled, clutching the bleeding wound, but the expression shifted into something dark and unyielding as she beheld Celaena. Ansel scrambled for her fallen blade.

But Celaena was already running.

Ansel grabbed her sword, dashing back to the Master and lifting it high over her head. She plunged the sword toward the Master's neck.

Celaena managed to tackle her before the blade struck, sending them both crashing to the floor. Cloth and steel and bone, twisting and rolling. She brought her legs up high enough to kick Ansel. The girls split apart, and Celaena was on her feet the moment she stopped moving.

But Ansel was already standing, her sword still in her hands, still between Celaena and the paralyzed Master. The blood from Ansel's arm dripped to the floor.

They panted, and Celaena steadied her reeling head. "Don't do it," she breathed.

Ansel let out a low laugh. "I thought I told you to go home."

Celaena drew the sword from her belt. If only she had a blade like Ansel's, not some bit of scrap metal. It shook in her hands as she realized who, exactly, stood between her and the Master. Not some nameless soldier, not some stranger, or a person she'd been hired to kill. But Ansel.

"Why?" Celaena whispered.

Ansel cocked her head, raising her sword a bit higher. "Why?"

Celaena had never seen anything more hideous than the hate that twisted Ansel's face. "Because Lord Berick promised me a thousand men to march into the Flatlands, that's why. Stealing those horses was exactly the public excuse he needed to attack this fortress. And all I had to do was take care of the guards and leave the gate open last night. And bring him this." She gestured with her sword to the Master behind her. "The Master's head." She ran an eye up and down Celaena's body, and Celaena hated herself for trembling further. "Put down your sword, Celaena."

Celaena didn't move. "Go to hell."

Ansel chuckled. "I've been to hell. I spent some time there when I was twelve, remember? And when I march into the Flatlands with Berick's troops, I'll see to it that High King Loch sees a bit of hell, too. But first . . ."

She turned to the Master and Celaena sucked in a breath. "*Don't,*" Celaena said. From this distance, Ansel would kill him before she could do anything to stop her.

"Just look the other way, Celaena." Ansel stepped closer to the man.

"If you touch him, I'll put this sword through your neck," Celaena snarled. The words shook, and she blinked away the building moisture in her eyes.

Ansel looked over her shoulder. "I don't think you will."

Ansel took another step closer to the Master, and Celaena's second dagger flew. It grazed the side of Ansel's armor, leaving a long mark before it clattered to a stop at the foot of the dais.

Ansel paused, giving Celaena a faint smile. "You missed."

"Don't do it."

"Why?"

Celaena put a hand over her heart, tightly gripping her sword with the other. "Because I know what it feels like." She dared another step. "Because I *know* how it feels to have that kind of hate, Ansel. I know how it feels. And this isn't the way. *This*," she said louder, gesturing to the fortress and all the corpses in it, all the soldiers and assassins still fighting. "This is not the way."

"Says the assassin," Ansel spat.

"I've become an assassin because I had no choice. But *you* have a choice, Ansel. You've always had a choice. Please don't kill him."

Please don't make me kill you was what she truly meant to say.

Ansel shut her eyes. Celaena steadied her wrist, testing the balance of her blade, trying to get a sense of its weight. When Ansel opened her eyes, there was little of the girl she'd grown to care for over the past month.

"These men," Ansel said, her sword rising higher. "These men destroy *everything*."

"I know."

"You know, and yet you do nothing! You're just a dog chained to your master." She closed the distance between them, her sword lowering. Celaena almost sagged with relief, but didn't lighten her grip on her own blade. Ansel's breathing was ragged. "You could come with me." She brushed back a strand of Celaena's hair. "The two of us alone could conquer the Flatlands—and with Lord Berick's troops . . ." Her hand grazed Celaena's cheek, and Celaena tried not to recoil at the touch and at the words that came out of Ansel's mouth. "I would make you my right hand. We'd take the Flatlands back."

"I can't," Celaena answered, even though she could see Ansel's plan with perfect clarity—even if it was tempting.

Ansel stepped back. "What does Rifthold have that's so special? How long will you bow and scrape for that monster?"

"I can't go with you, and you know it. So take your troops and leave, Ansel."

She watched the expressions flitter across Ansel's face. Hurt. Denial. Rage.

"So be it," Ansel said.

She struck, and Celaena only had time to tilt her head to dodge the hidden dagger that shot out of Ansel's wrist. The blade grazed her cheek, and blood warmed her face. Her *face*.

Ansel swiped with her sword, so close that Celaena had to flip herself backward. She landed on her feet, but Ansel was fast and near enough that Celaena could only bring up her blade. Their swords met.

Celaena spun, shoving Ansel's sword from hers. Ansel stumbled, and Celaena used the moment to gain the advantage, striking again and again. Ansel's superior blade was hardly impacted.

They passed the prostrate Master and the dais. Celaena dropped to the ground, swiping at Ansel with a leg. Ansel leapt back, dodging the blow. Celaena used the precious seconds to snatch her fallen dagger from where it lay on the dais steps.

When Ansel struck again, she met the crossed blades of Celaena's sword and dagger.

Ansel let out a low laugh. "How do you imagine this ending?" She pressed Celaena's blades. "Or is it a fight to the death?"

Celaena braced her feet against the floor. She'd never known Ansel was so strong—or so much taller than her. And Ansel's armor—how would she get through *that*? There was a joint between the armpit and the ribs—and then around her neck . . .

"You tell me," Celaena said. The blood from her cheek slid down her throat. "You seem to have everything planned."

"I tried to protect you." Ansel shoved hard against Celaena's blades, but not strongly enough to dislodge them. "And you came back anyway."

"You call that protection? Drugging me and leaving me in the desert?" Celaena bared her teeth.

But before she could launch another assault, Ansel struck with her free hand, right across the X made by their weapons, her fist slamming between Celaena's eyes.

Celaena's head snapped back, the world flashing, and she landed hard on her knees. Her sword and dagger clattered to the floor.

Ansel was on her in a second, her bloodied arm across Celaena's chest, the other hand pressing the edge of her sword against Celaena's unmarred cheek.

"Give me one reason not to kill you right here," Ansel whispered into her ear, kicking away Celaena's sword. Her fallen dagger still lay near them, just out of reach.

Celaena struggled, trying to put some distance between Ansel's sword and her face.

"Oh, how vain can you *be*?" Ansel said, and Celaena winced as the sword dug into her skin. "Afraid I'll scar your face?" Ansel angled the sword downward, the blade now biting into Celaena's throat. "What about your neck?"

"Stop it."

"I didn't want it to end this way between us. I didn't want you to be a part of this."

Celaena believed her. If Ansel wanted to kill her, she would have done it already. If she wanted to kill the Master, she would have done that already, too. And all of this waffling between sadistic hate and passion and regret . . . "You're insane," Celaena said.

Ansel snorted.

"Who killed Mikhail?" Celaena demanded. Anything to keep her talking, to keep her focused on herself. Because just a few feet away lay her dagger . . .

"I did," Ansel said. A little of the fierceness faded from her voice. Her back pressed against Ansel's chest, Celaena couldn't be sure without seeing Ansel's face, but she could have sworn the words were tinged with remorse. "When Berick's men attacked, I made sure that

I was the one who notified the Master; the fool didn't sniff once at the water jug he drank from before he went to the gates. But then Mikhail figured out what I was doing and burst in here—too late to stop the Master from drinking, though. And then Ilias just . . . got in the way."

Celaena looked at Ilias, who still lay on the ground—still breathing. The Master watched his son, his eyes wide and pleading. If someone didn't staunch Ilias's bleeding, he'd die soon. The Master's fingers twitched slightly, making a curving motion.

"How many others did you kill?" Celaena asked, trying to keep Ansel distracted as the Master made the motion again. A kind of slow, strange wriggling . . .

"Only them. And the three on the night watch. I let the soldiers do the rest."

The Master's finger twisted and slithered . . . like a snake.

One strike—that was all it would take. Just like the asp.

Ansel was fast. Celaena had to be faster.

"You know what, Ansel?" Celaena breathed, memorizing the motions she'd have to make in the next few seconds, imagining her muscles moving, praying not to falter, to stay focused.

Ansel pressed the edge of the blade into Celaena's throat. "What, *Celaena*?"

"You want to know what the Master taught me during all those lessons?"

She felt Ansel tense, felt the question distract her. It was all the opportunity she needed.

"This." Celaena twisted, slamming her shoulder into Ansel's torso. Her bones connected against the armor with a jarring thud, and the sword cut into Celaena's neck, but Ansel lost her balance and teetered back. Celaena hit Ansel's fingers so hard they dropped the sword right into Celaena's waiting hand.

In a flash, like a snake turning in on itself, Celaena pinned Ansel facedown on the ground, her father's sword now pressed against the back of her neck.

Celaena hadn't realized how silent the room was until she was kneeling there, one knee holding Ansel to the ground, the other braced on the floor. Blood seeped from where the sword tip rested against Ansel's tan neck, redder than her hair. "Don't do it," Ansel whispered, in that voice that she'd so often heard—that girlish, carefree voice. But had it always been a performance?

Celaena pushed harder and Ansel sucked in a breath, closing her eyes.

Celaena tightened her grip on the sword, willing steel into her veins. Ansel should die; for what she'd done, she deserved to die. And not just for all those assassins lying dead around them, but also for the soldiers who'd spent their lives for her agenda. And for Celaena herself, who, even as she knelt there, felt her heart breaking. Even if she didn't put the sword through Ansel's neck, she'd still lose her. She'd already lost her.

But maybe the world had lost Ansel long before today.

Celaena couldn't stop her lips from trembling as she asked, "Was it ever real?"

Ansel opened an eye, staring at the far wall. "There were some moments when it was. The moment I sent you away, it was real."

Celaena reined in her sob and took a long, steadying breath. Slowly, she lifted the sword from Ansel's neck—only a fraction of an inch.

Ansel made to move, but Celaena pressed the steel against her skin again, and she went still. From outside came cries of victory—and concern—in voices that sounded hoarse from disuse. The assassins had won. How long before they got here? If they saw Ansel, saw what she had done . . . they'd kill her.

"You have five minutes to pack your things and leave the fortress,"

Celaena said quietly. "Because in twenty minutes, I'm going up to the battlements and I'm going to fire an arrow at you. And you'd better hope that you're out of range by then, because if you're not, that arrow is going straight through your neck."

Celaena lifted the sword. Ansel slowly got to her feet, but didn't flee. It took Celaena a heartbeat to realize she was waiting for her father's sword.

Celaena looked at the wolf-shaped hilt and the blood staining the steel. The one tie Ansel had left to her father, her family, and whatever twisted shred of hope burned in her heart.

Celaena turned the blade and handed it hilt-first to Ansel. The girl's eyes were damp as she took the sword. She opened her mouth, but Celaena cut her off. "Go home, Ansel."

Ansel's face went white again. She sheathed the sword at her side. She glanced at Celaena only once before she took off at a sprint, leaping over Mikhail's corpse as if he were nothing more than a bit of debris.

Then she was gone.

CHAPTER 12

Celaena rushed to Ilias, who moaned as she turned him over. The wound in his stomach was still bleeding. She ripped strips from her tunic, which was already soaked with blood, and shouted for help as she bound him tightly.

There was a scrape of cloth on stone, and Celaena looked over her shoulder to see the Master trying to drag himself across the stones to his son. The paralytic must be wearing off.

Five bloodied assassins came rushing up the stairs, eyes wide and faces pale as they beheld Mikhail and Ilias. Celaena left Ilias in their care as she dashed to the Master.

"Don't move," she told him, wincing as blood from her face dripped onto his white clothes. "You might hurt yourself." She scanned the podium for any sign of the poison, and rushed to the fallen bronze goblet. A few sniffs revealed that the wine had been laced with a small amount of gloriella, just enough to paralyze him, not kill him. Ansel must have wanted him completely prone before she killed him—she must have wanted him to *know* she was the one who had betrayed him. To have him conscious while she severed his head. How had he not noticed it before he drank? Perhaps he wasn't as humble as he seemed; perhaps he'd been arrogant enough to believe that he was safe here. "It'll wear off soon," she told the Master, but she still called for an antidote to speed up the process. One of the assassins took off at a run.

She sat by the Master, one hand clutching her bleeding neck. The assassins at the other end of the room carried Ilias out, stopping to reassure the Master that his son would be fine.

Celaena nearly groaned with relief at that, but straightened as a dry, calloused hand wrapped around hers, squeezing faintly. She looked down into the face of the Master, whose eyes shifted to the open door. He was reminding her of the promise she'd made. Ansel had been given twenty minutes to clear firing range.

It was time.

Ansel was already a dark blur in the distance, Hisli galloping as if demons were biting at her hooves. She was heading northwest over the dunes, toward the Singing Sands, to the narrow bridge of feral jungle that separated the Deserted Land from the rest of the continent, and then the open expanse of the Western Wastes beyond them. Toward Briarcliff.

Atop the battlements, Celaena drew an arrow from her quiver and nocked it into her bow.

The bowstring moaned as she pulled it back, farther and farther, her arm straining.

Focusing upon the tiny figure atop the dark horse, Celaena took aim.

In the silence of the fortress, the bowstring twanged like a mournful harp.

~

The arrow soared, turning relentlessly. The red dunes passed beneath in a blur, closing the distance. A sliver of winged darkness edged with steel. A quick, bloody death.

~

Hisli's tail flicked to the side as the arrow buried itself in the sand just inches behind her rear hooves.

But Ansel didn't dare look over her shoulder. She kept riding, and she did not stop.

~

Celaena lowered her bow and watched until Ansel disappeared beyond the horizon. One arrow, that had been her promise.

But she'd also promised Ansel that she had twenty minutes to get out of range.

Celaena had fired after twenty-one.

~

The Master called Celaena to his chamber the following morning. It had been a long night, but Ilias was on the mend, the wound having narrowly missed puncturing any organs. All of Lord Berick's soldiers were dead, and were in the process of being carted back to Xandria as a reminder to Berick to seek the King of Adarlan's approval elsewhere. Twenty assassins had died, and a heavy, mourning silence filled the fortress.

Celaena sat on an ornately carved wooden chair, watching the Master as he stared out the window at the sky. She nearly fell out of her seat when he began speaking.

"I am glad you did not kill Ansel." His voice was raw, and his accent thick with the clipped yet rolling sounds of some language she'd never heard before. "I have been wondering when she would decide what to do with her fate."

"So you knew—"

The Master turned from the window. "I have known for years. Several months after Ansel's arrival, I sent inquiries to the Flatlands. Her family had not written her any letters, and I was worried that something might have happened." He took a seat in a chair across from Celaena. "My messenger returned to me some months later, saying that there was no Briarcliff. The lord and his eldest daughter had been murdered by the High King, and the youngest daughter—Ansel—was missing."

"Why didn't you ever . . . confront her?" Celaena touched the narrow scab on her left cheek. It wouldn't scar if she looked after it properly. And if it *did* scar . . . then maybe she'd hunt down Ansel and return the favor.

"Because I hoped she would eventually trust me enough to tell me. I had to give her that chance, even though it was a risk. I hoped she would learn to face her pain—that she'd learn to endure it." He smiled sadly at Celaena. "If you can learn to endure pain, you can survive anything. Some people learn to embrace it—to love it. Some endure it through drowning it in sorrow, or by making themselves forget. Others turn it into anger. But Ansel let her pain become hate, and let it consume her until she became something else entirely—a person I don't think she ever wished to be."

Celaena absorbed his words, but set them aside for consideration at a later time. "Are you going to tell everyone about what she did?"

"No. I would spare them that anger. Many believed Ansel was their friend—and part of me, too, believes that at times she was."

Celaena looked at the floor, wondering what to do with the ache in her chest. Would turning it into rage, as he said, help her endure it?

"For what it is worth, Celaena," he rasped, "I believe you were the closest thing to a friend Ansel has ever allowed herself to have. And I think she sent you away because she truly cared for you."

She hated her mouth for wobbling. "That doesn't make it hurt any less."

"I didn't think it would. But I think you will leave a lasting imprint on Ansel's heart. You spared her life, and returned her father's sword. She will not soon forget that. And maybe when she makes her next move to reclaim her title, she will remember the assassin from the North and the kindness you showed her, and try to leave fewer bodies in her wake."

He walked to a latticework hutch, as if he were giving her the time to regain her composure, and pulled out a letter. By the time he returned to her, Celaena's eyes were clear. "When you give this to your master, hold your head high."

She took the letter. Her recommendation. It seemed inconsequential in the face of everything that had just happened. "How is it that you're speaking to me now? I thought your vow of silence was eternal."

He shrugged. "The world seems to think so, but as far as my memory serves me, I've never officially sworn to be silent. I choose to be silent most of the time, and I've become so used to it that I often forget I have the capacity for speech, but there are some times when words are necessary—when explanations are needed that mere gestures cannot convey."

She nodded, trying her best to hide her surprise. After a pause, the Master said, "If you ever want to leave the North, you will always have a home here. I promise you the winter months are far better than the summer. And I think my son would be rather happy if you decided to return, too." He chuckled, and Celaena blushed. He took her hand. "When you leave tomorrow, you'll be accompanied by a few of my people."

"Why?"

"Because they will be needed to drive the wagon to Xandria. I know that you are indentured to your master—that you still owe him a good deal of money before you are free to live your own life. He's making you pay back a fortune that he forced you to borrow." He squeezed her hand before approaching one of three trunks pushed against the wall. "For saving my life—and sparing hers." He flipped open the lid of a trunk, then another, and another.

Sunlight gleamed on the gold inside, reflecting through the room like light on water. All that gold . . . and the piece of Spidersilk the merchant had given her . . . she couldn't think of the possibilities that wealth would open to her, not right now.

"When you give your master his letter, also give him this. And tell him that in the Red Desert, we do not abuse our disciples."

Celaena smiled slowly. "I think I can manage that."

She looked to the open window, to the world beyond. For the first time in a long while, she heard the song of a northern wind, calling her home. And she was not afraid.

THE ASSASSIN AND THE UNDERWORLD

Chapter 1

The cavernous entrance hall of the Assassins' Keep was silent as Celaena Sardothien stalked across the marble floor, a letter clutched between her fingers. No one had greeted her at the towering oak doors save the housekeeper, who'd taken her rain-sodden cloak—and, after getting a look at the wicked grin on Celaena's face, opted not to say anything.

The doors to Arobynn Hamel's study lay at the other end of the hall, and were currently shut. But she knew he was in there. Wesley, his bodyguard, stood watch outside, dark eyes unreadable as Celaena strode toward him. Though Wesley wasn't officially an assassin, she had no doubt that he could wield the blades and daggers strapped to his massive body with deadly skill.

She also had no doubt that Arobynn had eyes at every gate in this city. The moment she'd stepped into Rifthold, he'd been alerted that she'd at last returned. She trailed mud from her wet, filthy boots as she made her way toward the study doors—and Wesley.

It had been three months since the night Arobynn had beaten her unconscious—punishment for ruining his slave-trade agreement with the Pirate Lord, Captain Rolfe. It had been three months since he'd shipped her off to the Red Desert to learn obedience and discipline and to earn the approval of the Mute Master of the Silent Assassins.

The letter clutched in her hand was proof that she had done it. Proof that Arobynn hadn't broken her that night.

And she couldn't *wait* to see the look on his face when she gave it to him.

Not to mention when she told him about the three trunks of gold she'd brought with her, which were on their way up to her room at this moment. With a few words, she'd explain that her debt to him was now repaid, that she was going to walk out of the Keep and move into the new apartment she'd purchased. That she was free of him.

Celaena reached the other end of the hall, and Wesley stepped in front of the study doors. He looked about five years younger than Arobynn, and the slender scars on his face and hands suggested that the life he'd spent serving the King of the Assassins hadn't been easy. She suspected there were more scars beneath his dark clothing—perhaps brutal ones.

"He's busy," said Wesley, his hands hanging loosely at his sides, ready to reach for his weapons. She might be Arobynn's protégée, but Wesley had always made it clear that if she became a threat to his master, he wouldn't hesitate to end her. She didn't need to see him in action to know he'd be an interesting opponent. She supposed that was why he did his training in private—and kept his personal history a secret, too. The less she knew about him, the more advantage Wesley would have if that fight ever came. Clever, and flattering, she supposed.

"Nice to see you, too, Wesley," she said, flashing him a smile. He tensed, but didn't stop her as she strode past him and flung open the doors of Arobynn's study.

The King of the Assassins was seated at his ornate desk, poring over the stack of papers before him. Without so much as a hello, Celaena strode right up to the desk and tossed the letter onto the shining wooden surface.

She opened her mouth, the words near-bursting out of her. But Arobynn merely lifted a finger, smiling faintly, and returned to his papers. Wesley shut the doors behind her.

Celaena froze. Arobynn flipped the page, rapidly scanning whatever document was in front of him, and made a vague wave with his hand. *Sit.*

With his attention still on the document he was reading, Arobynn picked up the Mute Master's letter of approval and set it atop a nearby stack of papers. Celaena blinked. Once. Twice. He didn't look up at her. He just kept reading. The message was clear enough: she was to wait until *he* was ready. And until then, even if she screamed until her lungs burst, he wouldn't acknowledge her existence.

So Celaena sat down.

Rain plinked against the windows of the study. Seconds passed, then minutes. Her plans for a grand speech with sweeping gestures faded into silence. Arobynn read three other documents before he even picked up the Mute Master's letter.

And as he read it, she could only think of the last time she'd sat in this chair.

She looked at the exquisite red carpet beneath her feet. Someone had done a splendid job of getting all the blood out. How much of the blood on the carpet had been hers—and how much of it had belonged to Sam Cortland, her rival and coconspirator in the destruction of Arobynn's slave agreement? She still didn't know what Arobynn had done to him that night. When she'd arrived just now, she hadn't seen Sam in the entrance hall. But then again, she hadn't seen any of the other assassins who lived here. So maybe Sam was busy. She *hoped* he was busy, because that would mean he was alive.

Arobynn finally looked at her, setting aside the Mute Master's letter as if it were nothing more than a scrap of paper. She kept her back straight and her chin upheld, even as Arobynn's silver eyes scanned every inch of her. They lingered the longest on the narrow pink scar across the side of her neck, inches away from her jaw and ear. "Well," Arobynn said at last, "I thought you'd be tanner."

She almost laughed, but she kept a tight rein on her features. "Head-to-toe clothes to avoid the sun," she explained. Her words were quieter—weaker—than she wanted. The first words she'd spoken to him since he'd beaten her into oblivion. They weren't exactly satisfying.

"Ah," he said, his long, elegant fingers twisting a golden ring around his forefinger.

She sucked in a breath through her nose, remembering all that she'd been burning to say to him these past few months and during the journey back to Rifthold. A few sentences, and it would be over. More than eight years with him, finished with a string of words and a mountain of gold.

She braced herself to begin, but Arobynn spoke first.

"I'm sorry," he said.

Yet again, the words vanished from her lips.

His eyes were intent on hers, and he stopped toying with his ring. "If I could take back that night, Celaena, I would." He leaned over the edge of the desk, his hands now forming fists. The last time she'd seen those hands, they'd been smeared with her blood.

"I'm sorry," Arobynn repeated. He was nearly twenty years her senior, and though his red hair had a few strands of silver, his face remained young. Elegant, sharp features, blazingly clear gray eyes . . . He might not have been the handsomest man she'd ever seen, but he was one of the most alluring.

"Every day," he went on. "Every day since you left, I've gone to the temple of Kiva to pray for forgiveness." She might have snorted at the idea of the King of the Assassins kneeling before a statue of the God of Atonement, but his words were so raw. Was it possible that he actually regretted what he had done?

"I shouldn't have let my temper get the better of me. I shouldn't have sent you away."

"Then why didn't you retrieve me?" It was out before she had a chance to control the snap in her voice.

Arobynn's eyes narrowed slightly, as close to a wince as he'd let himself come, she supposed. "With the time it'd take for the messengers to track you down, you probably would have been on your way home, anyway."

She clenched her jaw. An easy excuse.

He read the ire in her eyes—and her disbelief. "Allow me to make it up to you." He rose from his leather chair and strode around the desk. His long legs and years of training made his movements effortlessly graceful, even as he swiped a box off the edge of the table. He sank to one knee before her, his face near level with hers. She'd forgotten how tall he was.

He extended the gift to her. The box in itself was a work of art, inlaid with mother-of-pearl, but she kept her face blank as she flipped open the lid.

An emerald-and-gold brooch glittered in the gray afternoon light. It was stunning, the work of a master craftsman—and she instantly knew what dresses and tunics it would best complement. He'd bought it because he also knew her wardrobe, her tastes, everything about her. Of all the people in the world, only Arobynn knew the absolute truth.

"For you," he said. "The first of many." She was keenly aware of each of his movements, and braced herself as he lifted a hand, carefully bringing it to her face. He brushed a finger from her temple down to the arc of her cheekbones. "I'm sorry," he whispered again, and Celaena raised her eyes to his.

Father, brother, lover—he'd never really declared himself any of them. Certainly not the lover part, though if Celaena had been another sort of girl, and if Arobynn had raised her differently, perhaps it might have come to that. He loved her like family, yet he put her in the most dangerous positions. He nurtured and educated her, yet he'd obliterated her innocence the first time he'd made her end a life. He'd given her everything, but he'd also taken everything away. She could no sooner sort out her feelings toward the King of the Assassins than she could count the stars in the sky.

Celaena turned her face away, and Arobynn rose to his feet. He leaned against the edge of the desk, smiling faintly at her. "I've another gift, if you'd like it."

All those months of daydreaming about leaving, about paying off her debts . . . Why couldn't she open her mouth and just *tell* him?

"Benzo Doneval is coming to Rifthold," Arobynn said. Celaena cocked her head. She'd heard of Doneval—he was an immensely powerful businessman from Melisande, a country far to the southwest, and one of Adarlan's newer conquests.

"Why?" she asked quietly—carefully.

Arobynn's eyes glittered. "He's a part of a large convoy that Leighfer Bardingale is leading to the capital. Leighfer is good friends with the former Queen of Melisande, who asked her to come here to plead their case before the King of Adarlan." Melisande, Celaena recalled, was one of the few kingdoms whose royal family had not been executed. Instead, they'd handed over their crowns and sworn loyalty to the King of Adarlan and his conquering legions. She couldn't tell what was worse: a quick beheading, or yielding to the king.

"Apparently," Arobynn went on, "the convoy will attempt to

demonstrate all that Melisande has to offer—culture, goods, wealth—in order to convince the king to grant them the permission and resources required to build a road. Given that the young Queen of Melisande is now a mere figurehead, I'll admit that I'm impressed by her ambition—and her brazenness in asking the king."

Celaena bit her lip, visualizing the map of their continent. "A road to connect Melisande to Fenharrow and Adarlan?" For years, trade with Melisande had been tricky due to its location. Bordered by near-impassable mountains and the Oakwald Forest, most of their trade had been reduced to whatever they could get out of their ports. A road might change all of that. A road could make Melisande rich—and influential.

Arobynn nodded. "The convoy will be here for a week, and they have parties and markets planned, including a gala three days from now to celebrate the Harvest Moon. Perhaps if the citizens of Rifthold fall in love with their goods, then the king will take their case seriously."

"So what does Doneval have to do with the road?"

Arobynn shrugged. "He's here to discuss business arrangements in Rifthold. And probably also to undermine his former wife, Leighfer. And to complete one very specific piece of business that made Leighfer want to dispatch him."

Celaena's brows rose. *A gift*, Arobynn had said.

"Doneval is traveling with some very sensitive documents," Arobynn said so quietly that the rain lashing the window nearly drowned out his words. "Not only would you need to dispatch him, but you'd also be asked to retrieve the documents."

"What sort of documents?"

His silver eyes brightened. "Doneval wants to set up a slave-trade business between himself and someone in Rifthold. If the road is approved and built, he wants to be the first in Melisande to profit off the import and export of slaves. The documents, apparently, contain proof that certain influential Melisanders in Adarlan are opposed to the slave trade. Considering the lengths the King of Adarlan has already gone to punish those who speak against his policies . . . Well, knowing who stands against him regarding the slaves—especially when it seems like they're taking steps to *help* free the slaves from his grasp—is information that the king would be *extremely* interested in learning. Doneval and his new business partner in Rifthold plan to use that list to blackmail those people into changing their minds—into stopping their resistance and investing with him to build the slave trade in Melisande. Or, if they refuse, Leighfer believes her former husband will make sure the king gets that list of names."

Celaena swallowed hard. Was this a peace offering, then? Some indication that Arobynn actually had changed his mind about the slave trade and forgiven her for Skull's Bay?

But to get tangled up in this sort of thing again . . . "What's Bardingale's stake in this?" she asked carefully. "Why hire us to kill him?"

"Because Leighfer doesn't believe in slavery, and she wants to protect the people on that list—people who are preparing to take the necessary steps to soften the blow of slavery in Melisande. And possibly even smuggle captured slaves to safety." Arobynn spoke like he knew Bardingale personally—like they were more than business partners.

"And Doneval's partner in Rifthold? Who is it?" She had to consider all the angles before she accepted, had to think it through.

"Leighfer doesn't know; her sources haven't been able to find a name in Doneval's coded correspondences with his partner. All she's gleaned is that Doneval will exchange the documents with his new business partner six days from now at his rented house, at some point in the day. She's uncertain what documents his partner is bringing to the table, but she's betting that it includes a list of important people opposed to slavery in Adarlan. Leighfer says Doneval will probably have a private room in his house to do the swap—perhaps an upstairs study or something of the sort. She knows him well enough to guarantee that."

She was beginning to see where this was going. Doneval was practically wrapped in a ribbon for her. All she had to do was find out what time the meeting would take place, learn his defenses, and figure out a way around them. "So I'm not only to take out Doneval, but also to wait until he's done the exchange so I can get his documents *and* whatever documents his partner brings to the table?" Arobynn smiled slightly. "What about his partner? Am I to dispatch this person as well?"

Arobynn's smile became a thin line. "Since we don't know who he'll be dealing with, you haven't been contracted to eliminate them. But, it's been strongly hinted that Leighfer and her allies want the contact dead as well. They might give you a bonus for it."

She studied the emerald brooch in her lap. "And how well will this pay?"

"Extraordinarily well." She heard the smile in his voice, but kept her attention on the lovely green jewel. "And I won't take a cut of it. It's all yours."

She raised her head at that. There was a glimmer of pleading in his eyes. Perhaps he truly was sorry for what he'd done. And perhaps he'd picked this mission just for her—to prove, in his way, that he understood why she'd freed those slaves in Skull's Bay. "I can assume Doneval is well-guarded?"

"Very," Arobynn said, fishing a letter from the desk behind him. "He's waiting to do the deal until after the citywide celebrations, so he can run home the next day."

Celaena glanced toward the ceiling, as if she could see through the wood beams and into her room on the floor above, where her trunks of gold now sat. She didn't *need* the money, but if she were going to pay off her debt to Arobynn, her funds would be severely depleted. And to take this mission wouldn't just be about killing—it would be about helping others, too. How many lives would be destroyed if she didn't dispatch Doneval and his partner and retrieve those sensitive documents?

Arobynn approached her again, and she rose from her chair. He brushed her hair back from her face. "I missed you," he said.

He opened his arms to her, but didn't make a further move to embrace her. She studied his face. The Mute Master had told her that people dealt with their pain in different ways—that some chose to drown it, some chose to love it, and some chose to let it turn into rage. While she had no regrets about freeing those two hundred slaves from Skull's Bay, she had betrayed Arobynn in doing it. Perhaps hurting her had been his way of coping with the pain of that.

And even though there was no excuse in this world for what he had done, Arobynn was all she had. The history that lay between them, dark and twisted and full of secrets, was forged by more than just gold. And if she left him, if she paid off her debts right now and never saw him again . . .

She took a step back, and Arobynn casually lowered his arms, not at all fazed by her rejection. "I'll think about taking on Doneval." It wasn't a lie. She always took time to consider her missions—Arobynn had encouraged that from the start.

"I'm sorry," he said again.

Celaena gave him another long look before she left.

Her exhaustion hit her the moment she began climbing the polished marble steps of the sweeping grand staircase. A month of hard travel—after a month of grueling training and heartache. Every time she saw the scar on her neck, or touched it, or felt her clothes brush against it, a tremor of pain went through her as she remembered the betrayal that had caused it. She'd believed Ansel was her friend—a life-friend, a friend of the heart. But Ansel's need for revenge had been greater than anything else. Still, wherever Ansel now was, Celaena hoped that she was finally facing what had haunted her for so long.

A passing servant bowed his head, eyes averted. Everyone who worked here knew more or less who she was, and would keep her identity secret on pain of death. Not that there was much of a point to it now, given that every single one of the Silent Assassins could identify her.

Celaena took a ragged breath, running a hand through her hair. Before entering the city this morning, she'd stopped at a tavern just outside Rifthold to bathe, to wash her filthy clothes, to put on some cosmetics. She hadn't wanted to stride into the Keep looking like a gutter rat. But she still felt *dirty*.

She passed one of the upstairs drawing rooms, her brows rising at the sound of a pianoforte and laughing people inside. If Arobynn had company, then why had he been in his study, *ever so busy*, when she arrived?

Celaena ground her teeth. So that nonsense where he'd made her wait while he finished his work . . .

She clenched her hands into fists and was about to whirl and stomp back down the stairs to tell Arobynn that she was leaving and that he no longer owned her, when someone stepped into the elegantly appointed hall.

Sam Cortland.

Sam's brown eyes were wide, his body rigid. As if it took some effort on his part, he shut the door to the hall washroom and strode toward her, past the teal velvet curtains hanging on the floor-to-ceiling windows, past the framed artwork, closer and closer. She remained still, taking in every inch of him before he stopped a few feet away.

No missing limbs, no limp, no indication of anything haunting him. His chestnut hair had gotten a little longer, but it suited him. And he was tan—gloriously tan, as if he'd spent the whole summer basking in the sun. Hadn't Arobynn punished him at all?

"You're back," Sam said, as if he couldn't quite believe it.

She lifted her chin, stuffing her hands in her pockets. "Obviously."

He tilted his head slightly to the side. "How was the desert?"

There wasn't a scratch on him. Of course, her face had healed, too, but . . . "Hot," she said. Sam let out a breathy chuckle.

It wasn't that she was *mad* at him for being uninjured. She was so relieved she could have vomited, actually. She just never imagined that seeing him today would feel so . . . strange. And after what had happened with Ansel, could she honestly say that she trusted him?

In the drawing room a few doors down, a woman let out a shrill giggle. How was it possible that she could have so many questions and yet so little to say?

Sam's eyes slipped from her face to her neck, his brows drawing together for a heartbeat as he saw the thin new scar. "What happened?"

"Someone held a sword to my throat."

His eyes darkened, but she didn't want to explain the long, miserable story. She didn't want to talk about Ansel, and she certainly didn't want to talk about what had happened with Arobynn that night they'd returned from Skull's Bay.

"Are you hurt?" Sam asked quietly, taking another step closer.

It took her a moment to realize that his imagination had probably taken him to a far, far worse place when she said someone had held a blade to her throat.

"No," she said. "No, not like that."

"Then like what?" He was now looking more closely at her, at the almost invisible white line along her cheek—another gift from Ansel—at her hands, at everything. His lean, muscled body tensed. His chest had gotten broader, too.

"Like none of your business, that's what," she retorted.

"Tell me what happened," he gritted out.

She gave him one of those simpering little smiles that she knew he hated. Things hadn't been bad between them since Skull's Bay, but after so many years of treating him awfully, she didn't know how to slide back into that newfound respect and camaraderie they'd discovered for each other. "Why should I tell you anything?"

"Because," he hissed, taking another step, "the last time I saw you, Celaena, you were unconscious on Arobynn's carpet and so bloodied up that I couldn't see your damn face."

He was close enough that she could touch him now. Rain continued beating against the hall windows, a distant reminder that there was still a world around them. "Tell me," he said.

I'll kill you! Sam had screamed it at Arobynn as the King of the Assassins beat her. He'd roared it. In those horrible minutes, whatever bond had sprung up between her and Sam hadn't broken. He'd switched loyalties—he'd chosen to stand by her, fight for *her*. If anything, *that* made him different from Ansel. Sam could have hurt or betrayed her a dozen times over, but he'd never jumped at the opportunity.

A half smile tugged at a corner of her lips. She'd missed him. Seeing the expression on her face, he gave her a bewildered sort of grin. She swallowed, feeling the words bubbling up through her—*I missed you*—but the door to the drawing room opened.

"Sam!" a dark-haired, green-eyed young woman chided, laughter on her lips. "There you—" The girl's eyes met Celaena's. Celaena stopped smiling as she recognized her.

A feline sort of smirk spread across the young woman's stunning features, and she slipped out of the doorway and slunk over to them. Celaena took in each swish of her hips, the elegant angle of her hand, the exquisite dress that dipped low enough to reveal her generous bosom. "Celaena," she cooed, and Sam eyed the two girls warily as she stopped beside him. Too close beside him for a casual acquaintance.

"Lysandra," Celaena echoed. She'd met Lysandra when they were both ten, and in the seven years that they'd known each other, Celaena couldn't recall a time when she didn't want to beat in the girl's face with a brick. Or throw her out a window. Or do any of a number of things she'd learned from Arobynn.

It didn't help that Arobynn had spent a good deal of money assisting Lysandra in her rise from street orphan to one of the most anticipated courtesans in Rifthold's history. He was good friends with Lysandra's madam—and had been Lysandra's doting benefactor for years. Lysandra and her madam remained the only courtesans aware that the girl Arobynn called his "niece" was actually his protégée. Celaena had never learned why Arobynn had told them, but whenever she complained about the risk of Lysandra revealing her identity, he seemed certain she would not. Celaena, not surprisingly, had trouble believing it; but perhaps threats from the King of the Assassins were enough to keep even the loud-mouthed Lysandra silent.

"I thought you'd been packed off to the desert," Lysandra said, running a shrewd eye over Celaena's clothes. Thank the Wyrd she'd bothered to change at that tavern. "Is it possible the summer passed *that* quickly? I guess when you're having so much fun . . ."

A deadly, vicious sort of calm filled Celaena's veins. She'd snapped once at Lysandra—when they were thirteen and Lysandra had snatched a lovely lace fan right out of Celaena's hands. The ensuing fight had sent them tumbling down a flight of stairs. Celaena had spent a night in the Keep's dungeon for the welts she'd left on Lysandra's face by beating her with the fan itself.

She tried to ignore how close the girl stood to Sam. He'd always been kind to the courtesans, and they all adored him. His mother had been one of them, and had asked Arobynn—a patron of hers—to look after her son. Sam had only been six when she was murdered by a jealous client. Celaena crossed her arms. "Should I bother to ask what you're doing here?"

Lysandra gave her a knowing smile. "Oh, Arobynn"—she purred his name like they were the most intimate of friends—"threw me a luncheon in honor of my upcoming Bidding."

Of course he did. "He invited your future clients here?"

"Oh, no." Lysandra giggled. "This is just for me and the girls. And Clarisse, of course." She used her madam's name, too, like a weapon, a word meant to crush and dominate—a word that whispered: *I am more important than you; I have more influence than you; I am everything and you are nothing.*

"Lovely," Celaena replied. Sam still hadn't said anything.

Lysandra lifted her chin, looking down her delicately freckled nose at Celaena. "My Bidding is in six days. They expect me to break all the records."

Celaena had seen a few young courtesans go through the Bidding process—girls trained until they were seventeen, when their virginity was sold to the highest bidder.

"Sam," Lysandra went on, putting a slender hand on his arm, "has been *so* helpful with making sure all the preparations are ready for my Bidding party."

Celaena was surprised at the swiftness of her desire to rip that hand right off Lysandra's wrist. Just because he sympathized with the courtesans didn't mean he had to be so . . . friendly with them.

Sam cleared his throat, straightening. "Not that helpful. Arobynn wanted to make sure that the vendors and location were secure."

"Important clientele *must* be given the best treatment," Lysandra trilled. "I *do* wish I could tell you who will be in attendance, but

Clarisse would kill me. It's extraordinarily hush-hush and need-to-know."

It was enough. One more word out of the courtesan's mouth, and Celaena was fairly certain she'd punch Lysandra's teeth down her throat. Celaena angled her head, her fingers curling into a fist. Sam saw the familiar gesture and pried Lysandra's hand off his arm. "Go back to the luncheon," he told her.

Lysandra gave Celaena another one of those smiles, which she then turned on Sam. "When are you coming back in?" Her full, red lips formed a pout.

Enough, enough, *enough.*

Celaena turned on her heel. "Enjoy your quality company," she said over her shoulder.

"Celaena," Sam said.

But she wouldn't turn around, not even when she heard Lysandra giggle and whisper something, not even when all she wanted in the entire world was to grab her dagger and *throw*, as hard as she could, right toward Lysandra's impossibly beautiful face.

She'd always hated Lysandra, she told herself. *Always* hated her. Her touching Sam like that, *speaking* to Sam like that, it didn't change things. But . . .

Though Lysandra's virginity was unquestionable—it *had* to be—there were plenty of other things that she could still do. Things that she might have done with Sam . . .

Feeling sick and furious and small, Celaena reached her bedroom and slammed the door hard enough to rattle the rain-splattered windows.

CHAPTER 2

The rain didn't stop the next day, and Celaena awoke to a grumble of thunder and a servant setting a long, beautifully wrapped box on her dresser. She opened the gift as she drank her morning cup of tea, taking her time with the turquoise ribbon, doing her best to pretend that she wasn't *that* interested in what Arobynn had sent her. None of these presents came close to earning any sort of forgiveness. But she couldn't contain her squeal when she opened the box and found two gold hair combs glinting at her. They were exquisite, formed like sharp fish fins, each point accentuated with a sliver of sapphire.

She nearly upset her breakfast tray as she rushed from the table by the window to the rosewood vanity. With deft hands, she dragged one of the combs through her hair, sweeping it back before she nimbly flipped it into place. She quickly repeated it on the other side of her head, and when she had finished, she beamed at her reflection. Exotic, beguiling, imperious.

Arobynn might be a bastard, and he might associate with Lysandra, but he had damn good taste. Oh, it was so *nice* to be back in civilization, with her beautiful clothes and shoes and jewels and cosmetics and all the luxuries she'd had to spend the summer without!

Celaena examined the ends of her hair and frowned. The frown deepened when her attention shifted to her hands—to her shredded cuticles and jagged nails. She let out a low hiss, facing the windows along one wall of her ornate bedroom. It was early autumn—that meant rain usually hung around Rifthold for a good couple of weeks.

Through the low-hanging clouds and the slashing rain, she could see the rest of the capital city gleaming in the gray light. Pale stone houses stood tucked together, linked by broad avenues that stretched from the alabaster walls to the docks along the eastern quarter of the city, from the teeming city center to the jumble of crumbling buildings in the slums at the southern edge, where the Avery River curved inland. Even the emerald roofs on each building seemed cast in silver. The glass castle towered over them all, its upper turrets shrouded in mist.

The convoy from Melisande couldn't have picked a worse time to visit. If they wanted to have street festivals, they'd find few participants willing to brave the merciless downpour.

Celaena slowly removed the combs from her hair. The convoy would arrive today, Arobynn had told her last night over a private dinner. She still hadn't given him an answer about whether she'd take down Doneval in five days, and he hadn't pushed her about it. He had been kind and gracious, serving her food himself, speaking softly to her like she was some frightened pet.

She glanced again at her hair and nails. A very unkempt, wild-looking pet.

She strode into her dressing room. She'd decide what to do about

Doneval and his agenda later. For now, not even the rain would keep her from a little pampering.

The shop she favored for her upkeep was ecstatic to see her—and utterly horrified at the state of her hair. And nails. *And her eyebrows! She couldn't have bothered to pluck her eyebrows while she was away?* Half a day later—her hair cut and shining, her nails soft and gleaming—Celaena braved the sodden city streets.

Even with the rain, people found excuses to be out and about as the giant convoy from Melisande arrived. She paused beneath the awning of a flower shop where the owner was standing on the threshold to watch the grand procession. The Melisanders snaked along the broad avenue that stretched from the western gate of the city all the way to the castle doors.

There were the usual jugglers and fire-eaters, whose jobs were made infinitely harder by the confounded rain; the dance girls whose billowing pants were sodden up to the knees; and then the line of Very Important, Very Wealthy People, who were bundled under cloaks and didn't sit quite as tall as they'd probably imagined they would.

Celaena tucked her numbed fingers into her tunic pockets. Brightly painted covered wagons ambled past. Their hatches had all been shut against the weather—and that meant Celaena would start back to the Keep immediately.

Melisande was known for its tinkerers, for clever hands that created clever little devices. Clockwork so fine you could swear it was alive, musical instruments so clear and lovely they could shatter your heart, toys so charming you'd believe magic hadn't vanished from the continent. If the wagons that contained those things were shut, then she had no interest in watching a parade of soaked, miserable people.

Crowds were still flocking toward the main avenue, so Celaena took to narrow, winding alleys to avoid them. She wondered if Sam was making his way to see the procession—and if Lysandra was with him. So much for Sam's unwavering loyalty. How long had it taken after she'd gone to the desert before he and Lysandra had become dear, *dear* friends?

Things had been better when she relished the thought of gutting him. Apparently, Sam was just as susceptible to a pretty face as Arobynn was. She didn't know why she'd thought he would be different. She scowled and walked faster, her freezing arms crossed over her chest as she hunched her shoulders against the rain.

Twenty minutes later, she was dripping water all over the marble floor of the Keep's entranceway. And one minute after that, she was dripping water all over Arobynn's study carpet as she told him that she would take on Doneval, his slave-trade blackmail documents, and whoever his co-conspirator might be.

The next morning, Celaena looked down at herself, her mouth caught between a smile and a frown. The neck-to-toe black outfit was all made from the same, dark fabric—as thick as leather, but without the sheen. It was like a suit of armor, only skintight and made from some strange cloth, not metal. She could feel the weight of her weapons where they were concealed—so neatly that even someone patting her down might think they were merely ribbing—and she swung her arms experimentally.

"Careful," the short man in front of her said, his eyes wide. "You might take off my head."

Behind them, Arobynn chuckled from where he leaned against the paneled wall of the training room. She hadn't asked questions when he'd summoned her, then told her to put on the black suit and matching boots that were lined with fleece.

"When you want to unsheathe the blades," the inventor said, taking a large step back, "it's a downward sweep, and an extra flick of the wrist." He demonstrated the motion with his own scrawny arm, and Celaena echoed it.

She grinned as a narrow blade shot out of a concealed flap in her forearm. Permanently attached to the suit, it was like having a short sword welded to her arm. She made the same motion with the other wrist, and the twin blade appeared. Some internal mechanism had to be responsible for it—some brilliant contraption of springs and gears. She gave a few deadly swings in the air in front of her, reveling in the *whoosh-whoosh-whoosh* of the swords. They were finely made, too. She raised her brows in admiration. "How do they go back?"

"Ah, a little more difficult," the inventor said. "Wrist angled up, and press this little button here. It should trigger the mechanism—there you go." She watched the blade slide back into the suit, then released and returned the blade several times.

The deal with Doneval and his partner was in four days, just long enough for her to try using the new suit. Four days was plenty to figure out his house's defenses and learn what time the meeting would take place, especially since she already knew that it was occurring in some private study.

At last she looked at Arobynn. "How much is it?"

He pushed off the wall. "It's a gift. As are the boots." She knocked a toe against the tiled floor, feeling the jagged edges and grooves of the soles. Perfect for climbing. The sheepskin interior would keep her feet at body temperature, the inventor had said, even if she got them utterly soaked. She'd never even *heard* of a suit like this. It would completely change the way she conducted her missions. Not that she needed the suit to give her an edge. But she was Celaena Sardothien, gods be damned, so didn't she deserve the very best equipment? With this suit, no one would question her place as Adarlan's Assassin. Ever. And if they did . . . Wyrd help them.

The inventor asked to take her final measurements, though the ones Arobynn had supplied were almost perfect. She lifted her arms out as he did the measuring, asking him bland questions about his trip from Melisande and what he planned to sell here. He was a master tinkerer, he said—and specialized in crafting things that were believed to be impossible. Like a suit that was both armor *and* an armory, and lightweight enough to wear comfortably.

Celaena looked over her shoulder at Arobynn, who had watched her interrogation with a bemused smile. "Are you getting one made?"

"Of course. And Sam, too. Only the best for my best." She noticed that he didn't say "assassin"—but whatever the tinkerer thought about who they were, his face yielded no sign.

She couldn't hide her surprise. "You never give Sam gifts."

Arobynn shrugged, picking at his nails. "Oh, Sam will be paying for the suit. I can't have my second-best completely vulnerable, can I?"

She hid her shock better this time. A suit like this had to cost a small fortune. Materials aside, just the hours it must have taken the tinkerer to create it . . . Arobynn had to have commissioned them immediately after he'd sent her to the Red Desert. Perhaps he truly felt bad about what happened. But to force Sam to buy it . . .

The clock chimed eleven, and Arobynn let out a long breath. "I have a meeting." He waved a ringed hand to the tinkerer. "Give the bill to my manservant when you're done." The master tinkerer nodded, still measuring Celaena.

Arobynn approached her, each step as graceful as a movement of a dance. He planted a kiss on the top of her head. "I'm glad to have you back," he murmured onto her hair. With that, he strolled from the room, whistling to himself.

The tinkerer knelt to measure the length between her knee and boot tip, for whatever purpose that had. Celaena cleared her throat, waiting until she was sure Arobynn was out of earshot. "If I were to give you a piece of Spidersilk, could you incorporate it into one of these uniforms? It's small, so I'd just want it placed around the heart." She used her hands to show the size of the material that she'd been given by the merchant in the desert city of Xandria.

Spidersilk was a near-mythical material made by horse-sized stygian spiders—so rare that you had to brave the spiders yourself to get it. And they didn't trade in gold. No, they coveted things like dreams and memories and souls. The merchant she'd met had traded twenty years of his youth for a hundred yards of it. And after a long, strange conversation with him, he'd given her a few square inches of Spidersilk. *A reminder*, he'd said. *That everything has a price.*

The master tinkerer's bushy brows rose. "I—I suppose. To the interior or the exterior? I think the interior," he went on, answering his own question. "If I sewed it to the exterior, the iridescence might ruin the stealth of the black. But it'd turn any blade, and it's just barely the right size to shield the heart. Oh, what I'd give for ten yards of Spidersilk! You'd be invincible, my dear."

She smiled slowly. "As long as it guards the heart."

~

She left the tinkerer in the hall. Her suit would be ready the day after tomorrow.

It didn't surprise her when she ran into Sam on her way out. She'd spotted the dummy that bore his own suit waiting for him in the training hall. Alone with her in the hallway, he examined her suit. She still had to change out of it and bring it back downstairs to the tinkerer so he could make his final adjustments in whatever shop he'd set up while he was staying in Rifthold.

"Fancy," Sam said. She made to put her hands on her hips, but stopped. Until she mastered the suit, she had to watch how she moved—or else she might skewer someone. "Another gift?"

"Is there a problem if it is?"

She hadn't seen Sam at all yesterday, but, then again, she'd also made herself pretty scarce. It wasn't that she was avoiding him; she just didn't particularly want to see him if it meant running into Lysandra, too. But it seemed strange that he wasn't on any mission. Most of the other assassins were away on various jobs or so busy they were hardly at home. But Sam seemed to be hanging around the Keep, or helping Lysandra and her madam.

Sam crossed his arms. His white shirt was tight enough that she could see the muscles shifting beneath. "Not at all. Though I'm a little surprised that you're accepting his gifts. How can you forgive him after what he did?"

"Forgive him! I'm not the one cavorting with Lysandra and attending luncheons and doing . . . doing whatever in hell it is you spent the summer doing!"

Sam let out a low growl. "You think I actually enjoy any of that?"

"You weren't the one sent off to the Red Desert."

"Believe me, I would rather have been thousands of miles away."

"I *don't* believe you. How can I believe anything you say?"

His brows furrowed. "What are you *talking* about?"

"Nothing. None of your business. I don't want to talk about this. And I don't particularly want to talk to *you*, Sam Cortland."

"Then go ahead," he breathed. "Go crawl back to Arobynn's study and talk to *him*. Let him buy you presents and pet your hair and offer you the best-paying missions we get. It won't take him long to figure out the price for your forgiveness, not when—"

She shoved him. "Don't you *dare* judge me. Don't you say one more word."

A muscle feathered in his jaw. "That's fine with me. You wouldn't listen anyway. Celaena Sardothien and Arobynn Hamel: just the two of you, inseparable, until the end of the world. The rest of us might as well be invisible."

"That sounds an awful lot like jealousy. Especially considering you had three uninterrupted months with him this summer. What happened, hmm? You failed to convince him to make *you* his favorite? Found you lacking, did he?"

Sam was in her face so quickly that she fought the urge to jump back. "You know *nothing* about what this summer was like for me. *Nothing*, Celaena."

"Good. I don't particularly care."

His eyes were so wide that she wondered if she'd struck him without realizing it. At last he stepped away, and she stormed past him. She halted when he spoke again. "You want to know what price I asked for forgiving Arobynn, Celaena?"

She slowly turned. With the ongoing rain, the hall was full of shadows and light. Sam stood so still that he might have been a statue. "My price was his oath that he'd never lay a hand on you again. I told him I'd forgive him in exchange for that."

She wished he'd punched her in the gut. It would have hurt less. Not trusting herself to keep from falling to her knees with shame right there, she just stalked down the hall.

She didn't want to speak to Sam ever again. How could she look him in the eye? He'd made Arobynn swear that *for her*. She didn't know what words could convey the mixture of gratitude and guilt. Hating him had been so much easier . . . And it would have been far simpler if he'd blamed her for Arobynn's punishment. She had said such cruel things to him in the hallway; how could she ever begin to apologize?

Arobynn came to her room after lunch and told her to have a dress pressed. Doneval, he'd heard, was going to be at the theater that night, and with four days until his exchange, it would be in her best interest to go.

She'd formulated a plan for stalking Doneval, but she wasn't proud enough to refuse Arobynn's offer to use his box at the theater for spying—to see who Doneval spoke to, who sat near him, who guarded him. And to see a classical dance performed with a full orchestra . . . well, she'd never turn that down. But Arobynn failed to say who would be joining them.

She found out the hard way when she climbed into Arobynn's carriage and discovered Lysandra and Sam waiting inside. With four days until her Bidding, the young courtesan needed all the exposure she could get, Arobynn calmly explained. And Sam was there to provide additional security.

Celaena dared a glance at Sam as she slumped onto the bench beside him. He watched her, his eyes wary, shoulders tensed, as if he expected her to launch a verbal attack right there. Like she'd mock him for what he'd done. Did he really think she was that cruel? Feeling a bit sick, she dropped Sam's stare. Lysandra just smiled at Celaena from across the carriage and linked her elbow through Arobynn's.

Chapter 3

Two attendants greeted them at Arobynn's private box, taking their sodden cloaks and exchanging them for glasses of sparkling wine. Immediately, one of Arobynn's acquaintances popped in from the hall to say hello, and Arobynn, Sam, and Lysandra remained in the velvet-lined antechamber as they chatted. Celaena, who had no interest in seeing Lysandra test out her flirting with Arobynn's friend, strode through the crimson curtain to take her usual seat closest to the stage.

Arobynn's box was on the side of the cavernous hall, near enough to the center so that she had a mostly unobstructed view of the stage and the orchestra pit, but still angled enough to make her look longingly at the empty Royal Boxes. All of them occupied the coveted center position, and all of them were vacant. What a waste.

She observed the floor seats and the other boxes, taking in the glittering jewels, the silk dresses, the golden glow of sparkling wine in fluted glasses, the rumbling murmur of the mingling crowd. If there was one place where she felt the most at home, a place where she felt happiest, it was here, in this theater, with the red velvet cushions and the glass chandeliers and the gilded domed ceiling high, high above them. Had it been coincidence or planning that had led to the theater being constructed in the very heart of the city, a mere twenty-minute walk from the Assassins' Keep? She knew it would be hard for her to adjust to her new apartment, which was nearly double the distance from the theater. A sacrifice she was willing to make—if she ever found the right moment to tell Arobynn she was paying her debt and moving out. Which she would. Soon.

She felt Arobynn's easy, self-assured gait strutting across the carpet, and straightened as he leaned over her shoulder. "Doneval is straight ahead," Arobynn whispered, his breath hot on her skin. "Third box in from the stage, second row of seats."

She immediately found the man she'd been assigned to kill. He was tall and middle-aged, with pale blond hair and tan skin. Not particularly handsome, but not an eyesore, either. Not heavy, but not toned. Aside from his periwinkle tunic—which, even from this distance, looked expensive—there was nothing remarkable about him.

There were a few others in the box. A tall, elegant woman in her late twenties stood near the partition curtain, a cluster of men around her. She held herself like a noble, though no diadem glittered in her lustrous, dark hair.

"Leighfer Bardingale," Arobynn murmured, following her gaze. Doneval's former wife—and the one who'd hired her. "It was an arranged marriage. She wanted his wealth, and he wanted her youth. But when they failed to have children and some of his less . . . desirable behavior was revealed, she managed to get out of the marriage, still young, but far richer."

It was smart of Bardingale, really. If she planned to have him assassinated, then pretending to be his friend would help keep fingers from pointing her way. Though Bardingale might have looked the part of a polite, elegant lady, Celaena knew there had to be some ice-cold steel running through her veins. And an unyielding sense of dedication to her friends and allies—not to mention to the common rights of every human being. It was hard not to immediately admire her.

"And the people around them?" Celaena asked. Through a small gap in the curtains behind Doneval, she could glimpse three towering men, all clad in dark gray—all looking like bodyguards.

"Their friends and investors. Bardingale and Doneval still have some joint businesses together. The three men in the back are his guards."

Celaena nodded, and might have asked him some other questions had Sam and Lysandra not filed into the box behind them, bidding farewell to Arobynn's friend. There were three seats along the balcony rail, and three seats behind them. Lysandra, to Celaena's dismay, sat next to her as Arobynn and Sam took the rear seats.

"Oh, *look* at how many people are here," Lysandra said. Her low-cut ice-blue dress did little to hide her cleavage as she craned her neck over the rail. Celaena blocked out Lysandra's prattling as the courtesan began tossing out important names.

Celaena could sense Sam behind her, feel his gaze focused solely on the gold velvet curtains concealing the stage. She should say something to him—apologize or thank him or just . . . say something kind. She felt him tensing, as if he, too, wanted to say something. Somewhere in the theater, a gong began signaling the audience to take their seats.

It was now or never. She didn't know why her heart thundered the way it did, but she didn't give herself a chance to second-guess as she twisted to look at him. She glanced once at his clothes and then said, "You look handsome."

His brows rose, and she swiftly turned back around in her seat, focusing hard on the curtain. He looked better than handsome, but . . . Well, at least she'd said one nice thing. She'd *tried* to be nice. Somehow, it didn't make her feel that much better.

Celaena folded her hands in the lap of her bloodred gown. It wasn't cut nearly as low as Lysandra's, but with the slender sleeves and bare shoulders, she felt particularly exposed to Sam. She'd curled and swept her hair over one shoulder, certainly *not* to hide the scar on her neck.

Doneval lounged in his seat, eyes on the stage. How could a man who looked so bored and useless be responsible for not just the fate of several lives, but of his entire country? How could he sit in this theater and not hang his head in shame for what he was about to do to his fellow countrymen, and to whatever slaves would be caught up in it? The men around Bardingale kissed her cheeks and departed for their own boxes. Doneval's three thugs watched the men very, very closely as they left. Not lazy, bored guards, then. Celaena frowned.

But then the chandeliers were hauled upward into the dome and dimmed, and the crowd quieted to hear the opening notes as the orchestra began playing. In the dark, it was nearly impossible to see Doneval.

Sam's hand brushed her shoulder, and she almost jumped out of her skin as he brought his mouth close to her ear and murmured, "You look beautiful. Though I bet you already know that." She most certainly did.

She gave him a sidelong glare and found him grinning as he leaned back into his seat.

Suppressing her urge to smile, Celaena turned toward the stage as the music established the setting for them. A world of shadows and mist. A world where creatures and myths dwelled in the dark moments before dawn.

Celaena went still as the gold curtain drew back, and everything she knew and everything she was faded away to nothing.

~

The music annihilated her.

The dancing was breathtaking, yes, and the story it told was certainly lovely—a legend of a prince seeking to rescue his bride, and the cunning bird he captured to help him to do it—but the *music.*

Had there ever been anything more beautiful, more exquisitely painful? She clenched the arms of the seat, her fingers digging into the velvet as the music hurtled toward its finale, sweeping her away in a flood.

With each beat of the drum, each trill of the flute and blare of the horn, she felt all of it along her skin, along her bones. The music broke her apart and put her back together, only to rend her asunder again and again.

And then the climax, the compilation of all the sounds she had loved best, amplified until they echoed into eternity. As the final note swelled, a gasp broke from her, setting the tears in her eyes spilling down her face. She didn't care who saw.

Then, silence.

The silence was the worst thing she'd ever heard. The silence brought back everything around her. Applause erupted, and she was on her feet, crying still as she clapped until her hands ached.

"Celaena, I didn't know you had a shred of human emotion in you," Lysandra leaned in to whisper. "And I didn't think the performance was *that* good."

Sam gripped the back of Lysandra's chair. "Shut up, Lysandra."

Arobynn clicked his tongue in warning, but Celaena remained clapping, even as Sam's defense sent a faint trickle of pleasure through her. The ovation continued for a while, with the dancers emerging from the curtain again and again to bow and be showered with flowers. Celaena clapped through it all, even as her tears dried, even as the crowd began shuffling out.

When she remembered to glance at Doneval, his box was empty.

Arobynn, Sam, and Lysandra left their box, too, long before she was ready to end her applause. But after she finished clapping, Celaena remained, staring toward the curtained stage, watching the orchestra begin to pack up their instruments.

She was the last person to leave the theater.

~

There was another party at the Keep that night—a party for Lysandra and her madam and whatever artists and philosophers and writers Arobynn favored at that moment. Mercifully, it was confined to one of the drawing rooms, but laughter and music still filled the entirety of the second floor. On the carriage ride home, Arobynn had asked Celaena to join them, but the last thing she wanted to see was Lysandra being fawned over by Arobynn, Sam, and everyone else. So she told him that she was tired and needed to sleep.

She wasn't tired in the least, though. Emotionally drained, perhaps, but it was only ten thirty, and the thought of taking off her gown and climbing into bed made her feel rather pathetic. She was Adarlan's Assassin; she'd freed slaves and stolen Asterion horses and won the respect of the Mute Master. Surely she could do something better than go to bed early.

So she slipped into one of the music rooms, where it was quiet enough that she could only hear a burst of laughter every now and then. The other assassins were either at the party or off on some mission or other. Her rustling dress was the only sound as she folded back the cover of the pianoforte. She'd learned to play when she was ten—under Arobynn's orders that she find at least *one* refined skill other than ending lives—and had fallen in love immediately. Though she no longer took lessons, she played whenever she could spare a few minutes.

The music from the theater still echoed in her mind. Again and again, the same cluster of notes and harmonies. She could feel them humming under the surface of her skin, beating in time with her heart. What she wouldn't give to hear the music once more!

She played a few notes with one hand, frowned, adjusted her fingers, and tried again, clinging to the music in her mind. Slowly, the familiar melody began to sound right.

But it was only a few notes, and it was the pianoforte, not an orchestra; she pounded the keys harder, working out the riffs. It was *almost* there, but not quite right. She couldn't remember the notes as perfectly as they sounded in her head. She didn't feel them the way she'd felt them only an hour ago.

She tried again for a few minutes, but eventually slammed the lid shut and stalked from the room. She found Sam lounging against a wall in the hallway. Had he been listening to her fumble with the pianoforte this whole time?

"Close, but not quite the same, is it?" he said. She gave him a withering look and started toward her bedroom, even though she had no desire to spend the rest of the night sitting in there by herself. "It must drive you mad, not being able to get it exactly the way you remember it." He kept pace beside her. His midnight-blue tunic brought out the golden hues in his skin.

"I was just fooling around," she said. "I can't be the best at *everything*, you know. It wouldn't be fair to the rest of you, would it?" Down the hall, someone had started a merry tune on the instruments in the gaming room.

Sam chewed on his lip. "Why didn't you trail Doneval after the theater? Don't you have only four days left?" She wasn't surprised he knew; her missions weren't usually *that* secret.

She paused, still itching to hear the music once more. "Some things are more important than death."

Sam's eyes flickered. "I know."

She tried not to squirm as he refused to drop her stare. "Why are you helping Lysandra?" She didn't know why she asked it.

Sam frowned. "She's not all that bad, you know. When she's away from other people, she's . . . better. Don't bite off my head for saying it, but even though you taunt her about it, she didn't choose this path for herself—like us." He shook his head. "She just wants your attention—and acknowledgment of her existence."

She clenched her jaw. Of course he'd spent plenty of time alone with Lysandra. And of course he'd find her sympathetic. "I don't particularly care *what* she wants. You still haven't answered my question. *Why* are you helping her?"

He shrugged. "Because Arobynn told me to. And since I have no desire to have my face beaten to a pulp again, I'm not going to question him."

"He—he hurt you that badly, too?"

Sam let out a low laugh, but didn't reply until after a servant bustled past, carrying a tray full of wine bottles. They were probably better off talking in a room where they'd be less likely to be overheard, but the idea of being utterly alone with him made her pulse pound.

"I was unconscious for a day, and dozed on and off for three more after that," Sam said.

Celaena hissed a violent curse.

"He sent you to the Red Desert," Sam went on, his words soft and low. "But *my* punishment was having to watch him beat you that night."

"Why?" Another question she didn't mean to ask.

He closed the distance between them, standing near enough

now that she could see the fine gold-thread detailing on his tunic. "After what we went through in Skull's Bay, you should know the answer."

She didn't *want* to know the answer, now that she thought about it. "Are you going to make a Bid for Lysandra?"

Sam burst out laughing. "Bid? Celaena, I don't have any money. And the money that I *do* have is going toward paying back Arobynn. Even if I *wanted* to—"

"*Do* you want to?"

He gave her a lazy grin. "Why do you want to know?"

"Because I'm curious whether Arobynn's beating damaged your brain, that's why."

"Afraid she and I had a summer romance?" That insufferable grin was still there.

She could have raked her nails down his face. Instead, she picked another weapon. "I hope you did. *I* certainly enjoyed myself this summer."

The smile faded at that. "What do you mean?"

She brushed an invisible fleck of dust off her red gown. "Let's just say that the son of the Mute Master was *far* more welcoming than the other Silent Assassins." It wasn't quite a lie. Ilias *had* tried to kiss her, and she *had* basked in his attention, but she hadn't wanted to start anything between them.

Sam's face paled. Her words had struck home, but it wasn't as satisfying as she thought it would be. Instead, the mere fact that it *had* affected him made her feel . . . feel . . . Oh, why had she even said *anything* about Ilias?

Well, she knew precisely why. Sam began to turn away, but she grabbed his arm. "Help me with Doneval," she blurted. Not that she needed it, but this was the best she could offer him in exchange for what he'd done for her. "I'll—I'll give you half of the money."

He snorted. "Keep your money. I don't need it. Ruining yet another slave-trade agreement will be enough for me." He studied her for a moment, his mouth quirking to the side. "You're sure you want my help?"

"Yes," she said. It came out a bit strangled. He searched her eyes for any sign of mockery. She hated herself for making him distrust her that much.

But he nodded at last. "Then we'll start tomorrow. We'll scope out his house. Unless you've already done that?" She shook her head. "I'll come by your room after breakfast."

She nodded. There was more she wanted to say to him, and she didn't want him to go, but her throat had closed up, too full of all those unspoken words. She made to turn away.

"Celaena." She looked back at him, her red gown sweeping around her. His eyes shone as he flashed her a crooked grin. "I missed you this summer."

She met his stare unflinchingly, returning the smile as she said, "I hate to admit it, Sam Cortland, but I missed your sorry ass, too."

He merely chuckled before he strode toward the party, his hands in his pockets.

CHAPTER 4

Crouched in the shadows of a gargoyle the following afternoon, Celaena shifted her numb legs and groaned softly. She usually opted to wear a mask, but with the rain, it would have limited her vision even further. Going without, though, made her feel somewhat exposed.

The rain also made the stone slick, and she took extra care while adjusting her position. Six hours. Six hours spent on this rooftop, staring across the street at the two-story house Doneval had rented for the duration of his stay. It was just off the most fashionable avenue in the city, and was enormous, as far as city homes went. Made of solid white stone and capped with green clay shingles, it looked just like any other wealthy home in the city, right down to its intricately carved windowsills and doorways. The front lawn was manicured, and even in the rain, servants bustled around the property, bringing in food, flowers, and other supplies.

That was the first thing she noticed—that people came and went all day. And there were guards everywhere. They looked closely at the faces of the servants who entered, scaring the daylights out of some of them.

There was a whisper of boots against the ledge, and Sam nimbly slipped into the shadows of the gargoyle, returning from scouting the other side of the house.

"A guard on every corner," Celaena murmured as Sam settled down beside her. "Three at the front door, two at the gate. How many did you spot in the back?"

"One on either side of the house, three more by the stables. And they don't look like cheap hands for hire, either. Will we take them out, or slip past them?"

"I'd prefer not to kill them," she admitted. "But we'll see if we can slip past when the time comes. Seems like they're rotating every two hours. The off-duty guards go into the house."

"Doneval's still away?"

She nodded, inching nearer to him. Of course, it was just to absorb his warmth against the freezing rain. She tried not to notice when he pressed closer to her, too. "He hasn't returned."

Doneval had left nearly an hour ago, closely flanked by a hulking brute of a man who looked hewn from granite. The bodyguard inspected the carriage, examined the coachman and the footman, held the door until Doneval was ensconced inside, and then slipped in himself. It seemed like Doneval knew very well just how coveted and delicate his list of slave sympathizers was. She'd seldom seen this kind of security.

They'd already surveyed the house and grounds, noting everything from the stones of the building to what sort of latches sealed the windows to the distance between the nearby rooftops and the roof of the house itself. Even with the rain, she could see well enough into the second-story window to make out a long hallway. Some servants came out of rooms bearing sheets and blankets—bedrooms, then. Four of them. There was a supply closet near the stairwell at the center of the hall. From the light that spilled into the hallway, she knew that the main stairwell had to be open and grand, just like the one in the Assassins' Keep. Not a chance of hiding, unless they found the servants' passages.

They got lucky, though, when she spied a servant going into one of the second-floor rooms, carrying a pile of the afternoon papers. A few minutes later, a maid lugged in a bucket and tools for sweeping out a fireplace, and then a manservant brought in what looked like a bottle of wine. She hadn't seen anyone changing the linens in that room, and so they took special notice of the servants who entered and exited.

It had to be the private study that Arobynn had mentioned. Doneval probably maintained a formal study on the first floor, but if he were doing dark dealings, then moving his real business to a more hidden quarter of the house would make sense. But they still needed to figure out what time the meeting would take place. Right now, it could be at any point on the arranged day.

"There he is," Sam hissed. Doneval's carriage pulled up, and the hulking bodyguard got out, scouring the street for a moment before he motioned for the businessman to emerge. Celaena had a feeling that Doneval's rush to get into the house wasn't just about the downpour.

They ducked back into the shadows again. "Where do you suppose he went?" Sam asked.

She shrugged. His former wife's Harvest Moon party was tonight; perhaps that had something to do with it, or the street festival that Melisande was hosting in the center of the city today. She and Sam were now crouching so close together that a toasty warmth was spreading up one side of her. "Nowhere good, I'm sure."

Sam let out a breathy laugh, his eyes still on the house. They were silent for a few minutes. At last, he said, "So, the Mute Master's son . . ."

She almost groaned.

"How close were you, exactly?" He focused on the house, though she noticed that he'd fisted his hands.

Just tell him the truth, idiot!

"Nothing happened with Ilias. It was only a bit of flirtation, but . . . nothing happened," she said again.

"Well," he said after a moment, "nothing happened with Lysandra. And nothing is going to. Ever."

"And *why*, exactly, do you think I care?" It was her turn to keep her eyes fixed on the house.

He nudged her with his shoulder. "Since we're *friends* now, I assumed you'd want to know."

She was grateful that her hood concealed most of her burning-hot face. "I think I preferred it when you wanted to kill me."

"Sometimes I think so, too. Certainly made my life more interesting. I wonder, though—if I'm helping you, does it mean I get to be your Second when you run the Assassins' Guild? Or does it just mean that I can boast that the famed Celaena Sardothien finally finds me worthy?"

She jabbed him with an elbow. "It means you should shut up and pay attention." They grinned at each other, and then they waited. Around sunset—which felt especially early that day, given the heavy cloud cover—the bodyguard emerged. Doneval was nowhere in sight, and the bodyguard motioned to the guards, speaking quietly to them before he strode down the street. "Off on an errand?" Celaena pondered. Sam inclined his head after the bodyguard, a suggestion that they follow. "Good idea."

Celaena's stiff limbs ached in protest as she slowly, carefully inched away from the gargoyle. She kept her eyes on the nearby guards, not once looking away as she grabbed the roof ledge and hauled herself up it, Sam following suit.

She wished she had the boots the master tinkerer was adjusting for her, but they wouldn't arrive until tomorrow. Her black leather boots, while supple and supportive, felt a bit traitorous on the rain-slick gutter of the roof. Still, she and Sam kept low and fast as they dashed along the roof edge, tracking the hulking man in the street below. Luckily, he turned down a back alley, and the next house was close enough that she could nimbly leap onto the adjacent roof. Her boots slid, but her gloved fingers grappled onto the green stone shingles. Sam landed flawlessly beside her, and, to her surprise, she didn't bite his head off when he grabbed the back of her cloak to help her stand.

The bodyguard continued along the alley, and they trailed on the rooftops, shadows against the growing dark. At last, he came to a broader street where the gaps between houses were too big to jump, and Celaena and Sam shimmied down a drainpipe. Their boots were soft as they hit the ground. They picked up a casual pace behind their quarry, arms linked, just two citizens of the capital on their way to somewhere, eager to get out of the rain.

It was easy to spot him in the crowd, even as they reached the main avenue of the city. People jumped out of his way, actually. Melisande's street festival in honor of the Harvest Moon was in full swing, and people flocked to it despite the rain. Celaena and Sam followed the bodyguard for a few more blocks, down a few more alleys. The bodyguard turned to look behind him only once, but he found them leaning casually against an alley wall, merely cloaked figures taking shelter from the rain.

With all the waste brought in by the Melisande convoy, and the smaller street festivals that had already occurred, the streets and sewers were nearly overflowing with garbage. As they stalked the bodyguard, Celaena heard people talking about how the city wardens had dammed up parts of the sewers to let them fill with rainwater. Tomorrow night they were going to unleash them, causing a torrent in the sewers wild enough to sweep all the clinging trash into the Avery River. They'd done it before, apparently—if the sewers weren't flushed out every now and then, the filth would grow stagnant and reek even more. Still, Celaena planned to be high, high above the streets by the time they unleashed those dams. There was sure to be some in-street flooding before it subsided, and she had no desire to walk through any of it.

The bodyguard eventually went into a tavern on the cusp of the crumbling slums, and they waited for him across the street. Through the cracked windows, they could see him sitting at the bar, drinking mug after mug of ale. Celaena began to wish fervently that she could be at the street festival instead.

"Well, if he has a weakness for alcohol, then perhaps that could be our way around him," Sam observed. She nodded, but didn't say anything. Sam looked toward the glass castle, its towers wreathed in mist. "I wonder if Bardingale and the others are having any luck convincing the king to fund their road," he said. "I wonder why she would even want it built, since she seems so eager to make sure the slave trade stays out of Melisande for as long as possible."

"If anything, it means she has absolute faith that we won't fail," Celaena said. When she didn't say anything else, Sam fell silent. An hour passed, and the bodyguard spoke to no one, paid the entire tab with a piece of silver, and headed back to Doneval's house. Despite the ale he'd consumed, his steps were steady, and by the time Sam and Celaena reached the house, she was almost bored to tears—not to mention shivering with cold and unsure if her numbed toes had fallen off inside her boots.

They watched from a nearby street corner as the bodyguard went up the front steps. He held a position of respect, then, if he wasn't made to enter through the back. But even with the bits of information they'd gathered that day, when they made the twenty-minute trek across the city to the Keep, Celaena couldn't help feeling rather useless and miserable. Even Sam was quiet as they reached their home, and merely told her that he'd see her in a few hours.

The Harvest Moon party was that night—and the deal with Doneval three days away. Considering how little they'd been able to actually glean that day, perhaps she'd have to work harder than she'd thought to find a way to take out her quarry. Maybe Arobynn's "gift" had been more of a curse.

What a waste.

She spent an hour soaking in her bathtub, running the hot water until she was fairly certain there wasn't any left for anyone else in the Keep. Arobynn himself had commissioned the running water outfit for the Keep, and it had cost as much as the building did, but she was forever grateful for it.

Once the ice had melted away from her bones, she slipped into the black silk dressing robe Arobynn had given her that morning—another of his presents, but still not enough that she'd forgive him anytime soon. She padded into her bedroom. A servant had started a fire, and she was about to begin dressing for the Harvest Moon party when she spotted the pile of papers on her bed.

They were tied with a red string, and her stomach fluttered as she pulled out the note placed on top.

Try not to stain them with your tears when you play. It took a lot of bribes to get these.

She might have rolled her eyes had she not seen what lay before her.

Sheet music. For the performance she'd seen last night. For the notes she couldn't get out of her mind, even a day later. She glanced again at the note. It wasn't Arobynn's elegant script, but Sam's hurried scrawl. When in hell had he found the time today to get these? He must have gone out right after they'd returned.

She sank onto the bed, flipping through the pages. The show had only debuted a few weeks ago; sheet music for it wasn't even in circulation yet. Nor would it be, until it proved itself to be a success. That could be months, even years, from now.

She couldn't help her smile.

Despite the ongoing rain that night, the Harvest Moon party at Leighfer Bardingale's riverfront house was so packed that Celaena hardly had room to show off her exquisite gold-and-blue dress, or the fish-fin combs she'd had positioned along the sides of her upswept hair. Everyone who was anyone in Rifthold was here. That is, everyone *without* royal blood, though she could have sworn she saw a few members of the nobility mingling with the bejeweled crowd.

The ballroom was enormous, its towering ceiling strung with paper lanterns of all colors and shapes and sizes. Garlands had been woven around the pillars lining one side of the room, and on the many tables, cornucopias overflowed with food and flowers. Young women in nothing more than corsets and lacy lingerie dangled from swings attached to the filigreed ceiling, and bare-chested young men with ornate ivory collars handed out wine.

Celaena had attended dozens of extravagant parties while growing up in Rifthold; she'd infiltrated functions hosted by foreign dignitaries and local nobility; she'd seen everything and anything until she thought nothing could surprise her anymore. But this party blew them all away.

There was a small orchestra accompanied by two identical-twin singers—both young women, both dark-haired, and both equipped with utterly ethereal voices. They had people swaying where they stood, their voices tugging everyone toward the packed dance floor.

With Sam flanking her, Celaena stepped from the stairs at the top of the ballroom. Arobynn kept on her left, his silver eyes scanning the crowd. They crinkled with pleasure when their hostess greeted them at the bottom of the steps. In his pewter tunic, Arobynn cut a dashing figure as he bowed over Bardingale's hand and pressed a kiss to it.

The woman watched him with dark, cunning eyes, a gracious smile on her red lips. "Leighfer," Arobynn crooned, half-turning to beckon to Celaena. "Allow me to introduce my niece, Dianna, and my ward, Sam."

His niece. That was always the story, always the ruse whenever they attended events together. Sam bowed, and Celaena curtsied. The glimmer in Bardingale's gaze said that she knew very well that Celaena was not Arobynn's niece. Celaena tried not to frown. She'd never liked meeting clients face-to-face; it was better if they went through Arobynn.

"Charmed," Bardingale said to her, then curtsied to Sam. "Both of them are delightful, Arobynn." A pretty, nonsense statement, said by someone used to wielding pretty, nonsense words to get what she wanted. "Walk with me?" she asked the King of the Assassins, and Arobynn extended an elbow.

Just before they slipped into the crowd, Arobynn glanced over his shoulder and gave Celaena a rakish smile. "Try not to get into too much trouble." Then Arobynn and the lady were swallowed up by the throng of people, leaving Sam and Celaena at the foot of the stairs.

"What now?" Sam murmured, staring after Bardingale. His dark green tunic brought up the faint flecks of emerald in his brown eyes. "Did you spot Doneval?"

They'd come here to see with whom Doneval associated, how many guards were waiting outside, and if he looked nervous. The exchange would happen three nights from now, in his upstairs study. But at what time? *That* was what she needed to find out more than anything. And tonight was the only chance she'd have to get close enough to him to do it.

"He's by the third pillar," she said, keeping her gaze on the crowd. In the shadows of the pillars lining one half of the room, little seating areas had been erected on raised platforms. They were separated by black velvet curtains—private lounges for Bardingale's most distinguished guests. It was to one of these alcoves that she spotted Doneval making his way, his hulking bodyguard close behind. As soon as Doneval plopped into the plush cushions, four of the corset-clad girls slid into place beside him, smiles plastered on their faces.

"Doesn't he look cozy," Sam mused. "I wonder how much Clarisse stands to make off this party." That explained where the girls came from. Celaena just hoped Lysandra wasn't here.

One of the beautiful serving boys offered Doneval and the courtesans glasses of sparkling wine. The bodyguard, who stood by the curtains, sipped first before nodding to Doneval to take it. Doneval, one hand already wrapped around the bare shoulders of the girl beside him, didn't thank either his bodyguard or the serving boy. Celaena felt her lip curl as Doneval pressed his lips to the neck of the courtesan. The girl couldn't have been older than twenty. It didn't surprise her at all that this man found the growing slave trade appealing—and that he was willing to destroy his opponents to make his business arrangement a success.

"I have a feeling he's not going to get up for a while," Celaena said, and when she turned to Sam, he was frowning. He'd always had a mixture of sorrow and sympathy for the courtesans—and such hatred for their clients. His mother's end hadn't been a happy one. Perhaps that was why he tolerated the insufferable Lysandra and her insipid companions.

Someone almost knocked into Celaena from behind, but she sensed the staggering man and easily sidestepped out of his path. "This is a madhouse," she muttered, her gaze rising to the girls on the swings as they floated through the room. They arched their backs so far that it was a miracle their breasts stayed in their corsets.

"I can't even imagine how much Bardingale spent on this party." Sam was so close his breath caressed her cheek. Celaena was actually more curious about how much the hostess was spending on keeping Doneval distracted; clearly, no cost was too great, if she'd hired Celaena to help destroy Doneval's trade agreement and get those documents into safe hands. But perhaps there was more to this assignment than just the slave-trade agreement and blackmailing list. Perhaps Bardingale was tired of supporting her former husband's decadent lifestyle. Celaena couldn't bring herself to blame her.

Even though Doneval's cushioned alcove was meant to be private, he certainly *wanted* to be seen. And from the bottles of sparkling wine that had been set on the low table before him, she could tell he had no intention of getting up. A man who wanted to be approached by others—who wanted to feel powerful. He liked to be worshipped. And at a party hosted by his former wife, he had some nerve associating with those courtesans. It was petty—and cruel, if she thought about it. But what good did knowing that do her?

He rarely spoke to other men, it seemed. But who said his business partner had to be a man? Maybe it was a woman. Or a courtesan.

Doneval was now slobbering over the neck of the girl on his other side, his hand roaming along her bare thigh. But if Doneval were in league with a courtesan, why would he wait until three days from now before making the document exchange? It couldn't be one of Clarisse's girls. Or Clarisse herself.

"Do you think he's going to meet with his conspirator tonight?" Sam asked.

Celaena turned to him. "No. I have a feeling that he's not foolish enough to actually do any dealings here. At least, not with anyone except Clarisse." Sam's face darkened.

If Doneval enjoyed female company, well, that certainly worked in favor of her plan to get close to him, didn't it? She began winding her way through the crowd.

"What are you doing?" Sam said, managing to keep up with her.

She shot him a look over her shoulder, nudging people out of the way as she made for the alcove. "Don't follow me," she said—but not harshly. "I'm going to try something. Just stay here. I'll come find you when I'm done."

He stared at her for a heartbeat, then nodded.

Celaena took a long breath through her nose as she mounted the steps and walked into the raised alcove where Doneval sat.

CHAPTER 5

The four courtesans noticed her, but Celaena kept her eyes on Doneval, who looked up from the neck of the courtesan currently on the receiving end of his affection. His bodyguard was alert, but didn't stop her. Fool. She forced a little smile to her lips as Doneval's eyes roved freely. Up and down, down and up. *That* was why she'd opted for a lower-cut dress than usual. It made her stomach turn, but she stepped closer, only the low-lying table between her and Doneval's sofa. She gave a low, elegant curtsy. "My lord," she purred.

He was not a lord in any sense, but a man like that had to enjoy fancy titles, however unearned they might be.

"May I help you?" he said, taking in her dress. She was definitely more covered-up than the courtesans around him. But sometimes there was more allure in *not* seeing everything.

"Oh, I'm so sorry to interrupt," she said, tilting her head so that the light from the lanterns caught in her eyes and set them sparkling.

She knew well enough which of her features men tended to notice—and appreciate—most. "But my uncle is a merchant, and he speaks so highly of you that I . . ." She now looked at the courtesans as if suddenly noticing them, as if she were a good, decent girl realizing the company he kept and trying not to become too embarrassed.

Doneval seemed to sense her discomfort and sat up, removing his hand from the thigh of the girl next to him. The courtesans all went a bit rigid, shooting daggers in her direction. She might have grinned at them had she not been so focused on her act.

"Go on, my dear," Doneval said, his eyes now fixed on hers. Really, it was too easy.

She bit her lip, tucking her chin down—demure, shy, waiting to be plucked. "My uncle is sick tonight and couldn't attend. He was *so* looking forward to meeting you, and I thought I might make an introduction on his behalf, but I'm so terribly sorry to have interrupted you." She made to turn, counting down the heartbeats until . . .

"No, no—I'd be pleased to make the acquaintance. What is your name, my dear girl?"

She turned back, letting the light catch in her blue-gold eyes again. "Dianna Brackyn; my uncle is Erick Brackyn . . ." She glanced at the courtesans, giving her best alarmed-innocent-maiden look. "I—I truly don't wish to interrupt you." Doneval kept drinking her in. "Perhaps, if it would not be an inconvenience or an impertinence, we could call on you? Not tomorrow or the day after, since my uncle has some contract with the viceroy of Bellhaven to work on, but the day after *that*? Three days from now, is what I mean." She made a little coo of a laugh.

"It wouldn't be an impertinence in the least," Doneval crooned, leaning forward. Mentioning Fenharrow's wealthiest city—and ruler—had done the trick. "In fact, I much admire you for having the nerve to approach me. Not many men would, let alone young women."

She almost rolled her eyes, but she just fluttered her eyelashes ever so slightly. "Thank you, my lord. What time would be convenient for you?"

"Ah," Doneval said. "Well, I have dinner plans that night." Not a hint of nerves, or a flicker of anxiety in his eyes. "But I am free for breakfast, or lunch," he added with a growing smile.

She sighed dramatically. "Oh, no—I think I might have committed myself then, actually. What about tea that afternoon? You say you have dinner plans, but perhaps something before . . . ? Or maybe we'll just see you at the theater that night."

He fell silent, and she wondered if he was growing suspicious. But she blinked, tucking her arms into her sides enough that her chest squeezed a bit more out of her neckline. It was a trick she'd used often enough to know it worked. "I would certainly like to have tea," he said at last, "but I'll also be at the theater after my dinner."

She gave him a bright smile. "Would you like to join us in our box? My uncle has two of his contacts from the viceroy of Bellhaven's court joining us, but I just *know* he'd be honored to have you with us as well."

He cocked his head, and she could practically see the cold, calculating thoughts churning behind his eyes. *Come on*, she thought, *take the bait* . . . Contacts with a wealthy businessman and Bellhaven's viceroy should be enough.

"I'd be delighted," he said, giving her a smile that reeked of trained charm.

"I'm sure you have a fine carriage to escort you to the theater, but we'd be doubly honored if you'd use ours. We could pick you up after your dinner, perhaps?"

"I'm afraid my dinner is rather late—I'd hate to make you or your uncle tardy for the theater."

"Oh, it wouldn't be a problem. What time does your dinner begin—or end, I suppose is the better question!" A giggle. A twinkle in her eye that suggested the sort of curiosity in what a man like Doneval would be eager to show an inexperienced girl. He leaned farther forward. She wanted to claw at the skin his gaze raked over with such sensual consideration.

"The meal should be over within an hour," he drawled, "if not sooner; only a quick meal with an old friend of mine. Why don't you stop by the house at eight thirty?"

Her smile grew, genuine this time. Seven thirty, then. That's when the deal would occur. How could he be *that* foolish, that arrogant? He deserved to die just for being so irresponsible—so easily lured by a girl who was far too young for him.

"Oh, yes!" she said. "Of course." She rattled off details about her uncle's business and how well they'd get along, and soon she was curtsying again, giving him another long look at her cleavage before she walked away. The courtesans were still glaring at her, and she could feel Doneval's gaze devouring her until the crowd swallowed her up. She made a show of going over to the food, keeping up the demure maiden facade, and when Doneval finally stopped watching, she let out a sigh. *That* had certainly gone well. She loaded a plate with food that made her mouth water—roast boar, berries and cream, warm chocolate cake . . .

From a few feet away, she found Leighfer Bardingale observing her, the woman's dark eyes remarkably sad. Pitying. Or was it regret for what she had hired Celaena to do? Bardingale approached, brushing against Celaena's skirts on her way to the buffet table, but Celaena chose not to acknowledge her. Whatever Arobynn had told the woman about her, she didn't care to know. Though she *would* have liked to know what perfume Bardingale was wearing; it smelled like jasmine and vanilla.

Sam was suddenly beside her, appearing in that silent-as-death way of his. "Did you get what you needed?" He followed Celaena as she added more food to her plate. Leighfer took a few scoops of berries and a dollop of cream and disappeared back into the crowd.

Celaena grinned, glancing to the alcove where Doneval had now returned to his hired company. She deposited her plate on the table. "I certainly did. It appears he's unavailable at seven thirty in the evening that day."

"So we have our meeting time," Sam said.

"Indeed we do." She turned to him with a triumphant smirk, but Sam was now watching Doneval, his frown growing as the man continued pawing at the girls around him.

The music shifted, becoming livelier, the twins' voices rising in a wraithlike harmony. "And now that I got what I came here for, I want to dance," Celaena said. "So drink up, Sam Cortland. We're not washing our hands in blood tonight."

~

She danced and danced. The beautiful youths of Melisande had gathered near the platform that held the twin singers, and Celaena had gravitated toward them. Bottles of sparkling wine passed from hand to hand, mouth to mouth. Celaena swigged from all of them.

Around midnight, the music changed, going from organized, elegant dances to a frenzied, sensual sound that had her clapping her hands and stomping her feet in time. The Melisanders seemed eager to writhe and fling themselves about. If there were music and movements that embodied the wildness and recklessness and immortality of youth, they were here, on this dance floor.

Doneval remained where he sat on the cushions, drinking bottle after bottle. He never once glanced in her direction; whoever he had thought Dianna Brackyn was, she was now forgotten. Good.

Sweat ran along every part of her body, but she tipped her head back, arms upraised, content to bask in the music. One of the courtesans on the swings flew by so low that their fingers brushed. The touch sent sparks shooting through her. This was more than a party:

it was a performance, an orgy, and a call to worship at the altar of excess. Celaena was a willing sacrifice.

The music shifted again, a riot of pounding drums and the staccato notes of the twins. Sam kept a respectful distance—dancing alone, occasionally detangling himself from the arms of a girl who saw his beautiful face and tried to seize him for her own. Celaena tried not to smirk when she saw him politely, but firmly, telling the girl to find someone else.

Many of the older partygoers had long since left, ceding the dance floor to the young and beautiful. Celaena focused long enough to check on Doneval—and to see Arobynn sitting with Bardingale in another one of the nearby alcoves. A few others sat with them, and though glasses of wine littered their table, they all had lowered brows and tight-lipped expressions. While Doneval had come here to feast off his former wife's fortune, it seemed like she had other thoughts on how to enjoy her party. What sort of strength had it taken to accept that assassinating her former husband was the only option left? Or was it weakness?

The clock struck three—three! How had so many hours passed? A glimmer of movement caught her eye by the towering doors atop the stairs. Four young men wearing masks stood atop the steps, surveying the crowd. It took all of two heartbeats for her to see that the dark-haired youth was their ringleader, and that the fine clothes and the masks they wore marked them as nobility. Probably nobles looking to escape a stuffy function and savor the delights of Rifthold.

The masked strangers swaggered down the steps, one of them keeping close to the dark-haired youth. That one had a sword, she noticed, and from his tensed shoulders, she could tell he wasn't entirely pleased to be here. But the lips of the ringleader parted in a grin as he stalked into the crowd. Gods above, even with the mask obscuring half of his features, he was handsome.

She danced as she watched him, and, as if he had somehow sensed her all this time, their eyes met from across the room. She gave him a smile, then deliberately turned back toward the singers, her dancing a little more careful, a little more inviting. She found Sam frowning at her. She gave him a shrug.

It took the masked stranger a few minutes—and a knowing smile from her to suggest that she, too, knew exactly where he was—but soon she felt a hand slide around her waist.

"Some party," the stranger whispered in her ear. She twisted to see sapphire eyes gleaming at her. "Are you from Melisande?"

She swayed with the music. "Perhaps."

His smile grew. She itched to pull off the mask. Any young nobles who were out at this hour were certainly not here for innocent purposes. Still—who was to say that she couldn't have some fun, too? "What's your name?" he asked above the roar of the music.

She leaned close. "My name is Wind," she whispered. "And Rain. And Bone and Dust. My name is a snippet of a half-remembered song."

He chuckled, a low, delightful sound. She was drunk, and silly, and so full of the glory of being young and alive and in the capital of the world that she could hardly contain herself.

"I have no name," she purred. "I am whoever the keepers of my fate tell me to be."

He grasped her by her wrist, running a thumb along the sensitive skin underneath. "Then let me call you Mine for a dance or two."

She grinned, but someone was suddenly between them, a tall, powerfully built person. Sam. He ripped the stranger's hand off her wrist. "She's spoken for," he growled, all too close to the young man's masked face. The stranger's friend was behind him in an instant, his bronze eyes fixed on Sam.

Celaena grabbed Sam's elbow. "Enough," she warned him.

The masked stranger looked Sam up and down, then held up his hands. "My mistake," he said, but winked at Celaena before he disappeared into the crowd, his armed friend close behind.

Celaena whirled to face Sam. "What in hell was that for?"

"You're drunk," he told her, so close her chest brushed his. "And he knew it, too."

"So?" Even as she said it, someone dancing wildly crashed into her and set her reeling. Sam caught her around the waist, his hands firm on her as he kept her from falling to the ground.

"You'll thank me in the morning."

"Just because we're working together doesn't mean I'm suddenly incapable of handling myself." His hands were still on her waist.

"Let me take you home." She glanced toward the alcoves. Doneval was passed out cold on the shoulder of a very bored-looking courtesan. Arobynn and Bardingale were still deep in their conversation.

"No," she said. "I don't need an escort. I'll go home when I feel like it." She slipped out of his grasp, slamming into the shoulder of someone behind her. The man apologized and moved away. "Besides," Celaena said, unable to stop the words or the stupid, useless jealousy that grabbed control of her, "don't you have Lysandra or someone equally for hire to be with?"

"I don't want to be with Lysandra, or *anyone else for hire*," he said through gritted teeth. He reached for her hand. "And you're a damned fool for not seeing it."

She shook off his grip. "I am what I am, and I don't particularly care what you think of me." Maybe once he might have believed that, but now . . .

"Well, I care what *you* think of *me*. I care enough that I stayed at this disgusting party just for you. And I care enough that I'd attend a thousand more like it so I can spend a few hours with you when you *aren't* looking at me like I'm not worth the dirt beneath your shoes."

That made her anger stumble. She swallowed hard, her head spinning. "We have enough going on with Doneval. I don't need to be fighting with you." She wanted to rub her eyes, but she would have ruined the cosmetics on them. She let out a long sigh. "Can't we just . . . try to enjoy ourselves right now?"

Sam shrugged, but his eyes were still dark and gleaming. "If you want to dance with that man, then go ahead."

"It's not about that."

"Then tell me what it's about."

She began wringing her fingers, then stopped herself. "Look," she said, the music so loud it was hard to hear her own thoughts. "I—Sam, I don't know how to be your friend yet. I don't know if I know how to be *anyone's* friend. And . . . Can we just talk about this tomorrow?"

He shook his head slowly, but gave her a smile, even though it didn't reach his eyes. "Sure. *If* you can remember anything tomorrow," he said with forced lightness. She made herself smile back at him. He jerked his chin toward the dancing. "Go have fun. We'll talk in the morning." He stepped closer, as if he'd kiss her cheek, but then thought better of it. She couldn't tell if she was disappointed or not as he squeezed her shoulder instead.

With that, he vanished into the crowd. Celaena stared after him until a young woman pulled her into a circle of dancing girls, and the revelry took hold of her again.

The rooftop of her new apartment looked out over the Avery River, and Celaena sat on the walled edge, her legs dangling off the side. The stone beneath her was chill and damp, but the rain had stopped during the night, and fierce winds had blown the clouds away as the stars faded and the sky lightened.

The sun broke over the horizon, flooding the snaking arm of the Avery with light. It became a living band of gold.

The capital began to stir, chimneys puffing up smoke from the first of the day's fires, fishermen calling to one another from the nearby docks, young children rushing through the streets with bundles of wood or the morning papers or buckets of water. Behind her, the glass castle shimmered in the dawn.

She hadn't been to her new apartment since she'd returned from the desert, so she'd taken a few minutes to walk through the spacious rooms hidden on the upper floor of a fake warehouse. It was the last place anyone would expect her to purchase a home, and the warehouse itself was filled with bottles of ink—a supply no one was likely to break in to steal. This was a place that was hers and hers alone. Or it would be, as soon as she told Arobynn she was leaving. Which she'd do as soon as she finished this business with Doneval. Or sometime soon after that. Maybe.

She inhaled the damp morning air, letting it wash through her. Seated on the roof ledge, she felt wonderfully insignificant—a mere speck in the vastness of the great city. And yet all of it was hers for the taking.

Yes, the party had been delightful, but there was more to the world than that. Bigger things, more beautiful things, more *real* things. Her future was hers, and she had three trunks of gold hidden in her room that would solidify it. She could make of her life what she wanted.

Celaena leaned back on her hands, drinking in the awakening city. And as she watched the capital, she had the joyous feeling that the capital watched her back.

CHAPTER 6

Since she'd forgotten to do it at the party the night before, she meant to thank Sam for the music during their usual tumbling lesson after breakfast. But several of the other assassins were also in the training hall, and she had no desire to explain the gift to any of the older men. They would undoubtedly take it the wrong way. Not that they particularly cared about what she was up to; they did their best to stay out of her way, and she didn't bother to get to know them, either. Besides, her head was throbbing thanks to staying up until dawn and drinking all that sparkling wine, so she couldn't even think of the right words just now.

She went through her training exercises until noon, impressing their instructor with the new ways she'd learned to move while she was in the Red Desert. She felt Sam watching her from the mats a few feet away. She tried not to look at his shirtless chest, gleaming with sweat, as he took a running jump, nimbly flipping through the air and landing almost soundlessly on the ground. By the Wyrd, he was fast. He'd certainly spent the summer training, too.

"Milady," the instructor coughed, and she turned to him, giving a glare that warned him not to comment. She slid into a backbend, then flipped out of it, her legs smoothly rising over her head and back to the floor.

She landed in a kneel, and looked up to see Sam approaching. Stopping before her, he gave the instructor a sharp jerk of his chin, and the stocky, compact man found somewhere else to be.

"He was helping me," Celaena said. Her muscles quivered as she stood. She'd trained hard this morning, despite how little sleep she'd gotten—which had nothing to do with the fact that she hadn't wanted to spend a moment alone with Sam in the training hall.

"He's here every other day. I don't think you're missing anything vital," Sam replied. She kept her gaze on his face. She'd seen Sam shirtless before—she'd seen all of the assassins in various stages of undress thanks to their training—but this felt different.

"So," she said, "are we breaking into Doneval's house tonight?" She kept her voice down. She didn't particularly like sharing anything with her fellow assassins. Ben she'd once told everything to, but he was dead and buried. "Now that we know the meeting time, we should get into that upstairs study and get a sense of what and how many documents there are before he shares them with his partner." Since the sun had finally decided to make an appearance, it made daytime stalking next to impossible.

He frowned, running a hand through his hair. "I can't. I *want* to, but I can't. Lysandra has a pre-Bidding rehearsal, and I'm on guard duty. I could meet you after, if you want to wait for me."

"No. I'll go myself. It shouldn't be that hard." She started from the training room, and Sam followed her, keeping close to her side.

"It's going to be dangerous."

"Sam, I freed two hundred slaves in Skull's Bay and took down

Rolfe. I think I can handle this." They reached the main entranceway of the Keep.

"And you did that with *my* help. Why don't I stop by Doneval's after I finish and see if you need me?"

She patted his shoulder, his bare skin sticky with sweat. "Do whatever you want. Though I have a feeling I'll already be done by that point. But I'll tell you all about it tomorrow morning," she crooned, pausing at the foot of the grand staircase.

He grabbed her hand. "Please be careful. Just get a look at the documents and go. We've still got two days until the exchange; if it's too dangerous, then we can try tomorrow. Don't put yourself at risk."

The doors to the Keep swung open and Sam dropped her hand as Lysandra and Clarisse came sweeping in.

Lysandra's face was flushed, making her green eyes sparkle. "Oh, *Sam*," Lysandra said, rushing toward him with outstretched hands. Celaena bristled. Sam grasped Lysandra's slender fingers politely. From the way she drank him in—especially his shirtless torso—Celaena had no trouble believing that two days from now, as soon as her Bidding Night was over and she could be with whoever she wanted, she'd seek out Sam. And who wouldn't?

"Another luncheon with Arobynn?" Sam asked, but Lysandra wouldn't let go of his hands. Madam Clarisse gave Celaena a curt nod as she bustled past, heading straight for Arobynn's study. The brothel madam and the King of the Assassins had been friends for as long as Celaena had been here, and Clarisse had never said more than a few words to her.

"Oh, no—we're here for tea. Arobynn promised a silver tea service," Lysandra said, her words somehow feeling tossed in Celaena's direction. "You *must* join us, Sam."

Ordinarily, Celaena would have bitten the girl's head off for the insult. Lysandra was still grasping Sam's hands.

As if he sensed it, Sam wriggled his fingers away. "I—" he started.

"You should go," Celaena said. Lysandra looked between them. "I have work to do, anyway. I don't get to be the best simply by lying on my back all day." A cheap shot, but Lysandra's eyes flashed. Celaena gave her a razor-sharp smile. Not that she had wanted to keep talking to Sam, or invite him to listen to her practice the music he'd gotten her, or spend *any* more time with him than was absolutely necessary.

He swallowed. "Have lunch with me, Celaena."

Lysandra clicked her tongue and strode off muttering, "Why would you want to have lunch with *her*?"

"I'm busy," Celaena said. It wasn't a lie; she *did* still have to finalize her plan to break into the house to find out more about Doneval's documents. She jerked her chin toward Lysandra and the sitting room beyond her. "Go enjoy yourself."

Without wanting to see what he chose, she kept her eyes on the marble floors, the teal drapes, and the gilded ceiling as she walked to her room.

The walls of Doneval's house were unguarded. Wherever he'd gone tonight—from the look of his clothes, probably to the theater or a party—he'd taken several of his guards with him, though she hadn't counted his hulking bodyguard in their ranks. Perhaps the bodyguard had the night off. It still left several guards patrolling the grounds, not to mention whoever was inside.

While she loathed the thought of getting her new black suit wet, Celaena was grateful for the rain that had started again at sundown, even if it meant forgoing her usual mask in order to keep her weather-limited senses open. Thankfully, the heavy downpour also meant that the guard on the side of the house didn't even notice her slipping right past him. The second floor was fairly high up, but the window was darkened, and the latch was easily unlocked from the outside. She'd mapped the house already. If she was correct—and she was certain she was—that window led right into the second-floor study.

Listening carefully, she waited until the guard was looking the other way, and began to climb. Her new boots found their grip on the stone, and her fingers had no trouble at all seeking out cracks. The suit was a little heavier than her usual tunic, but with the built-in blades in the gauntlets, she didn't have the additional encumbrance of a sword on her back or daggers at her waist. There were even two knives built into her boots. This was one gift from Arobynn that she'd get a lot of use out of.

But while the rain quieted and clouded *her*, it also masked the sound of anyone approaching. She kept her eyes and ears wide open, but no other guards rounded the corner of the house. The additional risk was worth it. Now that she knew what time the meeting would take place, she had two days to gather as much specific information as she could about the documents, namely how many pages there were and where Doneval hid them. In a few moments, she was at the sill of the study window. The guard below didn't even look up at the house towering behind him. Top-notch guards indeed.

One glance inside showed a darkened room—a desk littered with papers, and nothing else. He wouldn't be so foolish as to leave the lists out in plain sight, but . . .

Celaena hauled herself onto the ledge, and the slender knife from her boot gleamed dully as it wedged into the slight gap between the window doors. Two angled jabs, a flick of her wrist, and—

She eased the window open, praying for silent hinges. One of them creaked quietly, but the other swung away without a sound. She slid into the study, boots quiet on the ornate rug. Carefully, holding her breath, she eased the windows shut again.

She sensed the attack a heartbeat before it happened.

Chapter 7

Celaena whirled and ducked, the other knife from her boot instantly in her hand, and the guard went down with a groan. She struck fast as an asp—a move she'd learned in the Red Desert. As she yanked the knife from his thigh, hot blood pumped onto her hand. Another guard swiped a sword at her, but she met it with both her knives before kicking him squarely in the stomach. He staggered back, yet not fast enough to escape the blow to his head that knocked him out. Another maneuver the Mute Master had taught her while she'd been studying how the desert animals moved. In the darkness of the room, she felt the reverberations as the guard's body slammed into the floor.

But there were others, and she counted three more—three more grunting and moaning as they crumpled around her—before someone grabbed her from behind. There was a vicious thump against her head, and something wet and putrid pressed to her face, and then—

Oblivion.

Celaena awoke, but she didn't open her eyes. She kept her breathing steady, even as she inhaled the reek of filth and the damp, rotten air around her. And she kept her ears open, even as she heard the chuckle of male voices and the gurgle of water. She kept very still, even as she felt the ropes that bound her to the chair, and the water that was already up to her calves. She was in the sewer.

Splashes approached—heavy enough that the sewer water showered her lap.

"I think that's enough sleeping," said a deep voice. A powerful hand slapped her cheek. Through stinging eyes, she found the hatchet-hewn face of Doneval's bodyguard smiling at her. "Hello, lovely. Thought we didn't notice you spying on us for days, did you? You might be good, but you're not invisible."

Behind him, four guards loitered by an iron door—and beyond it was another door, through which she could see a set of steps that led upward. It must be a door into the cellar of the house. Several of the older houses in Rifthold had such doors: escape routes during wars, ways to sneak in scandal-worthy guests, or merely an easy way to deposit the household's waste. The double doors were to keep out the water—airtight, and made long ago by skilled craftsmen who had used magic to coat the thresholds with water-repellent spells.

"There are a lot of rooms to break into in this house," the bodyguard said. "Why'd you choose the upstairs study? And where's your friend?"

She gave him a crooked grin, all the while taking in the cavernous sewer around her. The water was rising. She didn't want to think about what was floating in it.

"Will this be an interrogation, then torture, *then* death?" she asked him. "Or am I getting the order wrong?"

The man grinned right back at her. "Smart-ass. I like it." His accent was thick, but she understood him well enough. He braced his hands on either arm of her chair. With her own arms bound behind her back, she only had the freedom to move her face. "Who sent you?"

Her heart beat wildly, but her smile didn't fade. Withstanding torture was a lesson she'd learned long ago. "Why do you assume anyone *sent* me? Can't a girl be independent?"

The wooden chair groaned under his weight as he leaned so close their noses were almost touching. She tried not to inhale his hot breath. "Why else would a little bitch like you break into this house? I don't think you're after jewels or gold."

She felt her nostrils flare. But she wouldn't make her move—not until she knew she had no chance to glean information from *him*.

"If you're going to torture me," she drawled, "then get it started. I don't particularly enjoy the smell down here."

The man pulled back, his grin unfaltering. "Oh, we're not going to torture you. Do you know how many spies and thieves and assassins have tried to take down Doneval? We're beyond asking questions. If you don't want to talk, then fine. Don't talk. We've learned how to deal with you filth."

"Philip," one of the guards said, pointing with his sword down the dark tunnel of the sewer. "We've got to go."

"Right," Philip said, turning back to Celaena. "See, I figure if someone was foolish enough to send you *here*, then you must be expendable. And I don't think anyone will look for you when they flood the sewers, not even your friend. In fact, most people are staying off the streets right now. You capital dwellers don't like getting your feet dirty, do you?"

Her heart pounded harder, but she didn't break his gaze. "Too bad they won't get *all* the trash," she said, batting her eyelashes.

"No," he said, "but they'll get you. Or at least, the river will get your remains, if the rats have left enough." Philip patted her cheek hard enough to sting. As if the sewers had heard him, a rush of water began sounding from the darkness.

Oh, no. No.

He splashed back to the landing where the guards stood. She watched them stride out through the second door, then up the stairs, then—

"Enjoy your swim," Philip said, and slammed the iron door shut behind him.

Darkness and water. In the moments it took for her to adjust to the dim streetlight leaking in through the grate high, high above, water gushed against her legs. It was up to her lap in an instant.

She cursed violently and wriggled hard against the ropes. But as the ropes cut into her arms, she remembered: the built-in blades. It was a testament to the inventor's skill that Philip hadn't found them, even though he must have searched her. Yet the bindings were almost too tight for her to release them . . .

She twisted her wrists, fighting for any shred of space to flick her hand. The water pooled around her waist. They must have built the sewer dam at the other end of the city; it would take a few minutes before it completely flooded this part.

The rope wouldn't budge, but she flicked her wrist, doing as the master tinkerer had told her, again and again. Then, at last, the whine and splash of the blade as it shot out. Pain danced down the side of her hand, and she swore. She'd cut herself on the damn thing. Thankfully, it didn't feel deep.

Immediately she started on the ropes, her arms aching while she twisted them as far as she could to angle against the bindings. They should have used iron shackles.

There was a sudden release of tension around her middle, and she almost fell face-first into the swirling black water as the rope gave. Two heartbeats later, the rest of the ropes were off, though she cringed as she plunged her hands into the filthy water to cut her feet from the chair legs.

When she stood, the water was at her thighs. And cold. Icy, icy cold. She felt things sliding against her as she splashed for the landing, struggling to keep upright in the fierce current. Rats were being swept past by the dozen, their squeals of terror barely audible over the roar of the water. By the time she reached the stone steps, the water was already pooling there, too. She tried the iron handle. It was locked. She tried to plunge one of her blades in alongside the threshold, but it bounced back. The door was sealed so tightly that nothing was getting through.

She was trapped.

Celaena looked down the length of the sewer. Rain was still pouring in from above, but the streetlights were bright enough that she could see the curved walls. There had to be some ladder to the street—there *had* to be.

She couldn't see any—not near her. And the grates were so high up that she'd have to wait until the sewer filled entirely before trying her luck. But the current was so strong that she'd probably be swept away.

"Think," she whispered. "Think, think."

Water rose higher on the landing, lapping now at her ankles.

She kept her breathing calm. Panicking would accomplish nothing. "*Think*." She scanned the sewer.

There might be a ladder, but it would be farther down. That meant braving the water—and the dark.

On her left, the water rose endlessly, rushing in from the other half of the city. She looked to her right. Even if there wasn't a grate, she might make it to the Avery.

It was a very, very big "might."

But it was better than waiting here to die.

Celaena sheathed her blades and plunged into the smelly, oily water. Her throat closed up, but she willed herself to keep from vomiting. She was *not* swimming through the entire capital's refuse. She was *not* swimming through rat-infested waters. She was *not going to die.*

The current was faster than she expected, and she pulled against it. Grates passed overhead, ever nearer, but still too distant. And then there, on the right! Midway up the wall, several feet above the water line, was a small tunnel opening. It was made for a solitary worker. Rainwater leaked out over the lip of the tunnel—somewhere, it *had* to lead to the street.

She swam hard for the wall, fighting to keep the current from sweeping her past the tunnel. She hit the wall and clung to it, easing down the side. The tunnel was high up enough that she had to reach, her fingers aching as they dug into the stone. But she had a grip, and even though pain lanced through her nails, she hauled herself into the narrow passage.

It was so small inside that she had to lie flat on her belly. And it was full of mud and the gods knew what else, but there—far ahead—was a shaft of lamplight. An upward tunnel that led to the street. Behind her, the sewer continued flooding, the roaring waters near deafening. If she didn't hurry, she'd be trapped.

With the ceiling so low, she had to keep her head down, her face nearly in the putrid mud as she stretched out her arms and *pulled.* Inch by inch, she dragged herself through the tunnel, staring at the light ahead.

Then the water reached the level of the tunnel. Within moments, it swept past her feet, past her legs, then her abdomen, and then her face. She crawled faster, not needing light to tell how bloody her hands were. Each bit of grit inside the cuts was like fire. *Go*, she thought to herself with each thrust and pull of her arms, each kick of her feet. *Go, go, go.* The word was the only thing that kept her from screaming. Because once she started screaming . . . that was when she'd concede to death.

The water in the passage was a few inches deep by the time she hit the upward tunnel, and she nearly sobbed at the sight of the ladder. It was probably fifteen feet to the surface. Through the circular holes in the large grate she spied a hovering streetlamp. She forgot the pain in her hands as she climbed the rusted ladder, willing it not to break. Water filled the tunnel bottom, swirling with debris.

She was quickly at the top, and even allowed herself a little smile as she pushed against the round grate.

But it didn't budge.

She balanced her feet on the rickety ladder and pushed with both hands. It still didn't move. She angled her body on the upper rung so that her back and shoulders braced against the grate and threw herself into it. Nothing. Not a groan, not a hint of metal giving way. It had to be rusted shut. She pounded against it until she felt something crack in her hand. Her vision flashed with pain, black-and-white sparks dancing, and she made sure the bone wasn't broken before pounding again. Nothing. *Nothing.*

The water was close now, its muddy froth so near that she could reach down and touch it.

She threw herself into the grate one last time. It didn't move.

If people were off the streets until the mandatory flooding was over . . . Rainwater poured into her mouth, her eyes, her nose. She banged against the metal, praying for anyone to hear her over the roar of the rain, for anyone to see the muddy, bloodied fingers straining upward from an ordinary city grate. The water hit her boots. She shoved her fingers through the grate holes and began screaming.

She screamed until her lungs burned, screamed for help, for anyone to hear. And then—

"Celaena?"

It was a shout, and it was close, and Celaena sobbed when she heard Sam's voice, nearly muffled by the rain and roaring waters beneath her. He said he'd come by after helping with Lysandra's party—he must have been on his way to or from Doneval's house. She wriggled her fingers through the grate hole, pounding with her other hand against the grate. "*HERE! In the sewer!*"

She could feel the rumble of steps, and then . . . "Holy gods." Sam's face swam into view through the grate. "I've been looking for you for twenty minutes," he said. "Hold on." His callused fingers latched onto the holes. She saw them go white with strain, saw his face turn red, then . . . He swore.

The water had reached her calves. "Get me the hell out of here."

"Shove with me," he breathed, and as he pulled, she pushed. The grate wouldn't move. They tried again, and again. The water hit her knees. By whatever luck, the grate was far enough away from Doneval's house that the guards couldn't hear them.

"Get as high as you can," he barked. She already was, but she didn't say anything. She caught the flash of a knife and heard the scrape of a blade against the grate. He was trying to loosen the metal by using the blade as a lever. "Push on the other side."

She pushed. Dark water lapped at her thighs.

The knife snapped in two.

Sam swore violently and began yanking on the grate cover again. "Come on," he whispered, more to himself than to her. "*Come on.*"

The water was around her waist now, and over her chest a moment after that. Rain continued streaming in through the grate, blinding her senses. "Sam," she said.

"I'm trying!"

"Sam," she repeated.

"No," he spat, hearing her tone. "*No.*"

He began screaming for help then. Celaena pressed her face to one of the holes in the grate. Help wasn't going to come—not fast enough.

She'd never given much thought to how she'd die, but drowning somehow felt fitting. It was a river in her native country of Terrasen that had almost claimed her life nine years ago—and now it seemed that whatever bargain she'd struck with the gods that night was finally over. The water would have her, one way or another, no matter how long it took.

"Please," Sam begged as he beat and yanked on the grate, then tried to wedge another dagger under the lid. "Please don't."

She knew he wasn't speaking to her.

The water hit her neck.

"*Please,*" Sam moaned, his fingers now touching hers. She'd have one last breath. Her last words.

"Take my body home to Terrasen, Sam," she whispered. And with a gasping breath, she went under.

CHAPTER 8

"*Breathe!*" someone was roaring as they pounded on her chest. "*Breathe!*"

And just like that, her body seized, and water rushed out of her. She vomited onto the cobblestones, coughing so hard she convulsed.

"Oh, gods," Sam moaned. Through her streaming eyes, she found him kneeling beside her, his head hung between his shoulders as he braced his palms on his knees. Behind him, two women were exchanging relieved, yet confused, expressions. One of them held a crowbar. Beside her lay the grate cover, and around them spilled water from the sewer.

She vomited again.

She took three baths in a row and ate food only with the intention of vomiting it up to clear out any trace of the vile liquid inside her. She plunged her torn, aching hands into a vat of hard liquor, biting down her scream but savoring the disinfectant burning through whatever had been in that water. Once that proved calming to her repulsion, she ordered her bathtub filled with the same liquor and submerged herself in it, too.

She'd never feel clean again. Even after her fourth bath—which had been immediately after her liquor bath—she felt like grime coated every part of her. Arobynn had cooed and fussed, but she'd ordered him out. She ordered *everyone* out. She'd take another two baths in the morning, she promised herself as she climbed into bed.

There was a knock on her door, and she almost barked at the person to go away, but Sam's head popped in. The clock read past twelve, but his eyes were still alert. "You're awake," he said, slipping inside without so much as a nod of permission from her. Not that he needed it. He'd saved her life. She was in his eternal debt.

On the way home, he'd told her that after Lysandra's Bidding rehearsal, he'd gone to Doneval's house to see if she needed any help. But when he got there, the house was quiet—except for the guards who kept sniggering about something that had happened. He'd been searching the surrounding streets for any sign of her when he heard her screaming.

She looked at him from where she lay in bed. "What do you want?" Not the most gracious words to someone who had saved her life. But, hell, she was supposed to be *better* than him. How could she say she was the best when she'd needed Sam to rescue her? The thought made her want to hit him.

He just smiled slightly. "I wanted to see if you were finally done with all the washing. There's no hot water left."

She frowned. "Don't expect me to apologize for that."

"Do I ever expect you to apologize for anything?"

In the candlelight, the lovely panes of his face seemed velvet-smooth and inviting. "You could have let me die," she mused. "I'm surprised you weren't dancing with glee over the grate."

He let out a low laugh that traveled along her limbs, warming her. "No one deserves that sort of death, Celaena. Not even you. And besides, I thought we were beyond that."

She swallowed hard, but was unable to break his gaze. "Thank you for saving me."

His brows rose. She'd said it once on their way back, but it had been a quick, breathless string of words. This time, it was different. Though her fingers ached—especially her broken nails—she reached for his hand. "And . . . And I'm sorry." She made herself look at him, even as his features crossed into incredulity. "I'm sorry for involving you in what happened in Skull's Bay. And for what Arobynn did to you because of it."

"Ah," he said, as if he somehow understood some great puzzle. He examined their linked hands, and she quickly let go.

The silence was suddenly too charged, his face too beautiful in the light. She lifted her chin and found him looking at the scar along her neck. The narrow ridge would fade—someday. "Her name was Ansel," she said, her throat tightening. "She was my friend." Sam slowly sat on the bed. And then the whole story came out.

Sam only asked questions when he needed clarification. The clock chimed one by the time she finished telling him about the final arrow she'd fired at Ansel, and how, even with her heart breaking, she'd given her friend an extra minute before releasing what would have been a killing shot. When she stopped speaking, Sam's eyes were bright with sorrow and wonder.

"So, that was my summer," she said with a shrug. "A grand adventure for Celaena Sardothien, isn't it?"

But he merely reached out and ran his fingers down the scar on her neck, as if he could somehow erase the wound. "I'm sorry," he said. And she knew he meant it.

"So am I," she murmured. She shifted, suddenly aware of how little her nightgown concealed. As if he'd noticed, too, his hand dropped from her neck and he cleared his throat. "Well," she said, "I suppose our mission just got a little more complicated."

"Oh? And why is that?"

She shook off the blush his touch had brought to her face and gave him a slow, wicked smile. Philip had *no* idea who he'd tried to dispatch, or of the world of pain that was headed his way. You didn't try to drown Adarlan's Assassin in a *sewer* and get away with it. Not in a thousand lifetimes. "Because," she said, "my list of people to kill is now one person longer."

CHAPTER 9

She slept until noon, took the two baths she'd promised herself, and then went to Arobynn's study. He was nursing a cup of tea as she opened the door.

"I'm surprised to see you out of the bathtub," he said.

Telling Sam the story about her month in the Red Desert had reminded her of why she'd wanted so badly to come home this summer, and of what she had accomplished. She had no reason now to tiptoe around Arobynn—not after what he'd done, and what she'd been through. So Celaena merely smiled at the King of the Assassins as she held open the door for the servants outside. They carried in a heavy trunk. Then another. And another.

"Do I dare ask?" Arobynn massaged his temples.

The servants hurried out, and Celaena shut the door behind them. Without a word, she opened the lids of the trunks. Gold shone in the noontime sun.

She turned to Arobynn, clinging to the memory of what it had felt like to sit on the roof after the party. His face was unreadable.

"I think this covers my debt," she said, forcing herself to smile. "And then some."

Arobynn remained seated.

She swallowed, suddenly feeling sick. Why had she thought this was a good idea?

"I want to keep working with you," she said carefully. He'd looked at her like this before—on the night he'd beaten her. "But you don't own me anymore."

His silver eyes flicked to the trunks, then to her. In a moment of silence that lasted forever, she stood still as he took her in. Then he smiled, a bit ruefully. "Can you blame me for hoping that this day would never come?"

She almost sagged with relief. "I mean it: I want to keep working with you."

She knew in that moment that she couldn't tell him about the apartment and that she was moving out—not right now. Small steps. Today, the debt. Perhaps in a few weeks, she could mention that she was leaving. Perhaps he wouldn't even care that she was getting her own home.

"And I'll always be happy to work with *you*," he said, but remained seated. He took a sip from his tea. "Do I want to know where that money came from?"

She became aware of the scar on her neck as she said, "The Mute Master. Payment for saving his life."

Arobynn picked up the morning paper. "Well, allow me to extend my congratulations." He looked at her over the top of the paper. "You're now a free woman."

She tried not to smile. Perhaps she wasn't free in the entire sense of the word, but at least he wouldn't be able to wield the debt against her anymore. That would suffice for now.

"Good luck with Doneval tomorrow night," he added. "Let me know if you need any help."

"As long as you don't charge me for it."

He didn't return her smile, and set down the paper. "I would never do that to you." Something like hurt flickered in his eyes.

Fighting her sudden desire to apologize, she left his study without another word.

The walk back to her bedroom was long. She'd expected to crow with glee when she gave him the money, expected to strut around the Keep. But seeing the way he'd looked at her made all that gold feel . . . cheap.

A glorious start to her new future.

Though Celaena never wanted to set foot in the vile sewer again, she found herself back there that afternoon. There was still a river flowing through the tunnel, but the narrow walkway alongside it was dry, even with the rain shower that was now falling on the street above them.

An hour before, Sam had just showed up at her bedroom, dressed and ready to spy on Doneval's house. Now he crept behind her, saying nothing as they approached the iron door she remembered all too well. She set down her torch beside the door and ran her hands along the worn, rusty surface.

"We'll have to get in this way tomorrow," she said, her voice barely audible above the gurgle of the sewer river. "The front of the house is too well-guarded now."

Sam traced a finger through the groove between the door and the threshold. "Aside from finding a way to haul a battering ram down here, I don't think we're getting through."

She shot him a dark look. "You could try knocking."

Sam laughed under his breath. "I'm sure the guards would appreciate that. Maybe they'd invite me in for an ale, too. That is, after they finished pumping my gut full of arrows." He patted the firm plane of his stomach. He was wearing the suit Arobynn had forced him to buy, and she tried not to look too closely at how well it displayed his form.

"So we can't get in this door," she murmured, sliding her hand along it again. "Unless we figure out when the servants dump the trash."

"Unreliable," he countered, still studying the door. "The servants might empty the trash whenever they feel like it."

She swore and glanced about the sewer. What a horrible place to have almost died. She certainly hoped that she'd run into Philip tomorrow. That arrogant ass wouldn't see what was coming until she was right in front of him. He hadn't even recognized her from the party the other night.

She smiled slowly. What better way to get back at Philip than to break in through the very door he'd revealed to her? "Then one of us will just have to sit out here for a few hours," she whispered, still staring at the door. "With the landing outside the door, the servants need to take a few steps to reach the water." Celaena's smile grew. "And I'm sure that if they're lugging a bunch of trash, they probably won't think to look behind them."

Sam's teeth flashed in the torchlight as he smiled. "And they'll be preoccupied long enough for someone to slip in and find a good hiding spot in the cellar to wait out the rest of the time until seven thirty."

"What a surprise they'll have tomorrow, when they find their cellar door unlocked."

"I think that'll be the least of their surprises tomorrow."

She picked up her torch. "It certainly will be." He followed her back down the sewer walkway. They'd found a grate in a shadowy alley, far enough away from the house that no one would suspect them. Unfortunately, it meant a long walk back through the sewers.

"I heard you paid off Arobynn this morning," he said, his eyes on the dark stones beneath their feet. He still kept his voice soft. "How does it feel to be free?"

She glanced at him sidelong. "Not the way I thought it would."

"I'm surprised he accepted the money without a fight."

She didn't say anything. In the dim light, Sam took a ragged breath.

"I think I might leave," he whispered.

She almost tripped. "Leave?"

He wouldn't look at her. "I'm going down to Eyllwe—to Banjali, to be precise."

"For a mission?" It was common for Arobynn to send them all over the continent, but the way Sam was speaking felt . . . different.

"Forever," he said.

"Why?" Her voice sounded a little shrill in her ears.

He faced her. "What do I have to tie me here? Arobynn already mentioned that it might be useful to firmly establish ourselves in the south, too."

"Arobynn—" she seethed, fighting to keep her voice to a whisper. "You talked to Arobynn about this?"

Sam gave her a half shrug. "Casually. It's not official."

"But—but Banjali is a thousand miles away."

"Yes, but Rifthold belongs to you and Arobynn. I'll always be . . . an alternative."

"I'd rather be an alternative in Rifthold than ruler of the assassins in Banjali." She hated that she had to keep her voice so soft. She was going to splatter someone against a wall. She was going to rip down the sewer with her bare hands.

"I'm leaving at the end of the month," he said, still calm.

"That's two weeks away!"

"Do I have any reason why I should stay here?"

"Yes!" she exclaimed as loudly as she could while still maintaining a hushed tone. "Yes, you do." He didn't reply. "You *can't* go."

"Give me a reason why I shouldn't."

"Because what was the *point* in anything if you just disappear forever?" she hissed, splaying her arms.

"The point in what, Celaena?" How could he be so calm when she was so frantic?

"The point in Skull's Bay, and the point in getting me that music, and the point in . . . the point in telling Arobynn that you'd forgive him if he never hurt me again."

"You said you didn't care what I thought. Or what I did. Or if I died, if I'm not mistaken."

"I lied! And you *know* I lied, you stupid bastard!"

He laughed quietly. "You want to know how I spent this summer?" She went still. He ran a hand through his brown hair. "I spent every single day fighting the urge to slit Arobynn's throat. And he *knew* I wanted to kill him."

I'll kill you! Sam had screamed at Arobynn.

"The moment I woke up after he beat me, I realized I *had* to leave. Because I was going to kill him if I didn't. But I couldn't." He studied her face. "Not until you came back. Not until I knew you were all right—until I saw that you were safe."

Breathing became very, very hard.

"He knew that, too," Sam went on. "So he decided to exploit it. He didn't recommend me for missions. Instead, he made me help Lysandra and Clarisse. He made me escort them around the city on picnics and to parties. It became a game between the two of us—how much of his horseshit I could take before I snapped. But we both knew he'd always have the winning hand. He'd always have *you*. Still, I spent every day this summer hoping you'd come back in one piece. More than that—I hoped you'd come back and take revenge for what he'd done to you."

But she hadn't. She'd come back and let Arobynn shower her with gifts.

"And now that you're fine, Celaena, now that you've paid off your debt, I can't stay in Rifthold. Not after all the things he's done to us."

She knew it was selfish, and horrible, but she whispered, "Please don't go."

He let out an uneven breath. "You'll be fine without me. You always have been."

Maybe once, but not now. "How can I convince you to stay?"

"You can't."

She threw down the torch. "Do you want me to beg, is that it?"

"No—never."

"Then tell me—"

"What more can I say?" he exploded, his whisper rough and harsh. "I've already told you everything—I've already told you that if I stay here, if I have to live with Arobynn, I'll snap his damned neck."

"But why? Why can't you let it go?"

He grabbed her shoulders and shook her. "Because I love you!"

Her mouth fell open.

"I love you," he repeated, shaking her again. "I have for *years*. And he *hurt* you and made me watch because he's always known how I felt, too. But if I asked you to pick, you'd choose Arobynn, and I. Can't. Take. It."

The only sounds were their breathing, an uneven beat against the rushing of the sewer river.

"You're a damned idiot," she breathed. "You're a moron and an ass and a *damned* idiot." He looked like she had hit him. But she went on, and grasped both sides of his face, "Because I'd pick *you*."

And then she kissed him.

CHAPTER 10

She'd never kissed anyone. And as her lips met his and he wrapped his arms around her waist, pulling her close against him, she honestly had no idea why she'd waited so long. His mouth was warm and soft, his body wondrously solid against hers, his hair silken as she threaded her fingers through it. Still, she let him guide her, forced herself to remember to breathe as he eased her lips apart with his own.

When she felt the brush of his tongue against hers, she was so full of lightning she thought she might die from the rush of it. She wanted more. She wanted *all* of him.

She couldn't hold him tight enough, kiss him fast enough. A growl rumbled in the back of his throat, so full of need she felt it in her core. Lower than that, actually.

She pushed him against the wall, and his hands roamed all over her back, her sides, her hips. She wanted to bask in the feeling—wanted to rip off her suit so she could feel his callused hands against her bare skin. The intensity of that desire swept her away.

She didn't give a damn about the sewers. Or Doneval, or Philip, or Arobynn.

Sam's lips left her mouth to travel along her neck. They grazed a spot beneath her ear and her breath hitched.

No, she didn't give a damn about anything right now.

It was nighttime when they left the sewers, hair disheveled and mouths swollen. He wouldn't let go of her hand during the long walk back to the Keep, and when they got there, she ordered the servants to send dinner for them to her room. Though they stayed up long into the night, doing a minimal amount of talking, their clothes remained on. Enough had happened today to change her life, and she was in no particular mood to alter yet another major thing.

But what had happened in the sewer . . .

Celaena lay awake that night, long after Sam had left her room, staring at nothing.

He loved her. For years. And he'd endured so much for her sake.

For the life of her, she couldn't understand why. She'd been nothing but horrible to him, and had repaid any kindness on his part with a sneer. And what she felt for him . . .

She *hadn't* been in love with him for years. Until Skull's Bay, she wouldn't have minded killing him.

But now . . . No, she couldn't think about this now. And she couldn't think about it tomorrow, either. Because tomorrow, they'd infiltrate Doneval's house. It was still risky, but the payoff . . . She couldn't turn down that money, not now that she would be supporting herself. And she wouldn't let the bastard Doneval get away with his slave-trade agreement, or blackmailing those who dared to stand against it.

She just prayed Sam wouldn't get hurt.

In the silence of her bedroom, she swore an oath to the moonlight that if Sam were hurt, no force in the world would hold her back from slaughtering everyone responsible.

After lunch the next afternoon, Celaena waited in the shadows beside the sewer door to the cellar. A ways down the tunnel, Sam also waited, his black suit making him almost invisible in the darkness.

With the household lunch just ending, it was a good bet that Celaena would soon have her best chance to slip inside. She'd been waiting for an hour already, each noise whetting the edge she'd been riding since dawn. She'd have to be quick and silent and ruthless. One mistake, one shout—or even a missing servant—might ruin everything.

A servant *had* to come down here to deposit the trash at some point soon. She pulled a little pocket watch out of her suit. Carefully, she lit a match to glance at the face. Two o'clock. She had five hours until she needed to creep into Doneval's study to await the seven-thirty meeting. And she was willing to bet he wouldn't enter the study until then; a man like that would want to greet his guest at the door, to see the look on his partner's face as he led him through the opulent halls. Suddenly, she heard the first, interior door to the sewers groan, and footsteps and grunts sounded. Her trained ear heard the noises of one servant—female. Celaena blew out the match.

She pressed herself into the wall as the lock to the outer door snapped open, and the heavy door slid against the ground. She could hear no other footsteps, save for the woman who hauled a vat of garbage onto the landing. The servant was alone. The cellar above was empty, too.

The woman, too preoccupied with depositing the metal pail of garbage, didn't think to look to the shadows beside the door. She didn't even pause as Celaena slipped past her. Celaena was through both doors, up the stairs, and into the cellar before she even heard the plop and splatter of the trash landing in the water.

As Celaena rushed toward the darkest corner of the vast, dimly lit cellar, she took in as many details as she could. Countless barrels of wine and shelves crammed full of food and goods from across Erilea. One staircase leading up. No other servants to be heard, save for somewhere above her. The kitchen, probably.

The outer door slammed shut, the lock sounding. But Celaena was already crouched behind a giant keg of wine. The interior door also shut and locked. Celaena slid on the smooth black mask she'd brought with her, tossing the hood of her cloak over her hair. The sound of footsteps and light panting, and then the servant reappeared at the top of the sewer stairs, empty garbage pail creaking as it swung from one hand. She walked right by, humming to herself as she mounted the stairs that led toward the kitchen.

Celaena loosed a breath when the woman's footsteps faded, then grinned to herself. If Philip had been smart, he would have slit her throat in the sewer that night. Perhaps when she killed him, she'd let him know exactly how she got into the house.

When she was absolutely certain that the servant wasn't returning with a second pail of garbage, Celaena hurried toward the small set of steps that led down to the sewer. Quiet as a jackrabbit in the Red Desert, she unlocked the first door, crept through, then unlocked the second. Sam wouldn't sneak in until right before the meeting—or else someone might come down and discover him preparing the cellar for the fire that would serve as a distraction. And if someone found the two unlocked doors before then, it could just be blamed on the servant who'd dumped the trash.

Celaena carefully shut both doors, making sure the locks remained disabled, and then returned to her place in the shadows of the cellar's vast wine collection.

Then she waited.

~

At seven, she left the cellar before Sam could arrive with his torches and oil. The ungodly amount of alcohol stocked inside would do the rest. She just hoped he made it out before the fire blew the cellar to bits.

She needed to be upstairs and hidden before that happened—and before the exchange was made. Once the fire started a few minutes after seven thirty, some of the guards would be called downstairs immediately, leaving Doneval and his partner with far fewer men to protect them.

The servants were eating their evening meal, and from the laughter inside the sub-level kitchen, none of them seemed aware of the deal that was to occur three flights above them. Celaena crept past the kitchen door. In her suit, cloak, and mask, she was a mere shadow on the pale stone walls. She held her breath the entire way up the servants' narrow spiral staircase.

With her new suit, it was far easier to keep track of her weapons, and she slid a long dagger out of the hidden flap in her boot. She peered down the second floor hallway.

The wooden doors were all shut. No guards, no servants, no members of Doneval's household. She eased a foot onto the wooden floorboards. Where the hell were the guards?

Swift and quiet as a cat, she was at the door to Doneval's study. No light shone from beneath the door. She saw no shadows of feet, and heard no sound.

The door was locked. A minor inconvenience. She sheathed her dagger and pulled out two narrow bits of metal, wedging and jamming them into the lock until—*click*.

Then she was inside, door locked again, and she stared into the inky black of the interior. Frowning, Celaena fished the pocket watch out of her suit. She lit a match.

She still had enough time to look around.

Celaena flicked out the match and rushed to the curtains, shutting them tight against the night outside. Rain still plinked faintly against the covered windows. She moved to the massive oak desk in the center of the room and lit the oil lamp atop it, dimming it until only a faint blue flame gave off a flicker of light. She shuffled through the papers on the desk. Newspapers, casual letters, receipts, the household expenses . . .

She opened every drawer in the desk. More of the same. Where were those documents?

Swallowing her violent curse, Celaena put a fist to her mouth. She turned in place. An armchair, an armoire, a hutch . . . She searched the hutch and armoire, but they had nothing. Just empty papers and ink. Her ears strained for any sound of approaching guards.

She scanned the books on the bookcase, tapping her fingers across the spines, trying to hear if any were hollowed out, trying to hear if—

A floorboard creaked beneath her feet. She was down on her knees in an instant, rapping on the dark, polished wood. She knocked all around the area, until she found a hollow sound.

Carefully, heart hammering, she dug her dagger between the floorboards and wedged it upward. Papers stared back at her.

She pulled them out, replaced the floorboard, and was back at the desk a moment later, spreading the papers before her. She'd only glance at them, just to be sure she had the right documents . . .

Her hands trembled as she flipped through the papers, one after another. Maps with red marks in random places, charts with numbers, and names—list after list of names and locations. Cities, towns, forests, mountains, all in Melisande.

These weren't just Melisanders opposed to slavery—these were locations for planned safe houses to smuggle slaves to freedom. This was enough information to get all these people executed or enslaved themselves.

And Doneval, that wretched bastard, was going to use this information to force those people to support the slave trade—or be turned over to the king.

Celaena gathered up the documents. She'd never let Doneval get away with this. Never.

She took a step toward the trick floorboard. Then she heard the voices.

CHAPTER 11

She had the lamp off and the curtains opened in a heartbeat, swearing silently as she tucked the documents into her suit and hid in the armoire. It would only take a few moments before Doneval and his partner found that the documents were missing. But that was all she needed—she just had to get them in here, away from the guards, long enough to take them both down. The fire would start in the cellar any minute now, hopefully distracting many of the other guards, and hopefully happening before Doneval noticed the papers were gone. She left the armoire door open a crack, peering out.

The study door unlocked and then swung open.

"Brandy?" Doneval was saying to the cloaked and hooded man who trailed in behind him.

"No," the man said, removing his hood. He was of average height and plain, his only notable features his sun-kissed face and high cheekbones. Who was he?

"Eager to get it over with?" Doneval chuckled, but there was a hitch to his voice.

"You could say that," the man replied coolly. He looked about the room, and Celaena didn't dare move—or breathe—as his blue eyes passed over the armoire. "My partners know to start looking for me in thirty minutes."

"I'll have you out in ten. I have to be at the theater tonight, anyway. There's a young lady I'm particularly keen to see," Doneval said with a businessman's charm. "I take it that your associates are prepared to act quickly and give me a response by dawn?"

"They are. But show me your documents first. I need to see what you're offering."

"Of course, of course," Doneval said, drinking from the glass of brandy that he'd poured for himself. Celaena's hands became slick and her face turned sweaty under the mask. "Do you live here, or are you visiting?" When the man didn't respond, Doneval said with a grin, "Either way, I hope you've stopped by Madam Clarisse's establishment. I've never seen such fine girls in all my life."

The man gave Doneval a distinctly displeased stare. Had Celaena not been here to kill them, she might have liked the stranger.

"Not one for chitchat?" Doneval teased, setting down the brandy and walking toward the floorboard. From the slight tremble in Doneval's hands, she could tell that his talking was all nervous babble. How had such a man come into contact with such incredibly delicate and important information?

Doneval knelt before the loose floorboard and pulled it up. He swore.

Celaena flicked the sword out of the hidden compartment in her suit and moved.

She was out of the closet before they even looked at her, and Doneval died a heartbeat after that. His blood sprayed from the spine-severing wound she gave him through the back of his neck, and the other man let out a shout. She whirled toward him, the sword flicking blood.

An explosion rocked the house, so strong that she lost her footing.

What in hell had Sam detonated down there?

That was all the man needed—he was out the study door. His speed was admirable; he moved like someone used to a lifetime of running.

She was through the threshold almost instantly. Smoke was already rising from the stairs. She turned left after the man, only to run into Philip, the bodyguard.

She rebounded away as he swiped with a sword for her face. Behind him, the man was still running, and he glanced over his shoulder once before he sprinted down the stairs.

"What have you *done*?" Philip spat, noticing the blood on her blade. He didn't need to see whose face was under the mask to identify her—he must have recognized the suit.

She deployed the sword in her other arm, too. "Get the hell out of my way." The mask made her words low and gravely—the voice of a demon, not a young woman. She slashed the swords in front of her, a deadly whine coming off of them.

"I'm going to rip you limb from limb," Philip growled.

"Just try it."

Philip's face twisted in rage as he launched himself at her.

She took the first blow on her left blade, her arm aching at the impact, and Philip barely moved away fast enough to avoid her punching the right blade straight through his gut. He struck again, a clever thrust toward her ribs, but she blocked him.

He pressed both her blades. Up close, she could see his weapon was of impressive quality.

"I wanted to make this last," Celaena hissed. "But I think it's going to be quick. Far cleaner than the death you tried to give me."

Philip shoved her back with a roar. "You have *no* idea what you've just done!"

She swung her swords in front of her again. "I know exactly what I've just done. And I know exactly what I'm about to do."

Philip charged, but the hallway was too narrow and his blow too undisciplined. She got past his guard instantly. His blood soaked her gloved hand.

Her sword whined against bone as she whipped it out again.

Philip's eyes went wide and he staggered back, clutching the slender wound that went up through his ribs and into his heart. "Fool," he whispered, slumping to the ground. "Did Leighfer hire you?"

She didn't say anything as he struggled for breath, blood bubbling from his lips.

"Doneval . . . ," Philip rasped, ". . . loved his country . . ." He took a wet breath, hate and grief mingling in his eyes. "You don't know anything." He was dead a moment later.

"Maybe," she said as she looked down at his body. "But I knew enough just then."

~

It had taken less than two minutes—that was it. She knocked out two guards as she catapulted down the stairs of the burning house and out the front door, disarming another three when she vaulted over the iron fence and into the streets of the capital.

Where in hell had the man gone?

There were no alleys from the house to the river, so he hadn't gone left. Which meant he had gone either straight through the alley ahead of her or to the right. He wouldn't have gone to the right—that was the main avenue of the city, where the wealthy lived. She took the alley straight ahead.

She sprinted so fast she could hardly breathe, snapping her swords back into their hidden compartment.

No one noticed her; most people were too busy rushing toward the flames now licking the sky above Doneval's house. What had happened to Sam?

She spotted the man then, sprinting down an alley that led toward the Avery. She almost missed him, because he was around the corner and gone the next instant. He'd mentioned his partners—was he headed to them now? Would he be that foolish?

She splashed through puddles and leapt over trash and grabbed the wall of a building as she hauled herself around the corner. Right into a dead end.

The man was trying to scale the large brick wall at the other end. The buildings surrounding them had no doors—and no windows low enough for him to reach.

Celaena popped out both of her swords as she slowed to a stalking gait.

The man made one last leap for the top of the wall, but couldn't reach. He fell hard against the cobblestone streets. Sprawled on the ground, he twisted toward her. His eyes were bright as he pulled out a pile of papers from his worn jacket. What sort of documents had he been bringing to Doneval? Their official business contract?

"Go to hell," he spat, and a match flared. The papers were instantly alight, and he threw them to the ground. So fast she could hardly see it, he grabbed a vial from his pocket and swallowed the contents.

She lunged toward him, but she was too late.

By the time she grabbed him, he was dead. Even with his eyes closed, the rage remained on his face. He was gone. Irrevocably gone. But for what—some business deal gone sour?

Easing him to the ground, she jumped swiftly to her feet. She stomped on the papers, extinguishing the flame in seconds. But half of them had already burned, leaving only scraps.

In the moonlight, she knelt on the damp cobblestones and picked up the remnants of the documents he'd been so willing to die for.

It wasn't merely a trade agreement. Like the papers she had in her pocket, these contained names and numbers and locations of safe houses. But these were in Adarlan—even stretching as far north as the border with Terrasen.

She whipped her head to the body. It didn't make any sense; why kill himself to keep this information secret, when he'd planned to share it with Doneval and use it for his own profit? Heaviness rushed through her veins. *You know nothing*, Philip had said.

Somehow, it suddenly felt very true. How much had Arobynn known? Philip's words sounded in her ears again and again. It didn't add up. Something was wrong—something was *off*.

No one had told her these documents would be this extensive, this damning to the people they listed. Her hands shaking, she shifted his body into a sitting position so he wouldn't be face-first on the filthy ground. Why had he sacrificed himself to keep this information safe? Noble or not, foolish or not, she couldn't let it go. She straightened his coat.

Then she picked up his half-destroyed documents, lit a match, and let them burn until they were nothing but ashes. It was the only thing she had to offer.

She found Sam slumped against the wall of another alley. She rushed to him where he knelt with a hand over his chest, panting heavily.

"Are you hurt?" she demanded, scanning the alley for any sign of guards. An orange glow spread behind them. She hoped the servants had gotten out of Doneval's house in time.

"I'm fine," Sam rasped. But in the moonlight, she could see the gash on his arm. "The guards spotted me in the cellar and shot at me." He grabbed at the breast of his suit. "One of them hit me right in the heart. I thought I was dead, but the arrow clattered right out. It didn't even touch my skin."

He peeled open the gash in the front of his suit, and a glimmer of iridescence sparkled. "Spidersilk," he murmured, his eyes wide.

Celaena smiled grimly and pulled off the mask from her face.

"No wonder this damned suit was so expensive," Sam said, letting out a breathy laugh. She didn't feel the need to tell him the truth. He searched her face. "It's done, then?"

She leaned down to kiss him, a swift brush of her mouth against his.

"It's done," she said onto his lips.

CHAPTER 12

The rain clouds had vanished and the sun was rising when Celaena strode into Arobynn's study and stopped in front of his desk. Wesley, Arobynn's bodyguard, didn't even try to stop her. He just shut the study doors behind her before resuming his sentry position in the hall outside.

"Doneval's partner burned his own documents before I could see them," she said to Arobynn by way of greeting. "And then poisoned himself." She'd slipped Doneval's documents under his bedroom door last night, but had decided to wait to explain everything to him until that morning.

Arobynn looked up from his ledger. His face was blank. "Was that before or after you torched Doneval's house?"

She crossed her arms. "Does it make a difference?"

Arobynn looked at the window and the clear sky beyond. "I sent the documents to Leighfer this morning. Did you look through them?"

She snorted. "Of course I did. Right in between killing Doneval and fighting my way out of his house, I found the time to sit down for a cup of tea and read them."

Arobynn still wasn't smiling.

"I've never seen you leave such a mess in your wake."

"At least people will think Doneval died in the fire."

Arobynn slammed his hands onto his desk. "Without an identifiable body, how can anyone be sure he's dead?"

She refused to flinch, refused to back down. "He's dead."

Arobynn's silver eyes hardened. "You won't be paid for this. I know for certain Leighfer won't pay you. She wanted a body and *both* documents. You only gave me one of the three."

She felt her nostrils flare. "That's fine. Bardingale's allies are safe now, anyway. And the trade agreement isn't happening." She couldn't mention that she hadn't even *seen* a trade agreement document among the papers—not without revealing that she'd read the documents.

Arobynn let out a low laugh. "You haven't figured it out yet, have you?"

Celaena's throat tightened.

Arobynn leaned back in his chair. "Honestly, I expected more from you. All the years I spent training you, and you couldn't piece together what was happening right before your eyes."

"Just spit it out," she growled.

"There was no trade agreement," Arobynn said, triumph lighting his silver eyes. "At least, not between Doneval and his source in Rifthold. The real meetings about the slave-trade negotiations have been going on in the glass castle—between the king and Leighfer. It was a key point of persuasion in convincing him to let them build their road."

She kept her face blank, kept herself from flinching. The man who poisoned himself—he hadn't been there to trade documents to sell out those opposed to slavery. He and Doneval had been working to—

Doneval loves his country, Philip had said.

Doneval had been working to set up a system of safe houses and form an alliance of people against slavery across the empire. Doneval, bad habits or not, had been working to *help* the slaves.

And she'd killed him.

Worse than that, she'd given the documents over to Bardingale—who didn't want to stop slavery at all. No, she wanted to profit from it and use her new road to do it. And she and Arobynn had concocted the perfect lie to get Celaena to cooperate.

Arobynn was still smiling. "Leighfer has already seen to it that Doneval's documents are secured. If it'll ease your conscience, she said she won't give them to the king—not yet. Not until she's had a chance to speak to the people on this list and . . . persuade them to support her business endeavors. But if they don't, perhaps those documents will find their way into the glass castle after all."

Celaena fought to keep from trembling. "Is this punishment for Skull's Bay?"

Arobynn studied her. "While I might regret beating you, Celaena, you *did* ruin a deal that would have been extremely profitable for us." "Us," like she was a part of this disgusting mess. "You might be free of me, but you shouldn't forget who I am. What I'm capable of."

"As long as I live," she said, "I'll never forget that." She turned on her heel, striding for the door, but stopped.

"Yesterday," she said, "I sold Kasida to Leighfer Bardingale." She'd visited Bardingale's estate in the morning of the day she was set to infiltrate Doneval's house. The woman had been more than happy to purchase the Asterion horse. She hadn't once mentioned her former husband's impending death.

And last night, after Celaena had killed Doneval, she'd spent a while staring at the signature at the end of the transfer of ownership receipt, so stupidly relieved that Kasida was going to a good woman like Bardingale.

"And?" Arobynn asked. "Why should I care about your horse?"

Celaena looked at him long and hard. Always power games, always deceit and pain. "The money is on its way to your vault at the bank."

He said nothing.

"As of this moment, Sam's debt to you is paid," she said, a shred of victory shining through her growing shame and misery. "From right now until forever, he's a free man."

Arobynn stared back, then shrugged. "I suppose that's a good thing." She felt the final blow coming, and she knew she should run, but she stood like an idiot and listened as he said, "Because I spent all the money you gave me when I was at Lysandra's Bidding last night. My vault feels a little empty because of it."

It took a moment for the words to sink in.

The money she had sacrificed so much to get . . .

He'd used it to win Lysandra's Bidding.

"I'm moving out," she whispered. He just watched her, his cruel, clever mouth forming a slight smile. "I've purchased an apartment, and I'm moving there. Today."

Arobynn's smile grew. "Do come back and visit us some time, Celaena."

She had to bite her lip to keep it from wobbling. "Why did you do it?"

Arobynn shrugged again. "Why shouldn't I enjoy Lysandra after all these years of investing in her career? And why do you care what I do with my own money? From what I've heard, you have Sam now. Both of you are free of me."

Of course he'd found out already. And of course he'd try to make this about her—try to make it *her* fault. Why shower her with gifts only to do this? Why deceive her about Doneval and then torture her with it? Why had he saved her life nine years ago just to treat her this way?

He'd spent *her* money on a person he *knew* she hated. To belittle her. Months ago, it would have worked; that sort of betrayal would have devastated her. It still hurt, but now, with Doneval and Philip and others dead by *her* hand, with those documents now in Bardingale's possession, and with Sam steadfastly at her side . . . Arobynn's petty, vicious parting shot had narrowly missed the mark.

"Don't come looking for me for a good, long while," she said. "Because I might kill you if I see you before then, Arobynn."

He waved a hand at her. "I look forward to the fight."

She left. As she strode through his study doors, she almost slammed into the three tall men who were walking in. They all took one look at her face and then muttered apologies. She ignored them, and ignored Wesley's dark stare as she strode past him. Arobynn's business was his own. She had her own life now.

Her boot heels clicked against the marble floor of the grand entrance. Someone yawned from across the space, and Celaena found Lysandra leaning against the banister of the staircase. She was wearing a white silk nightgown that barely covered her more private areas.

"You've probably already heard, but I went for a record price," Lysandra purred, stretching out the beautiful lines of her body. "Thank you for that; rest assured that your gold went a long, long way."

Celaena froze and slowly turned. Lysandra smirked at her.

Fast as lightning, Celaena hurled a dagger.

The blade imbedded itself into the wooden railing a hair's breadth from Lysandra's head.

Lysandra began screaming, but Celaena just walked out of the front doors, across the lawn of the Keep, and kept walking until the capital swallowed her up.

Celaena sat on the edge of her roof, looking out across the city. The convoy from Melisande had already left, taking the last of the rain clouds with them. Some of them wore black to mourn Doneval's death. Leighfer Bardingale had ridden Kasida, prancing down the main avenue. Unlike those in mourning colors, the lady had been dressed in saffron yellow—and was smiling broadly. Of course, it was just because the King of Adarlan had agreed to give them the funds and resources to build their road. Celaena had half a mind to go after her—to get those documents back and repay Bardingale for her deceit. And take back Kasida while she was at it, too.

But she didn't. She'd been fooled and had lost—badly. She didn't want to be a part of this tangled web. Not when Arobynn had made it perfectly clear that she could never win.

To distract her from that miserable thought, Celaena had then spent the whole day sending servants between the Keep and her apartment, fetching all the clothes and books and jewelry that now belonged to her and her alone. The late afternoon light shifted into a deep gold, setting all the green rooftops glowing.

"I thought you might be up here," Sam said, striding across the flat roof to where she sat atop the wall that lined the edge. He surveyed the city. "Some view; I can see why you decided to move."

She smiled slightly, turning to look at him over her shoulder. He came to stand behind her, and reached out a tentative hand to run through her hair. She leaned into the touch. "I heard what he did—about both Doneval and Lysandra," Sam murmured. "I never imagined he'd sink that low—or use your money like that. I'm sorry."

"It was what I needed." She watched the city again. "It was what I needed to make me tell him I was moving out."

Sam gave a nod of approval. "I've just sort of . . . left my belongings in your main room. Is that all right?"

She nodded. "We'll find space for it later."

Sam fell silent. "So, we're free," he said at last.

She turned fully to look at him. His brown eyes were vivid.

"I also heard that you paid off my debt," he said, his voice strained. "You—you sold your Asterion horse to do it."

"I had no choice." She pivoted from her spot on the roof and stood. "I'd never leave you shackled to him while I walked away."

"Celaena." He said her name like a caress, slipping a hand around her waist. He pressed his forehead against hers. "How can I ever repay you?"

She closed her eyes. "You don't have to."

He brushed his lips against hers. "I love you," he breathed against her mouth. "And from today onward, I want to never be separated from you. Wherever you go, I go. Even if that means going to Hell itself, wherever you are, that's where I want to be. Forever."

Celaena put her arms around his neck and kissed him deeply, giving him her silent reply.

Beyond them, the sun set over the capital, turning the world into crimson light and shadows.

THE ASSASSIN AND THE EMPIRE

AFTER

Curled into the corner of a prison wagon, Celaena Sardothien watched the splotches of shadows and light play on the wall. Trees—just beginning to shift into the rich hues of autumn—seemed to peer at her through the small, barred window.

She rested her head against the musty wooden wall, listening to the creak of the wagon, the clink of the shackles around her wrists and ankles, the rumbling chatter and occasional laughter of the guards who had been escorting the wagon along its route for two days now.

But while she was aware of it all, a deafening sort of silence had settled over her like a cloak. It shut out everything. She knew she was thirsty, and hungry, and that her fingers were numb with cold, but she couldn't feel it keenly.

The wagon hit a rut, jostling her so hard that her head knocked into the wall. Even that pain felt distant.

The freckles of light along the panels danced like falling snow.

Like ash.

Ash from a world burned into nothing—lying in ruins around her. She could taste the ash of that dead world on her chapped lips, settling on her leaden tongue.

She preferred the silence. In the silence she couldn't hear the worst question of all: had she brought this upon herself?

The wagon passed under a particularly thick canopy of trees, blotting out the light. For a heartbeat, the silence peeled back long enough for that question to worm its way into her skull, into her skin, into her breath and her bones.

And in the dark, she remembered.

CHAPTER 1

Eleven Days Earlier

Celaena Sardothien had been waiting for this night for the past year. Sitting on the wooden walkway tucked into the side of the gilded dome of the Royal Theater, she breathed in the music rising from the orchestra far below. Her legs dangled over the railing edge, and she leaned forward to rest her cheek on her folded arms.

The musicians were seated in a semicircle on the stage. They filled the theater with such wondrous noise that Celaena sometimes forgot how to breathe. She had seen this symphony performed four times in the past four years—but she'd always gone with Arobynn. It had become their annual autumn tradition.

Though she knew she shouldn't, she let her eyes drift to the private box where, until last month, she'd always been seated.

Was it from spite or sheer blindness that Arobynn Hamel now sat there, Lysandra at his side? He *knew* what this night meant to Celaena—knew how much she'd looked forward to it every year. And though Celaena hadn't wanted to go with him—and never wanted anything to do with him again—tonight he'd brought Lysandra. As if this night didn't mean anything to him at all.

Even from the rafters, she could see the King of the Assassins holding the hand of the young courtesan, his leg resting against the skirts of her rose-colored gown. A month after Arobynn had won the Bidding for Lysandra's virginity, it seemed that he was still monopolizing her time. It wouldn't be a surprise if he'd worked out something with her madam to keep Lysandra until he tired of her.

Celaena wasn't sure if she pitied Lysandra for it.

Celaena returned her attention to the stage. She didn't know why she'd come here, or why she'd told Sam that she had "plans" and couldn't meet him for dinner at their favorite tavern.

In the past month, she hadn't seen or spoken to Arobynn, nor had she wanted to. But this was her favorite symphony, the music so lovely that, to fill the yearlong wait between performances, she'd mastered a fair portion of it on the pianoforte.

The symphony's third movement finished, and applause thundered across the shimmering arc of the dome. The orchestra waited for the clapping to die down before it swept into the joyous allegro that led to the finale.

At least in the rafters, she didn't have to bother dressing up and pretending to fit in with the bejeweled crowd below. She had easily snuck in from the roof, and no one had looked up to see the black-clad figure seated along the railing, nearly hidden from view by the crystal chandeliers that had been raised and dimmed for the performance.

Up here, she could do what she liked. She could rest her head on her arms, or swing her legs in time with the music, or get up and *dance* if she wanted to. So what if she'd never again sit in that beloved box, so lovely with its red velvet seats and polished wooden banisters?

The music braided through the theater, and each note was more brilliant than the last.

She'd *chosen* to leave Arobynn. She'd paid off her debt to him, and Sam's debt to him, and had moved out. She'd walked away from her life as Arobynn Hamel's protégée. That had been her decision—and one she didn't regret, not after Arobynn had so sorely betrayed her. He'd humiliated and lied to her, and used her blood money to win Lysandra's Bidding just to spite her.

Though she still fancied herself Adarlan's Assassin, part of her wondered how long Arobynn would allow her to keep the title before he named someone else his successor. But no one could *truly* replace her. Whether or not she belonged to Arobynn, she was still the best. She'd always be the best.

Wouldn't she?

She blinked, realizing she'd somehow stopped hearing the music. She should change spots—move to a place where the chandeliers blocked out her view of Arobynn and Lysandra. She stood, her tailbone aching from sitting for so long on the wood.

Celaena took a step, the floorboards sagging under her black boots, but paused. Though it was as she'd remembered it, every note flawless, the music felt disjointed now. Even though she could play it from memory, it was suddenly like she'd never heard it before, or like her internal beat was now somehow *off* from the rest of the world.

Celaena glanced again at the familiar box far below—where Arobynn was now draping a long, muscled arm along the back of Lysandra's seat. *Her* old seat, the one closest to the stage.

It was worth it, though. She was free, and Sam was free, and Arobynn . . . He had done his best to hurt her, to break her. Forgoing these luxuries was a cheap price to pay for a life without him lording over her.

The music worked itself into the frenzy of its climax, becoming a whirlwind of sound that she found herself walking through—not toward a new seat, but toward the small door that led onto the roof.

The music roared, each note a pulse of air against her skin. Celaena threw the hood of her cloak over her head as she slipped out the door and into the night beyond.

It was nearing eleven when Celaena unlocked the door to her apartment, breathing in the already familiar scents of home. She'd spent much of the past month furnishing the spacious apartment—hidden on the upper floor of a warehouse in the slums—that she now shared with Sam.

He'd offered again and again to pay for half of the apartment, but each time, she ignored him. It wasn't because she didn't want his money—though she truly didn't—but rather because, for the first time ever, this was a place that was *hers*. And though she cared deeply for Sam, she wanted to keep it that way.

She slipped inside, taking in the great room that greeted her: to the left, a shining oak dining table large enough to fit eight upholstered chairs around it; to her right, a plush red couch, two armchairs, and a low-lying table set before the darkened fireplace.

The cold fireplace told her enough. Sam wasn't home.

Celaena might have gone into the adjacent kitchen to devour the remaining half of the berry tart Sam hadn't finished at lunch—might have kicked off her boots and reclined before the floor-to-ceiling window to take in the stunning nighttime view of the capital. She might have done any number of things had she not spied the note atop the small table beside the front door.

I've gone out, it said in Sam's handwriting. *Don't wait up*.

Celaena crumpled the note in her fist. She knew *exactly* where he'd gone—and *exactly* why he didn't want her to wait up.

Because if she were asleep, then she most likely wouldn't see the blood and bruises on him when he staggered in.

Swearing viciously, Celaena threw the crumpled note on the ground and stalked out of the apartment, slamming the door shut behind her.

~

If there was a place in Rifthold where the scum of the capital could always be found, it was the Vaults.

On a relatively quiet street of the slums, Celaena flashed her money to the thugs standing outside the iron door and entered the pleasure hall. The heat and reek hit her almost immediately, but she didn't let it crack her mask of cold calm as she descended into a warren of subterranean chambers. She took one look down at the teeming crowd around the main fighting pit and knew exactly who was causing them to cheer.

She swaggered down the stone steps, her hands in easy reach of the swords and daggers sheathed at the belt slung low over her hips. Most people would have opted to wear even more weapons to the Vaults—but Celaena had been here often enough to anticipate the threats the usual clientele posed, and she knew she could look after herself just fine. Still, she kept her hood over her head, concealing most of her face in shadow. Being a young woman in a place like this wasn't without its obstacles—especially when a good number of men came here for the *other* entertainment offered by the Vaults.

As she reached the bottom of the narrow stairs, the reek of unwashed bodies, stale ale, and worse things hit her full-on. It was enough to turn her stomach, and she was grateful that she hadn't eaten anything recently.

She slipped through the crowd packed around the main pit, trying not to look to the exposed rooms on either side—to the girls and women who weren't fortunate enough to be sold into an upper-class brothel like Lysandra. Sometimes, when Celaena was feeling particularly inclined to make herself miserable, she'd wonder if their fate would have been hers had Arobynn not taken her in. She'd wonder if she'd gaze into their eyes and see some version of herself staring back.

So it was easier not to look.

Celaena pushed past the men and women assembled around the sunken pit, keeping alert for grasping hands eager to part her from her money—or one of her exquisite blades.

She leaned against a wooden pillar and stared into the pit.

Sam moved so fast the hulking man in front of him didn't stand a chance, dodging each knock-out blow with power and grace—some of it natural, some learned from years of training at the Assassins' Keep. Both of them were shirtless, and Sam's toned chest gleamed with sweat and blood. Not his blood, she noticed—the only injuries she could see were his split lip and a bruise on his cheek.

His opponent lunged, trying to tackle Sam to the sandy floor. But Sam whirled, and as the giant stumbled past, Sam drove his bare foot into his back. The man hit the sand with a thud that Celaena felt through the filthy stone floor. The crowd cheered.

Sam could have rendered the man unconscious in a heartbeat. He could have snapped his neck just now, or ended the fight any number of ways. But from the half-wild, self-satisfied gleam in Sam's eyes, Celaena knew he was playing with his opponent. The injuries on his face had probably been intentional mistakes—to make it look like a somewhat even fight.

Fighting in the Vaults wasn't only about knocking out your opponent—it was about making a show out of it. The crowd near savage with elation, Sam probably had been giving them one hell of a performance. And, judging by the blood on Sam, it seemed like this performance was probably one of *several* encores.

A low growl rippled through her. There was only one rule in the Vaults: no weapons, just fists. But you could still get horribly hurt.

His opponent staggered to his feet, but Sam had finished waiting.

The poor brute didn't even have time to raise his hands as Sam lashed out with a roundhouse kick. His foot slammed into the man's face hard enough for the impact to sound over the shouts of the crowd.

The opponent reeled sideways, blood spurting from his mouth. Sam struck again, a punch to the gut. The man doubled over, only to meet Sam's knee to his nose. His head snapped skyward, and he stumbled back, back, back—

The crowd screamed its triumph as Sam's fist, coated in blood and sand, connected with the man's exposed face. Even before he finished swinging, Celaena knew it was a knockout punch.

The man hit the sand and didn't move.

Panting, Sam lifted his bloodied arms to the surrounding crowd.

Celaena's ears nearly shattered at the answering roar. She gritted her teeth as the master of ceremonies strode onto the sand, proclaiming Sam the victor.

It wasn't fair, really. No matter what opponents they threw his way, any person that went up against Sam would lose.

Celaena had half a mind to hop into the pit and challenge Sam herself.

That would be a performance the Vaults would never forget.

She gripped her arms. She hadn't had a contract in the month since she'd left Arobynn, and though she and Sam continued training as best they could . . . Oh, the urge to jump into that pit and take them *all* down was overwhelming. A wicked smile spread across her face. If they thought Sam was good, then she'd *really* give the crowd something to scream for.

Sam spotted her leaning against the pillar. His triumphant grin remained, but she saw a glimmer of displeasure flash in his brown eyes.

She inclined her head toward the exit. The gesture told him all he needed to know: unless he wanted *her* to get into the pit with him, he was done for tonight, and she'd meet him on the street when he had collected his earnings.

And then the real fight would begin.

"Should I be relieved or worried that you haven't said anything?" Sam asked her as they strode through the backstreets of the capital, weaving their way home.

Celaena dodged a puddle that could have been either rainwater or urine. "I've been thinking of ways to begin that don't involve screaming."

Sam snorted, and she ground her teeth. A bag of coins jangled at his waist. Although the hood of his cloak was pulled up over his head, she could still clearly see his split lip.

She fisted her hands. "You promised you wouldn't go back there."

Sam kept his eyes on the narrow alley ahead of them, always alert, always watching for any source of danger. "I didn't *promise*. I said I'd think about it."

"People *die* in the Vaults!" She said it louder than she meant to, her words echoing off the alley walls.

"People die because they're fools in search of glory. They're not trained assassins."

"Accidents still happen. Any of those men could have snuck in a blade."

He let out a quick, harsh laugh, full of pure male arrogance. "You really think so little of my abilities?"

They turned down another street, where a group of people were smoking pipes outside a dimly lit tavern. Celaena waited until they were past them before speaking. "Risking yourself for a few coins is absurd."

"We need whatever money we can get," Sam said quietly.

She tensed. "We have money." *Some* money, less and less each day.

"It won't last forever. Not when we haven't been able to get any other contracts. And especially not with your lifestyle."

"*My* lifestyle!" she hissed. But it was true. She could rough it, but her heart lay in luxury—in fine clothes and delicious food and exquisite furnishings. She'd taken for granted how much of that had been provided for her at the Assassins' Keep. Arobynn might have kept a detailed list of the expenses she owed him, but he'd never charged them for their food, or their servants, or their carriages. And now that she was on her own . . .

"The Vaults are easy fights," Sam said. "Two hours there, and I can make decent money."

"The Vaults are a festering pile of shit," she snapped. "We're better than that. We can make our money elsewhere." She didn't know where, or how, exactly, but she could find something better than fighting in the Vaults.

Sam grabbed her arm, making her stop to face him. "Then what if we left Rifthold?" Though her own hood covered most of her features, she raised her brows at him. "What's keeping us here?"

Nothing. Everything.

Unable to answer him, Celaena shook off his grasp and continued walking.

It was an absurd idea, really. Leaving Rifthold. Where would they even *go*?

They reached the warehouse and were quickly up the rickety wooden stairs at the back, then inside the apartment on the second floor.

She didn't say anything to him as she tossed off her cloak and boots, lit some candles, and went into the kitchen to down a piece of bread slathered in butter. And he didn't say anything as he strode into the bathing room and washed himself. The running water was a luxury the previous owner had spent a fortune on—and had been the biggest priority for Celaena when she was looking for places to live.

Benefits like running water were plentiful in the capital, but not widespread elsewhere. If they left Rifthold, what sorts of things would she have to go without?

She was still contemplating that when Sam padded into the kitchen, all traces of blood and sand washed away. His bottom lip was still swollen, and he had a bruise on his cheek, not to mention his raw knuckles, but he looked to be in one piece.

Sam slid into one of the chairs at the kitchen table and cut himself a piece of bread. Buying food for the house took up more time than she'd realized it would, and she'd been debating hiring a housekeeper, but . . . that'd cost money. *Everything* cost money.

Sam took a bite, poured a glass of water from the ewer she'd left sitting on the oak table, and leaned back in his chair. Behind him, the window above the sink revealed the glittering sprawl of the capital and the illuminated glass castle towering over them all.

"Are you just not going to speak to me ever again?"

She shot him a glare. "Moving is expensive. If we were to leave Rifthold, then we'd need a little more money so we could have something to fall back on if we can't get work right away." Celaena contemplated it. "One more contract each," she said. "I might not be Arobynn's protégée anymore, but I'm still Adarlan's Assassin, and you're . . . well, you're *you*." He gave her a dark look, and, despite herself, Celaena grinned. "One more contract," she repeated, "and we could move. It'd help with the expenses—give us enough of a cushion."

"Or we could say to hell with it and go."

"I'm not giving up everything just to slum it somewhere. *If* we leave, we'll do it my way."

Sam crossed his arms. "You keep saying *if*—but what else is there to decide?"

Again: nothing. Everything.

She took a long breath. "How will we establish ourselves in a new city without Arobynn's support?"

Triumph flashed in Sam's eyes. She leashed her irritation. She hadn't said outright that she was agreeing to move, but her question was confirmation enough for both of them.

Before he could answer, she went on: "We've grown up here, and yet in the past month, we haven't been able to get any hires. Arobynn always handled those things."

"Intentionally," Sam growled. "And we'd do just fine, I think. We're not going to need his support. *When* we move, we're leaving the Guild, too. I don't want to be paying dues for the rest of my life, and I don't want anything to do with that conniving bastard ever again."

"Yes, but you *know* that we need his blessing. We need to make . . . amends. And need him to agree to let us leave the Guild peacefully." She almost choked on it, but managed to get the words out.

Sam shot out of his seat. "Do I need to remind you what he did to us? What he's done to *you*? You know that the reason we can't find any hires is because Arobynn made sure word got out that we weren't to be approached."

"Exactly. And it will only get worse. The Assassins' Guild would punish us for beginning our own establishment elsewhere without Arobynn's approval."

Which was true. While they'd paid their debts to Arobynn, they were still members of the Guild, and still obligated to pay them dues every year. Every assassin in the Guild answered to Arobynn. Obeyed him. Celaena and Sam had both been dispatched more than once to hunt down Guild members who had gone rogue, refused to pay their dues, or broken some sacred Guild rule. Those assassins had tried to hide, but it had only been a matter of time before they'd been found. And the consequences hadn't been pleasant.

Celaena and Sam had brought Arobynn and the Guild a lot of

money and earned them a fair amount of notoriety, so their decisions and careers had been closely monitored. Even with their debts paid, they'd be asked to pay a parting fee, if they were lucky. If not . . . well, it'd be a very dangerous request to make.

"So," she went on, "unless you want to wind up with your throat cut, we need to get Arobynn's approval to break from the Guild before we leave. And since you seem in such a hurry to get out of the capital, we'll go see him tomorrow."

Sam pursed his lips. "I'm not going to grovel. Not to him."

"Neither am I." She stalked to the kitchen sink, bracing her hands on either side of it as she looked out the window. Rifthold. Could she truly leave it behind? She might hate it at times, but . . . this was *her* city. Leaving that, starting over in a new city somewhere on the continent . . . Could she do it?

Footsteps thudded on the wooden floor, a warm breath caressed her neck, and then Sam's arms slipped around her waist from behind. He rested his chin on the crook between her shoulder and neck.

"I just want to be with you," he murmured. "I don't care where we go. That's all I want."

She closed her eyes, and leaned her head against his. He smelled of her lavender soap—her *expensive* lavender soap that she'd once warned him to never use again. He probably had no idea what soap she'd even been scolding him about. She'd have to start hiding her beloved toiletries and leave out something inexpensive for him. Sam wouldn't be able to tell the difference, anyway.

"I'm sorry I went to the Vaults," he said onto her skin, planting a kiss beneath her ear.

A shiver went down her spine. Though they'd been sharing the bedroom for the past month, they hadn't yet crossed that final threshold of intimacy. She wanted to—and he *certainly* wanted to—but so much had changed so quickly. Something that monumental could wait a while longer. It didn't stop them from enjoying each other, though.

Sam kissed her ear, his teeth grazing her earlobe, and her heart stumbled a beat.

"Don't use kissing to swindle me into accepting your apology," she got out, even as she tilted her head to the side to allow him better access.

He chuckled, his breath caressing her neck. "It was worth a shot."

"If you go to the Vaults again," she said as he nibbled on her ear, "I'll hop in and beat you unconscious myself."

She felt him smile against her skin. "You could try." He bit her ear—not hard enough to hurt, but enough to tell her that he'd now stopped listening.

She whirled in his arms, glaring up at him, at his beautiful face illuminated by the glow of the city, at his eyes, so dark and rich. "And *you* used my lavender soap. Don't ever do that—"

But then Sam's lips found hers, and Celaena stopped talking for a good while after that.

Yet as they stood there, their bodies twining around each other, there was still one question that remained unasked—one question neither of them dared voice.

Would Arobynn Hamel let them leave?

CHAPTER 2

When Celaena and Sam entered the Assassins' Keep the next day, it was as if nothing had changed. The same trembling housekeeper greeted them at the door before scuttling away, and Wesley, Arobynn's bodyguard, was standing in his familiar position outside the King of the Assassins' study.

They strode right up to the door, Celaena using every step, every breath, to take in details. Two blades strapped to Wesley's back, one at his side, two daggers sheathed at his waist, the glint of one shining in his boot—probably one more hidden in the other boot, too. Wesley's eyes were alert, keen—not a sign of exhaustion or sickness or anything that she could use to her advantage if it came to a fight.

But Sam just strolled right up to Wesley, and despite how quiet he'd been on their long walk over here, he held out a hand and said, "Good to see you, Wesley."

Wesley shook Sam's hand and gave a half smile. "I'd say you look good, boyo, but that bruise says otherwise." Wesley looked at Celaena, who lifted her chin and huffed. "*You* look more or less the same," he said, a challenging gleam in his eyes. He'd never liked her—never bothered to be nice. As if he'd always known that she and Arobynn would wind up on opposite sides, and that he'd be the first line of defense.

She strode right past him. "And you still look like a jackass," she said sweetly, and opened the doors to the study. Sam muttered an apology as Celaena entered the room and found Arobynn waiting for them.

The King of the Assassins watched them with a smile, his hands steepled on the desk in front of him. Wesley shut the door behind Sam, and they silently took seats in the two chairs before Arobynn's massive oak desk.

One glance at Sam's drawn face told her that he, too, was remembering the last time the two of them had been in here together. That night had ended with both of them beaten into unconsciousness at Arobynn's hands. That had been the night that Sam's loyalty had switched—when he'd threatened to kill Arobynn for hurting her. It had been the night that changed everything.

Arobynn's smile grew, a practiced, elegant expression disguised as benevolence. "As overjoyed as I am to see you in good health," he said, "do I even want to know what brings the two of you back home?" *Home*—this wasn't her home now, and Arobynn knew it. The word was just another weapon.

Sam bristled, but Celaena leaned forward. They'd agreed that *she* would do the talking, since Sam was more likely to lose his temper when Arobynn was involved.

"We have a proposal for you," she said, keeping perfectly still. Coming face-to-face with Arobynn, after all his betrayals, made her stomach twist. When she'd walked out of this office a month ago, she'd sworn that she'd kill him if he bothered her again. And Arobynn, surprisingly, had kept his distance.

"Oh?" Arobynn leaned back in his chair.

"We're leaving Rifthold," she said, her voice cool and calm. "And we'd like to leave the Guild, too. Ideally, we'd establish our own business in another city on the continent. Nothing that would rival the Guild," she added smoothly, "just a private business for us to make ends meet." She might need his approval, but she didn't have to grovel.

Arobynn looked from Celaena to Sam. His silver eyes narrowed on Sam's split lip. "Lovers' quarrel?"

"A misunderstanding," Celaena said before Sam could snap a retort. Of course Arobynn would refuse to immediately give them an answer. Sam gripped the wooden arms of his chair.

"Ah," Arobynn replied, still smiling. Still calm, and graceful, and deadly. "And where, exactly, are you living now? Somewhere nice, I hope. It wouldn't do to have my best assassins living in squalor."

He'd make them play this game of exchanging niceties until *he* wanted to answer their question. Beside her, Sam was rigid in his seat. She could practically feel the hot rage rippling off of him as Arobynn said *my assassins*. Another razor-sharp use of words. She bit down on her own rising anger.

"You look well, Arobynn," she said. If he didn't answer her questions, then she certainly wouldn't answer his. Especially ones about their current location, though he probably already knew.

Arobynn waved a hand, leaning back in his seat. "This Keep feels too empty without you both."

He said it with such conviction—as if they'd left just to spite him—that she wondered if he meant it, if he'd somehow forgotten what he'd done to her and how he'd treated Sam.

"And now that you're talking of moving away from the capital and leaving the Guild . . ." Arobynn's face was unreadable. She kept her breathing even, kept her heartbeat from racing. A nonanswer to her question.

She kept her chin high. "Then is it acceptable to the Guild if we leave?" Every word balanced on the edge of a blade.

Arobynn's eyes glittered. "You are free to move away." Move away. He hadn't said anything about leaving the Guild.

Celaena opened her mouth to demand a clearer statement, but then—

"Give us a damned answer." Sam's teeth were bared, his face white with anger.

Arobynn looked at Sam, his smile so deadly that Celaena fought the urge to reach for a dagger. "I just did. You two are free to do whatever you want."

She had seconds, perhaps, before Sam truly exploded—before he'd start a brawl that would ruin everything. Arobynn's smile grew, and Sam's hands casually dropped to his sides—his fingers so, so near the hilts of his sword and dagger.

Shit.

"We're willing to offer this much to leave the Guild," Celaena interrupted, desperate for anything to get them from coming to blows. Gods above, she was aching for a fight, but not *this* one—not with Arobynn. Thankfully, both Arobynn and Sam turned to her as she named the sum. "That price is more than satisfactory for us to leave and set up our own business elsewhere."

Arobynn looked at her for a too-long moment before he made her a counteroffer.

Sam shot to his feet. "Are you *insane*?"

Celaena was too stunned to move. That much money . . . He had to know, somehow, how much she had left in the bank. Because paying him what he asked would wipe it out entirely. The only money they'd have would be Sam's meager savings, and whatever she could get from the apartment—which might be hard to sell, given its location and unusual layout.

She countered his offer with another, but he just shook his head and stared up at Sam. "You two are my best," Arobynn said with maddening calm. "If you leave, then the respect *and* the money you'd provide the Guild would be lost. I have to account for that. This price is generous."

"*Generous*," Sam hissed.

But Celaena, her stomach churning, lifted her chin. She could keep throwing figures at him until she was blue in the face, but he'd obviously picked this number for a reason. He would not budge. It was one last slap in the face—one final twist of the knife meant only to punish her.

"I accept," she said, giving him a bland smile. Sam whipped his head around, but she kept her eyes on Arobynn's elegant face. "I'll have the funds transferred to your account immediately. And once that's done, we're leaving—and I expect to never be bothered by you or the Guild again. Understood?"

Celaena rose to her feet. She had to get far away from here. Coming back had been a mistake. She shoved her hands in her pockets to hide how they were starting to tremble.

Arobynn grinned at her, and she realized he already knew. "Understood."

"You had no right to accept his offer," Sam raged, his face set with such fury that people along the broad city avenue practically jumped out of his way. "No right to do that without consulting me. You didn't even *bargain*!"

Celaena peered into the shop windows as she walked by. She loved the shopping district in the heart of the capital—the clean sidewalks lined with trees, the main avenue leading right up to the marble steps of the Royal Theater, the way she could find anything from shoes to perfumes to jewelry to fine weapons.

"If we pay that, then we definitely need to find a contract before we leave!"

If we pay that. She said, "I *am* paying that."

"Like hell you are."

"It's my money, and I can do what I want with it."

"You paid for your debt and mine already—I'm not letting you give him another copper. We can find some way around paying this parting fee."

They walked past the crowded entrance of a popular tea court, where finely dressed women were chatting with each other in the warm autumn sun.

"Is the issue that he demanded so much money, or that *I'm* paying it?"

Sam pulled up short, and though he didn't look twice at the tea court ladies, they certainly looked at him. Even with anger rolling off him, Sam was beautiful. And too angry to notice that this was *not* the spot to argue.

Celaena grabbed his arm, yanking him along. She felt the eyes of the ladies on her as she did so. She couldn't help a flicker of smugness as they took in her dark blue tunic with its exquisite gold embroidery along the lapels and cuffs, her fitted ivory pants, and her knee-high brown boots, made with butter-soft leather. While most women—especially the wealthy or noble-born ones—opted to wear dresses and miserable corsets, pants and tunics were common enough that her fine clothing wouldn't have escaped the appreciation of the women idling outside the tea courts.

"The issue," Sam said through his teeth, "is that I'm sick of playing his games, and I'd just as soon cut his throat as pay that money."

"Then you're a fool. If we leave Rifthold on bad terms, we'll never be able to settle anywhere—not if we want to keep our current occupation. And even if we decided to find honest professions instead, I'd always wonder if he or the Guild would show up one day and demand that money. So if I have to give him every last copper in my bank account to ensure that I can sleep in peace for the rest of my life, so be it."

They reached the enormous intersection at the heart of the shopping district, where the domed Royal Theater rose above streets packed with horses and wagons and people.

"Where do we draw the line?" Sam asked her quietly. "When do we say *enough*?"

"This is the last time."

He let out a derisive snort. "I'm sure it is." He turned down one of the avenues—in the opposite direction from home.

"Where are you going?"

He looked over his shoulder. "I need to clear my head. I'll see you at home." She watched him cross the busy avenue, watched until he was swallowed up by the hustle of the capital.

Celaena began walking, too, wherever her feet took her. She passed by the steps of the Royal Theater and kept walking, the shops and vendors blurring together. The day was blossoming into a truly lovely example of autumn—the air was crisp, but the sun was warm.

In some ways, Sam was right. But she'd dragged him into this mess—she'd been the one who had started things in Skull's Bay. Though he claimed to have been in love with her for years, if she'd only kept her distance these past few months, he wouldn't be in this situation. Perhaps, if she'd been smart, she would have just broken his heart and let him remain with Arobynn. Having him hate her was easier than this. She was . . . responsible for him now. And that was terrifying.

She cared for him more than she'd ever cared for anyone. Now that she'd ruined the career he'd worked for his whole life, she'd hand over all her money to make sure that he could at least be free. But she couldn't just explain that she paid for everything because she felt guilty. He'd resent that.

Celaena paused her walking and found herself at the other end of the broad avenue, across the street from the gates to the glass castle. She hadn't realized she'd walked so far—or been so lost in her thoughts. She usually avoided coming this close to the castle.

The heavily guarded iron gates led to a long, tree-lined path that snaked up to the infamous building itself. She craned her head back to take in the towers that brushed the sky, the turrets sparkling in the midmorning sun. It had been built atop the original stone castle, and was the crowning achievement in Adarlan's empire.

She hated it.

Even from the street, she could see people milling about the distant castle grounds—uniformed guards, ladies in voluminous dresses, servants clad in the clothes of their station . . . What sort of lives did they lead, dwelling within the shadow of the king?

Her eyes rose to the highest gray stone tower, where a small balcony jutted out, covered with creeping ivy. It was so easy to imagine that the people within had nothing to worry about.

But inside that shining building, decisions were made daily that altered the course of Erilea. Inside that building, it had been decreed that magic was outlawed, and that labor camps like Calaculla and Endovier were to be established. Inside that building, the murderer who called himself king dwelled, the man she feared above all others. If the Vaults were the heart of Rifthold's underworld, then the glass castle was the soul of Adarlan's empire.

She felt like it watched her, a giant beast of glass and stone and iron. Staring at it made her problems with Sam and Arobynn feel inconsequential—like gnats buzzing before the gaping maw of a creature poised to devour the world.

A chill wind blew past, ripping strands of hair from her braid. She shouldn't have let herself walk so close, even if the odds of ever encountering the king were next to none. Just the thought of him sent a wretched fear splintering through her.

Her only consolation was that most people from the kingdoms conquered by the king probably felt the same way. When he'd marched into Terrasen nine years ago, his invasion had been swift and brutal—so brutal that it made even Celaena sick to recall some of the atrocities that had been committed to secure his rule.

Shuddering, she turned on her heel and headed home.

Sam didn't return until dinner.

Celaena was sprawled on the couch before the roaring fireplace, book in hand, when Sam strode into the apartment. His hood still covered half of his face, and the hilt of the sword strapped to his back glinted in the orange light of the room. As he locked the door behind him, she caught the dull gleam of the gauntlets strapped to his forearms—thick, embroidered leather that concealed hidden daggers. He moved with such precise efficiency and controlled power that she blinked. Sometimes it was so easy to forget that the young man she shared the apartment with was also a trained, ruthless killer.

"I found a client." He pulled off his hood and leaned against the door, his arms crossed over his broad chest.

Celaena shut the book she'd been gobbling down and set it on the couch. "Oh?"

His brown eyes were bright, though his face was unreadable. "They'll pay. A lot. And they want to keep it from reaching the Assassins' Guild's ears. There's even a contract in it for you."

"Who's the client?"

"I don't know. The man I spoke to had the usual disguises—hood, unremarkable clothing. He could have been acting on behalf of someone else."

"Why do they want to avoid using the Guild?" She moved to perch on the arm of the couch. The distance between her and Sam felt too large, too full of lightning.

"Because they want me to kill Ioan Jayne and his second-in-command, Rourke Farran."

Celaena stared at him. "Ioan Jayne." The biggest Crime Lord in Rifthold.

Sam nodded.

A roaring filled her ears. "He's too well-guarded," she said. "And Farran . . . That man is a psychopath. He's a *sadist*."

Sam approached her. "You said that in order to move to another city, we need money. And since you're insisting on paying off the Guild, then we *really* need money. So unless you want to wind up as thieves, I suggest we take it."

She had to tilt her head back to look at him. "Jayne is dangerous."

"Then it's good that we're the best, isn't it?" Though he gave her a lazy smile, she could see the tension in his shoulders.

"We should find another contract. There's bound to be someone else."

"You don't know that. And no one else would pay this much." He named the figure, and Celaena's brows rose. They'd be *very* comfortable after that. They could live anywhere.

"You're sure you don't know who the client is?"

"Are you *looking* for excuses to say no?"

"I'm trying to make sure that we're safe," she snapped. "Do you know how many people have tried to take out Jayne and Farran? Do you know how many of them are still alive?"

Sam ran a hand through his hair. "Do you want to be with me?"

"What?"

"Do you want to be with me?"

"Yes." Right now, that was all she wanted.

A half smile tugged at one corner of his lips. "Then we'll do this, and we'll have enough money to tie up our loose ends in Rifthold and set ourselves up somewhere else on the continent. If you asked, I'd still leave tonight without giving Arobynn or the Guild a copper, but you're right: I don't want to spend the rest of our lives looking over our shoulders. It should be a clean break. I want that for us." Her throat tightened, and she looked toward the fire. Sam hooked a finger under her chin and tilted her head up to him again. "So will you go after Jayne and Farran with me?"

He was so beautiful—so full of all the things that she wanted, all that she hoped for. How had she never noticed that until this year? How had she spent so long hating him?

"I'll think about it," she rasped. It wasn't just bravado. She *did* need to think about it. Especially if their targets were Jayne and Farran.

Sam's smile grew and he leaned down to brush a kiss to her temple. "Better than a *no*."

Their breath mingled. "I'm sorry for what I said earlier today."

"An apology from Celaena Sardothien?" His eyes danced with light. "Do I dream?"

She scowled, but Sam kissed her. She wrapped her arms around his neck, opening her mouth to his, and a low growl escaped from him as their tongues met. Her hands tangled in the strap that held his sword against his back, and she withdrew long enough to unclasp the scabbard buckle across his chest.

His sword clattered to the wooden floor behind them. Sam looked her in the eyes again, and it was enough for her to grab him closer. He kissed her thoroughly, lazily, as if he had a lifetime of kisses to look forward to.

She liked that. A lot.

He slid one arm around her back and the other beneath her knees, sweeping her up in a fluid, graceful movement. Though she'd never tell him, she practically swooned.

He carried her from the living room and into the bedroom, gently setting her down on the bed. He withdrew only long enough to remove the deadly gauntlets from his wrists, followed by his boots, cloak, jerkin, and shirt beneath. She took in his golden skin and muscled chest, the slender scars that peppered his torso, her heart beating so fast she could hardly breathe.

He was hers. This magnificent, powerful creature was hers.

Sam's mouth found hers again, and he eased her farther onto the bed. Down, down, his clever hands exploring every inch of her until she was on her back and he braced himself on his forearms to hover over her. He kissed her neck, and she arched up into him as he ran his hand down the plane of her torso, unbuttoning her tunic as he went. She didn't want to know where he had learned to do these things. Because if she ever learned the names of those girls . . .

Her breath hitched as he reached the last button and pulled her out of the jacket. He looked down at her body, his breathing ragged. They had gone further than this before, but there was a question in his eyes—a question written over every inch of his body.

"Not tonight," she whispered, her cheeks flaring with heat. "Not yet."

"I'm in no rush," he said, bending down to graze his nose along her shoulder.

"It's just . . ." Gods above, she should stop talking. She didn't owe him an explanation, and he didn't push it with her, but . . . "If I'm only going to do this once, then I want to enjoy every step." He understood what she meant by *this*—this relationship between them, this bond that was forming, so unbreakable and unyielding that it made the entire axis of her world shift toward him. That terrified her more than anything.

"I can wait," he said thickly, kissing her collarbone. "We have all the time in the world."

Maybe he was right. And spending all the time in the world with Sam . . .

That was a treasure worth paying anything for.

CHAPTER 3

Dawn crept into their room, filling it with golden light that caught in Sam's hair and made it shine like bronze.

Propped on one elbow, Celaena watched him sleep.

His bare torso was still gloriously tanned from the summer—suggesting days spent training in one of the courtyards of the Keep, or maybe lounging on the banks of the Avery. Scars of varying lengths were scattered across his back and shoulders—some of them slender and even, some of them thicker and jagged. A life spent training and battling . . . His body was a map of his adventures, or proof of what growing up with Arobynn Hamel was like.

She ran a finger down the groove of his spine. She didn't want to see another scar added to his flesh. She didn't want *this* life for him. He was better than that. Deserved better.

When they moved, maybe they couldn't leave behind death and killing and all that came with it—not at first, but someday, far in the future, perhaps . . .

She brushed the hair from his eyes. Someday, they would both lay down their swords and daggers and arrows. And by leaving Rifthold, by leaving the Guild, they'd take the first step toward that day, even if they had to keep working as assassins for a few more years at least.

Sam's eyes opened, and, finding her watching him, he gave her a sleepy smile.

It hit her like a punch to the gut. Yes—for him, she could someday give up being Adarlan's Assassin, give up the notoriety and fortune.

He pulled her down, wrapping an arm around her bare waist and tucking her in close to him. His nose grazed her neck, and he breathed her in deeply.

"Let's take down Jayne and Farran," she said softly.

Sam purred a response onto her skin that told her he was only half-awake—and that his mind was on anything but Jayne and Farran.

She dug her nails into his back, and he grunted his annoyance, but made no move to awaken.

"We'll eliminate Farran first—to weaken the chain of command. It'd be too risky to take them both out at once—too many things could go wrong. But if we take out Farran first, even if it means Jayne's guards will be on alert, they'll still be in total chaos. And that's when we'll dispatch Jayne." It was a solid plan. She liked this plan. They merely needed a few days to figure out Farran's defenses and how to get around them.

Sam mumbled another response that sounded like *anything you want, just go back to sleep.*

Celaena looked up at the ceiling and smiled.

After breakfast, and after she'd gone to the bank to transfer a huge sum of money to Arobynn's account (an event that left both Celaena and Sam rather miserable and on edge), they spent the day gathering information on Ioan Jayne. As the biggest Crime Lord in Rifthold, Jayne was well-protected, and his minions were everywhere: orphan spies in the streets, harlots working in the Vaults, barkeeps and merchants and even some city guards.

Everyone knew where his house was: a sprawling three-story building of white stone on one of the nicest streets in Rifthold. The place was so well-watched that it was too risky to do more than walk past. Even stopping to observe for a few minutes might spark the interest of one of the disguised henchmen loitering on the street.

It seemed absurd that Jayne would have his house on this street. His neighbors were well-off merchants and minor nobility. Did they know who lived next door and what sort of evil went on beneath the emerald-tiled roof?

They had a stroke of good luck as they meandered past the house, looking for all the world like a well-dressed, handsome couple on a morning walk through the capital. Just as they were passing by, Farran, Jayne's Second, swaggered out the door, heading for the black carriage parked out front.

Celaena felt Sam's arm tense under her hand. He kept looking ahead, not daring to stare at Farran for too long in case someone noticed. But Celaena, pretending that she'd discovered a pull in her forest-green tunic, was able to glance over a few times.

She'd heard about Farran. Most everyone had. If she had a rival for notoriety, it was him.

Tall, broad-shouldered, and in his late twenties, Farran had been born and abandoned in the streets of Rifthold. He'd begun working for Jayne as one of his orphan spies, and over the years had clawed his way up the ranks of Jayne's twisted court, leaving a trail of bodies in his wake until he was appointed Second. Looking at him now, with his fine gray clothes and his gleaming black hair slicked into submission, it was impossible to tell that he'd once been one of the vicious little beasts that roamed the slums in feral packs.

As he walked down the stairs to the carriage that awaited him in the private drive, Farran's steps were smooth, calculated—his body rippling with barely restrained power. Even from across the street, Celaena could see how his dark eyes shone, his pale face set in a smile that made a shiver go down her spine.

The bodies Farran had left in his wake, she knew, hadn't been left in one piece. Somewhere in the years he'd spent rising from orphan to Second, Farran had developed a taste for sadistic torture. It had earned him his spot at Jayne's side—and kept his rivals from challenging him.

Farran slung himself into the carriage. The movement was so easy that his well-tailored clothes barely shifted out of place. The carriage started down the driveway, turned onto the street, and Celaena looked up as it ambled past.

Only to see Farran looking out the window—staring right at her.

Sam pretended not to notice. Celaena kept her face utterly blank—the disinterest of a well-bred lady who had no idea that the person staring at her like a cat watching a mouse was actually one of the most twisted men in the empire.

Farran gave her a smile. There was nothing human in it.

And *that* was why their client had offered a kingdom's ransom for Farran's and Jayne's deaths.

She bobbed her head in a demure deflection of his attention, and Farran's grin only grew before the carriage continued past and was swallowed up in the flow of city traffic.

Sam loosed a breath. "I'm glad we're taking him out first."

A dark, wicked part of her wished the opposite . . . wished she could see that feline grin vanish when Farran found out that Celaena Sardothien had killed Jayne. But Sam was right. She wouldn't sleep one wink if they took out Jayne first, knowing Farran would expend all his resources hunting them down.

They made a long, slow circle around the streets surrounding Jayne's house.

"It'd be easier to catch Farran on his way somewhere," Celaena said, all too aware of how many eyes were tracking them on these streets. "The house is too well-guarded."

"I'll probably need two days to figure it out," Sam said.

"*You'll* need?"

"I figured you'd want the glory of taking out Jayne. So I'll dispatch Farran."

"Why not work together?"

His smile faded. "Because I want you to stay out of this for as long as possible."

"Just because we're together doesn't mean I've become some weakling ninny."

"I'm not saying that. But can you blame me for wanting to keep the girl I love away from someone like Farran? And before you begin to rattle off your accomplishments, let me tell you that I *do* know how many people you've killed and the scrapes you've gotten out of. But *I* found this client, so we're doing it my way."

If there hadn't still been eyes on every corner, Celaena might have hit him. "How *dare* you—"

"Farran is a monster," Sam said, not looking at her. "You said so yourself. And if anything goes wrong, the *last* place I want you to be is in his hands."

"We'd be safer if we worked together."

A muscle feathered in his jaw. "I don't need you looking out for me, Celaena."

"Is this because of the money? Because I'm paying for things?"

"It's because I'm responsible for this hire, and because *you* don't always get to make the rules."

"At least let me do some aerial spotting for you," she said. She could let Sam take on Farran—she could become secondary for this mission. Hadn't she just accepted that she could someday let go of being Adarlan's Assassin? He could have the spotlight.

"No aerial spotting," Sam said sharply. "You'll be on the other side of the city—far away from this."

"You know how ridiculous that is, don't you?"

"I've had just as much training as you, Celaena."

She might have pushed it—might have kept arguing until he gave in—but she caught the flicker of bitterness in his eyes. She hadn't seen that bitterness in months, not since Skull's Bay, when they'd been all but enemies. Sam had always been forced to watch while glory was heaped upon her, and always taken whatever missions she didn't deign to accept. Which was absurd, really, given how talented he was.

If death-dealing could be called a talent.

And while she loved strutting around, calling herself Adarlan's Assassin, with Sam that sort of arrogance now sometimes felt like cruelty.

So though it killed a part of her to say it, and though it went against all her training to agree, Celaena nudged him with a shoulder and said, "Fine. You take down Farran by yourself. But I get to dispatch Jayne—and then we'll do it *my way*."

Celaena had her weekly dancing lesson with Madame Florine, who also trained all of the dancers at the Royal Theater, so she left Sam to finish his scouting as she headed to the old woman's private studio.

Four hours later, sweaty and aching and utterly spent, Celaena made her way back home across the city. She'd known the stern Madame Florine since she was a child: she taught all of Arobynn's assassins the latest popular dances. But Celaena liked to take extra lessons because of the flexibility and grace the classical dances instilled.

She'd always suspected the terse instructor had barely tolerated her—but to her surprise, Madame Florine had refused to take any pay for lessons now that she'd left Arobynn.

She'd have to find another dance instructor once they moved. More than that, a studio with a decent pianoforte player.

And the city would have to have a library, too. A great, wonderful library. Or a bookshop with a knowledgeable owner who could make sure her thirst for books was always sated.

And a good clothier. And perfumer. And jeweler. And confectionary.

Her feet dragged as she walked up the wooden steps to her apartment above the warehouse. She blamed it on the lesson. Madame Florine was a brutal taskmistress—she didn't accept limp wrists or sloppy posture or anything except Celaena's very best. Though she *did* always turn a blind eye to the last twenty minutes of their lesson, when she allowed Celaena to tell the student on the pianoforte to play her favorite music and set herself loose, dancing with wild abandon. And now that Celaena had no pianoforte of her own in the apartment, Madame Florine even let her remain after the lesson to practice.

Celaena found herself atop the stair landing, staring at the silvery-green door.

She *could* leave Rifthold. If it meant being free from Arobynn, she could leave behind all these things she loved. Other cities on the continent had libraries and bookshops and fine outfitters. Perhaps not as wonderful as Rifthold's, and perhaps the city's heart wouldn't beat with the familiar rhythm that she adored, but . . . for Sam, she could leave.

Sighing, Celaena unlocked the door and walked into the apartment.

Arobynn Hamel was sitting on the couch.

"Hello, darling," he said, and smiled.

CHAPTER 4

Alone in the kitchen, Celaena poured herself a cup of tea, trying to keep her hands from shaking. He'd probably gotten the address from the servants who had helped bring over her things. To find him here, having broken into her home . . . How long had he been sitting inside? Had he gone through her things?

She poured another cup of tea for Arobynn. Cups and saucers in hand, she walked back into the living room. He had his legs crossed, one arm sprawled across the back of the sofa, and seemed to have made himself quite at home.

She said nothing as she gave him the cup and then took a seat in one of the armchairs. The hearth was dark, and the day had been warm enough that Sam had left one of the living room windows open. A briny breeze off the Avery flowed into the apartment, rustling the crimson velvet curtains and teasing through her hair. She'd miss that smell, too.

Arobynn took a sip, then peered into his teacup to look at the amber liquid inside. "Who can I thank for the impeccable taste in tea?"

"Me. But you already know that."

"Hmm." Arobynn took another sip. "You know, I *did* know that." The afternoon light caught in his gray eyes, turning them to quicksilver. "What I *don't* know is why you and Sam think it's a good idea to dispatch Ioan Jayne and Rourke Farran."

Of course he knew. "It's none of your business. Our client wanted to operate outside of the Guild, and now that I've transferred the money to your account, Sam and I are no longer a part of it."

"Ioan Jayne," Arobynn repeated, as if she somehow didn't know who he was. "*Ioan Jayne.* Are you *insane*?"

She clenched her jaw. "I don't see why I should trust your advice."

"Even *I* wouldn't take on Jayne." Arobynn's gaze burned. "And I'm saying that as someone who has spent *years* thinking of ways to put that man in a grave."

"I'm not playing another one of your mind games." She set down her tea and rose from her seat. "Get out of my house."

Arobynn just stared up at her as if she were a sullen child. "Jayne is the undisputed Crime Lord in Rifthold for a reason. And Farran is his Second for a damn good reason, too. You might be excellent, Celaena, but you're not invincible."

She crossed her arms. "Maybe you're trying to dissuade me because you're worried that when I kill him, I will have truly surpassed you."

Arobynn shot to his feet, towering over her. "The reason I'm trying to dissuade you, you stupid, ungrateful girl, is because Jayne and Farran are *lethal.* If a client offered me the glass castle itself, I wouldn't touch an offer like that!"

She felt her nostrils flare. "After all that you've done, how can you expect me to believe a word that comes out of your mouth?" Her hand had started drifting toward the dagger at her waist. Arobynn's eyes remained on her face, but he was aware—he knew every movement her hands made and didn't have to look at her to track them. "*Get out of my house,*" she growled.

Arobynn gave her a half smile and looked around the apartment with deliberate care. "Tell me something, Celaena: do you trust Sam?"

"What sort of a question is that?"

Arobynn casually slid his hands into the pockets of his silver tunic. "Have you told him the truth about where you came from? I have a feeling that's something he'd like to know. Perhaps before he dedicates his life to you."

She focused on keeping her breathing even, and pointed at the door again. "*Go.*"

Arobynn shrugged, waving a hand as if to dismiss the questions he'd raised, and walked toward the front door. She watched his every move, took in every step and shift of his shoulders, noted what he looked at. He reached for the brass doorknob, but turned to her. His eyes—those silver eyes that would probably haunt her for the rest of her life—were bright.

"No matter what I have done, I really do love you, Celaena."

The word hit her like a stone to the head. He'd never said that word to her before. Ever.

A long silence fell between them.

Arobynn's neck shifted as he swallowed. "I do the things that I do because I'm afraid . . . and because I don't know how to express what I feel." He said it so quietly that she barely heard it. "I did all of those things because I was angry with you for picking Sam."

Was it the King of the Assassins who spoke, or the father, or the lover who had never manifested himself?

Arobynn's carefully cultivated mask fell, and the wound she'd given him flickered in those magnificent eyes. "Stay with me," he whispered. "Stay in Rifthold."

She swallowed, and found it particularly hard to do so. "I'm going."

"No," he said softly. "Don't go."

No.

That was what she'd said to him that night he'd beaten her, in the moment before he'd struck her, when she thought he was going to hurt Sam instead. And then he'd beaten her so badly she'd been knocked unconscious. Then he'd beaten Sam, too.

Don't.

That was what Ansel had said to her in the desert, when Celaena had pressed the sword into the back of her neck, when the agony of Ansel's betrayal had been almost enough to make Celaena kill the girl she'd called a friend. But that betrayal still paled in comparison to what Arobynn had done to her when he'd tricked her into killing Doneval, a man who could have freed countless slaves.

He was using words as chains to bind her again. He'd had so many chances over the years to tell her that he loved her—he'd *known* how much she'd craved those words. But he hadn't spoken them until he needed to use them as weapons. And now that she had Sam, Sam who said those words without expecting anything in return, Sam who loved her for reasons she would never understand . . .

Celaena tilted her head to the side, the only warning she gave that she was still ready to attack him. "Get out of my house."

Arobynn just nodded slowly and left.

The Black Cygnet tavern was packed wall-to-wall, as it was most nights. Seated with Sam at a table in the middle of the busy room, Celaena didn't particularly feel like eating the beef stew in front of her. Or like talking, even though Sam had told her all about the information he'd gathered on Farran and Jayne. She hadn't mentioned Arobynn's surprise visit.

A cluster of giggling young women sat nearby, tittering about how the Crown Prince was gone on a holiday to the Surian coast, and how *they* wished they could join the prince and his dashing friends, and on and on until Celaena contemplated chucking her spoon at them.

But the Black Cygnet wasn't a violent tavern. It catered to a crowd who came to enjoy good food, good music, and good company. There were no brawls, no dark dealings, and certainly no prostitutes milling about. Perhaps that was what brought her and Sam back here for dinner most nights—it felt so *normal.*

It was another place she'd miss.

When they arrived home after dinner, the apartment feeling strangely not hers now that Arobynn had broken in, Celaena went straight to the bedroom and lit a few candles. She was ready for this day to be over. Ready to dispatch Jayne and Farran, and then leave.

Sam appeared in the doorway. "I've never seen you so quiet," he said.

She looked at herself in the mirror above the dresser. The scar from her fight with Ansel had faded from her cheek, and the one on her neck was well on its way to disappearing, too.

"I'm tired," she said. It wasn't a lie. She began unbuttoning her tunic, her hands feeling strangely clumsy. Was this why Arobynn had visited? Because he'd known he'd impact her like this? She straightened, hating the thought so much that she wanted to shatter the mirror in front of her.

"Did something happen?"

She reached the final button of her tunic, but didn't take it off. She turned to face him, looking him up and down. *Could* she ever tell him everything?

"Talk to me," he said, his brown eyes holding only concern. No twisted agendas, no mind games . . .

"Tell me your deepest secret," she said softly.

Sam's eyes narrowed, but he pushed off the threshold and took a seat on the edge of the bed. He ran a hand through his hair, setting the ends sticking up at odd angles.

After a long moment, he spoke. "The only secret I've borne my entire life is that I love you." He gave her a slight smile. "It was the one thing I believed I'd go to the grave without voicing." His eyes were so full of light that it almost stopped her heart.

She found herself walking toward him, then placing one hand along his cheek and threading the other through his hair. He turned his head to kiss her palm, as if the phantom blood that coated her hands didn't bother him. His eyes found hers again. "What's yours, then?"

The room felt too small, the air too thick. She closed her eyes. It took her a minute, and more nerve than she realized, but the answer finally came. It had always been there—whispering to her in her sleep, behind every breath, a dark weight that she couldn't ever escape.

"Deep down," she said, "I'm a coward."

His brows rose.

"I'm a coward," she repeated. "And I'm scared. I'm scared all the time. Always."

He removed her hand from his cheek to kiss the tips of her fingers. "I get scared, too," he murmured onto her skin. "You want to hear something ridiculous? Whenever I'm scared out of my wits, I tell myself: *My name is Sam Cortland . . . and I will not be afraid*. I've been doing it for years."

It was her turn to raise her brows. "And that actually works?"

He laughed onto her fingers. "Sometimes it does, sometimes it doesn't. But it usually makes me feel better to some degree. Or it just makes me laugh at myself a bit."

It wasn't the sort of fear she'd been talking about, but . . .

"I like that," she said.

He laced his fingers with hers and pulled her onto his lap. "I like *you*," he murmured, and Celaena let him kiss her until she'd again forgotten the dark burden that would always haunt her.

CHAPTER 5

Rourke Farran was a busy, busy man. Celaena and Sam were waiting a block away from Jayne's house before dawn the next morning, both of them wearing nondescript clothing and cloaks with hoods deep enough to cover most of their features without giving alarm. Farran was out and about before the sun had fully risen. They trailed his carriage through the city, observing him at each stop. It was a wonder he even had *time* to indulge in his sadistic delights, because Jayne's business certainly took up plenty of his day.

He took the same black carriage everywhere—more proof of his arrogance, since it made him an easily marked target. Unlike Doneval, who was constantly guarded, Farran seemed to deliberately go without guards, daring anyone to take him on.

They followed him to the bank, to the dining rooms and taverns owned by Jayne, to the brothels and the black-market stalls hidden in crumbling alleys, then back to the bank again. He made several stops at Jayne's house in between, too. And then he surprised Celaena once by going into a bookshop—not to threaten the owner or collect dues, but to buy books.

She'd hated that, for some reason. Especially when, despite Sam's protests, she'd quickly snuck in while the bookseller was in the back and spied the receipt ledger behind the desk. Farran hadn't bought books about torture or death or anything wicked. Oh, no. They'd been adventure novels. Novels that *she* had read and enjoyed. The idea of Farran reading them too felt like a violation, somehow.

The day slipped by, and they learned little except for how brazenly he traveled about. Sam should have no trouble dispatching him tomorrow night.

When the sun was shifting into the golden hues of late afternoon, Farran pulled up at the nondescript iron door that led down into the Vaults.

At the end of the street, Celaena and Sam watched him as they pretended to be washing dung off their boots at a public spigot.

"It seems fitting that Jayne owns the Vaults," Sam said quietly over the gushing water.

Celaena gave him a glare—or she would have, if the hood hadn't been in the way. "Why do you think I got so mad about you fighting there? If you ever got into any trouble with the people at the Vaults, ever pissed them off, you're significant enough that Farran himself would come to punish you."

"I can handle Farran."

She rolled her eyes. "I didn't expect him actually to make a visit, though. Seems too dirty here, even for him."

"Should we take a look?" The street was quiet. The Vaults came alive at night, but during the day, there wasn't anyone in the alley except for a few stumbling drunks and the half-dozen guards always posted outside.

It was a risk, she supposed—going into the Vaults after Farran—but . . . If Farran truly rivaled her for notoriety, it would be interesting to get a sense of what he was really like before Sam ended his life tomorrow night. "Let's go," she said.

They flashed silver at the guards outside, then tossed it to the guards inside, and they were in. The thugs asked no questions, and didn't demand they remove their weapons or their hoods. Their usual clientele wanted discretion while partaking in the twisted delights of the Vaults.

From the top of the stairs just inside the front door, Celaena instantly spotted Farran sitting at one of the scarred and burned wooden tables in the center of the room, talking to a man she recognized as Helmson, the master of ceremonies during the fights. A small lunchtime crowd had gathered at the other tables, though they'd all cleared a ring around Farran. At the back of the chamber, the pits were dark and quiet, slaves working to scrape off the blood and gore before the night's revelries.

Celaena tried not to look too long at the shackles and broken posture of the slaves. It was impossible to tell where they'd come from—if they'd begun as prisoners of war or had just been stolen from their kingdoms. She wondered if it was better to wind up as a slave here, or a prisoner in a brutal labor camp like Endovier. Both seemed like similar versions of a living hell.

Compared to the teeming crowds the other night, the Vaults were practically deserted today. Even the prostitutes in the exposed chambers flanking the sides of the cavernous space were resting while they could. Many of the girls slept in tangled heaps on the narrow cots, barely hidden from view by the shabby curtains designed to give the illusion of privacy.

She wanted to burn this place into nothing but ashes. And then let everyone know that this wasn't the sort of thing Adarlan's Assassin stood for. Perhaps after they'd taken out Farran and Jayne, she'd do just that. One final bit of glory and retribution from Celaena Sardothien—one last chance to make them remember her forever before she left.

Sam kept close to her as they reached the bottom of the stairs and strode to the bar tucked into the shadows beneath. A wisp of a man stood behind it, pretending to wipe down the wooden surface while his watery blue eyes stayed fixed on Farran.

"Two ales," Sam growled. Celaena thumped a silver coin down on the bar, and the barkeep's attention snapped to them. She was grossly overpaying, but the barkeep's slender, scabbed hands vanished the silver in the blink of an eye.

There were enough people still inside the Vaults that Celaena and Sam could blend in—mostly drunks who never left the premises and people who seemed to enjoy this sort of wretched environment while eating their lunch. Celaena and Sam pretended to drink their ales—sloshing the alcohol on the ground when no one was looking—and watched Farran.

There was a locked wooden chest resting on the table beside Farran and the squat master of ceremonies—a chest that Celaena had no doubt was full of the Vaults' earnings from the night before. Farran's attention was fixed with feline intensity on Helmson, the chest seemingly forgotten. It was practically an invitation.

"How mad do you think he'd be if I stole that chest?" Celaena pondered.

"Don't even entertain the idea."

She clicked her tongue. "Spoilsport."

Whatever Farran and Helmson were discussing, it was over quickly. But instead of going back up the stairs, Farran walked over to the warren of girls. He prowled past every alcove and stone chamber, and the girls all straightened. Sleeping ones were hastily awakened, any sign of sleep vanished by the time Farran stalked past. He looked them over, inspecting, making comments to the man who hovered behind him. Helmson nodded and bowed and barked orders at the girls.

Even from across the room, the terror on the girls' faces was evident.

Both Celaena and Sam struggled to keep from going rigid. Farran crossed the large chamber and inspected the dens on the other side. By that time, the girls there were prepared. When Farran had finished, he looked over his shoulder and nodded to Helmson.

Helmson sagged with what could only be relief, but then paled and quickly found somewhere else to be as Farran snapped his fingers at one of the sentries near a small door. Immediately, the door opened and a shackled, dirty, muscular man was dragged out by another sentry. The prisoner looked half-dead already, but the moment he saw Farran, he started begging, thrashing against the sentry's grip.

It was hard to hear, but Celaena discerned enough from the man's frantic pleading to get the gist of it: he was a fighter in the Vaults, owed Jayne more money than he could ever repay, and had tried to cheat his way out of it.

Although the prisoner promised to repay Jayne with interest, Farran just smiled, letting the man babble until at last he paused for a shuddering breath. Then Farran jerked his chin toward a door hidden behind a ragged curtain, and his smile grew as the sentry dragged the still-pleading man toward it. As the door opened, Celaena caught a glimpse of a stairwell that swept downward.

Without so much as a look in the direction of the patrons discreetly watching from their tables, Farran led the sentry and his prisoner inside and shut the door. Whatever was about to happen was Jayne's version of justice.

Sure enough, five minutes later, a scream pierced through the Vaults.

It was more animal than human. She'd heard screams like that before—had witnessed enough torture at the Keep to know that when people screamed like that, it meant that the pain was just beginning. By the end, when that sort of pain happened, the victims had usually blown out their vocal cords and could only emit hoarse, shattered shrieks.

Celaena gritted her teeth so hard her jaw hurt. The barkeep gave a sharp wave to the minstrels in the corner, and they immediately started up a song to cover the noise. But screams still echoed up from beneath the stone floor. Farran wouldn't kill the man right away. No, his pleasure came from the pain itself.

"It's time to leave," Celaena said, noting how tightly Sam gripped his mug.

"We can't just—"

"We *can*," she said sharply. "Believe me, I'd like to burst in there, too. But this place is designed like a death trap, and I've no desire to make my final stand here, or right now." Sam was still staring at the stairwell door. "When the time comes," she added, putting a hand on his arm, "you'll make sure he pays his debt."

Sam turned to her, his face concealed within the shadows of the hood, but she could read the aggression in his body well enough. "He'll pay his debt for *all* of this," Sam snarled. And that's when Celaena noticed that some of the girls were weeping, some shook, some just stared at nothing. Yes, Farran had visited before, had used that room to do Jayne's dirty work—while reminding everyone else not to cross the Crime Lord. How many horrors had these girls witnessed—or at least heard?

The screams were still rising up from below when they left the Vaults.

She had intended to lead them home, but Sam insisted on going to the public park built along a well-off neighborhood beside the Avery

River. After meandering along the neat gravel walkways, he slumped onto a bench facing the water. He pulled off his hood and rubbed his face with his broad hands.

"We're not like that," he whispered through his fingers.

Celaena sank onto the wooden bench. She knew exactly what he meant. The same thought had been echoing through her head as they walked here. They had been taught how to kill and maim and torture—she knew how to skin a man and keep him alive while doing it. She knew how to keep someone awake and coherent during long hours of torment—knew where to inflict the most pain without having someone bleed out.

Arobynn had been so, so clever about it, too. He'd brought in the most despicable people—rapists, murderers, rogue assassins who had butchered innocents—and he'd made her read all of the information he'd gathered on them. Made her read about all of the awful things they'd done until she was so enraged she couldn't think straight, until she was *aching* to make them suffer. He'd honed her anger into a lethal blade. And she'd let him.

Before Skull's Bay, she'd done it all and had rarely questioned it. She'd pretended that she had some moral code, lied to herself and said that since she didn't *enjoy* it, it meant that she had some excuse, but . . . she had still stood in that chamber beneath the Assassins' Keep and seen the blood flow toward the drain in the sloped floor.

"We *can't* be like that," Sam said.

She took his hands, easing them away from his face. "We're not like Farran. We know how to do it, but we don't enjoy it. That's the difference."

His brown eyes were distant as he watched the gentle current of the Avery making its way toward the nearby sea. "When Arobynn ordered us to do things like that, we never said no."

"We had no choice. But we do now." Once they left Rifthold,

they'd never have to make a choice like that again—they could create their own codes.

Sam looked at her, his expression so haunted and bleak it made her sick. "But there was always that part. That part that *did* enjoy it when it was someone who truly deserved it."

"Yes," she breathed. "Yes, there was always that part. But we still had a line, Sam—we still stayed on the other side of it. Lines don't exist for someone like Farran."

They weren't like Farran—*Sam* wasn't like Farran. She knew that in her bones. Sam would never be like Farran. He'd never be like *her*, either. She sometimes wondered if he knew just how dark she could turn.

Sam leaned against her, resting his head on her shoulder. "When we die, do you think we'll be punished for the things we've done?"

She looked at the far bank of the river, where a row of ramshackle houses and docks had been built. "When we die," she said, "I don't think the gods will even know what to do with us."

Sam glanced at her, a hint of amusement shining in his eyes.

Celaena smiled at him, and the world, for one flickering heartbeat, felt right.

The dagger whined as Celaena sharpened it, the reverberations shooting through her hands. Seated beside her on the floor of the great room, Sam pored over a map of the city, tracing streets with his fingers. The fireplace before them cast everything into flickering shadows, a welcome warmth on a chill night.

They had returned to the Vaults in time to see Farran entering his carriage again. So they spent the rest of the afternoon stalking him—more trips to the bank and other locations, more stops back at Jayne's house. She'd gone off on her own for two hours to trail Jayne—to get another subtle glimpse at the house and see where the Crime Lord went. It was two uneventful hours of figuring out where his spies hid on the streets, since Jayne didn't emerge from the building at all.

If Sam planned to dispatch Farran tomorrow night, they agreed that the best time to do it would be when he took a carriage from the house to wherever else he had dealings, either for himself or Jayne. After a long day of running errands for Jayne, Farran was sure to be drained, his defenses sloppy. He wouldn't know what was coming until his lifeblood spilled.

Sam would be wearing the special suit that the Master Tinkerer from Melisande had made for him, which in itself was its own armory. The sleeves possessed concealed built-in swords, the boots were specially designed for climbing, and, thanks to Celaena, Sam's suit was equipped with an impenetrable patch of Spidersilk right over his heart.

Celaena had her own suit, of course—used only sparingly now that the convoy from Melisande had returned home. If either suit needed repairs, it'd be near impossible to find someone in Rifthold skilled enough. But dispatching Farran was definitely an occasion worth the risk. In addition to the suit's defenses, Sam would also be equipped with the extra blades and daggers that Celaena was now sharpening. She tested an edge against her hand, smiling grimly as her skin stung. "Sharp enough to cut air," she said, sheathing it and setting it down beside her.

"Well," Sam said, eyes still flitting across the map, "let's hope I don't have to get close enough to use it."

If all went according to plan, Sam would only need to fire four arrows: one each to disable the carriage driver and the footman, one for Farran—and one more just to make sure Farran was dead.

Celaena picked up another dagger and began sharpening that as well. She jerked her chin toward the map. "Escape routes?"

"A dozen planned already," Sam said, and showed her. With Jayne's house as a starting point, Sam had picked multiple streets in every direction where he could fire his arrows—which led to multiple escape routes that would get Sam away as quickly as possible.

"Remind me again why I'm not going?" The dagger in her hands let out a long whine.

"Because you'll be here, packing?"

"Packing?" She stilled the sharpening knife in her hand.

He returned his attention to the map. Then he said, very carefully, "I secured us passage on a ship to the southern continent, leaving in five days."

"The southern continent."

Sam nodded, still focusing on the map. "If we're going to get away from Rifthold, then we're going to get away from this entire continent, too."

"That wasn't what we discussed. We decided to move to another city on *this* continent. And what if there's *another* Assassins' Guild on the southern continent?"

"Then we'll ask to join them."

"I'm not going to grovel to join some no-name guild and be subservient to some would-be infamous assassins!"

Sam looked up. "Is this really about your pride, or is it because of the distance?"

"Both!" She slammed down the dagger and the honing stone on the rug. "I was willing to move to a place like Banjali or Bellhaven or Anielle. Not to an entirely new continent—a place we hardly know *anything* about! That wasn't part of the plan."

"At least we'd be out of Adarlan's empire."

"I don't give a damn about the empire!"

He sat back, propping himself on his hands. "Can't you just admit that this is about Arobynn?"

"No. You don't know what you're talking about."

"Because if we sail for the southern continent, then he will *never* find us again—and I don't think you're quite ready to accept that."

"My relationship with Arobynn is—"

"Is *what*? Over? Is that why you didn't tell me that he came to visit yesterday?"

Her heart skipped a beat.

Sam went on. "While you were trailing Jayne today, he approached me in the street, and seemed surprised that you hadn't said anything about his visit. He also told me to ask about what really happened before he found you half-dead on that riverbank when we were children." Sam leaned forward, bracing a hand on the floor as he brought his face close to hers. "And you know what I told him?" His breath was hot on her mouth. "That I didn't care. But he just kept trying to bait me, to make me not trust you. So after he walked away, I went right to the docks and found the first ship that would take us away from this damned continent. Away from *him*, because even though we're out of the Guild, he will *never* leave us alone."

She swallowed hard. "He said those things to you? About . . . about where I came from?"

Sam must have seen something like fear in her eyes, because he suddenly shook his head, his shoulders slumping. "Celaena, when you're good and ready to tell me the truth, you'll do it. And no matter what it is, when that day comes, I'll be honored that you trust me enough to do so. But until then, it's not my business, and it's not Arobynn's business. It's not anyone's business but your own."

Celaena leaned her forehead against his, and some of the tightness in his body—and hers—melted away. "What if moving to the southern continent is a mistake?"

"Then we'll move somewhere else. We'll keep moving until we find the place where we're meant to be."

She shut her eyes and took a steadying breath. "Will you laugh if I say that I'm scared?"

"No," he said softly, "never."

"Maybe I should try your little trick." She took another breath. "My name is Celaena Sardothien, and I will not be afraid."

He did laugh then, a tickle of breath on her mouth. "I think you have to say it with a bit more conviction than that."

She opened her eyes and found him watching her, his face a mixture of pride and wonder and such open affection that she could see that far-off land where they'd find a home, see that future that awaited them, and that glimmer of hope that promised happiness she'd never considered or dared yearn for. And even though the southern continent was a drastic change in their plans . . . Sam was right. A new continent for a new beginning.

"I love you," Sam said.

Celaena wrapped her arms around him and held him close, breathing in his scent. Her only reply was, "I hate packing."

CHAPTER 6

The next night, the clock on the mantel seemed to be stuck at nine o'clock. It had to be, because there was no way in hell that a minute could take *this* long.

She been trying to read for the past two hours—trying and failing. Even an utterly sinful romance novel hadn't held her interest. And neither had playing cards, or digging out her atlas and reading about the southern continent, or eating all the candy she'd hidden from Sam in the kitchen. Of course, she was *supposed* to be organizing the belongings she wanted to pack. When she'd complained to Sam about what a chore it'd be, he'd even gone so far as to take all their empty trunks out of the closet. And then pointed out that he would *not* be traveling with her dozens of shoes, and she could have them shipped to her once they found their home. After saying *that*, he'd wisely left the apartment to kill Farran.

She didn't know why she hesitated to pack—she'd contacted

the solicitor that morning. He had told her the apartment might be hard to sell, but she was glad to do the dealings over a long distance, and she told him she'd contact him as soon as she found her new home.

A new home.

Celaena sighed as the clock arms shifted. A whole minute had passed.

Of course, with Farran's schedule being somewhat erratic, Sam might have to wait a few hours for him to leave the house. Or maybe he'd already done the job and needed to lie low for a while, just in case someone traced him back here.

Celaena checked the dagger beside her on the couch, then glanced around the room for the hundredth time that evening, making sure all the concealed weapons were in their proper places.

She wouldn't check on Sam. He'd wanted to do this on his own. And he could be anywhere now.

The trunks lay by the window.

Maybe she *should* start packing. Once they dispatched Jayne tomorrow night, they'd need to be ready to leave the city as soon as that ship was available to board. Because while she certainly wanted the world to know that Celaena Sardothien had made the kill, getting far from Rifthold would be in their best interest.

Not that she was running away.

The clock arms shifted again. Another minute.

Groaning, Celaena stood and walked to the bookshelf along the wall, where she began pulling out books and stacking them into the nearest empty trunk. She'd have to leave her furniture and most of her shoes behind for now, but there was no way in hell she was going to move to the southern continent without all of her books.

The clock struck eleven, and Celaena headed into the streets, wearing the suit the Master Tinkerer had made for her, plus several other weapons strapped to her body.

Sam should have been back by now. And even though there was still another hour until the time when they'd agreed she'd look for him if he hadn't returned, if he was truly in trouble, then she certainly wasn't going to sit around for another minute—

The thought sent her sprinting down alleys, heading toward Jayne's house.

The slums were silent, but no more so than usual. Whores and barefoot orphans and people struggling to make a few honest coppers glanced at her as she ran past, no more than a shadow. She kept an ear out for any snippets of conversation that might suggest Farran was dead, but overheard nothing useful.

She slowed to a stalking gait, her steps near-silent on the cobblestones as she neared the wealthy neighborhood in which Jayne's house stood. Several affluent couples were walking around, heading back from the theater, but there were no signs of a disturbance . . . Though if Farran had been killed, then surely Jayne would try to keep the assassination hidden for as long as possible.

She made a long circuit through the neighborhood, checking on all the points where Sam had planned to be. Not a spot of blood or sign of a struggle. She even dared to walk across the street from Jayne's house. The house was brightly lit and almost merry, and the guards were at their posts, all looking bored.

Perhaps Sam had found out that Farran wasn't leaving the house tonight. She might very well have missed him on his way home. He wouldn't be pleased when he learned she'd gone out to find him, but he would have done the same for her.

Sighing, Celaena hurried back home.

Chapter 7

Sam wasn't at the apartment.

But the clock atop the mantel read one in the morning.

Celaena stood before the embers of the fireplace and stared at the clock, wondering if she was somehow reading it wrong.

But it continued ticking, and when she checked her pocket watch, it also read one. Then two minutes past the hour. Then five minutes . . .

She threw more logs on the fire and took off her swords and daggers, but remained in the suit. Just in case.

She had no idea when she began pacing in front of the fire—and only realized it when the clock chimed two and she found herself still standing before the clock.

He would come home any minute.

Any minute.

Celaena jolted awake at the faint chime of the clock. She'd somehow wound up on the couch—and somehow fallen asleep.

Four o'clock.

She would go out again in a minute. Maybe he'd hidden in the Assassins' Keep for the night. Unlikely, but . . . it was probably the safest place to hide after you'd killed Rourke Farran.

Celaena closed her eyes.

The dawn was blinding, and her eyes felt gritty and sore as she hurried through the slums, then the wealthy neighborhoods, scanning every cobblestone, every shadowed alcove, every rooftop for any sign of him.

Then she went to the river.

She didn't dare breathe as she walked up and down the banks that bordered the slums, searching for anything. Any sign of Farran, or . . . or . . .

Or.

She didn't let herself finish that thought, though crippling nausea gripped her as she scanned the banks and docks and sewer depositories.

He would be waiting for her at home. And then he'd chide her and laugh at her and kiss her. And then she'd dispatch Jayne tonight, and then they'd set sail on this river and then out to the nearby sea, and then be gone.

He would be waiting at home.

He'd be home.

Home.

Noon.

It couldn't be noon, but it was. Her pocket watch was properly wound, and hadn't once failed her in the years she'd had it.

Each of her steps up the stairs to her apartment was heavy and light—heavy and light, the sensation shifting with each heartbeat. She'd stop by the apartment only long enough to see if he'd returned.

A roaring silence hovered around her, a cresting wave that she'd been trying to outrun for hours. She knew that the moment the silence finally hit her, everything would change.

She found herself atop the landing, staring at the door.

It had been unlocked and left slightly ajar.

A strangled sort of noise broke out of her, and she ran the last few feet, barely noticing as she threw open the door and burst into the apartment. She was going to scream at him. And kiss him. And scream at him some more. A *lot* more. How *dare* he make her—

Arobynn Hamel was sitting on her couch.

Celaena halted.

The King of the Assassins slowly got to his feet. She saw the expression in his eyes and knew what he was going to say long before he opened his mouth and whispered, "I'm sorry."

The silence struck.

CHAPTER 8

Her body started moving, walking straight toward the fireplace before she really knew what she was going to do.

"They thought he was still living in the Keep," Arobynn said, his voice pitched at that horrible whisper. "They left him as a message."

She reached the mantel and grabbed the clock from where it rested.

"Celaena," Arobynn breathed.

She hurled the clock across the room so hard it shattered against the wall behind the dining table.

Its fragments landed atop the buffet table against the wall, breaking the decorative dishes displayed there, scattering the silver tea set she'd bought for herself.

"Celaena," Arobynn said again.

She stared at the ruined clock, the ruined dishes and tea set. There was no end to this silence. There would never be an end, only this beginning.

"I want to see the body." The words came from a mouth she wasn't sure belonged to her anymore.

"No," Arobynn said gently.

She turned her head toward him, baring her teeth. "*I want to see the body.*"

Arobynn's silver eyes were wide, and he shook his head. "No, you don't."

She had to start moving, had to start walking *anywhere*, because now that she was standing still . . . Once she sat down . . .

She walked out the door. Down the steps.

The streets were the same, the sky was clear, the briny breeze off the Avery still ruffled her hair. She had to keep walking. Perhaps . . . perhaps they'd sent the wrong body. Perhaps Arobynn had made a mistake. Perhaps he was lying.

She knew Arobynn followed her, staying a few feet behind as she strode across the city. She also knew that Wesley joined them at some point, always looking after Arobynn, always vigilant. The silence kept flickering in and out of her ears. Sometimes it'd stop long enough for her to hear the whinny of a passing horse, or the shout of a peddler, or the giggle of children. Sometimes none of the noises in the capital could break through.

There had been a mistake.

She didn't look at the assassins guarding the iron gates to the Keep, or at the housekeeper who opened the giant double doors of the building, or at the assassins who milled about the grand entrance and who stared at her with fury and grief mingling in their eyes.

She slowed long enough for Arobynn—trailed by Wesley—to step in front of her, to lead the rest of the way.

The silence peeled back, and thoughts tumbled in. It had been a mistake. And when she figured out where they were keeping him—where they were hiding him—she'd stop at nothing to find him. And then she'd slaughter them all.

Arobynn led her down the stone stairwell at the back of the entrance hall—the stairs that led into the cellars and the dungeons and the secret council rooms below.

The scrape of boots on stone. Arobynn in front of her, Wesley trailing behind.

Down and down, then along the narrow, dark passageway. To the door across from the dungeon entrance. She knew that door. Knew the room behind it. The mortuary where they kept their members until—No, it had been a mistake.

Arobynn took out a ring of keys and unlocked the door, but paused before opening it. "Please, Celaena. It's better if you don't."

She elbowed past him and into the room.

The square room was small and lit with two torches. Bright enough to illuminate . . .

Illuminate . . .

Each step brought her closer to the body on the table. She didn't know where to look first.

At the fingers that went the wrong way, at the burns and careful, deep slices in his flesh, at the face, the face she still knew, even when so many things had been done to destroy it beyond recognition.

The world swayed beneath her feet, but she kept upright as she finished the walk to the table and looked down at the naked, mutilated body she had—

She had—

Farran had taken his time. And though that face was in ruins, it betrayed none of the pain he must have felt, none of the despair.

This was some dream, or she had gone to Hell after all, because she *couldn't* exist in the world where this had been done to him, where she'd paced like an idiot all night while he suffered, while Farran tortured him, while he ripped out his eyes and—

Celaena vomited on the floor.

Footsteps, then Arobynn's hands were on her shoulder, on her waist, pulling her away.

He was dead.

Sam was dead.

~

She wouldn't leave him like this, in this cold, dark room.

She yanked out of Arobynn's grasp. Wordlessly, she unfastened her cloak and spread it over Sam, covering the damage that had been so carefully inflicted. She climbed onto the wooden table and lay beside him, stretching an arm across his middle, holding him close.

The body still smelled faintly like Sam. And like the cheap soap she'd made him use, because she was so selfish that she couldn't let him have her lavender soap.

Celaena buried her face in his cold, stiff shoulder. There was a strange, musky scent all over him—a smell that was so distinctly *not* Sam that she almost vomited again. It clung to his golden-brown hair, to his torn, bluish lips.

She wouldn't leave him.

Footsteps heading toward the door—then the *snick* of it closing as Arobynn left.

Celaena closed her eyes. She wouldn't leave him.

She wouldn't leave him.

CHAPTER 9

Celaena awoke in a bed that had once been hers, but somehow no longer felt that way. There was something missing in the world, something vital. She arose from the depths of slumber, and it took her a long moment to sort out what had changed.

She might have thought that she was awakening in her bed in the Keep, still Arobynn's protégée, still Sam's rival, still content to be Adarlan's Assassin forever and ever. She might have believed it if she hadn't noticed that so many of her beloved belongings were missing from this familiar bedroom—belongings that were now in her apartment across the city.

Sam was gone.

Reality opened wide and swallowed her whole.

She didn't move from the bed.

She knew the day was drifting along because of the shifting light on the wall of the bedroom. She knew the world still passed by, unaffected by the death of a young man, unaware that he'd ever existed and breathed and loved her. She hated the world for continuing on. If she never left this bed, this room, maybe she'd never have to continue on with it.

The memory of his face was already blurring. Had his eyes been more golden brown, or soil brown? She couldn't remember. And she'd never get the chance to find out.

Never get to see that half smile. Never get to hear his laugh, never get to hear him say her name like it meant something special, something more than being Adarlan's Assassin ever could.

She didn't want to go out into a world where he didn't exist. So she watched the light shift and change, and let the world pass by without her.

Someone was speaking outside her door. Three men with low voices. The rumble of them shook her from sleep to find the room was dark, the city lights glowing beyond the windows.

"Jayne and Farran will be expecting retaliation," a man said. Harding, one of Arobynn's more talented assassins, and a fierce competitor of hers.

"Their guards will be on alert," said another—Tern, an older assassin.

"Then we'll take out the guards, and while they're distracted, some of us will go for Jayne and Farran." Arobynn. She had a foggy memory of being carried—hours or years or a lifetime ago—up from that dark room that smelled of death and into her bed.

Muffled replies from Tern and Harding, then—

"We strike tonight," Arobynn growled. "Farran lives at the

house, and if we time it right, we'll kill them both while they're in their beds."

"Getting to the second floor isn't as simple as walking up the stairs," Harding challenged. "Even the exteriors are guarded. If we can't get through the front, then there's a small second-story window that we can leap through using the roof of the house next door."

"A leap like that could be fatal," Tern countered.

"*Enough*," Arobynn cut in. "I'll decide how to break in when we arrive. Have the others ready to go in three hours. I want us on our way at midnight. And tell them to keep their mouths *shut*. Someone must have tipped off Farran if he knew to set a trap for Sam. Don't even tell your servants where you're going."

Grunted acquiescence, then footsteps as Tern and Harding walked away.

Celaena kept her eyes closed and her breathing steady as the lock turned in her bedroom door. She recognized the even, confident gait of the King of the Assassins striding toward her bed. Smelled him as he stood over her, watching. Felt his long fingers as they stroked through her hair, then along her cheek.

Then the steps leaving, the door shutting—and locking. She opened her eyes, the glow of the city offering enough light for her to see that the lock on the door had been altered since she'd left—it now locked only from the outside.

He had locked her in.

To keep her from going with them? To keep her from helping to pay back Farran for every inch of flesh he'd tortured, every bit of pain Sam had endured?

Farran was a master of torture, and he'd kept Sam all night.

Celaena sat up, her head spinning. She couldn't remember the last time she'd eaten. Food could wait. Everything could wait.

Because in three hours, Arobynn and his assassins would venture out to exact vengeance. They'd rob her of her claim to revenge—the satisfaction of slaughtering Farran and Jayne and *anyone* who stood in her way. And she had no intention of letting them do it.

She stalked to the door and confirmed that it was locked. Arobynn knew her too well. Knew that when the blanket of grief had been ripped away . . .

Even if she could spring the lock, she had no doubt that there was at least one assassin watching the hall outside her bedroom. Which left the window.

The window itself was unlocked—but the two-story drop was formidable. While she'd been sleeping, someone had taken off her suit and given her a nightgown. She ripped apart the armoire for any sign of the suit—its boots were designed for climbing—but all she found were two black tunics, matching pants, and ordinary black boots. Fine.

There were no weapons in sight, and she hadn't brought any in with her. But years of living in this room had its advantages. She kept her motions quiet as she pulled up the loose floorboards where she'd long ago hidden a set of four daggers. She sheathed two at her waist and tucked the other two into her boots. Then she found the twin swords she'd kept disguised as part of the bed frame since she was fourteen. Neither the daggers nor the sword had been good enough to bring with her when she moved. Today they would do.

When she'd finished strapping the blades across her back, she rebraided her hair and fitted on her cloak, throwing the hood over her head.

She'd kill Jayne first. And then she'd drag Farran to a place where she could properly repay him and take however long she wanted. Days, even. When that debt was paid, when Farran had no more agony or blood to offer, she'd place Sam in the embrace of the earth and send him to the afterlife knowing he'd been avenged.

She eased open the window, scanning the front courtyard. The dew-slick stones gleamed in the lamplight, and the sentries at the iron gate seemed focused on the street beyond.

Good.

This was her kill, her revenge to take. No one else's.

A black fire rippled in her gut, spreading through her veins as she hopped onto the windowsill and eased outside.

Her fingers found purchase in the large white stones, and, with one eye on the guards at the distant gate, she climbed down the side of the house. No one noticed her, no one looked her way. The Keep was silent, the calm before the storm that would break when Arobynn and his assassins began their hunt.

Her landing was soft, no more than a whisper of boots against slick cobblestones. The guards were so focused on the street that they wouldn't notice when she jumped the fence near the stables around the back.

Creeping around the exterior of the house was as simple as getting out of her room, and she was well within the shadows of the stables when a hand reached out and grabbed her.

She was hurled into the side of the wooden building, and had a dagger drawn by the time the thump finished echoing.

Wesley's face, set with rage, seethed at her in the dark.

"Where in hell do you think you're going?" he breathed, not loosening his grip on her shoulders even as she pressed her dagger to the side of his throat.

"Get out of my way," she growled, hardly recognizing her own voice. "Arobynn can't keep me locked up."

"I'm not talking about Arobynn. Use your head and *think*, Celaena!" A flicker of her—a part of her that had somehow vanished since she'd shattered that clock—realized that this might be the first time he'd ever addressed her by her name.

"Get out of my way," she repeated, pushing the edge of the blade harder against his exposed throat.

"I know you want revenge," he panted. "I do, too—for what he did to Sam. I know you—"

She flicked the blade, angling it enough that he reared back to avoid her slicing a deep line across his throat.

"Don't you understand?" he pleaded, his eyes gleaming in the dark. "It's all just a—"

But the fire rose up in Celaena and she whirled, using a move the Mute Master had taught her that summer, and Wesley's eyes lost focus as she slammed the pommel of her dagger into the side of his head. He dropped like a stone.

Before he'd even finished collapsing, Celaena was sprinting for the fence. A moment later, she jumped it and vanished into the city streets.

She was fire, she was darkness, she was dust and blood and shadow.

She hurtled through the streets, each step faster than the last as that black fire burned through thought and feeling until all that remained was her rage and her prey.

She took back alleys and leapt over walls.

She'd slaughter them all.

Faster and faster, sprinting for that beautiful house on its quiet street, for the two men who had taken her world apart piece by piece, bone by shattered bone.

All she had to do was get to Jayne and Farran—everyone else was collateral. Arobynn had said they'd both be in their beds. That meant she had to get past all those guards at the front gate, the front door, and on the first floor . . . not to mention the guards that were sure to be outside the bedrooms.

But there was an easier way to get past all of them. A way in that didn't involve possibly alerting Farran and Jayne if the guards at the front door raised the alarm. Harding had mentioned something about a window on the second floor that he could leap through . . . Harding was a good tumbler, but she was better.

When she was a few streets away, she climbed the side of a house until she was on the roof and running again, fast enough to make the leap across the gap between houses.

She'd walked past Jayne's house enough times in the past few days to know that it was separated from its neighbors by alleys probably fifteen feet wide.

She leapt across another gap between roofs.

Now that she thought of it, she *knew* there was a second-floor window facing one of those alleys—and she didn't give a damn where that window opened to, just that it would get her inside before the guards on the first floor could notice.

The emerald roof of Jayne's house gleamed, and Celaena skidded to a halt on the roof next door. A wide, flat stretch of the gabled roof stood between her and the long jump across the alley. If she aimed correctly and ran fast enough, she could make that leap and land through that second-floor window. The window was already thrown open, though the curtains had been drawn, blocking any view of what was within.

Despite the fog of rage, years of training made her instinctively scan the neighboring rooftops. Was it arrogance or stupidity that kept Jayne from having guards on the nearby roofs? Even the guards on the street didn't look up at her.

Celaena untied her cloak and let it slide to the ground behind her. Any additional drag might be fatal, and she had no intention of dying until Jayne and Farran were corpses.

The roof on which she stood was three stories high and faced the second-floor window across the alley. She factored in the distance and how fast she'd be falling, and made sure the swords crossed to her back were neatly tucked in. The window was wide, but she still needed to avoid the blades catching on the threshold. She backed up as far as she could to give herself running space.

Somewhere on that second floor slept Jayne and Farran. And somewhere in this house, they had destroyed Sam.

After she had killed them, perhaps she'd tear the house down stone by stone.

Perhaps she'd tear this entire city down, too.

She smiled. She liked the sound of that.

Then she took a deep breath and broke into a run.

The roof was no longer than fifty feet—fifty feet between her and the jump that would either land her right through that open window a level below, or splatter her on the alley between.

She sprinted for the ever-nearing edge.

Forty feet.

There was no room for error, no room for fear or sorrow or anything except that blinding rage and cold, vicious calculation.

Thirty feet.

She raced, straight as an arrow, each pump of her legs and arms bringing her closer.

Twenty.

Ten.

The alley below loomed, the gap looking far bigger than she'd realized.

Five.

But there was nothing left of her to even consider stopping.

Celaena reached the edge of the roof and leapt.

Chapter 10

The cold kiss of night air on her face, the glitter of the wet streets under lamplight, the sheen of moonlight on the black curtains inside the open window as she arced toward it, hands already reaching for her daggers . . .

She tucked her head into her chest, bracing for impact as she burst through the curtains, ripping them clean off their hangings, hit the floor, and rolled.

Right into a meeting room full of people. In a heartbeat, she took in the details: a somewhat small room where Jayne, Farran, and others sat around a square table, and a dozen guards now staring at her, already formed into a wall of flesh and weaponry between her and her prey.

The curtains were thick enough to have blocked out any light within the room—to make it look like it was dark and empty inside. A trick.

It didn't matter. She'd take them all down anyway. The two daggers in her boots were thrown before she was even on her feet, and the guards' dying shouts brought a wicked grin to her lips.

Her swords whined, both in her hands as the nearest guard charged for her.

He immediately died, a sword punched through his ribs and into his heart. Every object—every person—between her and Farran was an obstacle or a weapon, a shield or a trap.

She whirled to the next guard, and her grin turned feral as she caught a glimpse of Jayne and Farran at the other end of the room, seated across the table. Farran was smiling at her, his dark eyes bright, but Jayne was on his feet, gaping.

Celaena buried one of her swords into the chest of a guard so she could reach for her third dagger.

Jayne was still gaping when that dagger imbedded itself to the hilt in his neck.

Utter pandemonium. The door flung open, and more guards poured in as she retrieved her second sword from the chest cavity of the fallen guard. It couldn't have been more than ten seconds since she'd leapt through the open window. Had they been waiting?

Two guards lunged for her, swords slicing the air. Her twin blades flashed. Blood sprayed.

The room wasn't large—only twenty feet separated her from Farran, who remained seated, watching her with wild delight.

Three more guards went down.

Someone hurled a dagger at her, and she knocked it aside with a blade, sending it right into the leg of another guard. Unintentional, but lucky.

Another two guards fell.

There were only a few left between her and the table—and Farran at the other side. He didn't even look at Jayne's corpse, slumped on the table beside him.

Guards were still rushing in from the hall, but they were all wearing strange black masks, masks with clear glass eyepieces, and some sort of cloth mesh over the mouths . . .

And then the smoke started, and the door shut, and as she gutted another guard, she glanced at Farran in time to see him slide on a mask.

She knew this smoke—knew this smell. It had been on Sam's corpse. That musky, strange—

Someone sealed the window, shutting out the air. Smoke everywhere, fogging everything.

Her eyes stung, but she dropped a sword to reach for that last dagger, the one that would find its home in Farran's skull.

The world jolted to the side.

No.

She didn't know if she said it or thought it, but the word echoed through the darkness that was devouring her.

Another masked guard had reached her, and she straightened in time to drive a sword into his side. Blood soaked her hand, but she kept her grip on the blade. Kept her grip on the dagger in her other hand as she cocked it back, angling for Farran's head.

But the smoke invaded every pore, every breath, every muscle. As she arched her arm, a shudder went through her body, making her vision twist and falter.

She swayed to the side, losing her grip on the dagger. A guard swiped for her, but missed, slicing off an inch from her braid instead. Her hair broke free in a golden wave as she careened to the side, falling so, so slowly, Farran still smiling at her . . .

A guard's fist slammed into her gut, knocking the air out of her. She reeled back, and another fist like granite met her face. Her back, her ribs, her jaw. So many blows, so fast the pain couldn't keep up, and she was falling so slowly, breathing in all that smoke . . .

They had been waiting for her. The invitingly open window, the smoke and the masks, were all a part of a plan. And she had fallen right into it.

She was still falling as the blackness consumed her.

"None of you are to touch her," a cool, bored voice was saying. "She's to be kept alive."

There were hands on her, prying her weapons out of her grip, then setting her into a sitting position against the wall. Fresh air poured into the room, but she could hardly feel it on her tingling face.

She couldn't feel anything. Couldn't move anything. She was paralyzed.

She managed to open her eyes, only to find Farran crouched in front of her, that feline smile still on his face. The smoke had cleared from the room, and his mask lay discarded behind him.

"Hello, Celaena," he purred.

Someone had betrayed her. Not Arobynn. Not when he hated Jayne and Farran so much. If she'd been betrayed, it would have been one of the wretches in the Guild—someone who would have benefited most from her death. It *couldn't* be Arobynn.

Farran's dark gray clothes were immaculate. "I've been waiting a few years to meet you, you know," he said, sounding rather cheerful despite the blood and bodies.

"To be honest," he went on, his eyes devouring every inch of her in a way that made her stomach start to twist, "I'm disappointed. You walked right into our little trap. You didn't even stop to think twice about it, did you?" Farran smiled. "Never underestimate the power of love. Or is it revenge?"

She couldn't convince her fingers to shift. Even blinking was an effort.

"Don't worry—the numbness from the gloriella is already fading, though you won't be able to move much at all. It *should* wear off in about six hours. At least, that's how long it lasted on your companion after I caught him. It's a particularly effective tool for keeping people sedated without the constraints of shackles. Makes the process much more . . . enjoyable, even if you can't scream as much."

Gods above. Gloriella—the same poison Ansel had used on the Mute Master, somehow warped into incense. He must have caught Sam, brought him back here, used the smoke on him, and . . . He was going to torture her, too. She could withstand some torture, but considering what had been done to Sam, she wondered how quickly she'd break. If she'd had control over herself, she'd have ripped out Farran's throat with her teeth.

Her only glimmer of hope came from the fact that Arobynn and the others would arrive soon, and even if one of her kind had betrayed her, when Arobynn found out . . . when he saw whatever Farran had started to do to her . . . He'd keep Farran alive, if only so when she recovered, she could gut him herself. Gut him, and take a damn long time to do it.

Farran stroked the hair out of her eyes, tucking it behind her ears. She'd shatter that hand, too. The way Sam's hands had been methodically shattered. Behind Farran, guards began dragging the bodies away. No one touched Jayne's corpse, still sprawled on the table.

"You know," Farran murmured, "you're really quite beautiful." He ran a finger down her cheek, then along her jaw. Her rage became a living thing thrashing inside of her, fighting for just *one* chance to break free. "I can see why Arobynn kept you as a pet for so many years." His finger went lower, sliding across her neck. "How old are you, anyway?"

She knew he didn't expect an answer. His eyes met hers, dark and ravenous.

She wouldn't beg. If she were to die like Sam, she'd do so with dignity. With that rage still burning. And maybe . . . maybe she'd get the chance to butcher him.

"I'm half-tempted to keep you for myself," he said. He brushed his thumb over her mouth. "Instead of handing you over, perhaps I'll take you downstairs, and if you survive . . ." He shook his head. "But that wasn't part of the bargain, was it?"

Words boiled up in her, but her tongue didn't move. She couldn't even open her mouth.

"You're dying to know what the bargain was, aren't you? Let's see if I remember correctly . . . We kill Sam Cortland," Farran recited, "you go berserk and break in here, then *you* kill Jayne"—he gave a nod toward the huge body on the table—"and I take Jayne's place." His hands were roving over her neck now, sensual caresses that promised unbearable agony. With each passing second, some of the numbness did indeed wear off—but hardly any control of her body returned. "Pity that I need you to take the blame for Jayne's death. And if only handing you over to the king wouldn't make *such* a nice gift."

The king. He wasn't going to torture her, or kill her, but give her to the king as a bribe to keep royal eyes from looking Farran's way. She could have faced torture, endured the violations she could practically see in Farran's eyes, but if she went to the king . . . She shoved the thought away, refusing to follow its path.

She had to get out.

He must have seen the panic enter her eyes. Farran smiled, a hand closing around her throat. Too-sharp nails pricked her skin. "Don't be afraid, Celaena," he whispered into her ear, digging his nails in deeper. "If the king lets you survive, I'm in your eternal debt. You've handed me my crown, after all."

There was one word on her lips, but she couldn't get it out, no matter how much she tried.

Who?

Who had betrayed her so foully? She could understand hating her, but *Sam* . . . Everyone had adored Sam, even Wesley . . .

Wesley. He had tried to tell her: *It's all just a—* And his face hadn't been set with irritation, but with grief—grief and rage, directed not at her, but at someone else. Had Arobynn sent Wesley to warn her? Harding, the assassin who had been talking about the window, had always had an eye on her position as Arobynn's heir. And he'd practically spoon-fed her the details about where to break in, *how* to break in . . . It had to be him. Maybe Wesley had figured it out just as she was breaking out of the Keep. Because the alternative . . . No, she couldn't even think of the alternative.

Farran pulled back, loosening his grip on her throat. "I do wish I'd been allowed to play with you for a bit, but I swore not to harm you." He cocked his head to the side, taking in the injuries she'd already suffered. "I think a few bruised ribs and a split lip are excusable." He pulled out a pocket watch. "Alas, it's eleven, and you and I both have places to be." Eleven. An hour before Arobynn would even *leave* the Keep. And if Harding had actually been the one to betray her, then he'd probably do his best to delay them even further. Once she was brought to the royal dungeons, what odds did Arobynn have of successfully breaking her out? When the gloriella wore off, what odds did *she* have of breaking out?

Farran's eyes were still on hers, glittering with delight. And then, without warning, his arm slashed through the air.

She heard the sound of a hand against flesh before she felt the stinging throb in her cheek and mouth. The pain was faint. She was thankful the numbness was still clinging to her, especially as the coppery tang of blood filled her mouth.

Farran gracefully rose from his crouch. "That was for getting blood on the carpet."

Despite the sideways angle of her head, she managed to glare up at him, even as her blood slid down her throat. Farran straightened his gray tunic, then leaned down to turn her head forward. His smile returned.

"You would have been delightful to break," he told her, and strode from the room, motioning to three tall, well-dressed men as he passed. Not petty guards. She'd seen those three men before. Somewhere—at some point that she couldn't quite recall . . .

One of the men approached, smiling, despite the gore pooled around her. Celaena glimpsed the rounded pommel of his sword before it connected with her head.

CHAPTER 11

Celaena awoke with a pulsing headache.

She kept her eyes shut, letting her senses take in her surroundings before she announced to the world that she was awake. Wherever she was, it was quiet, and damp, and cold, and reeked of mildew and refuse.

She knew three things before she even opened her eyes.

The first was that at least six hours had passed, because she could wriggle her toes and her fingers, and those movements were enough to tell her that all of her weapons had been removed.

The second was that because at least six hours had passed and Arobynn and the others clearly had not found her, she was either in the royal dungeons across the city or in some cell beneath Jayne's house, awaiting transport.

The third was that Sam was still dead, and even her rage had been a pawn in some betrayal so twisted and brutal she couldn't begin to wrap her aching head around it.

Sam was still dead.

She opened her eyes, finding herself indeed in a dungeon, dumped onto a rotten pallet of hay and chained to the wall. Her feet had also been shackled to the floor, and both sets of chains had just enough slack that she could make it to the filthy bucket in the corner to relieve herself.

That was the first indignity she allowed herself to suffer.

Once she'd taken care of her bladder, she looked about the cell. No windows, and not enough space between the iron door and the threshold for anything more than light to squeeze through. She couldn't hear anything—not through the walls, nor coming from outside.

Her mouth was parched, her tongue leaden in her mouth. What she wouldn't give for a mouthful of water to wash away the lingering taste of blood. Her stomach was painfully empty, too, and the throbbing in her head sent splinters of light through her skull.

She had been betrayed—betrayed by Harding or someone like him, someone who would benefit from her being *permanently* gone, with no hope of ever coming back. And Arobynn still hadn't rescued her.

He'd find her, though. He *had* to.

She tested the chains on her wrists and ankles, examining where they were anchored into the stone floor and walls, looking over every link, studying the locks. They were solid. She felt all the stones around her, tapping for loose bits or possibly a whole block that she could use as a weapon. There was nothing. All the pins had been pulled out of her hair, robbing her of a chance to even try to pick the lock. The buttons on her black tunic were too small and delicate to be useful.

Perhaps if a guard came in, she could get him close enough to use the chains against him—strangle him or knock him unconscious, or hold him hostage long enough for someone to let her out.

Perhaps—

The door groaned open, and a man filled the threshold, three others behind him.

His tunic was dark and embroidered with golden thread. If he was surprised to see her awake, he didn't reveal it.

Royal guards.

This was the royal dungeon, then.

The guard in the doorway placed the food he was carrying on the floor and slid the tray toward her. Water, bread, a hunk of cheese. "Dinner," he said, not stepping one foot in the room.

He and his companions knew the threat of getting too close.

Celaena glanced at the tray. Dinner. How long had she been down here? Had it been nearly a whole day—and Arobynn *still* hadn't come for her? He had to have found Wesley by the stables—and Wesley would have told him what she'd gone to do. He *had* to know she was here.

The guard was watching her. "This dungeon is impenetrable," he said. "And those chains are made with Adarlanian steel."

She stared at him. He was middle-aged, perhaps forty. He wore no weapons—another precaution. Usually, the royal guards joined young and stayed until they were too old to carry a sword. That meant this man had years of extensive training. It was too dark to see the three guards behind him, but she knew they wouldn't trust just anyone to watch her.

And even if he'd said the words to intimidate her into behaving, he was probably telling the truth. No one got out of the royal dungeons, and no one got in.

If it had been a whole day and Arobynn hadn't yet found her, she wasn't getting out either. If her betrayer had been able to fool her, and Sam, and Arobynn, then they'd find a way to keep the King of the Assassins from knowing she was in here, too.

Now that Sam was dead, there wasn't anything left outside of the dungeons worth fighting for, anyway. Not when Adarlan's Assassin was crumbling apart, and her world with her. The girl who'd taken on a Pirate Lord and his entire island, the girl who'd stolen Asterion horses and raced along the beach in the Red Desert, the girl who'd sat on her own rooftop, watching the sun rise over the Avery, the girl who'd felt alive with possibility . . . that girl was gone.

There wasn't anything left. And Arobynn wasn't coming.

She'd failed.

And worse, she'd failed Sam. She hadn't even killed the man who'd ended his life so viciously.

The guard shifted on his feet, and she realized she'd been staring at him. "The food is clean," was all the guard said before he backed out of the room and shut the door.

She drank the water and ate as much of the bread and cheese as she could stomach. She couldn't tell if the food itself was bland, or if her tongue had just lost all sense of taste. Every bite tasted like ash.

She kicked the tray toward the door when she was finished. She didn't care that she could have used it as a weapon, or a lure to get one of the guards closer.

Because she wasn't getting out, and Sam was dead.

Celaena leaned her head against the freezing, damp wall. She'd never be able to make sure he was safely buried in the earth. She'd failed him even in that.

When the roaring silence came to claim her again, Celaena walked into it with open arms.

The guards liked to talk. About sporting events, about women, about the movement of Adarlan's armies. About her, most of all.

Sometimes, flickers of their conversations broke through the wall of silence, holding her attention for a moment before she let the quiet sweep her back out to its endless sea.

"The captain's going to be furious he wasn't here for the trial."

"Serves him right for gallivanting with the prince along the Surian coast."

Sniggers.

"I heard the captain's racing back to Rifthold, though."

"What's the point? Her trial is tomorrow. He won't even make it in time to see her executed."

~

"You think she's really Celaena Sardothien?"

"She looks my daughter's age."

"Better not tell anyone—the king said he'd flay us all alive if we breathe one word."

"Hard to imagine that it's her—did you see the list of victims? It went on and on."

"You think she's wrong in the head? She just *looks* at you without really *looking* at you, you know?"

"I bet they needed someone to pay for Jayne's death. They probably grabbed a simple girl to pretend it was her."

Snorts. "Won't matter to the king, will it? And if she won't talk, then it's her own damn fault if she's innocent."

"I don't think she's really Celaena Sardothien."

~

"I heard it'll be a closed trial and execution because the king doesn't want anyone seeing who she really is."

"Trust the king to deny everyone else the chance to watch."

"I wonder if they'll hang or behead her."

CHAPTER 12

The world flashed. Dungeons, rotten hay, cold stones against her cheek, guards talking, bread and cheese and water. Then guards entered, crossbows aimed at her, hands on their swords. Two days had passed, somehow. A rag and a bucket of water were thrown at her. Clean herself up for her trial, they said. She obeyed. And she didn't struggle when they gave her new shackles on her wrists and ankles—shackles she could walk in. They took her down a dark, cold hallway that echoed with distant groans, then up the stairs. Sunlight shone through a barred window—harsh, blinding—as they went up more stairs, and eventually into a room of stone and polished wood.

The wooden chair was smooth beneath her. Her head still ached, and the places where Farran's men had struck her were still sore.

The room was large, but sparsely appointed. She'd been shoved into a chair set in the center of the room, a safe distance from the massive table on the far end—the table at which twelve men sat facing her.

She didn't care who they were, or what their role was. She could feel their eyes on her, though. Everyone in the room—the men at the table and the dozens of guards—was watching her.

A hanging or a beheading. Her throat closed up.

There was no point in fighting, not now.

She deserved this. For more reasons than she could count. She should never have allowed Sam to convince her to dispatch Farran on his own. It was her fault, all of it, set in motion the day she'd arrived in Skull's Bay and decided to make a stand for something.

A small door at the back of the room opened, and the men at the table got to their feet.

Heavy boots stomping across the floor, the guards straightening and saluting . . .

The King of Adarlan entered the room.

She wouldn't look at him. Let him do what he wanted to her. If she looked into his eyes, what semblance of calm she had would be shredded. So it was better to feel nothing than to cower before him—the butcher who had destroyed so much of Erilea. Better to go to her grave numb and dazed than begging.

A chair at the center of the table was pulled back. The men around the king didn't sit until he did.

Then silence.

The wooden floor of the room was so polished that she could see the reflection of the iron chandelier hanging far above her.

A low chuckle, like bone against rock. Even without looking at him, she could sense his sheer mass—the darkness swirling around him.

"I didn't believe the rumors until now," the king said, "but it seems the guards were not lying about your age."

A faint urge to cover her ears, to shut out that wretched voice, flickered in the back of her mind.

"How old are you?"

She didn't reply. Sam was gone. Nothing she could do—even if she fought, even if she raged—could change that.

"Did Rourke Farran get his claws on you, or are you just being willful?"

Farran's face, leering at her, smiling so viciously as she was helpless before him.

"Very well, then," the king said. Papers being shuffled, the only sound in the deathly silent room. "Do you deny that you are Celaena Sardothien? If you do not speak, then I will take your silence for acquiescence, girl."

She kept her mouth shut.

"Then read the charges, Councilor Rensel."

A male throat was cleared. "You, Celaena Sardothien, are charged with the deaths of the following people . . ." And then he began a long recitation of all those lives she'd taken. The brutal story of a girl who was now gone. Arobynn had always seen to it that the world knew of her handiwork. He always got word out through secret channels when another victim had fallen to Celaena Sardothien. And now, the very thing that had earned her the right to call herself Adarlan's Assassin would be what sealed her doom. When it was over, the man said, "Do you deny any of the charges?"

Her breathing was so slow.

"Girl," the councilman said a bit shrilly, "we will take your lack of response to mean you do not deny them. Do you understand that?"

She didn't bother to nod. It was all over, anyway.

"Then I will decide your sentence," the king growled.

Then there was murmuring, more rustling papers, and a cough. The light on the floor flickered. The guards in the room remained focused on her, weapons at the ready.

Footsteps suddenly thudded toward her from the table, and she heard the sound of weapons being angled. She recognized the footsteps before the king even reached her chair.

"Look at me."

She kept her gaze on his boots.

"Look at me."

It made no difference now, did it? He'd already destroyed so much of Erilea—destroyed parts of her without even knowing it.

"*Look at me.*"

Celaena raised her head and looked at the King of Adarlan.

The blood drained from her face. Those black eyes were poised to devour the world; the features were harsh and weathered. He wore a sword at his side—the sword whose name everyone knew—and a fine tunic and fur cloak. No crown rested on his head.

She had to get away. Had to get out of this room, get away from him.

Get away.

"Do you have any last requests before I announce your sentence?" he asked, those eyes still searing through every defense she'd ever learned. She could still smell the smoke that had suffocated every inch of Terrasen nine years ago, still smell the sizzling flesh and hear the futile screams as the king and his armies wiped out every last trace of resistance, every last trace of magic. No matter what Arobynn had trained her to do, the memories of those last weeks as Terrasen fell were imprinted upon her blood. So she just stared at him.

When she didn't reply, he turned on his heel and walked back to the table.

She had to get away. Forever. Brash, foolish fire flared up, and turned her—only for a moment—into that girl again.

"I do," she said, her voice hoarse from disuse.

The king paused and looked over his shoulder at her.

She smiled, a wicked, wild thing. "*Make it quick.*"

It was a challenge, not a plea. The king's council and the guards shifted, some of them murmuring.

The king's eyes narrowed slightly, and when he smiled at her, it was the most horrific thing she'd ever seen.

"Oh?" he said, turning to face her fully.

That foolish fire went out.

"If it is an easy death you desire, Celaena Sardothien, I will certainly not give it to you. Not until you have adequately suffered."

The world balanced on the edge of a knife, slipping, slipping, slipping.

"You, Celaena Sardothien, are sentenced to nine lives' worth of labor in the Salt Mines of Endovier."

Her blood turned to ice. The councilmen all glanced at one another. Obviously, this option hadn't been discussed beforehand.

"You will be sent with orders to keep you alive for as long as possible—so you will have the chance to enjoy Endovier's special kind of agony."

Endovier.

Then the king turned away.

Endovier.

There was a flurry of motion, and the king barked an order to have her on the first wagon out of the city. Then there were hands on her arms, and crossbows pointed at her as she was half-dragged out of the room.

Endovier.

She was thrown in her dungeon cell for minutes, or hours, or a day. Then more guards came to fetch her, leading her up the stairs, into the still-blinding sun.

Endovier.

New shackles, hammered shut. The dark interior of a prison wagon. The turn of multiple locks, the jostle of horses starting into a walk, and many other horses surrounding the wagon.

Through the small window high in the door wall, she could see the capital, the streets she knew so well, the people milling about and glancing at the prison wagon and the mounted guards, but not thinking about who might be inside. The golden dome of the Royal Theater in the distance, the briny scent of a breeze off the Avery, the emerald-tiled roofs and white stones of every building.

All passing by, all so quickly.

They passed the Assassins' Keep where she had trained and bled and lost so much, the place where Sam's body lay, waiting for her to bury him.

The game had been played, and she had lost.

Now they came to the looming alabaster walls of the city, their gates thrown wide to accommodate their large party.

As Celaena Sardothien was led out of the capital, she sank into a corner of the wagon and did not get up.

Standing atop one of the many emerald roofs of Rifthold, Rourke Farran and Arobynn Hamel watched as the prison wagon was escorted out of the city. A chill breeze swept off the Avery, ruffling their hair.

"Endovier, then," Farran mused, his dark eyes still upon the wagon. "A surprising twist of events. I thought you had planned a grand rescue from the butchering block."

The King of the Assassins said nothing.

"So you're not going after the wagon?"

"Obviously not," Arobynn said, glancing at the new Crime Lord of Rifthold. It had been on this very rooftop that Farran and the King of the Assassins had first run into each other. Farran had been going to spy on one of Jayne's mistresses, and Arobynn . . . well, Farran had never learned why Arobynn had been meandering across the roofs of Rifthold in the middle of the night.

"You and your men could free her in a matter of moments," Rourke went on. "Attacking a prison wagon is far safer than what you had originally planned. Though, I'll admit—sending her to Endovier is far more interesting to me."

"If I wanted your opinion, Farran, I would have asked for it."

Farran gave him a slow smile. "You might want to consider how you speak to me now."

"And you might want to consider who gave you your crown."

Farran chuckled, and silence fell for a long moment. "If you wanted her to suffer, you should have left her in my care. I could have had her begging for you to save her in a matter of minutes. It would have been exquisite."

Arobynn just shook his head. "Whatever gutter you grew up in, Farran, it must have been an unparalleled sort of hell."

Farran studied his new ally, his gaze glittering. "You have no idea." After another moment of quiet, he asked, "Why did you do it?"

Arobynn's attention drifted back to the wagon, already a small dot in the rolling foothills above Rifthold. "Because I don't like sharing my belongings."

AFTER

She had been in the wagon for two days now, watching the light shift and dance on the walls. She only moved from the corner long enough to relieve herself or to pick at the food they threw in for her.

She had believed she could love Sam and not pay the price. *Everything has a price*, she'd once been told by a Spidersilk merchant in the Red Desert. How right he was.

Sun shone through the wagon again, filling it with weak light. The trek to the Salt Mines of Endovier took two weeks, and each mile led them farther and farther north—and into colder weather.

When she dozed, falling in and out of dreams and reality and sometimes not knowing the difference, she was often awoken by the shivers that racked her body. The guards offered her no protection against the chill.

Two weeks in this dark, reeking wagon, with only the shadows and light on the wall for company, and the silence hovering around her. Two weeks, and then Endovier.

She lifted her head from the wall.

The growing fear set the silence flickering.

No one survived Endovier. Most prisoners didn't survive a month. It was a death camp.

A tremor went down her numb fingers. She drew her legs in tighter to her chest, resting her head against them.

The shadows and the light continued to play on the wall.

Excited whispers, the crunch of rushing feet on dried grass, moonlight shining through the window.

She didn't know how she got upright, or how she made it to the tiny barred window, her legs stiff and aching and wobbly from disuse.

The guards were gathered near the edge of the clearing they'd camped in for the night, staring out into the tangle of trees. They'd entered Oakwald Forest sometime on the first day, and now it would be nothing but trees-trees-trees for the two weeks that they would travel north.

The moon illuminated the mist swirling along the leaf-strewn ground, and made the trees cast long shadows like lurking wraiths.

And there—standing in a copse of thorns—was a white stag.

Celaena's breath hitched.

She clenched the bars of the small window as the creature looked at them. His towering antlers seemed to glow in the moonlight, crowning him in wreaths of ivory.

"Gods above," one of the guards whispered.

The stag's enormous head turned slightly—toward the wagon, toward the small window.

The Lord of the North.

So the people of Terrasen will always know how to find their way home, she'd once told Ansel as they lay under a blanket of stars and traced the constellation of the Stag. *So they can look up at the sky, no matter where they are, and know Terrasen is forever with them.*

Tendrils of hot air puffed from the stag's snout, curling in the chill night.

Celaena bowed her head, though she kept her gaze upon him.

So the people of Terrasen will always know how to find their way home . . .

A crack in the silence—spreading wider and wider as the stag's fathomless eyes stayed steady on her.

A glimmer of a world long since destroyed—a kingdom in ruins. The stag shouldn't be here—not so deep into Adarlan or so far from home. How had he survived the hunters who had been set loose nine years ago, when the king had ordered all the sacred white stags of Terrasen butchered?

And yet he was here, glowing like a beacon in the moonlight.

He was here.

And so was she.

She felt the warmth of the tears before she realized she was crying.

Then the unmistakable groan of bowstrings being pulled back.

The stag, her Lord of the North, her beacon, didn't move.

"*Run!*" The hoarse scream erupted out of her. It shattered the silence.

The stag remained staring at her.

She banged on the side of the wagon. "*Run, damn you!*"

The stag turned and sprinted, a bolt of white light weaving through the trees.

The twang of bowstrings, the hiss of arrows—all missing their mark.

The guards cursed, and the wagon shook as one of them struck it in frustration. Celaena backed away from the window, backed up, up, up, until she ran into the wall and collapsed to her knees.

The silence had gone. In its absence, she could feel the barking pain echo through her legs, and the ache of the injuries Farran's men had given her, and the dull stinging of wrists and ankles rubbed raw by chains. And she could feel the endless hole where Sam had once been.

She was going to Endovier—she was to be a slave in the Salt Mines of Endovier.

Fear, ravenous and cold, dragged her under.

BEGINNING

Celaena Sardothien knew she was nearing the Salt Mines when, two weeks later, the trees of Oakwald gave way to gray, rough terrain, and jagged mountains pierced the sky. She'd been lying on the floor since dawn and had already vomited once. And now she couldn't bring herself to stand up.

Sounds in the distance—shouting and the faint crack of a whip.

Endovier.

She wasn't ready.

The light turned brighter as they left the trees behind. She was glad Sam wasn't here to see her like this.

She let out a sob so violent she had to press her fist to her mouth to keep from being heard.

She'd never be ready for this, for Endovier and the world without Sam.

A breeze filled the wagon, lifting away the smells of the past two weeks. Her trembling paused for a heartbeat. She knew that breeze.

She knew the chill bite beneath it, knew it carried the hint of pine and snow, knew the mountains from which it hailed. A northern breeze, a breeze of Terrasen.

She *must* stand up.

Pine and snow and lazy, golden summers—a city of light and music in the shadow of the Staghorn Mountains. She must stand, or be broken before she even entered Endovier.

The wagon slowed, wheels bouncing over the rough path. A whip snapped.

"My name is Celaena Sardothien . . . ," she whispered onto the floor, but her lips shook hard enough to cut off the words.

Somewhere, someone started screaming. From the shift in the light, she knew they were nearing what had to be a giant wall.

"My name is Celaena Sardothien . . . ," she tried again. She gasped down uneven breaths.

The breeze grew into a wind, and she closed her eyes, letting it sweep away the ashes of that dead world—of that dead girl. And then there was nothing left except something new, something still glowing red from the forging.

Celaena opened her eyes.

She would go into Endovier. Go into Hell. And she would not crumble.

She braced her palms on the floor and slid her feet beneath her.

She had not stopped breathing yet, and she had endured Sam's death and evaded the king's execution. She would survive this.

Celaena stood, turning to the window and looking squarely at the mammoth stone wall rising up ahead of them.

She would tuck Sam into her heart, a bright light for her to take out whenever things were darkest. And then she would remember how it had felt to be loved, when the world had held nothing but possibility. No matter what they did to her, they could never take that away.

She would not break.

And someday . . . someday, even if it took her until her last breath, she'd find out who had done this to her. To Sam. Celaena wiped away her tears as the wagon entered the shade of the tunnel through the wall. Whips and screams and the clank of chains. She tensed, already taking in every detail she could.

But she squared her shoulders. Straightened her spine.

"My name is Celaena Sardothien," she whispered, "*and I will not be afraid*."

The wagon cleared the wall and stopped.

Celaena raised her head.

The wagon door was unlocked and thrown open, flooding the space with gray light. Guards reached for her, mere shadows against the brightness. She let them grab her, let them pull her from the wagon.

I will not be afraid.

Celaena Sardothien lifted her chin and walked into the Salt Mines of Endovier.

ACKNOWLEDGMENTS

Elements of these stories have been floating through my imagination for the past decade, but getting the chance to write them all down was something I never believed I'd be blessed enough to do. It was a delight to originally share these novellas as e-books, but seeing them printed as a physical book is a dream come true. So it's with immense gratitude that I thank the following people:

My husband, Josh—for making dinner, bringing me coffee (and tea . . . and chocolate . . . and snacks), walking Annie, and for all of the unconditional love. I could not do this without you.

My parents—for buying multiple copies of every novel and novella, for being my #1 fans, and for all of the adventures (a few of which inspired these stories).

My incomparable agent, Tamar Rydzinski, who called one summer afternoon with a crazy idea that would eventually become these novellas.

My editor, Margaret Miller, who never fails to challenge me to be a better writer.

And the entire worldwide team at Bloomsbury—for the unfailing enthusiasm, brilliance, and support. Thank you for all that you've done for the Throne of Glass series. I am so proud to call myself a Bloomsbury author.

Writing a book is definitely not a solitary task, and without the following people, these novellas would not be what they are:

Alex Bracken, whom I'll never stop owing for the genius suggestion regarding *The Assassin and the Underworld* (and for all the other incredible feedback, too).

Jane Zhao, whose unwavering enthusiasm for the world of Throne of Glass was one of the things I clung to most on the long path to publication. Kat Zhang, who always finds time to critique despite an impossibly hectic schedule. Amie Kaufman, who cried and swooned in all the right places.

And Susan Dennard—my wonderful, honest, fierce Sooz. You remind me that sometimes—just sometimes—the universe can get things right. No matter what happens, I will always be grateful for the day you came into my life.

Additional love and thanks to my incredible friends: Erin Bowman, Dan Krokos, Leigh Bardugo, and Biljana Likic.

And you, dear reader: thank you for coming with me on this journey. I hope that you've enjoyed this glimpse into Celaena's past—and I hope that you'll enjoy seeing where her adventures take her in *Throne of Glass*!

SHE STOLE A LIFE. NOW SHE MUST PAY WITH HER HEART.

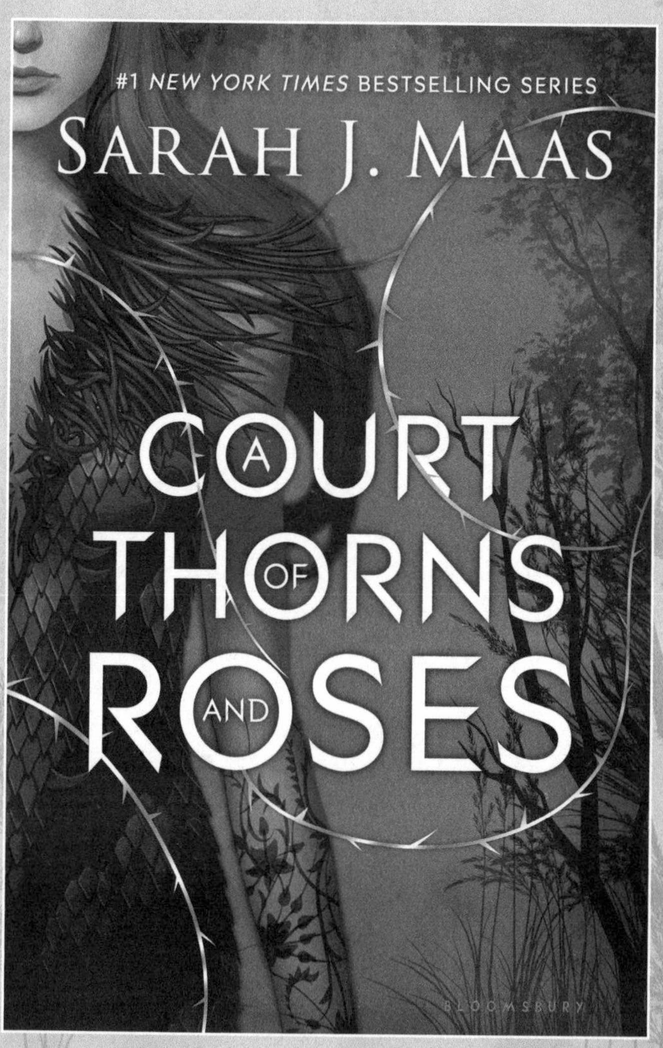

READ ON FOR A PREVIEW OF ANOTHER CAPTIVATING SERIES FROM #1 *NEW YORK TIMES* BESTSELLING AUTHOR SARAH J. MAAS—A BLEND OF "BEAUTY AND THE BEAST" AND FAERIE LORE.

The forest had become a labyrinth of snow and ice.

I'd been monitoring the parameters of the thicket for an hour, and my vantage point in the crook of a tree branch had turned useless. The gusting wind blew thick flurries to sweep away my tracks, but buried along with them any signs of potential quarry.

Hunger had brought me farther from home than I usually risked, but winter was the hard time. The animals had pulled in, going deeper into the woods than I could follow, leaving me to pick off stragglers one by one, praying they'd last until spring.

They hadn't.

I wiped my numb fingers over my eyes, brushing away the flakes clinging to my lashes. Here there were no telltale trees stripped of bark to mark the deer's passing—they hadn't yet moved on. They would remain until the bark ran out, then travel north past the wolves' territory and perhaps into the faerie lands of Prythian—where no mortals would dare go, not unless they had a death wish.

A shudder skittered down my spine at the thought, and I shoved it away, focusing on my surroundings, on the task ahead. That was all I could do, all I'd been able to do for years: focus on surviving the week, the day, the hour ahead. And now, with the snow, I'd be lucky to spot anything—especially from my position up in the tree, scarcely able to see fifteen feet ahead. Stifling a groan as my stiff limbs protested at the movement, I unstrung my bow before easing off the tree.

The icy snow crunched under my fraying boots, and I ground my teeth. Low visibility, unnecessary noise—I was well on my way to yet another fruitless hunt.

Only a few hours of daylight remained. If I didn't leave soon, I'd have to navigate my way home in the dark, and the warnings of the town hunters still rang fresh in my mind: giant wolves were on the prowl, and in numbers. Not to mention whispers of strange folk spotted in the area, tall and eerie and deadly.

Anything but faeries, the hunters had beseeched our long-forgotten gods—and I had secretly prayed alongside them. In the eight years we'd been living in our village, two days' journey from the immortal border of Prythian, we'd been spared an attack—though traveling peddlers sometimes brought stories of distant border towns left in splinters and bones and ashes. These accounts, once rare enough to be dismissed by the village elders as hearsay, had in recent months become commonplace whisperings on every market day.

I had risked much in coming so far into the forest, but we'd finished our last loaf of bread yesterday, and the remainder of our dried meat the day before. Still, I would have rather spent another night with a hungry belly than found myself satisfying the appetite of a wolf. Or a faerie.

Not that there was much of me to feast on. I'd turned gangly by this time of the year, and could count a good number of my ribs. Moving as nimbly and quietly as I could between the trees, I pushed a hand against my hollow and aching stomach. I knew the expression that would be on my two elder sisters' faces when I returned to our cottage empty-handed yet again.

After a few minutes of careful searching, I crouched in a cluster of snow-heavy brambles. Through the thorns, I had a half-decent view of a clearing and the small brook flowing through it. A few holes in the ice suggested it was still frequently used. Hopefully something would come by. Hopefully.

I sighed through my nose, digging the tip of my bow into the ground, and leaned my forehead against the crude curve of wood. We wouldn't last another week without food. And too many families had already started begging for me to hope for handouts from the wealthier townsfolk. I'd witnessed firsthand exactly how far their charity went.

I eased into a more comfortable position and calmed my breathing, straining to listen to the forest over the wind. The snow fell and fell, dancing and curling like sparkling spindrifts, the white fresh and clean against the brown and gray of the world. And despite myself, despite my numb limbs, I quieted that relentless, vicious part of my mind to take in the snow-veiled woods.

Once it had been second nature to savor the contrast of new grass against dark, tilled soil, or an amethyst brooch nestled in folds of emerald silk; once I'd dreamed and breathed and thought in color and light and shape. Sometimes I would even indulge in envisioning a day when my sisters were married and it was only me and Father, with enough food to go around, enough money to buy some paint, and enough time to put those colors and shapes down on paper or canvas or the cottage walls.

Not likely to happen anytime soon—perhaps ever. So I was left with moments like this, admiring the glint of pale winter light on snow. I couldn't remember the last time I'd done it—bothered to notice anything lovely or interesting.

Stolen hours in a decrepit barn with Isaac Hale didn't count; those times were hungry and empty and sometimes cruel, but never lovely.

The howling wind calmed into a soft sighing. The snow fell lazily now, in big, fat clumps that gathered along every nook and bump of the trees.

Mesmerizing—the lethal, gentle beauty of the snow. I'd soon have to return to the muddy, frozen roads of the village, to the cramped heat of our cottage. Some small, fragmented part of me recoiled at the thought.

Bushes rustled across the clearing.

Drawing my bow was a matter of instinct. I peered through the thorns, and my breath caught.

Less than thirty paces away stood a small doe, not yet too scrawny from winter, but desperate enough to wrench bark from a tree in the clearing.

A deer like that could feed my family for a week or more.

My mouth watered. Quiet as the wind hissing through dead leaves, I took aim.

She continued tearing off strips of bark, chewing slowly, utterly unaware that her death waited yards away.

I could dry half the meat, and we could immediately eat the rest—stews, pies . . . Her skin could be sold, or perhaps turned into clothing for one of us. I needed new boots, but Elain needed a new cloak, and Nesta was prone to crave anything someone else possessed.

My fingers trembled. So much food—such salvation. I took a steadying breath, double-checking my aim.

But there was a pair of golden eyes shining from the brush adjacent to mine.

The forest went silent. The wind died. Even the snow paused.

We mortals no longer kept gods to worship, but if I had known their lost names, I would have prayed to them. All of them. Concealed in the thicket, the wolf inched closer, its gaze set on the oblivious doe.

He was enormous—the size of a pony—and though I'd been warned about their presence, my mouth turned bone-dry.

But worse than his size was his unnatural stealth: even as he inched closer in the brush, he remained unheard, unspotted by the doe. No animal that massive could be so quiet. But if he was no ordinary animal, if he was of Prythian origin, if he was somehow a faerie, then being eaten was the least of my concerns.

If he was a faerie, I should already be running.

Yet maybe . . . maybe it would be a favor to the world, to my village, to myself, to kill him while I remained undetected. Putting an arrow through his eye would be no burden.

But despite his size, he *looked* like a wolf, moved like a wolf. *Animal*, I reassured myself. *Just an animal*. I didn't let myself consider the alternative—not when I needed my head clear, my breathing steady.

I had a hunting knife and three arrows. The first two were ordinary arrows—simple and efficient, and likely no more than bee stings to a wolf that size. But the third arrow, the longest and heaviest one, I'd bought from a traveling peddler during a summer when we'd had enough coppers for extra luxuries. An arrow carved from mountain ash, armed with an iron head.

From songs sung to us as lullabies over our cradles, we all knew from infancy that faeries hated iron. But it was the ash wood that made their immortal, healing magic falter long enough for a human to make a killing blow. Or so legend and rumor claimed. The only proof we had of the ash's effectiveness was its sheer rarity. I'd seen drawings of the trees, but never one with my own eyes—not after the High Fae had burned them all long ago. So few remained, most of them small and sickly and hidden by the nobility within high-walled groves. I'd spent weeks after my purchase debating whether that overpriced bit of wood had been a waste of money, or a fake, and for three years, the ash arrow had sat unused in my quiver.

Now I drew it, keeping my movements minimal, efficient—anything to avoid that monstrous wolf looking in my direction. The arrow was long and heavy enough to inflict damage—possibly kill him, if I aimed right.

My chest became so tight it ached. And in that moment, I realized my life boiled down to one question: Was the wolf alone?

I gripped my bow and drew the string farther back. I was a decent shot, but I'd never faced a wolf. I'd thought it made me lucky—even blessed. But now . . . I didn't know where to hit or how fast they moved. I couldn't afford to miss. Not when I had only one ash arrow.

And if it was indeed a faerie's heart pounding under that fur, then good riddance. Good riddance, after all their kind had done to us. I wouldn't risk this one later creeping into our village to slaughter and maim and torment. Let him die here and now. I'd be glad to end him.

The wolf crept closer, and a twig snapped beneath one of his paws—each bigger than my hand. The doe went rigid. She glanced to either side, ears straining toward the gray sky. With the wolf's downwind position, she couldn't see or smell him.

His head lowered, and his massive silver body—so perfectly blended into the snow and shadows—sank onto its haunches. The doe was still staring in the wrong direction.

I glanced from the doe to the wolf and back again. At least he was alone—at least I'd been spared that much. But if the wolf scared the doe off, I was left with nothing but a starving, oversize wolf—possibly a faerie—looking for the next-best meal. And if he killed her, destroying precious amounts of hide and fat . . .

If I judged wrongly, my life wasn't the only one that would be lost. But my life had been reduced to nothing but risks these past eight years that I'd been hunting in the woods, and I'd picked correctly most of the time. Most of the time.

The wolf shot from the brush in a flash of gray and white and black, his yellow fangs gleaming. He was even more gargantuan in the open, a marvel of muscle and speed and brute strength. The doe didn't stand a chance.

I fired the ash arrow before he destroyed much else of her.

The arrow found its mark in his side, and I could have sworn the ground itself shuddered. He barked in pain, releasing the doe's neck as his blood sprayed on the snow—so ruby bright.

He whirled toward me, those yellow eyes wide, hackles raised. His low growl reverberated in the empty pit of my stomach as I surged to my feet, snow churning around me, another arrow drawn.

But the wolf merely looked at me, his maw stained with blood, my ash arrow protruding so vulgarly from his side. The snow began falling again. He *looked*, and with a sort of awareness and surprise that made me fire the second arrow. Just in case—just in case that intelligence was of the immortal, wicked sort.

He didn't try to dodge the arrow as it went clean through his wide yellow eye.

He collapsed to the ground.

Color and darkness whirled, eddying in my vision, mixing with the snow.

His legs were twitching as a low whine sliced through the wind. Impossible—he should be dead, not dying. The arrow was through his eye almost to the goose fletching.

But wolf or faerie, it didn't matter. Not with that ash arrow buried in his side. He'd be dead soon enough. Still, my hands shook as I brushed off snow and edged closer, still keeping a good distance. Blood gushed from the wounds I'd given him, staining the snow crimson.

He pawed at the ground, his breathing already slowing. Was he in much pain, or was his whimper just his attempt to shove death away? I wasn't sure I wanted to know.

The snow swirled around us. I stared at him until that coat of charcoal and obsidian and ivory ceased rising and falling. Wolf—definitely just a wolf, despite his size.

The tightness in my chest eased, and I loosed a sigh, my breath clouding in front of me. At least the ash arrow had proved itself to be lethal, regardless of who or what it took down.

A rapid examination of the doe told me I could carry only one animal—and even that would be a struggle. But it was a shame to leave the wolf.

Though it wasted precious minutes—minutes during which any predator could smell the fresh blood—I skinned him and cleaned my arrows as best I could.

If anything, it warmed my hands. I wrapped the bloody side of his pelt around the doe's death-wound before I hoisted her across my shoulders. It was several miles back to our cottage, and I didn't need a trail of blood leading every animal with fangs and claws straight to me.

Grunting against the weight, I grasped the legs of the deer and spared a final glance at the steaming carcass of the wolf. His remaining golden eye now stared at the snow-heavy sky, and for a moment, I wished I had it in me to feel remorse for the dead thing.

But this was the forest, and it was winter.

The sun had set by the time I exited the forest, my knees shaking. My hands, stiff from clenching the legs of the deer, had gone utterly numb miles ago. Not even the carcass could ward off the deepening chill.

The world was awash in hues of dark blue, interrupted only by shafts of buttery light escaping from the shuttered windows of our dilapidated cottage. It was like striding through a living painting—a fleeting moment of stillness, the blues swiftly shifting to solid darkness.

As I trudged up the path, each step fueled only by near-dizzying hunger, my sisters' voices fluttered out to meet me. I didn't need to discern their words to know they most likely were chattering about some young man or the ribbons they'd spotted in the village when they should have been chopping wood, but I smiled a bit nonetheless.

I kicked my boots against the stone door frame, knocking the snow from them. Bits of ice came free from the gray stones of the cottage, revealing the faded ward-markings etched around the threshold. My father had once convinced a passing charlatan to trade the engravings against faerie harm in exchange for one of his wood carvings. There was so little that my father was ever able to do for us that I hadn't possessed the heart to tell him the engravings were useless . . . and undoubtedly fake. Mortals didn't possess magic—didn't possess any of the superior strength and speed of the faeries or High Fae. The man, claiming some High Fae blood in his ancestry, had just carved the whorls and swirls and runes around the door and windows, muttered a few nonsense words, and ambled on his way.

I yanked open the wooden door, the frozen iron handle biting my skin like an asp. Heat and light blinded me as I slipped inside.

"Feyre!" Elain's soft gasp scraped past my ears, and I blinked back the brightness of the fire to find my second-eldest sister before me. Though she was bundled in a threadbare blanket, her gold-brown hair—the hair all three of us had—was coiled perfectly about her head. Eight years of poverty hadn't stripped from her the desire to look lovely. "Where did you get that?" The undercurrent of hunger honed her words into a sharpness that had become too common in recent weeks. No mention of the blood on me. I'd long since given up hope of them actually noticing whether I came back from the woods every evening. At least until they got hungry again. But then again, my mother hadn't made *them* swear anything when they stood beside her deathbed.

I took a calming breath as I slung the doe off my shoulders. She hit the wooden table with a thud, rattling a ceramic cup on its other end.

"Where do you think I got it?" My voice had turned hoarse, each word burning as it came out. My father and Nesta still silently warmed their hands by the hearth, my eldest sister ignoring him, as usual. I peeled the wolf pelt from the doe's body, and after removing my boots and setting them by the door, I turned to Elain.

Her brown eyes—my father's eyes—remained pinned on the doe. "Will it take you long to clean it?" Me. Not her, not the others. I'd never once seen their hands sticky with blood and fur. I'd only learned to prepare and harvest my kills thanks to the instruction of others.

Josh Wasserman

SARAH J. MAAS is the #1 *New York Times* and internationally bestselling author of the young adult series Throne of Glass and A Court of Thorns and Roses, as well as her upcoming adult series, Crescent City. Her books are published in over thirty-six languages. A New York native, Sarah lives near Philadelphia with her husband, son, and dog.

www.sarahjmaas.com
facebook.com/worldofsarahjmaas
instagram.com/therealsjmaas